PENGUIN BOOKS

Queen Bee

Queen Bee

JANE FALLON

PENGUIN BOOKS

PENGUIN BOOKS

UK | USA | Canada | Ireland | Australia
India | New Zealand | South Africa

Penguin Books is part of the Penguin Random House group of companies
whose addresses can be found at global.penguinrandomhouse.com.

First published 2020
001

Copyright © Jane Fallon, 2020

The moral right of the author has been asserted

Set in 12.5/14.75 pt Garamond MT Std
Typeset by Jouve (UK), Milton Keynes
Printed and bound in Great Britain by Clays Ltd, Elcograf S.p.A.

A CIP catalogue record for this book is available from the British Library

ISBN: 978-1-405-94334-5

Dedicated to the amazing
people of NOWZAD for their incredible
work with animals in Afghanistan.
www.nowzad.com

Prologue

Am I really going to do this?

Angie gives me an almost imperceptible nod. I pull open the drawer. At first glance, it's crammed full of what look like official documents. Contracts and letters.

'It's just more paperwork,' I say. 'Probably stuff about the business that's confidential.'

'Anything else?' she asks, disappointed.

I scrabble to the bottom of the pile. There's something underneath. A metal box, like one of those ones people use to put petty cash in. Red. About thirty centimetres wide. 'Where's that other key?' I say, and even to my own ears my voice sounds wobbly. 'You really won't tell anyone about this, will you, Ange? Anyone?'

'Of course I won't,' she says, going for the top-right-hand drawer again. 'It'd make me look as bad as you.'

It takes her a moment to locate the tiny key. I know just from looking at the lock that it's going to fit, and it does. I open the box before I can change my mind.

There's not much in there. Disappointingly little, in fact. I glance out at the main office again, and then I tip the contents out on to the floor. There are a couple of envelopes, a receipt from Cartier, a small box containing a tacky gold sovereign ring, large enough to fit a man's finger. I open the first envelope. A card. A print of a garish painting of Paris. Inside, in curly, cursive handwriting, a note.

Thank you for the best 2 days ever. Love u. F xx

There are crudely drawn hearts covering the bottom half of the card.

'Whoever she is, she's young,' I say.

'Does the pope shit in the woods?' Angie says, reaching for the second envelope. 'F. Have you come across any Fs? Any Fionas or Fays hanging round your way?'

I shake my head. I snap a quick photo of the message on my phone. Angie has pulled another card from the second envelope. A photo of a kitten sitting in a large coffee cup.

She goes to open it.

There's a shout. A man's voice. 'Ange! Angie!'

The pair of us freeze.

I

February: one month earlier

The house is magnificent.

Even in the pouring rain it's impossible not to appreciate the sheer scale of it. The horseshoe drive with a gate marked in and a whole other gate marked out, the perfectly manicured box balls not a leaf out of place, the symmetry either side of the large columned porch. A small stone water fountain standing proudly in the middle of a complicated arrangement of low hedges. Three storeys high and the width of five terraced houses, it's vast. Never in my wildest dreams did I think I would end up living somewhere like this. I drag the last of my boxes from the boot of my car and look around me in awe as I carry it in. The other seven houses in the close are all similar but different enough to give them the illusion of individuality. McMansions, really, if I were being critical. No history, but each one equally majestic. Set in a leafy private cul de sac at the far north edge of the heath. It seems slightly surreal that this is going to be my home. I pause for a second, my wet hair falling into my eyes, and listen. Beyond the rain there's nothing. Silence. It's hard to believe I'm still in London. Then I half run up the drive, circumvent the black shiny front door and duck to the side of the house, where there is a metal staircase up to my new rented flat above the garage. One bedroom, a living room/kitchen and a tiny bathroom. The granny flat. The annexe. That's how Gail had referred to it, when she and her husband, Ben, had interviewed me as a prospective tenant.

At one point he'd said something about staff quarters and she'd grimaced at me.

'We don't have staff,' she said apologetically, shooting him a look.

'No. I just meant, that's what some of them do.' Ben waved his hand vaguely to indicate the rest of The Close. 'I didn't mean . . . sorry, Laura, that sounded patronizing.' He looked genuinely apologetic and I laughed.

'God, I don't care,' I'd said. And I didn't. I needed somewhere to live. Somewhere I could afford. It really didn't matter to me if I would be staying somewhere all the other residents of The Close stuck their nanny. 'As long as you don't mind Betsy staying over a few nights a week . . .'

I had explained on the phone that I had a daughter. Seven years old. Currently living with her father in his smart new flat because the little house I was buying had fallen through at the last minute, leaving me with nowhere to go once our family home was sold. His midlife-crisis flat is how I think of it. His flat where he wanted to live, not with a shiny young girlfriend – he had told me there was no one else and I believed him; honesty had always been a big deal in our marriage, and I had no reason to think that had changed – but alone. Without me. Because apparently that was preferable to living with me. A mistress would almost have been easier to deal with.

'No, of course not,' Gail had said, smiling. 'You have to think of it as yours. Don't feel you have to ask permission for everything . . .'

And just like that the flat was mine. A six-month lease while I tried to find myself – and my daughter – a new permanent home.

I don't have the energy to unpack. I don't even have the energy to make a cup of tea. I change out of my wet clothes, wrap a towel around my head and slump on the sofa. My share of the marital furniture is in storage for now, but there's a comfortable, smart two-seater in here, with a small coffee table. I am Gail and Ben's first ever tenant, so everything is pristine, which is a bonus. God knows they don't need the money from the rent. What I'm paying must be small change to them. But Gail told me she felt nervous sometimes, alone in the huge house when Ben is away on business. They're both lawyers. Both wildly successful. He's a partner in a big international practice, and she has a high-powered job in the City, although they must be heading for retirement soon. She just wanted to feel there was someone else around. I've lucked out, there's no doubt about it. She could have just settled for getting a dog.

There's a sweet-smelling bunch of flowers on the coffee table. It's a nice touch. Kind. It makes me smile. I allow myself to breathe out. It's going to be OK.

After ten minutes I force myself up. I need to unpack my work stuff, set up an office in a corner of the room. There's no desk, and no room for one, but luckily I only have a few files and a laptop that houses the rest of my empire. I run a small cleaning company – just me and eleven part-timers, single mums mostly, and contracts for three office buildings. It's never going to make me a fortune, but I get by. Then I ring round the six who are due to be working tonight and check there are no problems, make a note of the swapped shifts. Half my job seems to be keeping track of everyone's hours, who's covering for who because their daughter has a parents' evening or their son is sick. They've all known each other for so long now that they self-police. There are always the minimum number available; those who aren't working babysit for those who are. We've become a community. Last September we were joined by students Paul and Tomas, who steer clear of the childcare but are so desperate for cash that they'll cover any shift at any amount of notice, often doubling up and working late into the night. I'm lucky. There have only been a handful of occasions in the past five years when I didn't have enough staff to do the job and I've had to stand in myself. That's not going to be so easy from now on, if it's a night I have Betsy and no David to leave her with. I push the thought from my mind. He's still her dad. He'll still have to help out. Today, thankfully, there are no problems, no potential no-shows, although anything could happen between now and when they all start at six.

I find some sheets in one of my suitcases and make up the bed, shoving the empty case underneath it. And then I locate the box with 'Important Stuff' written on the side in Sharpie and unpack the kettle, tea and coffee, milk, my toothbrush and a few basic toiletries. That'll do for now. The sound of a car breaks through the silence and I peer out of the front window, above the sink. Something smart and sporty – a Mercedes? – pulls into the drive opposite. One of my new neighbours. I wonder briefly what they'll make of my battered old bright yellow Corsa, parked out on the street. If I'm lowering the tone. I watch as a woman about my age climbs elegantly out of the driver's seat. She's dressed as if for a night out and it's only two in the afternoon. Short, figure-hugging, structured dress under a close-fitting, tailored leather jacket. Spiky heels, long hair sleek, long legs shiny. She looks like a fantasy. One set in a slightly tacky nightclub full of overweight late-middle-aged men, maybe. But a fantasy nonetheless. I look down at my leggings, ill-fitting hoody and purple trainers. I'm in the middle of moving house, I tell myself, ignoring the fact that I dress like this pretty much every day. One of the joys of working for myself.

The woman lets herself in through the front door, slams it behind her, and The Close is silent again.

Gail has invited me over for a glass of wine when she gets home from work. I could do without it, to be honest. Grateful as I am to be living in such a salubrious street for such an affordable rent, I don't want to feel that puts me at my landlady's beck and call. But it was hard to say no without feeling I then have to go out somewhere, or hide in my flat with the lights off all evening. I tell myself I'll just say yes this once. It's nice of her to ask, after all. Ben is in Brussels for a couple of days; she told me when I collected the keys first thing this morning. She'll be glad of the company.

I tear myself away from the pull of the sofa when I hear

her car turn into the drive. All I want to do is to lie in a heap with a glass of Sauvignon Blanc. To contemplate the circumstances that have brought me here, while my daughter has her tea at her friend Zara's house as she waits for her father to pick her up. David's new place is near her school – as was the house I was hoping to buy. As is her Monday-night ballet class (I say ballet – it's similar to watching a small herd of elephants on a drunken rampage) and her Thursday-night painting club. Her whole short life is contained within those few streets. It makes sense that she stays with him most of the time. I know it does. But that doesn't mean it feels right. I tried to rent somewhere closer, but everything was too expensive or resembled a crime scene, and then time ran out, our maisonette was sold and I had to look further afield. I found my studio on a noticeboard in the kitchen at one of the companies we clean for – AJT Music – nestled between flyers for hot yoga and comedy at a local pub. It's temporary, I remind myself. Six months at the most, and those contain the Easter holidays, half-term and the summer break, when Betsy can stay with me most of the time. And, let's face it, there are far worse places to live than this.

Ten minutes later I'm at the front door, smoothing down my hair and wishing I'd bothered to run a comb through the frizz. Rain and my natural curls do not play nicely together. Gail answers, still in her dark work suit, lipstick in place.

'I didn't get the dress-code memo,' I say, and luckily she laughs, showing gleaming, even teeth.

'Five more minutes and I'd be wearing exactly the

same. In fact, if you don't mind, I'll go and change. It's usually the first thing I do when I walk through the door, but Ben just called and it put me off my stride.'

'Sure,' I say. 'I can come back . . .'

'No. Come on in. You can start on the wine.'

I follow her through the cavernous hallway into the kitchen. There are two wine glasses on the island beside an open bottle of red. I'd much prefer white, but it seems rude to say so. She pours us both a generous measure, takes a swig of hers and leaves me to it, unbuttoning her jacket as she goes. I sit at the vast pale wooden table and try to resist the urge to rummage through the small pile of post that sits at the centre. Not that I'm nosy, but I've always had difficulty not looking at things I'm not supposed to look at. It's like when someone tells you not to touch something because it's hot. Who doesn't at least tap the tip of a finger on it?

I occupy myself by taking in the details of the room, saving them up to share with Betsy on the phone later. She's very amused by the idea of me living in a mansion. This kitchen probably cost many hundreds of thousands of pounds. It's almost certainly the most expensive one I've ever been in. It's all white floor-to-ceiling cupboards and shiny black surfaces. The central island – tastefully contrasting in walnut – is about the size of the living room/kitchen in my rented studio. I start trying to work out whether my whole flat could fit into this room (it definitely could), and that keeps me occupied till Gail reappears, dressed almost identically to me, except her hoody is coral-coloured and snugly fitted, and the telltale Lululemon logo lets me know that her ensemble probably cost three times as much as my H&M get-up. I can't help taking in what a stunning figure she has. She must be twenty-five years older than me but she's in better shape than I've ever managed. Her long blonde hair is loose now, heavy fringe almost touching her lashes. She looks like one of those rock star's wives from the seventies who gave up the drugs and found hot yoga. And Botox.

'So,' she says, taking another large gulp from her glass then topping us both up. 'Are you settled in?'

'Getting there.' I wrack my brain for conversation, but everything I can think of seems so drab and insignificant compared to her fabulous life.

'Well, if you need any help . . .' she says, which is nice of her, even though I'm pretty sure she didn't mean it literally. I think about saying, *Yes, please. Could you help me build an IKEA flat-pack TV stand*, but of course I don't. We sit there in silence for a moment. I've already decided that I need to stay for an hour so as not to appear rude. I resist the temptation to look at the wall clock I noticed earlier. Keep my eyes firmly on my glass.

Gail gives a little laugh and I look up. 'This is how I imagine a Tinder date might be.'

'What? The type where you invent an emergency at home just to get away?' I hope she takes it as the joke I mean it to be, and I'm gratified to see her smile broaden.

'Obviously, I've never done Tinder,' she says. 'Ben and I met through work. I mean, how old-fashioned does that sound now?'

'I'm an expert,' I say. 'Since my separation, you know . . .'

Her eyes light up. 'Oh my goodness, let me live vicariously through you. Tell me everything.'

There's actually nothing much to tell. I've rarely taken it beyond chatting online. Never met up with any of them more than once. But I've been close. I've had some near misses. Men I thought I might be interested in until I realized I wasn't. So I fill her in on Joe number one, who, after a couple of weeks of talking online, and a cancelled date (by me, I'd like to add. It had seemed like a good idea until I started waking up in a cold sweat thinking about it) starting asking me how I felt about anal; Joe number two, who was great company if you wanted to discuss gas-gathering systems in the North Sea; and Martin, who had potential but was too hung up on his ex. Gail is fascinated by each and every one of them and wants all the gory details, which I am only too happy to supply. I even show her some of the conversations on my phone. I make it all sound like a big joke. As if I've been running round town in a blaze of hedonistic singledom, having fun. The truth is that I've approached every date like it's an affront. This man isn't David, so why would I even consider him? OK, so Joe number one was a hopeless case but, in truth, Joe number two was a nice guy, just nervous and consequently rather dull. Martin might have just needed more time. As did I. I talked about David far more than he did his former wife. I feel my face colour as I remember myself, two drinks too many down, asking, 'Why am I not enough for him?', as Martin looked on, horrified. I didn't give either of them a chance. I was offhand, rude, uninterested. Even if I had wanted to meet up with one of them again, I'm pretty sure they would have turned me down. I tell Gail none of this.

She tells me that she and Ben have been together for

twenty-three years ('late starters, we were both so focussed on work'), married for twenty-one, one child – Daisy – who is now at Cambridge, hence the desire for another presence around the place.

'It's so quiet without her. I mean, there was only one of her, but the house felt full when she was here, you know . . .'

'I do.' I know exactly what she means. Just knowing your child is sleeping in the next room makes a home feel alive. Makes it feel like a home.

'There are a few children on The Close, so Betsy will have someone to play with when she comes to stay. Jan and Roman at number 5 have a daughter, but actually, she's quite a bit older. Nearly Daisy's age. The couple at number 1 have a baby, although it's still tiny, I think. They don't mix much. Stella and Al across the street have two girls. Eight and ten going on eighteen and twenty. Oh, that reminds me . . .' She looks at me with an amused expression on her face. 'Stella told me I was crazy to invite a newly divorced woman to move in. She thinks you'll be after all our husbands . . .'

'What?' I explode. Though I've noticed that since David and I split up invitations from our couple friends have dwindled. I put it down to them feeling uneasy about which one of us their loyalties ought to lie with, but maybe I'm suddenly viewed as some kind of potential predatory man-stealer, just by virtue of finding myself on my own.

Gail laughs. 'Don't worry. No one's taking her seriously.'

I manage a smile. 'She sounds nice.'

'She actually is. But she's Al's trophy wife – what can I say? Eleven years younger than him. Well, except that they're not married yet. Wedding of the century coming up. They've been together years, though. He was married to someone else when they met, blah blah blah. You get the picture.'

'Ah, so he's got form.'

'Exactly. So I imagine now she's paranoid about the same thing happening to her.'

'Is she the one right opposite? Peter Stringfellow's dream woman, if she was fifteen years younger?'

Gail laughs. 'That's her. She's harmless. In fact, I really like her. She has a good heart. Al, not so much, but anyway. I'll introduce you to them when I get the chance.' She looks at her wrist, on which there's an actual watch, not a fitness device. It looks weirdly quaint. 'Oh, I should eat something. Do you fancy staying?'

I glance at the clock. It's twenty past eight. Somehow, we've chatted for over an hour and a half. 'Gosh, no. I should go. I promised Betsy we'd FaceTime before she went to bed. Thanks, though.'

Gail stands up and gives me a hug. 'Well, welcome to The Close.'

I feel a bit bad leaving her to rattle around in her 10,000-square-foot mansion on her own (who am I kidding? I'm sure I'd get used to it. I could get a skateboard and practise in the hallway). My studio at least feels cosy. Probably because half of it is still taken up by boxes. I forgot to ask Gail when to put the recycling out. I haven't even caught sight of a bin yet. I imagine The Close is not the sort of place where they're left outside all week. I don't want to be marked down as an anarchist by leaving the recyclables on the kerb on a Monday.

Betsy answers on the second ring, looking scrubbed and shiny in her favourite yellow spotty pyjamas. My heart lurches at the thought that this is my new reality. Even when I find a new home for the two of us, even when she has a bedroom of her own next to mine, there are still going to be nights like these, when the only access I'll have to my daughter is through a screen.

'Hi, Mummy.' I'm 'Mum' at least fifty per cent of the time these days, so I'm pathetically grateful for those two extra letters. I settle down on the sofa, ready to hear about her day.

I hardly sleep at all. It's too quiet. I'm used to the sounds of cars and the occasional shouty drunk. At about half past three I give in and get up to make myself a cup of tea. The kitchen end of my living space looks out over The Close and I feel exposed standing there when everything outside is so black, as if anyone could be out there watching me, so I turn the light off and boil the kettle in the dark. There are no streetlamps. At one point the house opposite lights up like a fairground ride and I gasp, half expecting to see balaclava'd burglars scaling the walls, but then a lanky fox saunters casually down the front path, stopping and looking right at me before racing off along the middle of the street and into the woods. The light snaps off again. I can see why Gail gets nervous here when she's alone.

I take my tea back to bed and lie there wondering what happens now. I've already decided I need to throw myself into my work, not just as a distraction but because I do need to drum up some more business. It's been ticking over for years, but it's hardly been a money-making machine. And the competition is fierce, especially now that cleaning is the new baking. There are TV shows dedicated to how to do it to perfection and achieve Zen-like levels of mindfulness at the same time. Although I guarantee Mrs Hinch has never had to mop up vomit from round the urinals after an office Christmas party. That'll kill anyone's buzz. Now I'm a single mum and, despite the fact that I know David will always be fair, our expenses have doubled. Two households. Two mortgages, once I find my house. The spring is always my busiest time – we can make enough extra on top of our regular office contracts to carry us through the leaner times in the winter. I have to get out there every day, capitalize on that. Part of the reason I agreed to Betsy's current living arrangements was so that I would have no excuse – precious little else to do; I hardly have a bulging social calendar. David and I shared our life outside of work, but there's no doubt that our friends were made up more of his pals and their other halves than mine. And even after eleven years that seems to matter. His oldest mates – mostly from uni – were all still in London, still a tight bunch, whereas mine were scattered across the country. None of us even considered staying in Derby once our college days were over. They're out there somewhere, they're just not a cohesive group. And it's always been hard to add someone random I've met along the way – a work colleague, a neighbour, another mum – to such a closed shop. That's something else I need to address. I curse myself for letting old friendships dwindle away. Tell myself that tomorrow I'll start making an effort. It's time to move on with my life.

2

My Corsa is still the only car parked out on the street. I assume none of the annexe-dwelling nannies and house-keepers have transport of their own, or else they're being paid enough to drive one of the many Bentleys and BMWs on the cobbled forecourts. To make matters worse, mine has 'Sunshine Cleaning' emblazoned on the side in cheer-ful orange letters, along with the website address and phone number. It's classy – what can I say?

I look around self-consciously as I beep the doors unlocked. Lean into the passenger side to deposit my bag on the seat. I always carry a bag of epic proportions. I have no idea what's in it beyond my phone and keys. Cer-tainly nothing I need on a daily basis. I hear the clop-clop of high-heeled shoes and look up to see Stella, the woman from the house opposite, heading to her shiny vehicle. Today she's in eye-wateringly tight skinny jeans, huge heels and a smart checked fitted jacket. The abundant hair is in a loose, effortless (for which read it took hours or she got someone else to do it) half up, half down style. Up close, I see she has the blank, smooth, high-cheeked look of someone who knows her way around the inside of a surgeon's office. Her oversized lips pout puffily. Despite the fact that I know she's wary of me, I smile and wave and start to say, 'Hello', but stop short when she blanks me. Maybe she just didn't see me. I lower my hand and pretend to look occupied. She revs up the engine like she's a teenage drag-racer and glides out of the drive while looking down at her phone. Still, at least I tried.

Angie, my longest-serving employee, has emailed me a stock update for each building, so I fill in the gaps at the warehouse (nine bottles of bleach for the price of six! What a time to be alive!) and drive to the first of our regulars – a four-storey seventies block near Lord's Cricket Ground housing a different company on each floor, which have miraculously all got together and agreed to use the services of Sunshine Cleaning. They have a small car park out the front and I open the entrance door with the code, prop it open and unload some of my booty, checking Angie's list, before taking it down to our tiny storeroom in the basement. I repeat the process further down the street (three-storey Victorian, housing one media company, no parking but a swanky reception, and a kind doorman who helps me with my boxes then keeps an eye out for traffic wardens while I head down to the basement again). Then again, round the corner on St John's Wood High Street (modern block, five storeys, two companies, but we only have the contract for the financiers on the lower three floors. I'm working on the insurance brokers upstairs. No basement this time; I'm allocated space in a hallway cupboard. I have to be flexible in my line of work. Every company has different needs and facilities, and there's no point throwing a fit because there's not enough room to store my Vileda Super Mop. There are a hundred other cleaning companies waiting to snatch my contracts from my hands if I'm not adaptable enough.

The afternoon stretches out ahead of me. I think of

all the times I've longed for more hours to myself, but, without the prospect of my daughter barrelling in through the door at half past three, I don't know what to fill them with. I should go home and start ringing round, making appointments to pitch for new contracts, but I have no impetus to do anything. David's flat is not far from here, near Maida Vale, in a grand mansion block, complete with concierge. We used to laugh at the kind of people who thought they needed a concierge on call, as if every day they had a theatre-ticket emergency that needed dealing with urgently. ('Julian! They've put us in row K! Whatever shall we do?' 'Don't fret, Harriet, the concierge will make everything better.') Betsy's school is close by, off Shirland Road. Before I know what I'm doing, I'm driving in that direction, almost on autopilot. How many times have I done this journey from my work to our old maisonette, just along the street from David's new place?

I park outside the school, look up at the huge Victorian building. Somewhere inside, Betsy will be reciting French verbs or painting one of her many pictures of our ginger cat Felix. David currently has custody of Felix, but once our roles are reversed and Betsy is back with me during the week he'll be back living with me too. Betsy and Felix are inseparable. I stare hopefully at the mullioned windows, trying to catch a glimpse of my daughter's wayward curls. Wondering if she has her hair in a ponytail or plaits today. There's a long debate about the merits of each every morning, and it feels strange not to know today's outcome. Not to know how to picture her.

Eventually, I make myself start the car again. No point

sitting out here like a weirdo. I need to take control of my life. I drive on towards Queen's Park and the estate agents who are looking out for a rarely available two-storey terrace house that is within my price range.

As luck would have it, Rahina, my main point of contact, is at her desk. She smiles when she sees me. I think she still feels guilty that I was gazumped on my dream home – tiny but perfectly formed, two bedrooms, end terrace, small south-facing garden, walking distance to Betsy's school – and I know I'd be first on her list to alert if anything similar came in. I know there will be nothing new. But what if something perfect came in half an hour ago and I could snap it up without it even going on their website, without anyone else seeing it?

'Laura! Hi.' She stands up to greet me, hand extended.

'I was just passing,' I say, pretty sure she'll know it's a lie. 'Anything . . . ?'

She shakes her head. 'Sorry. There's a flat . . .'

When my little house fell through, I looked at flats, but I couldn't get the idea out of my head of having a place that was entirely my own, however minuscule, with its own garden. Somewhere for Betsy to play. I'm not ready to give up yet. 'No, thanks.'

She touches my arm. Rahina has a four-year-old son, and I know she understands my desperation. 'I'll call you as soon as there's anything. Something'll come up. It's spring. It's a good time . . .'

I fake a smile. 'Thanks.'

On the drive home I keep my head down as I turn off Maida Vale and pass the block where David now lives. Except that, of course, I look up at the last minute, locate his fourth-floor windows and the Juliet balcony. I know he'll be at work, but I somehow can't look away.

Gail has a surprise for me. She's invited some of the other residents of The Close round for drinks, and she'd like me to come along. It'll be my chance to get to know them she tells me when I bump into her on the drive.

'Are you not at work today?' I ask, trying to change the subject. I can't imagine anything I want to do less. Even though I know I need to find myself a social life, I'm pretty sure I'm not going to find it here. I'd had hopes of maybe befriending some of the staff – the nannies and housekeepers and cooks. Maybe meeting a rugged gardener or two. But I never see any of them. No one seems to have told the employers of The Close about the laws entitling their employees to time off.

'Working at home.' She does that fingers-in-the-air thing when she says 'working'. 'So pop round at six. No excuses.'

I'm saved from having to answer by the appearance of a woman and a large brown Labrador from the house next door. She's somehow making skinny jeans and green wellingtons look like something on the catwalk. Like my opposite neighbour, she has way too much hair for one human being. I'm thankful that at least I've tamed my curls into a ponytail this morning. She waves a hello. Gail beckons her over and I make a fuss of the dog. 'Eva, this is Laura, who's just moved into our annexe.'

Eva gives me a hesitant smile. I wonder if Stella has shared her wariness of me with her too. 'How are you settling in?'

'Great,' I say. 'It's lovely here.'

'Well, welcome.' She turns to Gail. 'Six o'clock, right?'

'Perfect.'

'We'll be there. Nice to meet you, Laura. See you later.' She moves off in the direction of the woods, Labrador in tow.

'She seems nice,' I say to Gail.

'She is. Eva and Rafa. They have two grown-up kids, both married and living abroad.'

I watch Eva sashaying away. 'How old is she, then?'

Gail shrugs. 'Late forties.'

'She looks about twenty-five.'

Gail laughs. 'Bits of her probably are. Her boobs are only about four, I think.'

'What does she do?'

She looks at me, confused. 'Do? Oh, for work? God, no. I'm the only working female in The Close, unless you count the staff. And now you, thank god. It's like the land that time forgot. If I have to have one more conversation about the best fillers and laser eyelid lifts versus surgery, I won't be responsible for my actions. Not that I haven't dabbled myself. I mean, who hasn't?'

I don't bother to say, 'Not me,' because I think it's probably evident from the multitude of lines that spring up on my face when I grimace. 'What do they do all day?'

'Who knows? Have lunch? Except none of them really eats anything. You watch their faces tonight when I offer them snacks.'

'I can't wait,' I say, beginning to think this could be more fun than I imagined. If nothing else, I might get some funny stories out of it to share with Angie. And at least Eva was friendly. I shouldn't be judgemental.

*

Betsy FaceTimes me at four from Zara's to show me her new masterpiece.

'Is it an orangutan?' I say, and she giggles.

'Of course not. It's Felix.'

I know it's Felix. It's always Felix. He must be the most documented cat in history. 'It's what? Sorry, sweetie, you cut out halfway through. A sea lion?'

Betsy guffaws. 'Felix. Feeeelix!'

'Oh, Miss Friedricks! Yes, I can see it now.' Whatever comedy gods ensured that my daughter's teacher's name semi-rhymed with her favourite muse, I thank them for the thousandth time. Betsy is inconsolable with laughter. She one hundred per cent knows that I'm winding her up.

'Miss Friedricks doesn't have a tail, silly.'

'I bet she does. Have you had a proper look?'

I tell her I'm going to drinks at the big house and, once she's established that there won't be any actual princesses there, she instructs me to make a mental note of what everyone is wearing so I can share the details with her. Zara's mum Michaela appears over her shoulder and waves at me. I wave back. She ruffles Betsy's hair. 'Teatime when you're ready. No rush.'

'I'll see you tomorrow!' Betsy shouts happily to me. I've agreed with David that I'll pick her up from school on Wednesdays and take her to mine for tea before dropping her back at his in time for bed. I'm as excited as she is.

'I love you,' I say, blowing her a kiss, and she rewards me by doing the same.

*

I spend the rest of the afternoon agonizing about what to wear. Sweatpants are not going to cut it. In the end, I settle for a dress I only usually have the chance to show off at weddings. Reiss. Fitted and sleek, in a dramatic flowery fabric. Or, at least, it used to be fitted. Now it's a bit too snug. I've discovered comfort eating in the wake of the separation. Still, needs must. It doesn't look too bad. I dig around in the cases under the bed to find my one pair of heels, scowl at my pale legs, slap on some haphazard make-up and smooth argan oil through my hair. I look like a weird, more girly version of me. It'll do.

I'm early, but I decide to head over to see if Gail needs any last-minute help. She opens the door and for a second I think I've got the time wrong. She's wearing skinny jeans and an old T-shirt with 'Lynyrd Skynyrd' written on it. She looks effortlessly rock-chick gorgeous.

She beams a smile at me. 'Hi! Come on in.'

'I . . . um . . . I'm overdressed, aren't I?'

'What? No, you look fabulous.' I follow her inside, wondering if I should nip home and change. Gail is handing me a drink, though, an elegant flute of fizz. I put it down. 'Oh, no, I came to see if you wanted any help . . .'

'All done,' she says, leading me into the living room, picking up my glass as she goes. It's gigantic, with the biggest, whitest sofa I have ever seen, heavy, dark wood side tables, an open fire, framed abstract art. The patio doors leading on to the garden are gaping wide.

'Too cold?' she says.

'A little bit, maybe, but it's . . .' I'm interrupted by the doorbell. I feel ridiculously nervous, like a prize cow that's about to be examined and appraised. Gail goes to answer it. I hear voices, a man and a woman. Air-kissing. I take a sip of my drink.

I stand there for what seems like an awfully long time while they go via the kitchen to get a drink. I wonder if I should go in there to greet them, but it feels presumptuous, so I just stay where I am, listening to them all talking and laughing. Eventually, I hear Gail saying, 'Oh, come and meet Laura,' and I stand to attention, shifting from foot to foot in my uncomfortable heels.

It's the woman from opposite. Stella. And, I assume, her fiancé Al. He's clearly a good bit older than her – eleven years, I think Gail said – but toned and tanned and buffed to perfection, with that glow that says, 'I'm rich and successful.' He's handsome under there somewhere, but his eyes appear to have been stretched round and open and he has blinding white veneers on his teeth, so now he looks like a startled baby bird who's wearing dentures. Like Stella, he has an unfeasibly large head of hair. Just a shade too dark, in his case. I make a note to ask Gail about the hair. Maybe it's something in the local water. I could bottle it and make a fortune. He looks familiar. I'm not sure why.

Stella looks immaculate, in faded jeans, with flat, bejewelled thong sandals revealing golden ankles and perfectly manicured toes and, guess what, a soft-fitted retro T-shirt. I feel like someone's aunt, making way too much effort, while all the cool kids are naturally chic in whatever they threw on.

'Laura, this is Stella and Al,' Gail says as she comes in. Stella and Al look me up and down; she with a bit of a sneer, he, I would say, with a slightly wolfish smile.

'Hi,' I manage.

'Hello,' Stella says, somehow imbuing the two syllables with disdain. The huge hair is tied up like the most luxurious horse's tail you ever seen. Every bit of her glows with health and self-care. Apart from her lips, which are just . . . well . . . weird, in my opinion. Two mutant slugs that have taken up residence on her face. And her eyes, the outside corners of which are pulled up at a sharp angle. It looks painful.

'Laura's going to be living in the annexe for a while,' Gail says. 'Do you remember, I told you? Her house fell through.'

'There are definitely worse places to end up,' Al says.

'Yes, it's lovely.' I'm wracking my brains as to where I know him from.

Stella turns to Gail, ignoring me. 'Did you hear that Roman and Jan are moving away for a year? He's opening an office in Nice.'

It's a blatant attempt to exclude me from the conversation.

'Oh no, I didn't know,' Gail says. I'm willing the doorbell to ring and more guests to arrive, to dilute the awkwardness.

'The girls are so upset. They've become such good friends with Sophia.'

'Oh,' Gail says. 'Laura has a daughter. She's seven, isn't that right, Laura?'

I nod. 'Betsy. How old are yours?'

Stella graces me with her attention. 'Eight and ten, but they're very sophisticated.'

Clearly, Betsy is not considered worthy. 'Oh well, Betsy isn't. She's a typical little girl, you know. Her idea of sophistication is eating Nandos with a knife and fork. But I'm sure they'll get on.'

'Hmmm,' is all that Stella can manage. She turns back to Gail. 'I suppose Sophia will be off to uni in the autumn, anyway, but still . . .'

I sip my champagne nervously. I have a tendency to drink a little too much in social situations when I'm feeling uncomfortable. Especially if I feel I'm on show. I remind myself to go slow. But I'm irritated by the way I know she's prejudged me. 'Maybe Betsy could have a play-date with them? She'll be with me every weekend.'

Stella raises a sceptical eyebrow. At least, I think that's what she's trying to do; it's hard to tell on her frozen face. 'My girls have a very busy schedule. They don't really do impromptu playdates. Or playdates at all, actually. They're a bit old for that.'

I want to say, *Poor them*, but I don't want to make things awkward for Gail. Stella eliminates the threat, though, by more or less turning her back on me. 'Of course, they won't be leaving before the autumn. And they're not selling up, so that's something –'

'You look very familiar, Al,' I interrupt. Stella stops talking and shoots him a look that could turn milk.

'I was just thinking the same,' he says. He has one of those voices actors have in TV shows from the seventies. Smooth. Silky. Seductive. I bet he practises it when he's alone.

'You don't work in St John's Wood, maybe?'

He takes a slow sip of his drink. 'I do, actually. Do you?' Stella looks from him to me and back again.

'Yes,' I say. 'Well, yes and no . . .'

'Laura runs a cleaning company,' Gail pipes up.

Stella turns to me, pillowy lips pouted. 'Oh, you're a cleaner.'

'I run a cleaning company,' I say, as politely as I can.

'Mmm,' she says, unconvinced.

'In St John's Wood?' Al says.

'Mainly. Maybe you work for one of the companies . . .'

He puffs his chest up proudly. 'AJT Music. I'm the CEO.'

'Oh well, you're one of my clients,' I say. Stella glares at me. I ignore her. Fuck her. All I'm doing is having a civil conversation. 'You've probably seen me dropping off supplies or popping in to check everything is OK.'

'That must be it. I never forget a face,' he says. He's being friendly, but there's something unsettling about him, something flirty in his tone that makes me uncomfortable, as if this is a dynamic he and Stella play out often and I'm just a mouse to be toyed with.

'That makes sense,' Gail says. 'I gave Al one of my ads for the annexe to put up at work. I gave them to everyone on The Close. I thought, that way, I'd end up with someone respectable.' She laughs to show that this is a joke, although I imagine there's a grain of truth in it somewhere.

'That's it. That's where I saw it.'

'Ah, so I'm responsible for you moving in,' Al says, with a raised eyebrow. Stella's nostrils flare.

'Oh! I keep meaning to tell you. We've secured Ottolenghi to do the catering,' she says to Gail, out of nowhere. 'It's not something he would usually do, but . . .' She leaves the sentence hanging, for us to draw our own conclusions about how they persuaded him. Cold hard cash, I assume. To be fair, it does sound like a bit of a coup.

'Wow,' Gail says. 'Fabulous.'

Stella is obviously disappointed that we don't ask more questions. 'Al won't tell me what it's costing.' She lays a hand on Al's arm.

'Nothing but the best,' he says, smiling at her cheesily. I have to force myself not to pull a face. C—ringe, as Betsy would say.

I decide I need to try to claw back some goodwill, so I take a chance. 'Oh yes, Gail told me you were getting married. Congratulations.'

I wait for her to tell me that she was talking about a birthday party for one of her daughters or just a routine Sunday lunch, but she ignores me. Al at least has the good grace to be polite. 'Thank you. It only took her twelve years to persuade me.' He laughs heartily at his own joke, and I smile weakly. Thankfully, the doorbell rings. Gail puts her glass down on the mantelpiece.

'It's OK,' Al says, making a move towards the door. 'I'll let them in. I need the little boys' room anyway.'

Gail, Stella and I stand there in silence for a moment. I give Stella a forced smile. 'How about you? Do you work?' I ask, although I already know what the answer will be.

She looks at me as if I've just asked her if she gives blow jobs for small change. 'No. I don't.'

'Oh,' I say disingenuously. 'You're unemployed. That's tough.'

Beside me, Gail snorts, then attempts to disguise it as a cough. Stella narrows her eyes at me, and, if I was taken in for questioning, I would swear that this is the moment that she decides she hates me.

3

By the time I go home later – having again made the excuse that I need to FaceTime with my daughter – I've met four more residents of The Close. Eva's husband, Rafa – as blankly pleasant as she is. He's a cosmetic dentist with a private practice on Harley Street, and I can see him checking out my molars whenever I smile. I wonder if he's responsible for the oversized veneers they all sport. Roman and Jan – similar in age to Eva and Rafa – who clearly used the same surgeon, because they look almost identical: high-cheeked and wide-eyed, mandatory thick hair, his in a swept-back bouffant and hers in loose blonde waves. The main difference is that she has an arse like a shelf that in no possible universe grew on its own. I have no idea how she sits down, but, on the plus side, Roman always has somewhere to put his drink. They're friendly enough, but distant, as if they've decided it's hardly worth getting to know me, since they're moving away. And Katya, from number 2 – younger than the others by a good few years, so I assume a second or even third wife. She tells me she's 'married to Guy, who's away on business' when I ask her what she does, but is, at least, sweet and welcoming.

They all look like pictures of glowing, privileged health who have then let a slightly drunken surgeon run roughshod over their facial features. I swear there's not an original nose among them. Even Katya, who can't be more than twenty-five, has obviously already had either Botox or a severe facelift, because when she smiles her face looks as if it's about to split open with the effort. And her lips – like Stella's, like Eva's, like Jan's – are unnaturally full.

Apparently, the couple from number 1 never accept invitations; 7 spend most of their time in Russia; and Bill and Anya from number 8 are on holiday in Dubai. Stella and Al are clearly the sun around which all these planets revolve. The golden couple. They hold court, each in the centre of a circle of their own gender. Even in this sea of fabulously rich and successful people, it's indisputable that Stella and Al are the unacknowledged – or maybe it is acknowledged; who knows? – Queen and King of The Close.

As social occasions go, it's hardly the highlight of my year, but at least there are now a few people who will say hello to me in the street if I bump into them. In fact, Eva and Rafa have invited me to their thirtieth-anniversary party in a couple of weeks' time, and Katya has asked me if I'd like to join her at the day spa for a pampering (which I definitely can't afford to do, although I didn't actually say so, I just made non-committal noises about work and Betsy. Katya looked at me wide-eyed – something I'm not sure she could help, so stretched is her skin, so tight her ponytail – and said, 'You're so lucky to have a little girl. Don't you just want to spend all day dressing her up?' and I laughed, thinking how Betsy's idea of hell is being made to wear something she's not supposed to climb trees in) so my social diary is positively bursting. Tonight I'm just relieved to go back to my own space, though.

About half an hour later I hear noises in the street and peer through my front window to see Stella and Al, and Eva and Rafa, saying their goodbyes in front of the house. There's a lot of cheek-kissing and friendly promises to meet up again soon, but the minute Eva and Rafa head off in the direction of number 5 I notice Stella's demeanour change. The smile drops from her face and she stalks off towards her front door, leaving Al in her wake. Clearly, they are not in for a night of marital bliss. He goes to follow her, but then glances up at my window and catches me watching before I have the chance to duck down. He gives me a lecherous grin and a wave and I feel compelled to wave back, feeling as if I've been caught spying. Which, let's face it, I have.

I busy myself washing up a mug that's in the sink, as if, if he looks back, he'll think that's what I was doing all along. Luckily, he's distracted by Jan, Roman and Katya all leaving together and I step back out of sight.

My phone rings and I jump. I pick it up and see it's Angie. I don't often get calls once they've all commenced work for the evening. A few times, when they've accidentally tripped alarms, or forgotten how to set one as they leave. Once, when there was water dripping through the ceiling of one of the offices and they had no idea who to call. Once, when someone sliced their finger open on a piece of metal in one of the bins and had to be taken to A&E and I went in to cover for them. Sometimes it's just to let me know one of them has had to go home early because they're sick, or some unusual circumstance means they'll need to do extra hours. Tonight is one of those times. Angie tells me that the finance office were in the middle of a party when they arrived and the last stragglers have only just left, leaving behind a trail of destruction. She wants to know if I can authorize the extra hours it's going to take to clean it up. I tell her yes, ask her to take a few photos of the mess on her phone, just in case they quibble. Then I offer to come down and help – an extra pair of hands – but she's happy they can manage. I often go in and help out if there's an emergency. It's important the customers are satisfied.

On Wednesday I get to school way too early. I'm so desperate to give Betsy a hug. I hang around in my car for a bit, but then I see Michaela join the ever-increasing throng of parents, so I make my way over to her.

She gives me a big smile when she sees me. 'Hey. How are you?'

'Good,' I say. Michaela is only a couple of years younger than me, but you'd believe her if she told you she was a teenager. Just a very tired one. Button-nosed, with fair hair and freckles, she has girl-next-door down to a T. I've always thought we could be friends, given the chance. I mean, we are, but we're not confidantes. She has two other children, both younger than Zara, and time is not her friend. 'I hope she's been behaving.'

'Well, it's only been two days,' Michaela says, laughing. 'But honestly, it's a godsend. They keep each other amused so I have one less kid to worry about entertaining.'

'And David's been getting there on time to pick her up? He's not taking advantage?'

'He's been fine, Laura. Stop worrying.'

Michaela refused to accept any offer of payment when

she agreed to take Betsy home with her and Zara after school – or after ballet or painting, both of which Zara attends, too – three nights a week. It was one of those awkward things where I didn't know whether to offer or not, and then I did and she refused, and then I was a bit embarrassed in case she thought I was treating her like the hired help. They live in a block just along the road from David's. It made sense. 'Well,' I say now, 'just let me know if it gets to be too much.'

'I promise I will. You should come round one afternoon – I mean, if you're at a loose end. Don't feel you can't drop in and see Bets just because . . . you know . . .'

I feel my face break into a big smile. 'I will. Thank you. Oh look, here they are . . .'

Betsy steamrollers into me, throwing her arms round my waist as if she hasn't seen me for weeks, rather than days. I bury my face in her dark blonde hair, inhaling the familiar smell of strawberry shampoo, her favourite.

'Ready?' I say, and she nods.

'See you soon,' I say to Michaela. 'And thanks again.'

At this time of day, the drive to my place takes a good forty-five minutes. We sit in a queue of cars, most containing one parent and one child, edging slowly forwards. I used to rail against the laziness of those who drove their offspring to and from school rather than walking, clogging up the roads for those who needed them, but here I am: one of them. I don't care, though, because I'm here with Betsy while she prattles on, my own small ray of sunshine.

She gasps when she sees the house. 'Is this ours? Can we get a dog?'

'No. Just above the garage, remember.'

She runs up the stairs ahead of me, waits while I unlock the door. 'This is cool,' she says, taking in the whole place in about three seconds. She hares into the bedroom. 'Is this my bed when I stay here?'

'Both of ours,' I say. 'We're sharing.'

'Brilliant. Can I have this side?' She puts her schoolbag down on the side of the bed where I have been sleeping.

'Of course.'

She looks out of the window behind the headboard, on to the large expanse of grass and the woods at the edge of the heath beyond. 'Can I play out there?'

''Fraid not. That's Gail and Ben's garden. Do you have homework?'

'A bit. Spelling. Can we explore?'

'Homework first.' I open her bag, and her teddy pops out at me like a jack in the box. 'Oh good, Bruno came.'

'Of course he did.'

I prop him up on the pillow, blink back a tear. 'Right. Homework, explore, tea. How does that sound?'

There's a gate at the end of The Close that leads to the woods. I'm slightly panicked that I don't know my way around yet, that we could end up lost, like a pair of doomed fairy-tale characters. 'Stick to the path,' I say to her, for the millionth time. It's beautiful; there's no doubt about it. The daffodils are out, the birds are singing, there's even a woodpecker tapping out a rhythm nearby. I take a deep breath. The air is fresh; there's the smell of new growth and a hint of coconut from the gorse. It's hard to imagine living with this on your doorstep.

'If we got a dog, we could bring him over here every day,' Betsy says.

'We're not getting a dog.'

'But if we did, we could walk him over here every day.'

'We don't live here.'

'Technicality,' she says, rolling her eyes exaggeratedly. This is her new favourite expression. I have no idea where she learned it. My guess is from Morgan, the most precocious girl in her class. Whatever Morgan says, the rest of them are all parroting it a few days later. She's the one who's going to lead them all storming into early adolescence in a couple of years' time. I'm thankful that, although Betsy admires her and they get on fine, she's not in her inner circle. Yet.

I'm saved by the appearance of Eva and her chocolate lab. Betsy goes flying over to greet the dog, throwing herself to the ground in front of it so it couldn't really avoid her if it wanted to. Luckily, it wags its big heavy tail and Eva seems pleased to see us, too, although she shows it more subtly.

'Ah, you must be Betsy,' she says, and I'm touched that she remembers her name. Betsy rewards her with a big toothless smile, arms around the dog.

'What's she called?'

'Cocoa. She's a he.'

'Betsy, this is Eva. She lives next door.' Betsy is too busy telling Cocoa she loves him to take much notice. I give Eva an apologetic smile.

'My two were the same with animals,' she says sympathetically. 'They practically camped out here and accosted any creature that went past.'

'You've lived here that long?' I ask, slightly in awe.

Eva nods, smiling. 'Twenty-eight years. It's a hard place to leave. How did you enjoy last night?'

'Great. Everyone seems lovely.' I'm dying to ask her what she thinks of Stella, whether she's as awful as she seems, but for all I know she might be her best friend.

'We do these get-togethers quite regularly,' she tells me. Betsy is throwing Cocoa's soggy tennis ball and watching him amble off to retrieve it. 'Well, a few of us do. It's nice to have a sense of community, don't you think? Don't forget our thirtieth, by the way. I'll let you know as soon as we have a definite date for the party, but it'll be in a couple of weeks.'

'I'll look forward to it,' I say. If nothing else, it'll be fascinating to get more insight into how the other half live.

She hooks a loose strand of hair behind her ear. 'How are you liking the woods?'

'Gorgeous. Although I'm a bit scared we'll get lost. I feel like I need to tie a bit of string to a tree.'

'You're welcome to walk with us,' she says. 'We don't go far. Cocoa's hips aren't what they were.'

I look over at Betsy, playing with the dog's ears. If Cocoa minds, he's not showing it. 'Oh. That'd be lovely. Thanks.'

She fills me in on more gossip about The Close as we walk, Betsy and Cocoa following behind. I'm not a gossip fan. I always assume that if someone is badmouthing someone else to you, they'll do the same about you the minute you leave the room. But Eva's chatter is all positive. Bill and Anya are adopting a baby, Stella and Al's wedding is going to be a do to die for (I'm not expecting an invitation any time soon), Gail and Ben are just about the nicest people she's ever met. I find myself telling her what brought me here, about the way my marriage ended. How devastated I was. Still am. Every now and then I turn back to check that Betsy is a) still there and b) not listening, but she's blissfully absorbed in playing with the dog. We walk in a big circle, out of the woods, which turn out to be smaller than I'd imagined, and around a huge field. Eventually, we end up back where we started and we say goodbye at her gate.

'I walk him twice a day, so feel free to join me any time. It's nice to have company.'

'I definitely will,' I say, feeling more positive than I have in days. I drag Betsy reluctantly away from Cocoa and we turn towards home. Her school uniform is covered in mud. I should have told David to pack something for her to change into after school, because now I just have to hope he has a clean, ironed set at his for tomorrow. We're still working out the details of who does what in our new world, but I hate that I've already lost my sixth sense for what Betsy needs and when.

'They're nice,' she says, slipping her hand into mine.

'Eva or Cocoa?' I say with a smile. I know exactly who she really means.

She laughs. 'Cocoa. But the lady seems nice too. Is she posh?'

'Very,' I say. 'Well, she's rich. They're not necessarily the same.'

As we approach our own gate Stella's car rolls into the drive opposite us and two small Mini Mes exit the back seats. High, gleaming dark brown ponytails – in their case, I assume, natural – and faces full of make-up, I realize with horror as we get closer. Betsy stops dead on the spot. 'Who are they?' she says in awe, mouth open. I don't have time to answer because Stella has seen us. I plaster a smile on my face. Walk towards her, Betsy in tow. I'm going to make an effort, be the bigger person, set a good example to my daughter.

'Hey. How are you? This is Betsy, I told you about her . . .'

I wait for Stella to introduce her two, but she just says hello and goes back to unloading designer bags from the boot of her car.

'I think you and Betsy are about the same age,' I say to the slightly smaller of the two girls. 'She's going to be staying here sometimes. At number 6.' I realize I'm prattling, trying at least to get them to acknowledge my child, who is staring at them both as if they're two previously undiscovered Wonders of the World.

The smaller girl looks her up and down. 'I don't think so. I'm eight.'

'I'm seven!' Betsy says. I look at her eager face, mud-streaked now, her hair springing from her ponytail in all directions, her glasses wonky on her nose, and I feel a rush of protective love.

Big Mini Me looks unimpressed. 'Why are you wearing your school uniform?' she says. I notice her top has a logo on. Chanel, maybe?

Betsy looks confused. 'Because I've been at school.'

'Girls, can you help me carry these inside?' Stella pipes up. She hands them each a large paper carrier. 'So nice to see you, Laura,' she says unconvincingly as she slams the boot shut with an elbow.

They parade towards the front door like a row of unpacked Russian dolls. Betsy waves a hand. 'Bye.'

The smaller one at least has the good manners to wave back.

I wait in the lobby while the sullen concierge phones up to tell David his daughter is home. A few minutes later the lift opens and there he is. My soon-to-be ex-husband. He gives me a big smile, as if we're just two good friends bumping into each other in the street. My heart, as usual, flip-flops all over the place.

'Hi,' he says. 'Hi, Bets.'

She throws herself into his hug. David looks at me over her shoulder. 'All OK?'

'Yep. Sorry her uniform is a mess.'

'I met a dog,' Betsy announces. I know David will hear the whole story later.

'Did you indeed?' he says. He looks back at me with those amber-flecked dark brown eyes that I used to think I could read so well. 'No problem. We've got a clean set.'

'Don't forget you need to take everything you want for the weekend to school with you on Friday,' I say to Betsy. Then I turn back to David. 'I'll see you on Sunday night.'

'OK.'

Betsy looks at me, face about to crumble. 'Do you have to go back tonight? Can't you stay with us?'

I swoop her into me. 'I do, sweetie. I'll see you on Friday. Have fun with Dad.' He takes her hand and they walk off to the lift. 'OK, so this dog. Do you know its name . . .'

I turn and walk out. Remind myself he's a good father.

Turns out he was a shit husband, but he's definitely a good father.

Because I'm in the area, I stop off to check in with – who am I kidding? – to check up on my cleaners. I often do unannounced visits. Not because I don't trust them. I absolutely do. But it still feels sensible to keep them on their toes. I can't afford to lose any of my hard-won clients. I pull up outside the three-storey media company – Al's company, I remember now. They use us every weekday night. Three cleaners working for two hours. The receptionist and doorman have long since gone home, but I have a set of keys, so I let myself in. I find Angie hoovering the stairs between the ground and first floors.

'Jesus Christ, you made me jump!' she says when I shout hello over the noise. I snort with laughter at her flustered face.

'Sorry. Unintentional.'

She turns off the machine. 'You'll be one member of staff down if you do that too often.'

'It's good for you. Gets your heart going. Everything OK?'

She brushes her short chestnut hair off her face. 'All fine. The others are upstairs.'

'How are the kids?'

She gives me a big smile. Angie has one of those faces that has only two modes: resting bitch and full-on happy. Any mention of her two sons always brings on face number two. Her body is wiry. Muscly and tanned, like she's been plastinated. She's older than me – her fiftieth was a couple of years ago – and she has a fourteen- and a sixteen-year-old at home and the sinewy body of someone who does a hundred press-ups every morning for fun. 'Nightmare, the pair of them. Bobby just won his judo tournament, though.'

'Amazing.'

She asks me about Betsy and I have to blink back tears. 'It'll be over before you know it,' she says. I nod, unable to talk about it.

'I'll go and frighten the others,' I say.

I hear the vacuum start up again as I head up towards the first floor. The offices here are open-plan. Sixteen desks. Bright primary colours. At one end is a glass-walled room containing a large circular wooden table. There's a printed sign stuck to the door: 'Meeting Room. Please Book'. And underneath it another, handwritten: 'We all share this room. It's not here for you to use as your office!!!' I wonder who the culprit is. Which of the sixteen desks belongs to the person who can't stand being in the communal space so much they set up camp in there on a regular basis. That'd be me. I find Tomas scrubbing the kitchen on the landing.

'Oh, hi, Mrs Anthony,' he says when he spots me. I remind him again that I'm not Mrs Anthony any more. That I'm back to Ms Martin, but actually, he should call me Laura anyway.

'Sure, Mrs Anthony,' he says. I give up. Tomas is a hard worker. The kitchen is as gleaming as one used by twenty-odd people can be. I can see he's doing a good job.

'Everything OK?'

He nods. 'All good.'

I leave him to it. Go up one more flight to the top floor.

Here, there are individual offices for, I assume, the executives. I'm guessing one of these must be Al's. I peer in through the glass walls. There's an open area here, too, for the assistants. Sharon, my newest and youngest employee – she can't be more than twenty, and she's on her own with twins – is dusting one of the desks gingerly. The rule is, don't disturb anyone's stuff. I've had enough complaints that someone can't find some valuable piece of paper, because an over-zealous cleaner must have moved it, so my staff are instructed to clean only the gaps where the desks are concerned.

She starts telling me a seemingly interminable story about her kids and something her mother said about the way they were dressed ('Like something off of *Love Island*! Just because Jayden was wearing a crop top!') and I remember – too late, as always – that it's a mistake to engage Sharon in conversation when she's supposed to be working. I keep my eyes on the duster in her flapping hand in the hope she gets the message that it's time for it to make contact with the desk again.

'Anyway, I'd better go,' I say when she takes a rare breath. 'I don't want to hold you up.'

Downstairs, I have a quick check round the ground-floor reception and the admin offices at the back. Then I shout my goodbyes to Angie and leave. I repeat the same process at the four-storey, four-company building round the corner, making sure I check in with all three workers there, and then I head for home to my empty flat and an early night. I try to calculate the hours till I see Bets again. It's less than forty-eight, but it feels like a lifetime.

4

I have no idea what to say.

I stand there, mouth opening and shutting. I know I should say, *No. It wasn't me. I don't have a clue what you're talking about.* But I don't know how I can. I'd be calling Al a liar and probably making myself look as if I actually do have something to hide. So I just say nothing.

Stella looks at me with what can only be described as undisguised loathing.

What happened was this. I was getting out of my car at the same time Stella and Al were heading out to get into theirs. Dressed up to the nines. Them, not me. I was tired and miserable, missing Betsy already, longing for my PJs and a cup of tea. The last thing I wanted was another awkward encounter with Stella. So I just waved. Smiled and said hello.

Next thing I knew, Al was calling out to me across the street.

'Laura, thank you for the book, by the way.'

I was about to ask him what he meant, say that he must be mistaken, that I hadn't given him any book, but he kept right on talking before I had the chance. Loudly, so that Stella would hear. 'I told Stella that we'd been talking about it when I bumped into you the other day, and that you'd very kindly given me your spare copy . . .'

I tuned out. I hadn't bumped into him. I hadn't

43

exchanged a word with him since Gail's drinks. I glanced at Stella as if she might give me a clue as to what was going on, but she just looked between me and Al, like an owl deciding which vole to pounce on and tear apart first. I felt my forehead creasing up. A frown. Confusion. Al must have seen it too, because he turned on his heels and strode back towards the car.

'Anyway, we'd better get a move on or we're going to be late. Bye, Laura. Thanks again.'

Now I stand there frozen to the spot, watching them leave. Knowing I should have said something. Knowing this is going to come back and haunt me. Feeling like an idiot.

I seethe about it all night. Clearly, Al does not really think I gave him a book. Clearly, he knows he didn't bump into me the other day. Clearly, he has something he wants to hide from Stella. I want to confront him with it, to ask him never to put me on the spot like that again, but I know I can't go round with Stella there. It'd only make things worse.

I know he works long hours, but from half past five on the dot the next day I hover, looking out of my kitchen window in the hope of catching him home alone. The gods must be on my side because about an hour and a half later, just as I'm thinking of taking a break because my legs have gone to sleep, I finally see him arrive home in his sports Bentley and then, five minutes later, Stella exits the front door in her designer yoga gear and heads towards her own car.

Before I really know what I'm doing, I'm down the

stairs and stomping across the road. I assume the kids are home – I haven't seen any signs of them leaving – but I also assume that they have a nanny who does the after-school care. I can't imagine Al being Dad of the Year and entertaining them while he cooks dinner. I ring the bell and, after a few moments, Mini Me the Elder answers. She looks at me blankly.

'Yes?'

'Hi,' I say, feeling stupidly intimidated by her overconfidence. Her poise.

'Is your dad around? I just want a quick word.'

She looks back over her shoulder without saying anything. 'Dad!'

I'm hoping she won't hang around listening to what I have to say, but actually, I don't think she could muster up any interest in me if I keeled over, frothing at the mouth, on her doorstep. She struts off towards the back of the house and I wait in the open doorway, looking around every now and again in case Stella decides to cut her yoga class short. I've come out without a cardigan and it's a chilly evening, so I'm tempted to step into their swirly, marble-floored hallway but, like a vampire, I feel I should be invited first. I can just make out a large painting of Stella – dressed in what looks like her underwear – on the landing wall. I'm gawping at it when a shiny pair of men's shoes rounds the corner in the stairs, followed by the rest of Al himself.

'Laura,' he says. I can't make out his tone. I don't know what I was expecting – apologetic? Repentant? Flirtatious? – but it just sounds flat. Matter of fact.

'Could I have a quick word?' I say, trying to keep the

annoyance out of my voice. I remind myself that I have to tread carefully. AJT Music are one of my best clients. I have far more competitors than I used to since cleaning became a spectator sport. It's only a matter of time before there's a reality show – *Celebrity Clean Off* – with four show-offy judges going round peering down people's toilets and sneering. And AJT with their three floors and five days a week are not a contract I can afford to lose.

'Of course,' he says. 'Do you want to come in?'

'No. I . . . This is OK. I just want to ask you what was all that about the book yesterday. I mean, did you get me mixed up with someone else?'

He steps out into the porch. Pulls the door behind him. 'Sorry about that. Stella put me on the spot, you know . . .' He looks at me as if I'm meant to know what the hell he's going on about.

'About a book?'

'Someone gave me the book, and she found it and asked me who it was from . . .'

Ah. I'm starting to see where this is going. 'Why didn't you tell her?'

He raises his eyebrows as if to say, *Why do you think?* Gives me what I imagine he believes is a charming smile. I force myself to look him directly in the eye. 'Or just tell her you bought it? Surely that would have been the best idea?'

'There's an inscription . . .'

I cut him off. 'Oh no, Al . . . You've let Stella think . . . what?' What exactly has he let her think? I try to keep my voice light. 'That we have some kind of little secret going on?'

'Of course not,' he says. 'I just told her we talked about the book and I said it sounded interesting, and then next thing I knew, you'd given me a copy.'

'With an inscription in. What does it say?'

'It doesn't matter.'

'It actually really does,' I say a bit too loudly, and he shushes me nervously. 'It matters whether it says, *Here's that book I was telling you about* or something way more personal. I'm guessing something way more personal.'

He says nothing, but he looks guilty so I suppose I have my answer.

'So, at the very least, Stella now thinks I have a thing for you? Well, that's just brilliant. That's going to make my life here so much more pleasant.'

'The thing is, Laura,' he says, rolling my name around his tongue in what I assume he thinks is a suggestive way. 'Stella can be a little jealous. She has a tendency to see something where there's nothing . . . do you know what I mean? She'll blow up, but then she'll forget about it in a couple of days.' And I think that, while I may have known Stella for less than a week, I already know her better than he does.

I let out a sigh. I know I'm not in a position to push it. 'I hope so. Listen, please don't involve me again. I mean . . . I'm trying to fit in here.'

'Don't tell her, will you?' he says, slightly threateningly, as I walk away. I don't bother to answer.

Back in my annexe, I flick the kettle on, fuming. Then I flick it off again and I'm down the stairs and round to Gail's front door before I can stop myself. I know I shouldn't turn up announced. I wouldn't want her to start doing the same to me. But I have to share this with someone. Have to work out if I'm being reasonable, being so furious. I ring the bell and shuffle from foot to foot as I wait. I know Ben isn't home until tomorrow, but she might be in the middle of eating, in the bath, anything. I'm about to turn away, go back upstairs, when the door opens and there she is. She looks genuinely pleased to see me, which is something.

'Hi. This is a nice surprise . . .'

'I don't want to disturb you,' I say, probably sounding deranged, 'but do you have a moment?'

She steps back to allow me to enter. 'Of course. Everything OK?'

'Yes. I mean, no. But yes. With the flat, I mean. All's fine.' I take a deep breath. Try to calm my voice. 'I just wanted to share something with you. See if I'm overreacting. I'm really sorry to just turn up.' I follow her into the kitchen. She has a glass of wine on the go, but I decline when she offers me one. I don't want her to think I'm intending to hijack her whole evening.

'So . . . ?' she says, sitting at the table. I join her, pouring out the whole story in one long, ill-formed sentence. Gail's eyes grow wide, and I know I'm not overreacting.

'I'm not surprised you're cross,' she says when I get to the end. 'What a weird thing to do. He must know how paranoid Stella is.'

'He's obviously got some woman on the side and he panicked,' I say. 'I mean, I know I shouldn't be saying this to you . . . you're their friend . . .' It occurs to me that this might be a huge mistake, telling Gail what just happened. Her loyalties lay with them long before she even met me.

'In all honesty, I've never been so sure about him,' she says. 'There's an element of . . . I don't know. I said to Ben once that I think he likes to keep Stella on the back foot. So she doesn't ever get too comfortable, you know?'

I nod. It sounds plausible. I also think Stella's a psycho, but I'm not about to share that with Gail. 'But why me? Why involve me in it?'

She thinks for a moment. 'Because you're not going to be here long? Because Stella is already a bit suspicious of you, seeing as you're the predatory divorcee? Because you were the first person he could think of and it keeps the heat away from whoever he's really seeing?'

'I think it's because he knows I won't make a fuss. I work for him, in a roundabout way, after all.'

She ponders this. 'You're right.'

'So . . . what? . . . He's going to let her think me and him are having a fling? I've only known him a few days.'

'I doubt Stella's being that rational,' she says, running her fingers up the stem of her glass. 'Are you sure you won't have one?' It takes me a second to work out what she means.

'Go on then.'

She gets up and fetches another glass. 'You're going to hate this, but I imagine he's presented it like you've got a crush on him, not like there's anything happening.'

'Oh my god,' I groan. 'That's almost worse.'

Gail laughs. Hands me a large red. 'Up in your garret, pining away with lust . . .'

'Don't!'

49

'The thing about Stella is . . .' She thinks for a moment. 'She's ridiculously jealous, but then, she has reason to be. So who can blame her? Can you accuse someone of being jealous if their suspicions are right half the time?"

I put my head in my hands. 'What do you think I should do?'

Gail thinks about it for a second. 'Personally, I'd forget about it. I know that probably goes against everything you're feeling, but do you really want to end up being drawn in further?'

'No. But I can't stand that she would think that of me. That anyone would.'

'I think she's already probably decided not to like you anyway. What's the difference?'

I shrug. 'Because now she thinks she has a legitimate reason. Now she thinks she was right about me all along.'

Gail puts a hand over mine. 'Sleep on it. That would be my main advice. Don't go storming back over there saying things you might regret.'

Of course, I don't sleep. Of course, I lie there, tossing and turning, veering from fury at Al to anger at Stella that she would so readily believe the bad light he's painted me in. Somehow, in the morning, despite the fact that I'm exhausted, I feel calmer. Gail was right. There's nothing to be gained by starting a fight. If Stella asks me outright, maybe I'll tell her it's not true. Maybe I'll tell her the book wasn't from me. I'll definitely make it clear that I have no interest in her sleazy husband. But, until that happens, I'll just keep to myself. Wait for it all to blow over.

Famous last words.

5

Betsy is dragging her bright yellow overnight case behind her when I collect her from school on Friday afternoon, and my heart almost breaks at the sight of it. I resolve to have a chat with David about splitting her wardrobe between the two homes so she doesn't have to lug it back and forth. She doesn't seem bothered, though.

'Is Felix in there?' I say as we load it in the boot.

She giggles. 'No. Can I bring him next time?'

'You'd have to take him to school for the day first. I don't think he'd like that. He hasn't got a uniform, for a start. He'd feel left out.'

'We could stop off at Dad's and get him now,' she says, looking at me hopefully.

'Dad will be at work,' I say, wishing I'd never opened this particular can of worms. Betsy won't understand why I don't have keys to David's new place, why it wouldn't be OK for us to go there now and help ourselves to the cat. She has never really seen us argue, beyond the normal squabbles of two people who live together about who's turn it is to cook or what to watch on TV. We had the most civilized separation in history, mostly – I realized, in retrospect – because David didn't care enough about me to be passionate.

*

I keep my head down as I drive into The Close, as I have every time I've come and gone since Wednesday evening. Thankfully, I haven't come into contact with either Al or Stella, mostly because I've been hiding, waiting for them to go out before I emerge. I'm beginning to think Gail was right and it might all have blown over. At least I've stopped waiting for Stella to steam up to my front door accusing me of god knows what. She's had ample chances. Even the most hot-headed person must have calmed down by now.

'Do you think those girls from over the road will play with me?'

Ah.

I give Betsy what I hope is a reassuring smile. 'I'm not sure . . . I'm a bit . . . I don't really know them and I'm not sure their mum and dad would be too keen . . .'

'Why not?'

'Well, I don't know. They're just not terribly friendly.'

'Can we go over there and ask? Please, Mum? I haven't got any friends here.'

I turn and lock the car. 'Not tonight, anyway. Let's get your homework out of the way, and then we've got the whole of the rest of the weekend to do stuff.'

'Tomorrow, then?' She looks at me so hopefully that I almost say yes, but I know I can't. No way is Stella going to let my daughter near hers now.

'I don't know, Bets. I think I'd have to ask the parents first. They're a bit snobby about me being the lodger.' It's not a lie. It's just not the whole truth. As soon as I say it, I regret it, though. Betsy looks at me as if I've just told her some humans don't like animals. She has no concept of people looking down on other people's status at this point in her short life.

'That's nasty,' she says as I unlock my front door. She scowls over at their house. 'What's wrong with being the lodger? Just because they have a big house . . .'

I seem to have awoken my daughter's social conscience. That's not such a bad thing. 'Exactly,' I say. 'Right. Who wants to go for a walk in the woods before homework?'

'We can look for Cocoa,' she says, Stella's family forgotten. I breathe a sigh of relief. We dump her case inside and head straight back out. As luck would have it, we spot Eva and Cocoa up ahead almost as soon as we go through the gate. Betsy takes off after the dog and I increase my pace to catch up with Eva.

'Hey,' I say as I come up behind her. She turns round. Is it my imagination, or does she not look particularly happy to see me?

'Oh,' she says in a monotone. 'Laura. It's you.'

I'm momentarily confused, but then I think she's probably just having a bad day. I look over, and Betsy is on her knees in the dirt, nuzzling Cocoa's big brown face. 'Everything OK?' I ask. I wonder if Eva's had some bad news or something.

She looks me straight in the eye and, if I'm being honest, it's a bit disconcerting. 'Yes. Why shouldn't it be?'

'Oh . . . um . . . you just seem a bit distracted . . .'

'No. I've just . . . I'm in rather a hurry. Will you excuse me, Laura? Cocoa!'

The dog lumbers after her, leaving Betsy scrabbling to her feet. 'See you soon,' I call after Eva. I'm worried that she doesn't seem herself, that maybe she's had bad news.

Not that it would be any of my business, but I like her; I hope nothing's wrong. She raises a hand in response.

Betsy and I trample through the woods. I'm more confident already about finding my way back. We meet an Irish terrier called Marcel and a small hairy thing called Dora (it's vitally important to Betsy that she finds out their names; the owners', not so much) so, all in all, it's a success, and it takes her mind off the idea of inviting herself round to Stella and Al's, at least for a while. We go home, do homework, eat pasta, watch *Coronation Street*, and when she goes to bed I go to bed, revelling in cuddling up next to her, even though I'm not remotely tired.

The thing about The Close is that you almost never see anyone on the street. The children don't play out there because they all have gardens the size of tennis courts out the back; the staff must either come and go in the middle of the night or they're all locked inside for twenty-four hours a day in case one of the residents has a sudden shirt-ironing emergency. I never see them either way. No one passes through because the gate to the woods has 'Private' written on it in large letters and there's a much friendlier public entrance a hundred metres or so along the main road, and no one – by that, I mean no one apart from me – walks to the shops because it's just that bit too far to carry anything home. And why would you, when you have a giant 4x4 the size of a Sherman tank and you could use it to transport a seven-stone human and a bag of lettuce? So the only time you're likely to bump into anyone is when they're getting into or out of their cars on their drives or – for the few that have them – walking their dogs. Consequently, Betsy and I go through the rest of the weekend without speaking to anyone. Because she hasn't seen me all week, Betsy seems fine with it, but I worry that as time goes on she'll come to dread her days with me. All of her friends live near her school, near David.

I hand her over in front of the concierge again. David promises to dig out some clothes for next weekend and give them to me when I drop her off on Wednesday so she doesn't have to cart half her wardrobe to school. It's all very polite. I cry most of the way home in the car.

6

March

I'm sitting in my kitchen listening to the sounds of music, chatter and laughter coming from next door. Cars have been arriving all evening and The Close is lined with Bentleys, Mercedes and Rolls-Royces, some of them with uniformed drivers sitting inside, idly scrolling through their phones. I've seen Stella and Al cross from the other side, Katya and – I assume – Guy stroll along the street, and a smart older man/younger woman big-haired, tanned-skinned, luminous-teethed couple I assume are Bill and Anya emerge from number 8. It's a good turn-out for a school night.

The Close has been a hive of activity all day. From my bedroom window I watched as a marquee was erected in next door's vast back garden. Gas heaters and wood burners have been strategically placed both inside and out, and fairy lights draped in the trees. A van with 'Clarendon Catering Services (Bespoke Party and Dinner Catering)' emblazoned on the side has been parked on the street all afternoon. I can't see inside the marquee, but I watched as white, gold-decorated tables and chairs were carried in, along with several fridges and countless crates of wine, followed, at about seven o'clock, by platters and platters of sumptuous food.

There's no doubting that this is Eva and Rafa's thirtieth-anniversary party. The one to which I thought I was invited. Except that when it came to it, I wasn't. If I hadn't seen Eva hand-delivering the invitations, I would have thought that maybe her mention of it the other week was enough. That the fact she had never told me the actual date was an oversight. But I'd watched as she went house to house, posting an envelope through each and every door except mine, surreptitiously glancing up at my window as she walked up the drive and past the stairs to my front door to deliver a summons to Gail and Ben.

A couple of days later Gail had confirmed my suspicions by asking if I was intending to go.

'I haven't had an invite,' I said, trying not to sound like a sulky child. To be honest, I didn't really care about the party. I would know hardly anyone, and I'd probably spend the whole evening hiding in a dark corner anyway, but it was the principle – the idea that someone I'd thought I was starting to get friendly with had decided to exclude me.

'They probably just forgot,' she said. We were sitting in her kitchen again, glasses of wine on the go.

'I don't think so,' I said, picking at the corner of the label on the bottle. 'Last time I saw her she was a bit off with me . . .'

'Eva? That doesn't sound like her.'

I'd been thinking about this since I saw Eva circumvent my flat on her rounds. Maybe she hadn't been having a bad day when I'd bumped into her in the woods. Maybe her problem was with me. I'd wracked my brain, trying to think of what I might have done, and the only thing I could come up with was Stella. Was it just a coincidence that Al had used me as some kind of smokescreen and then the next minute I was being treated like a pariah by Eva? OK, so I knew I was exaggerating the situation, even to myself, but something had shifted, I could feel it. Had Stella been bad-mouthing me? Did she really believe that I was throwing myself at Al, or worse, that there was something actually going on between us? I shared my worries with Gail. I hadn't known her for long, but I was pretty sure I could trust her to be straight with me.

'Well.' She leaned back in her chair, hooking her long hair behind one ear. 'No one's said anything to me. But then, they all know I've got no time for gossip.'

'Do you think I might be right?'

She was silent for a moment while, I assumed, she considered it. I expected an equivocal answer, but she surprised me with a 'Yes'.

'Really?'

'Stella can be pretty . . . not mean, that's way too strong. But she makes it known when she doesn't like someone. And she and Eva have been friends for a long time. I can imagine her pulling an "It's her or me" if she really believed you were making a play for Al.'

'I've barely even met him.' I was incensed.

'Well, so far as both Stella and Al are concerned, he's pretty irresistible . . .'

I screwed up my face. 'He's really not.'

'I know that, and you know that. But he doesn't seem to have any trouble getting women to fall for his charms. There have been at least three that I can remember. At least, according to Stella. Nothing serious – I mean, well, it depends on how you define serious, I suppose – but nothing that lasted beyond a few weeks. And, of course, there might be more that she's never found out about. Awful, really . . .'

'But the point is, even if it's happening again now, it's not with me. Should I just go and talk to her, do you think?'

'Up to you. Are you going to tell her Al was lying about the book?'

I drained the last of my wine, refused Gail's offer of another. I didn't feel like drinking. 'Shit. I don't know.'

'I imagine she'll go straight to him, demanding to know who it was . . .'

'And now he knows it's my company that cleans his offices . . .'

She nods. 'Exactly.'

I really can't afford to lose my contract with AJT Music. Not without another one lined up to take its place. It's a third of my business. Gail carries our glasses over to the sink. 'Coffee?'

'Thanks.'

'I don't think he's that vindictive. He probably just panicked, and he knew Stella was already suspicious of you . . .'

'For no reason.'

'For no reason. My guess is he just thought she'd buy it. The predatory single woman hitting on her wealthy fiancé. And it looks like she did.'

'This is ridiculous. It's like school. Worse.'

'Don't do anything hasty. Sleep on it. You don't want to make things worse, when it might just blow over.'

I knew it wouldn't, though. I knew that Stella and Al were poison.

I sit watching more guests arrive. Cinderella in her kitchen. I tell myself it doesn't matter. That I'll be out of here in six months, hopefully. Less now. That these people will never matter to me again. But the injustice is eating me up. I'm not the kind of person who would make a play for someone else's husband. I never have, and I never would. I can't bear the idea that anyone would think that of me, let alone anyone I liked. I think about all my neighbours over there now, probably discussing me and how awful I am. I think about Betsy being shunned when she runs after Cocoa or tries to befriend Stella's daughters in the street. It's so unjust. Before I know it, I have tears rolling down my face, sitting there with all the lights off, spying on my neighbours. It's not fair. I know I can't ignore it. I have to do something. I just have to work out what.

7

I barely sleep at all. The party goes on till after two in the morning. Obviously, none of these people is in the kind of job where they'll get fired if they turn up late or hungover. Every peal of laughter leaves me feeling more vulnerable, more convinced that it's aimed at me. Gradually, the chauffeur-driven cars leave, more than a few taxis turn up and the residents of The Close totter home, calling out to one another loudly as they go. Because who is there to disturb here, apart from me?

In the morning there's a posh-car graveyard out in the street and a steady stream of cabs dispensing weary-looking people who had the sense to realize they shouldn't drive themselves home last night. I see Katya leaving number 2 in her running gear and heading for the woods. She looks fresh-faced. Clearly, she's young enough not to be wiped out by a hangover. I decide to contrive to bump into her. Maybe she'll be pleased to see me. Maybe I've been over-reacting and everything is fine. I haven't seen her since that night at Gail and Ben's, when she was so sweet and friendly, asking me about Betsy and telling me how she couldn't wait to have a daughter of her own. I force myself into the bedroom and dress quickly before I can change my mind. Then I pull on my trainers and head downstairs. Just going for a run. Nothing to see here.

I jog to the end of the street, the unpractised movement

making my tight muscles complain immediately. Once I've gone through the gate at the end of The Close I stop short. Enough of that. I have no idea which route Katya has taken, or how long she will be, but she'll have to pass this way to get home – unless she's gone out on to the main road somewhere, it suddenly occurs to me, although that seems unlikely when you have miles of uninterrupted beautiful woods and heath to run through – so my plan is to wait here, doing elaborate stretches, until she sees me, at which point I'll pretend I've just arrived and that I'm surprised to bump into her.

Ten minutes later I'm still waiting. Of course, Katya is probably super-fit and a short jog for her comprises ten miles cross-country. I could be here all day. I'm starting to get cold, so I do in fact start running on the spot and jumping up and down, flapping my arms back and forth across my chest like a chicken. I must look demented.

I'm just beginning to think I should give up when I hear pounding footsteps coming towards me. I stick one leg up on a tree stump and lean forward into a stretch. Thankfully, it's Katya. A delicate sweat on her flawless olive skin. Her outsized lips pursed in concentration. Not even remotely out of breath. I give her a big smile, stand up straight.

'Hey! How are you?'

She starts when she sees me. 'Oh, hi, Laura,' she says, with her slight hint of an accent. Latvian, she told me. I wait for her to come to a stop, but she doesn't. She just breezes on past me without looking back. I watch her disappear from view, feeling slighted. I'm just being paranoid, I tell myself. People are busy. They have things on their minds. Not everything is about me.

Later in the day, though, my worst fears are confirmed. I've collected Betsy from school, we've done homework and, because it's a beautiful sunny afternoon, she's playing on the steps to my front door. I can hear her running up and down them while I knock up macaroni and cheese, her favourite. I have Kisstory on the radio and I sing along to a Soul II Soul song from the eighties. I'm feeling, if not happy, then at least not unhappy either. It's amazing the difference having my daughter around makes to my mood. I'm rinsing a dirty saucepan in the sink when I see a huge 4x4 deposit Stella's two girls at the end of her drive. They wave to the person inside. I'm looking at them, wondering how they can be so close in age to Betsy but so different – both are dressed as if for dinner at Nobu followed by partying at whatever the hip West End nightclub *du jour* is, in cold shoulder tops, skinny jeans and heels – when I hear her voice, Betsy's, calling out hello. Big Mini Me – I now know her name is Taylor – looks over with a sneer. My hearts flips. Next thing I know, I see Betsy running across the street towards the two girls, waving happily. The danger of her hurling herself into the road without looking is eclipsed by the thought of her coming up against those two overgroomed sharks. I drop the pan I'm washing and run out of the door.

By the time I get to our gate I hear Stella's front door slam and then see Betsy plodding back down their drive with tears pouring down her face. I swoop her up. 'What happened?'

She sniffles. 'They won't play with me.'

I brush one of her curls away from her eyes. Straighten her glasses. 'I told you, sweetie, they're a bit snobby.

Forget about them. Do you want to go for a walk in the woods?'

She shakes her head. 'They said their mum said you're a slut and that I wasn't welcome in their house. What's a slut?'

'They . . . ?' I resist the urge to go and batter their front door down and punch any or all of them square in the face. For now, I hold Betsy at arm's length.

'Have you heard that word before?'

Another shake of the head. That's something, at least. Morgan must be slipping. 'Well, it's a very nasty thing grown-ups sometimes say about other people. It's a bad name. And I'm not, by the way. They're just trying to be mean. They don't even know me.'

'OK,' she says trustingly. I love her so much. I take her hand and, just as I turn to lead her back to the flat, I see Stella looking out of her front window. I look away. There's nothing I want to say to her now. Not while my daughter can hear.

Later, once I've taken Betsy back to her dad's – she cheered up after the mac and cheese and a few games of *Mario Kart* on the Wii I installed for her a couple of days ago, although she got a bit clingy when I turned to leave; she couldn't understand why I couldn't go upstairs and put her to bed – I lie in wait for Eva to take Cocoa for a walk. I've seen either her or Rafa take the dog for a late-night wee most nights since I've been here. I'm lucky that tonight it's Eva's turn, and I'm down the steps and running up the street after her before she even gets to the end of her drive.

'Eva!' I call when I'm a few feet behind her. Cocoa's head whips round and he starts wagging his tail. Eva turns more reluctantly. 'Good grief! You gave me a shock. What are you doing out here at this time of night?'

'Sorry. I wanted to speak to you.'

'I'm in a bit of a hurry, Laura, as I'm sure you'll appreciate.'

'It's OK,' I say decisively. 'I'll walk with you.'

She walks on, and I have to trot to keep up. Security lights for each house spring on as we pass. Eva doesn't say anything, so I just launch into it. 'I don't know what you've heard, but there's nothing going on with me and Al. I didn't give him that book . . .'

This clearly isn't what she's expecting me to say. She slows her pace a little, looks at me. 'I see.'

'I'm telling the truth, Eva. I went along with what Al was saying at first because he blindsided me and I couldn't think straight. I had no idea what he was on about. I didn't want to contradict him in front of Stella. And then . . . well, he owns one of the companies I work for . . . I one hundred per cent did not give him that book.'

'I assume you've told Stella this?'

I stop walking and, thankfully, Eva does too. She unclips Cocoa's lead and the dog shambles off happily and pees up the first tree he finds. 'How could I? She'd go straight to him and demand to know who did. And he'd probably tell the person who hired me to fire me.'

'Are you asking *me* to tell her it wasn't you who gave him the book?'

'No! Not unless you think she wouldn't say anything to Al. God, this is such a mess. I just wanted you to know

I'm not like that. That I haven't done anything wrong.' I'm furious with myself. If I'd never let on to Al that I recognized him, none of this would have happened. Or, if it had, I could have just denied it straight out without worrying about the consequences.

'Stella and I have been friends for years, and she's very upset,' Eva says, and I know I've lost. 'If you're not prepared to be honest with her, then I don't see what I can do.'

'Just don't judge me, please. Give me the benefit of the doubt.'

She shakes her head. 'I don't want to get involved. We'll all still be here when you move on . . .'

'I know. But meanwhile, Betsy's being made to feel like some kind of outsider. She's going through enough with the divorce, and then Stella's girls were really mean to her . . .' I can feel myself blinking back tears.

I think I see Eva's expression soften a little, but then she inhales sharply. 'I'm sorry about Betsy. Those girls are little madams. But at the end of the day, Stella is my friend and you and I barely know each other. Don't ask me to take sides.'

There's no point to this. 'I'm not. I just wanted to say my piece, that's all. Thanks for hearing me out.'

'I really do have to get back inside.' She calls out to Cocoa, who reappears from the woods immediately, like he knows the drill.

'Of course,' I say. 'You go on.'

I watch as she turns and strides off. Cocoa follows. I stand there in the dark as the last security light snaps off again. There's only one more thing I can try.

8

It's the next morning and I'm standing on Stella's doorstep. I've rung the bell and I'm trying to stop my hands from shaking. I feel sick, but I know I have to do this. I've thought carefully about what I can say that will, hopefully, get me off the hook without sending her running off to Al and dropping me in it. God knows if I'm capable of getting the words out, though.

A very small woman, probably in her sixties and wearing some kind of maid's uniform, answers. I assume this is the housekeeper and not a hooker fulfilling a very specialized fetish. Besides, I'm counting on Al being at work and Stella home alone. Apart from the staff.

'Yes?'

'Hi,' I stutter. 'Is Stella home? Mrs . . . I mean, Ms . . . um . . .' I realize I have no idea what Stella's surname is. '. . . Stella.'

'Please come.'

I follow her into the cavernous hallway that I caught a glimpse of the other week, past the portrait of Stella in her knickers and into a vast living room. Stella and Al's is the grandest house in The Close. The widest. The highest. The mansion *di tutti* mansions. The busy brown marble floor runs through here too. I always think marble floors look as if someone made a mess and can't be arsed to clear it up. I remember describing one to David after

I'd cleaned a very posh house once. 'You know, one of those ones that look like the cat's been sick all over it.' There are ornate pillars flecked with gold, and more paintings of Stella and the two girls on the wall. All of them horribly lifelike and lacking any artistry whatsoever. Two hard-looking, black, leggy sofas face each other on either side of an ornate mirror-topped fireplace in a completely different marble, a dark smoky-glass coffee table between them, a few large art books lined up neatly on top. One of them still has the plastic covering on, and I'm pretty sure the others have never been opened either. The overlong midnight-blue velvet drapes spill on to the floor in a carefully contrived puddle and I have to resist the temptation to go and pick them up to see if anyone has vacuumed underneath. The smell of lilies from two huge vases on side tables is overpowering. The room doesn't feel lived in at all. I assume they must have a cosy snug somewhere where they all hang out and watch TV and do normal family things. Upside down, like bats, probably.

'I get,' the woman says, and goes off. I hope she doesn't get sacked for letting me in without finding out who I am and whether Stella wants to see me. It's a bonus for me that she hasn't asked my name. Otherwise I'm pretty sure I'd be back out in the cold already.

'Meeees Stella,' I hear her calling, and then some muttering that I can't make out. I daren't sit down because I'm worried it looks too presumptuous, but I'm feeling a bit faint, so I steady myself on a corner of the fireplace. Moments later I hear the staccato tap of heels on marble. I can tell, even before she appears, that she's irritated because she doesn't know who is waiting for her.

Something about the quick little steps scream annoyance. I close my eyes for a second, try to calm myself down.

'What are you doing here?' My eyes spring open to see Stella standing there, glaring at me.

'Stella,' I say. 'I need to talk to you for a moment. 'You have to believe there's nothing going on with me and Al . . .'

The slug lips pout. 'Who said there was? Not for want of trying on your part, though, I hear.'

Oh, for fuck's sake. 'That's not true. I wouldn't . . . I would never do something like that.'

'What? So giving my husband-to-be a book with some stupid French inscription in it isn't overstepping the mark?'

French? Who said anything about French? I don't speak French. I stick to my script. 'It was a joke. A silly reference to something that came up when I mentioned the book to him.'

I don't know what the inscription says. I'm starting to feel like this was an even worse idea than I thought. What if she asks me for a translation to see if it matches his? I'm bizarrely thankful that she seems to have bigger fish to fry.

'What are you doing seeking him out at his work, anyway? Aren't you supposed to be cleaning?'

I resist the urge to remind her I own the company. 'I didn't. I just ran into him on the stairs, and I was carrying a copy of the book . . .'

'When you were meant to be working?'

'I'd just popped in to check on my staff.' OK, so I don't resist the urge to remind her I own the company. 'I hardly ever go there,' I add, thinking she might like to hear that. I have no idea if what I'm saying fits in with anything he's told her or, indeed, where and when I'm meant to have actually given him his gift.

'You're lucky I haven't insisted he find a new cleaning company. Not that he would usually involve himself in such menial things.'

'I . . .' I start to say, but she cuts me off.

'Do you often give random people copies of books?' she says, tossing her horse's mane. I half expect her to stamp her Christian Louboutin-clad hoof.

'Yes,' I say confidently. This, I have already decided, is to be my trump card. I'm the eccentric lady who loves to gift books she enjoys to vague acquaintances. You know Laura? The one who is always giving random people books? That's her. (I don't actually think I have ever given anybody a book outside of birthdays and Christmas, but what's that small detail between friends?) 'All the time. I love books. It's a thing I do. And I'd never even thought about it being inappropriate, so I'm really sorry if you think it was. I certainly didn't mean to upset you.'

'And do you always write provocative messages in French in them?'

'No. I mean, I do always write something. Just a little joke or whatever . . .' She's not buying a word of this, I can tell. I shift from foot to foot. I wish I could sit down. Not that I want to stay here a moment longer than is necessary.

'How adorable,' she says in a voice that lets me know she thinks it's anything but. 'For the record, though,

Laura, neither Al nor I are comfortable with such overfamiliarity.'

'I understand,' I say. 'And I apologize again if my gesture was crass.' She starts walking towards the front door, so I follow her. I take it this is my cue to leave.

'Just out of interest,' she says as I follow in her wake. 'What on earth were the two of you talking about that made you write that particular message?'

Shit, so she knows what it says. Which is more than I do. She turns round and locks her weirdly slanted eyes on mine. I can feel myself blush. 'Oh, I can't really remember. Like I said, it was just a stupid joke.'

'And like I said, Laura, it was overstepping the mark.' She opens the front door. 'Please don't call round again unannounced. Pilar's English isn't up to explaining that I don't want to see you.'

'Of course,' I say, all pretence of civility gone. If she's cold enough not to accept my – clearly genuine – pleading, then fuck her. 'And I'd appreciate if you'd ask your daughters not to be such little bitches to Betsy. Maybe try to show them by example. Although, on second thoughts, I imagine that'd be too much of a stretch.'

I step through the door and she slams it after me. That went well.

I'm desperate to talk to someone about what's happening. But Ben's car is on the drive when I get back, and I don't want to get in the way of him and Gail having a quiet night in together for once. Besides, I'm not sure she would want to hear that I'd just picked a fight with her friend, and she is my landlady, after all. Half an hour later I hear

71

voices coming from the back. Laughter. I look out of my bedroom window and see Stella sitting with Eva, Jan, Anya and Katya in Eva's garden next door. Bottle of Prosecco on the go. Even before I hear my name I know they're talking about me from the forced whispers, the little glances Katya and Anya steal up at my window. I can't make out what they're saying, and I know I shouldn't try. It's not going to be anything good. I don't know what else to do so, once I've checked everyone is at work and – barring accidents – nothing is likely to go wrong, I take a Sleepeaze and huddle under the duvet. I feel defeated. Deflated. Maybe I just have to accept my fate. Live out my time here shunned by the neighbours and looked down on as some kind of desperate scarlet woman. It's going to be miserable, but I'm strong, I can do it. But Betsy being treated like a pariah is something else. Something I don't think I can stand. I eventually drift into an unnatural, dreamless sleep.

I wake up at around three in the morning. Eyes wide open.

Someone gave Al that book. Someone wrote the inscription. She's the other woman. She's the one Stella should be upset about, not me.

If I can show Stella proof of who he's really seeing, then not only will she know it's not me, but she can confront Al all she likes about her without him thinking I've betrayed him. It's win–win.

I just need to find out who she is.

9

Of course, this is easier said than done. I am not a private detective. I can't dedicate my life to following Al around, even if I knew how to do so discreetly. I can't break into their house and poke through his things to see what I can find. I can't even get myself invited round there legitimately.

I do, however, have access to his office.

In the middle of the night this seems like a genius idea. I play out fantasies in my head, of me thrusting some damning piece of evidence in front of Stella's shocked face. *See! I am innocent!* I cry, and she has to admit how wrong she's been, what a bully. How could she have misunderstood me so badly? She insists that she will clear my name with Eva and Katya and anyone else she's badmouthed me to, and I am celebrated in The Close like a Death Row prisoner, hours from execution, who is finally able to prove her alibi. There are tears and hugs and apologies, and a party is held in my honour.

The night-time does strange things to my rationality.

Once I wake up in the morning, having slipped into a deep sleep on a wave of misplaced euphoria, the first thought I have is: This is the worst plan I have ever had. It is, however, all I've got.

I wish I had someone to talk it over with. This is definitely a step too far for Gail, sympathetic as she is. I'm her tenant; Stella is her friend. I don't think it would be fair to her to tell her what I'm thinking of doing. She'd just worry she'd invited some crazy loose cannon to live in her annexe. Someone who was going to cause a shitload of trouble and then move on, leaving her to deal with the fallout. I think about trying to explain the situation to one of my former 'close' friends, but first I'd have to get past the 'where have you been since David and I separated?' conversation I have in my head on repeat. Air those thoughts that keep me awake at night sometimes about the way they all sided with their husbands, David's friends. No, not sided with. That's unfair. But they chose the path of least resistance. I still get texts asking how I am, Facebook messages with pictures of their kids or cheesy memes of kittens, but I've given up asking if any of them are free for a coffee.

I'm going to have to do this on my own. Although quite what I'm going to do, I'm still not sure.

As a first port of call, and because I have nothing better to do, it feels foolish not to drop into AJT Music and at least get a sense of where Al's office is. I let myself into the foyer. I can hear someone moving around in the accounts offices at the back. Angie is on tonight, as always, along with Tomas and Catriona, so I assume it's one of them, although occasionally a keen young researcher toils into the late evening and, on a handful of nights over the years, one of my staff has stumbled across a pair of star-crossed lovers banging away in an after-hours office. Cleaners are treated as invisible for the most part. I remember once listening to some very heated phone sex while I washed a floor. On speakerphone. I always wondered what the woman on the other end thought the noise of the damp mop squeaking across the wood was. It doesn't bear thinking about. I wonder now if Al's bit on the side is someone who works with him. If I might have seen her when I've dropped off supplies during the day.

I bypass the first floor and make my way up to the second, where the smart offices are. There's nothing I can really do while my staff are here, and I can't risk one of them finding me poking about, so, when I get to the top of the stairs I call out 'Hello', and Angie appears from the Ladies, a bright scarf holding her hair back from her face.

'Back so soon?' she says with a smile.

'I just dropped Betsy off,' I say, as if that's an explanation. I'm lying, of course, but I feel as if I need to justify myself. Angie's smile drops as quickly as it appeared.

'Oh yes. That's tough.'

I feel bad using Betsy as an excuse, but it's also true that I don't really want to go back to an empty flat. Any distraction is good.

'I could do with a tea break,' she says, and I follow her through to the tiny kitchen, where she busies herself putting the kettle on and hunting out tea bags.

We chat about nothing much for a while. She asks me how I'm getting on in my new place and I tell her the Stella story without letting on that the boyfriend works a few feet away.

'Jesus,' she says, when I get to the bit about Stella's girls telling Betsy her mother is a slut. 'What a bitch.'

'It'd almost be funny if it weren't for Betsy.'

Angie huffs. 'I love the way people think single mums

75

have the time or the energy to even think about seducing anyone . . .'

Of course, I'm a single mum now. Although one whose child, thankfully, also has a supportive single dad to help out. Angie wasn't so lucky. She was widowed when her youngest was just a few months old. Car accident. She's been bringing them up on her own ever since. As far as I know she's never even dated. Don't get me wrong, she's had the odd hook-up, but nothing more. She couldn't be bothered, she'd said to me once. It all felt too much like hard work, on top of bringing up her boys and cleaning every night. I once asked why she didn't try Tinder and she'd laughed and said, 'Ah yes, cos that's working out so well for you,' which shut me up.

I lean back against the counter. 'And even if I did have – which I don't, or the inclination, just to be clear – I wouldn't do it by writing something soppy in French in a book.'

'Maybe she *is* French.'

For some reason this hasn't even occurred to me. Maybe she is. I surreptitiously flick a look around the kitchen, hoping for . . . what? A sign on the wall announcing 'Brigitte works here' or 'J'aime Paris'. Angie catches me looking, so I snap my attention back to her.

'That would make sense.'

She takes a sip of her tea. 'Why you, do you think?'

I let out a sigh. 'I don't . . .' I start to say, and then I think, sod it. I've known Angie for five years. She's my most trusted employee. And she's a friend. Just because we don't go out to lunch together very often doesn't mean we're not friends. I don't know why I didn't think of confiding in her before. I've asked her advice on a million different things over the years. In fact, she was the first person I told when David announced he was leaving. I was still trying to process it, to understand why.

'Don't go thinking this has anything to do with you,' was the first thing she said. 'This is his midlife crisis, not your failure.' It was exactly what I needed to hear.

'He works here. Al,' I say, now.

Her pencil-thin eyebrows shoot upwards. She's been trying to grow them thicker ever since I've known her, and they stubbornly refuse. Too many years of teenage over-plucking. Who knew the fashion would suddenly change and everyone would be sporting caterpillars? 'Really? That's a coincidence.'

The more I think about this, the more convinced I am. 'I don't think it is. I think that's why he thought he could get away with involving me, because I stupidly told him I'd seen him at work, and now he thinks I'll be scared I'll lose the contract if I don't go along with him . . .'

'He sounds nice.' She rinses her mug under the tap and holds her hand out for mine. 'Is he in a position to do that?'

I shrug. 'He owns the company. I doubt he even knows what cleaning firm they use, but I'm sure he could insist they got a new one.' It occurs to me that I might have made Angie worry about her own livelihood. 'Don't worry, I won't let that happen. I'll just have to ride it out and maybe see if I can drum up some more work some-where else meanwhile, just in case.'

'I know,' she says. 'I have total faith. Shall we have a poke round his office? See if the book's in there? You never know. You could at least see what it says.'

I think about feigning shock. Pretending that I'm horrified she would suggest such a thing. But who am I
kidding? 'That's what I was thinking of doing. Come on,
then. Don't tell the others, will you?'

She gives me an 'as if' look. 'What's his name? Al what?'

'I don't know. Do they have nameplates? I can't remember.' I follow her back into the main area, stopping on the
stairs to check neither of the others is on the way up.

'It's not that kind of office. This one's all wearing jeans
and expressing your creativity.'

'Well, hopefully he's the only Al. There'll be something
with his name on. Let's start with the biggest first.'

'Don't move stuff around!' she says as I head for one of
the three large glass-fronted rooms at the end. Now it's
my turn to give her an 'as if' look. We start in the one on
the right. There are framed tour posters of bands I've
heard of on the walls. A bookcase full of DVDs. 'I'm
pretty sure I've seen a woman in here,' Angie says.

'Was she French?'

I look behind the door and there's a telltale women's
coat. Chic black soft wool. Fitted. Angie is flicking
through a pile of papers in a tray on the desk. 'Judith
O'Brien.'

I hear a noise – a clattering – and we both freeze. We
look towards the door to the stairs. Nothing. 'It'll be
Tomas thumping around with the Hoover,' Angie says
finally. 'It's like a combat sport. I'm sure we're going to get
a bill for repainting their skirting boards one of these
days.' Still, we wait until we hear it again, fainter this time.

'Let's try the next one,' I say in a whisper, and then I

have to say it again more loudly because she didn't hear me. 'Keep an ear out.'

In the middle office I go straight to the coat hook behind the door, and Angie once again heads for the desk. There's no coat, but there's a masculine scarf and a big black umbrella. 'Anything?'

She looks up. 'Hold on.' I look round the walls. More band posters. I notice a couple of framed gold and silver discs. One huge album I remember from the nineties and the others more recent. All with signatures scrawled across them. There's a small bronze plaque. 'Presented to Alec Thornbury'.

'Look! Alec. I was thinking he was an Alan.' I check the second one. Check again. 'This is him. Alec Thornbury.'

Angie heads over and has a look. 'Perfect. What were we going to look for again?'

'The book. The inscription.'

She looks at the overstuffed bookcase along one wall. 'Ah, yes. Good luck with that. I'm just going to have a look at the other office, in case . . .'

She goes off and I start half-heartedly pulling books from the shelves. I can't imagine someone gave him Bear Grylls' memoirs as a romantic gift, or a paperback of *Spanish Made Simple*, but I check them anyway. This is hopeless. And pointless.

'Mark Freeborn,' Angie says, coming back in. She pulls her phone out of her pocket and checks it. 'We're going to need to be out of here soon. The others'll be finished . . .'

'You carry on and get done. Just give me a shout if you hear either of them coming up.'

'We need a code word,' she says, with a laugh.

'How about "pointless",' I say. 'Or "hopeless".'

'How about I just shout your name?'

'Good one. Very imaginative.' She leaves me to it and I work my way through the top shelf, being careful to put everything back exactly where I found it. None of the books has an inscription, let alone one in French. I'm about to embark on shelf two when I hear Angie call me.

'What?' I say, and then I remember and scrabble to my feet. I'm back in the main office, apparently in conversation with Angie, when Catriona appears from the corridor.

'I didn't know you were here,' she says, giving me a smile. Catriona has the world's quietest voice, and I usually have to guess the last few words in any sentence.

'Just catching up. How are you doing?'

'Oh, you know,' she says. 'Knackered. We're finished by the way.' This to Angie.

'Who's babysitting tonight?'

'Sharon,' both Angie and Catriona say at once.

Angie collects a dirty mug from a desk, wipes down underneath it. 'Two minutes. I got behind.'

'I waylaid her,' I say, feeling guilty.

Catriona takes the mug from her. 'I'll wash this. Anything else?' Angie shakes her head. 'Thanks.' I love my team and how supportive they are of each other.

Angie waits until Catriona is out of hearing. 'You could stay.' I know I could, in theory. I have the keys to lock up after me, and there's – in so far as I know – no overnight security beyond the alarm, the code to which I have in my phone.

'I don't know. It doesn't seem right . . .' Poking around while I'm there legitimately is one thing, but what if some overzealous person looks at the CCTV and sees me leaving way out of hours? What if there's something on the front door that sends a notification if it's opened at unusual times? 'I can't risk it.'

'I can have another go tomorrow –' she starts to say, but I interrupt. I don't want Angie putting herself in a risky situation for me.

'No! I'll come back when I can. Thanks, though.'

'Well, warn me,' she says, lowering her voice as the sound of Catriona's footsteps comes back along the hall. 'I can at least make sure I'm the one doing up here.'

As I wave the three off them off, watching them trudge up the road to begin another couple of hours' work at the financiers' around the corner, I can't help but glance up at the CCTV. I feel a rush of something like excitement. Nerves, probably. But at least I feel as if I'm doing something. I'm taking back control.

10

I don't go back until after the weekend. It rains solidly for the whole two days, which means there's no question of Betsy wanting to go and track down Cocoa on his walk, but it also means we feel trapped in the tiny studio, tripping over each other, me trying to find things for her to do to stop her from getting bored. Everything she thinks will keep her amused, every book she thinks she might like to read, is in her bedroom at her dad's flat. She thinks she might like to paint, but I don't have any paints here. There are a few crayons in her schoolbag, but then I can't find any paper. I feel as if I'm stifling her spontaneity, offering her the same three Wii games over and over again. I don't even have an iPad. She plays *Candy Crush* on my phone for a while, until she puts it aside, bored. She doesn't complain, but I can tell she's going stir crazy, as am I. I catch her gazing out of the window, and when I look at what she's watching I see Taylor and Amber, Stella's Mini Mes, getting into the back of a 4x4 in their ballet gear, Pilar holding a huge umbrella over their high-ponytailed heads, while her own hair clings soggily to her cheeks like an amorous octopus.

I'm concerned that Betsy might just sit there for hours watching for them to be dropped off again, so in the end we make a run for the car – both soaked before I even get the doors open – and head for Brent Cross, where we stock up on art supplies and baking materials (including a muffin tin and mixing bowl) so that we can make cupcakes in the afternoon. I'm going to need to get a bigger flat at this rate. Or at least, bigger cupboards. Maybe I can box up some more of my things and add them to the furniture that's in storage, I wonder. David and I divided everything scrupulously fairly, of course.

We get through the rest of the weekend snuggled up watching films on Netflix, and eating misshapen chocolate peanut-butter cupcakes. We might both end up obese, but at least I've taken her mind off the mean girls. Until, that is, they are unpacking yet more bags from their car at the same time as we are getting into ours to take Betsy back to David's. I keep my head down, ignore Stella before she can ignore me. I hear the girls laughing loudly. Betsy looks over.

'Let's go, Bets,' I say quickly. She's looking unbearably cute in her shiny yellow rain mac with red leggings and little DMs. I usher her into the car.

'What *is* she wearing?' I hear Taylor say loudly. Amber giggles theatrically. They want to make sure Betsy hears them. I turn the radio on and whack the volume up high.

On Monday afternoon, after I've been given a guided tour of a telecommunications company's two floors near Regent's Park, a client of the letting department at Rahina's company – she's always passing on tips, something that elevates her above the average estate agent in my eyes – and prepared a detailed quote for them, I send Angie a text – *Might come by tonight* – and I get a thumbs-up in return. I seem to spend half my life preparing pointless quotes. People underestimate how much effort you have to put in just to pitch for a job. You can't simply pluck a figure out of nowhere.

I go out of boredom more than a genuine hope, or even desire, that I might discover Al's secret. My days feel long now, but my evenings even longer. I never realized how much time I used to devote to thinking about what we were all going to have for dinner, experimenting with dishes that were both tasty for us grown-ups and appealing to my daughter. Because I work for myself, I was the one who cooked every night, who shopped for the ingredients. Preparing a meal only for myself just feels like a chore. It's just food. Fuel. It's not an event. Consequently, I'm spending most evenings stuffing in whatever random leftovers I have from Betsy's previous visit, then flopping around unable to settle to anything apart from regularly checking the property listings for my preferred area with an almost religious zeal. I know every property that's available by heart. I could lead tours around them without having to refer to notes. I could point out every 'potential wet room' (toilet) and 'cosy chill-out space' (no windows) from memory. At this point, I'd take any kind of distraction.

I get to AJT Music early, but not too early. My crew starts at six and, from experience, I know the offices are rarely empty of staff before seven. I don't want to risk bumping into Al, but I also want to give myself as much time as possible. So I sit in my car along the street waiting for Angie to text me. At ten to seven she does: *Everyone on this floor gone.* Still I'm cautious when I let myself in.

I say a quick hello to Sharon and Tomas. As promised, Angie is tackling the second floor. She beckons me over away from the stairs when she sees me.

'I've managed to do the second shelf since you were here last. Nothing.' She's wearing a flowery scarf round her head to keep her hair off her face while she works, and she looks weirdly like a glamorous wooden carving. I have no idea where she gets her tan in March, because she never takes a holiday. She's the visual opposite of the women from The Close. Her face is lived in, full of character. You can see she's had a life. I love it.

'Thank you. You shouldn't have, but thanks.'

She shrugs. 'If I shout your name, it means I've heard one of them coming up the stairs and you need to get out of there. If I shout, "Aagh! There's a spider," that means it's too late and you need to hide under his desk or somewhere.'

I can't help but laugh. 'You've really thought about this.'

'Bobby came up with the spider thing. I didn't tell him what was going on,' she adds, in case I think she's been blabbing.

'What if you really see a spider?' I ask, teasing her. 'What then?'

She raises an eyebrow at me. 'Get on with it.'

I work my way through the last two rows of books on Al's shelves pretty quickly, flicking a look up every now and then, just in case Angie has got absorbed in her work and failed to hear impending intruders. The last time I look she's not there, so I assume she's cleaning the toilets or the kitchen. She told me she had done the vacuuming first, to get the noisy stuff out of the way before I arrived. Much to the annoyance of the last few remaining office workers. That was probably part of the reason they all went home so early. I look round the room. There aren't many obvious hiding places. There's a vast grey metal desk – retro or actual vintage, I can't tell – with a small amount of clutter on top, and two drawers either side underneath. I poke through the surface paperwork half-heartedly. Stella and the Mini Mes stare judgementally out at me from a framed photo. It's disconcerting, to say the least. I've never really understood why people display pictures of their loved ones in their work spaces anyway. As if they might forget what they look like during the course of an eight-hour day. Or it's a way of saying, 'I am not a sociopath. Look! I know a human woman and two small children well enough to have taken their photograph!'

There's nothing to pique my interest. Al is either extremely efficient, or his job mainly consists of swanning around not doing any actual work, because there's precious little to sift through. I notice a movement in the main office and jump away from the desk. It's only Angie, spray can of Pledge in hand. I relax, look in the right-hand drawers. The top one is full of personal stuff, but a quick glance tells me it's all of the tissues, toothbrush, cold remedy, emergency snack variety. In the underneath, larger drawer there is a pile of paperwork about an upcoming tour by a famed boy band. Costings and schedules, some annotated. I check for anything incriminating between them. Nothing. I get momentarily distracted looking at their rider: four (extra-large) bags of Monster Munch, twelve one-litre bottles of cider, eight rounds of cheese-and-pickle sandwiches and four boxes of take-out KFC (to be kept warm). Clearly, fame has not rubbed their edges off yet. I snap a photo of the list, thinking it'll make David laugh, and then remember that's not really who we are any more.

I put it back in the drawer and move over to the left-hand side . . .

'Spider!!!!!!'

My heart (and my blood pressure, I imagine) shoots through the roof. I'm a rabbit caught in the headlights and then I remember the drill and fall to the floor underneath Al's desk.

I hear a kerfuffle. Sharon's voice. Angie reassuring her that what she thought was a killer arachnid has turned out to be a piece of cotton.

'Has Laura left?' I hear Sharon say.

'She's just in the loo.' Angie's voice sounds wobbly, nervous. I wonder if Sharon will notice.

Of all the things I should be worrying about, I find myself hoping Sharon doesn't say anything bitchy about me. I'm a firm believer in not listening at closed doors. I know that most people relish any chance to bash the boss, and Sharon strikes me as the most likely of all my employees to enjoy a good moan. I don't want to hear it, though. I'd rather not know.

'Is she OK, do you think?' is what Sharon actually says. 'I mean, you know, the divorce and everything.'

'She's fine,' Angie says, clearly not wanting to engage with this – albeit rather sweet – enquiry with me more or less in the room.

Sharon won't be derailed. 'She's looking a bit down, if you ask me. Poor love.'

I chide myself for assuming the worst. Feel a warm fuzzy glow of fondness for my team. 'Did you need something?' Angie says, changing the subject just as I was starting to enjoy it. Clearly, she's staying focused on the issue at hand.

'Oh. I've finished downstairs. I was just coming to see if you needed any help.'

Shit.

'That was quick,' Angie says. I assume she's buying herself time to think.

'I think half of them weren't in today,' Sharon says, unaware. 'Even the kitchen was clean already.'

'Tell you what, I promised Laura I'd give the supplies cupboard a clean-out when I got a chance. Do you want to do that? And make a list of whatever we're low on.' Genius. The supplies cupboard is down in the basement, far, far away from here.

'Sure,' Sharon says. 'It's a bit creepy down there, though.'

'Swap with Tomas, then. He won't mind. You can finish off the ground floor.'

I wait what seems like an age after Sharon agrees with this plan. I'm about to emerge when I hear a hoarse whisper from Angie. 'All clear.'

'Jesus,' I say, dragging myself up. 'Well done.'

'Anything?' she says, hopefully. I shake my head.

'OK, well, you've got about half an hour till we're done.'

'There's not much else I can look at,' I say. I nudge the mouse on Al's desk, just in case, but the computer is off. I pull open the top-left-hand drawer. Angie peers in with me. Pens, stationery, highlighters, Post-its. Nothing of any substance. I shut it again. Angie turns to go and get on with her work. I tug the handle of the final drawer, the deep one, bottom left. It doesn't move.

'Ange. This one's locked.' I say to her retreating back. She stops in her tracks.

11

We both stand there staring at the locked drawer like it's the holy grail. I tug on it again. It's only held closed by the flimsiest of locks, but it might as well be a Hatton Garden vault. 'Maybe we could open it with a hairgrip,' I say hopefully. I have a head full of them, as usual, trying to flatten the curls that spring out the side when I tie my hair back. Mind you, I also have absolutely no idea how I would use one to open a lock.

'You've been watching too many films,' Angie says. 'Maybe the key's in one of the other drawers. She starts rifling through the personal stuff top right, and I take the stationery, top left.

'A-ha!' I hear, and I look over to see Angie brandishing a small key.

'Amazing. Give it here.' I feed the key into the lock. Or, at least, I try to. But it's obvious the shape is all wrong.

'Damn. I wonder what this is for.' We both gaze around the room hopefully, but there's nothing that jumps out. I even move the framed discs, just in case there's a secret safe behind one of them.

'Let's keep looking,' Angie says. She puts the key back where she found it and carries on poking through the drawer. I do the same. A few seconds later I lift up a pile of unused envelopes and feel something in the bottom one.

'Wait . . .' I open the envelope and slide out another – flatter, slightly bigger – key. It fits smoothly into the lock. Turns easily. I look up at Angie.

Am I really going to do this?

She gives me an almost imperceptible nod. I pull open the drawer. At first glance, it's crammed full of what look like official documents. Contracts and letters.

'It's just more paperwork,' I say. 'Probably stuff about the business that's confidential.'

'Anything else?' she asks, disappointed.

I scrabble to the bottom of the pile. There's something underneath. A metal box, like one of those ones people use to put petty cash in. Red. About thirty centimetres wide. 'Where's that other key?' I say, and even to my own ears my voice sounds wobbly. 'You really won't tell anyone about this, will you, Ange? Anyone?'

'Of course I won't,' she says, going for the top-right-hand drawer again. 'It'd make me look as bad as you.'

It takes her a moment to locate the tiny key. I know just from looking at the lock that it's going to fit, and it does. I open the box before I can change my mind.

There's not much in there. Disappointingly little, in fact. I glance out at the main office then I tip the contents on to the floor. There are a couple of envelopes, a receipt from Cartier, a small box containing a tacky gold sovereign ring, large enough to fit a man's finger. I open the first envelope. A card. A print of a garish painting of Paris. Inside, in curly, cursive handwriting, a note.

Thank you for the best 2 days ever. Love u. F xx.

There are crudely drawn hearts covering the bottom half of the card.

'Whoever she is, she's young,' I say.

'Does the pope shit in the woods?' Angie says, reaching for the second envelope. 'F. Have you come across any Fs? Any Fionas or Fays hanging round your way?'

I shake my head. 'I don't think she's French either.' I snap a quick photo of the message on my phone. Angie has pulled another card from the second envelope. A photo of a kitten sitting in a large coffee cup.

She goes to open it.

There's a shout. A man's voice. 'Ange! Angie!'

The pair of us freeze.

It's Tomas.

'Put it all back,' she says, hauling herself to her feet. I stuff the second card and its envelope into my pocket. Scrabble the rest of the contents back into the box.

'What?' Angie shouts, as loudly as she can.

'We're finished down here.'

I lock the box and shove it back underneath the pile of paperwork.

'I'm coming,' Angie calls. 'Two secs.'

I lock the drawer and put the key back under the detritus top right and the other one in the envelope top left. I can hear Angie clattering around, gathering up her cleaning things. Hopefully, no one will notice that she's done a much less thorough job than usual. I check Al's desk, making sure nothing is out of place. Panic that I've put the keys in the wrong drawers, swap them. Swap them back. Panic again. Swap them again. Angie comes in, looking flustered. 'I have to go.'

'Coming,' I say. We both stand there, looking round the room for a minute. I straighten a picture. 'OK.'

'What did it say?' she mutters as we head for the stairs.

'I don't even know. I'll text you later.' It seems only natural to keep Angie updated now I've involved her this much. 'Wait,' I say. 'Retie your scarf. You look like you've been in a fight.' She pulls her headscarf off, stuffs it in her coat pocket and runs her fingers through her short hair.

Sharon and Tomas are lurking on the stairs up from the foyer. He's stuffing in a huge sandwich. He's about seven feet tall and eight stone (OK, six foot three and whatever skinny men that height weigh) and he eats almost constantly. No wonder he likes to work all hours. He has to spend more money on food than most humans. He waves matily.

'Oh, you still here?' Sharon says when she sees me. 'I didn't realize.' Tomas hands me a list of supplies. Unsurprisingly, we're not really low on anything, because it's only been a few days since I stocked up.

We all leave together. Angie sets the alarm and locks up. Just a normal day.

12

I barely even wait for the three of them to walk off before I pull the second card out of my pocket. It's the same handwriting, there's no doubt about that. This time, there's a longer message.

Happy Birthday, gorgeous boy . . .

I'm momentarily distracted by the thought of anyone referring to Al as a boy. Big, predatory, overconfident Al.

. . . I know you can't wear this yet, but you can put it on when your alone and think of me . . .

Your. She actually put 'your' instead of 'you're'. And she can't even blame autocorrect. She means the ring, I realize. The garish ring in the blue box.

. . . or just look at the photo haha! . . .

I scrabble around in the envelope. Find a Polaroid. Eww.
I stuff it back in the envelope quickly.

. . . I can't wait for our tomorrow. I love u 2 the moon and back!!!
F xxxx

94

More cartoony hearts.

C–ringe. The thought just pops into my head, and I smile, thinking of Betsy. God knows what she'd make of what I've just done. She has a very firm sense of what's right and what's wrong. I snap a picture of the message, decide to wait until Angie will have finished work to text it to her. Just in case she's with one of the others when it arrives. To kill time (and, I remind myself, to do my job, which should be my main priority at the moment, let's face it), I stop by the four-storey, four-company offices. The team there – Paul, Amita and Jean tonight – are just about finishing up. On the way home I send Angie a message: *Text me when you leave.*

The Close is deserted when I arrive home. I'm glad. I have no desire to run into any of them. Even Gail, because I'm scared I'll blurt out what I've just done.

Angie and I text back and forth, offering up names. Faith, Faye, Fran, Francesca, Florence. They get more and more ridiculous: Frenchie, Frou Frou, Fluffy. *Frankenstein*, she sends, and I send back *Fridge Freezer*. There's no doubt, whoever she is, Al's relationship with her is not one of which Stella would approve. But I still don't know her name. And I can hardly go to Stella and say, 'So, I was ransacking Al's office the other night . . .'

I tell her about the Polaroid.

So you'd recognize her if you saw her, she sends back, with a laughing face.

Not her face, obviously. If she came at me fanny first . . .

Angie sends back a series of emojis ranging from smiling to horror.

What was the Cartier receipt for?

Damn, I type back. *I forgot to look.*

We don't even know how old these notes are. For all I know, F could have been and gone to the great ex-lover graveyard in the sky. He might be on to G by now. Or even H.

Have you noticed any Fs anywhere else in the company? His assistant? I know it's a cliché, but sometimes clichés are made for a reason. And F is definitely young. Everything about her notes screams wide-eyed infatuation. The hearts and kisses. *Love u 2 the moon and back.* I doubt she's one of the other executives.

Never noticed. I'll look.

But we both know the truth is she could be anyone. His hairdresser. Someone who serves him coffee at Starbucks. A backing singer on a tour his company is promoting. Someone he met in a bar who has no other connection to him whatsoever. There's no clue.

'Have you heard the latest wedding news?' Gail says. We're drinking tea in her kitchen while she's meant to be working from home. She has an office elsewhere on the sprawling ground floor, she tells me, as does Ben. She checks her phone for emails every few minutes just in case. I wonder for a second if she's going to tell me it's all off. That Stella has finally had enough. 'No one's talking to me, remember.'

'Oh. Yes. I forgot. Well, they've got Lewis Capaldi singing at the reception. Al knows him through work, apparently.'

'Wow.' I can't deny that's impressive. 'When is it again?'

I'm hoping I'll be long gone. Secure and happy in my cosy new home, having forgotten about The Close and all its inhabitants. Except maybe for Gail.

'Early August. I can't remember which date. Third, maybe. We all had to sign up in blood that we'd be there at least a year ago.'

I make a mental note to up the intensity of my property search. It's almost April now. The chances of me finding my ideal home and securing it before August are getting slimmer by the day. 'Where are they having it?'

'Here.' She waves a hand around in the direction of Stella and Al's. 'They're building a small town in their back garden. Actual proper structures. No flimsy old marquee.'

David and I got married in a little church near my mum in Hastings. I'm an only child; he has just one brother. His parents were already gone. Even with all our friends, there were a maximum of thirty-five people there. We took over the room upstairs at the pub next door and the bar staff served us fish and chips and mushy peas. Everyone got very merrily drunk until we all got kicked out at midnight. It was perfect.

'Actually, they're expanding into Katya and Guy's next door too. The girls wanted miniature ponies so they're putting them in there. Some kind of petting zoo.'

'Jesus.' I wonder how much Al's heart is in this. How he can be planning a wedding and seeing someone else at the same time? 'Don't you think it's odd that this whole thing with the book happened so close to the wedding? I mean . . .'

Gail shrugs. 'Al's always going to be a massive flirt. I

don't think we should read too much into it. Someone giving him a book with a flirty message doesn't mean he's reciprocating.'

I think about the Polaroid. Keep my mouth firmly shut.

'I wish I knew what it said.' I drain the last of my tea. 'I wish I knew what I was being accused of writing.'

'Oh, well, I can just ask Stella,' Gail says, shrugging as if it's the most natural thing in the world. 'Although I'm not sure you want to know. It might just wind you up more.'

'I want to know what I'm up against,' I say, standing up. 'I should go. I need to do the rotas . . .'

Someone is heading up the drive as I open Gail's front door. Anya. We've only met in passing. Early days in the 'antebook' era, but I steel myself. I'm pretty sure I already know what to expect. She's Katya best buddy. They look like twins. Aspiring Stellas in thrall of the OG. Still, I plaster a smile on to my face.

'Hi!' I say enthusiastically.

Her first reaction is to smile. For a second, I think she hasn't got the memo. Either that or she has a mind of her own. But then it's as if she remembers, and her face drops. She makes a sort of non-committal noise and hesitates, as if she might turn round and walk off again.

'Don't worry,' I say. 'I'm on my way home. It's safe for you to come in.'

She blushes. Shakes her head. 'I don't know what you mean.'

I leave the door open for her. 'No, of course you don't.'

*

Doing the rotas is my equivalent of picking the perfect football team. You can come up with the winning combination in your head, but when it comes to it, someone always has a last-minute injury or, in the world of Sunshine Cleaning, a school play to attend or a poorly child. Everyone has different preferences, regular commitments I have to avoid, amounts of nights and hours they're willing to work. I first have to collate any texts I've had with requests for certain evenings on or off. Next week, Sharon wants Tuesday off; Catriona would rather not work on Tuesday either, or Friday; Maggie could do any day but would prefer Monday, Wednesday and Thursday, and she'd like to do the four-storey office on at least two of those days to get away earlier; Amita wants four nights' work, if possible; Jean three, but not Wednesday, and she'd like AJT Music and the financiers because she needs the hours; Kirsty also three, preferably Tuesday, Thursday, Friday; Aisha could do any evening but would like to coincide with Maggie.

It's like a huge game of Buckaroo. One false move and the whole thing comes crashing down. I'm thankful for the two students, Tomas and Paul, who will both work every day, as usual. It takes me the whole afternoon to come up with two teams of three for each evening in a form that – I hope – won't piss anyone off. I email it over to Angie to check over before I issue it to the others. I know it will all change anyway, once someone's kid gets the sniffles or someone suddenly remembers a commitment they entirely forgot to tell me about.

It's five o'clock before I remember I have a date tonight. As soon as I do, I also remember that I meant to cancel it.

It's been arranged for weeks, one of those things where you pluck a random day in the future, already knowing you'll make an excuse to cry off when the time comes. Only this time, I forgot. My heart's not in the dating thing. It feels reckless and frivolous. Not to mention pointless. Something I'm doing because I feel I'm supposed to rather than because I have any interest in it. I'd much rather put my PJs on and read a book or watch a film. I don't want to have to make forced conversation with someone who probably wishes they weren't there either. It all feels too much like hard work and, from my limited experience so far, I would put a bet on that nothing will come of it. I've often thought I'd rather just stick to the flirty banter stage. The light virtual conversations that pass an hour here or there. With the two conversions I've made so far, from online to actual human contact, the only result has been the end of a burgeoning friendship. Once we met in real life and realized that the chemistry was zero, that our pheromones were incompatible, we stopped chatting. What was the point? We were there to find love, not friends.

Except that friends are what I really need.

Tonight I am meeting Jeremy for the first time. We've been chatting for about six weeks. I agreed to move it on a stage and meet up face to face after dropping Betsy off with David one night. I got home, as I always do, feeling raw and rejected. I wanted to show him. Maybe you don't find me attractive any more, but look! Someone does. I have a social life. A sexual life. I am functioning without you. This is how all my 'dates' have happened, by the way. Off the back of an encounter with David, followed by a couple of glasses of wine. Bravado. It makes me feel better for a few hours, until I wake up in the small hours of the next day and think, *What the fuck have I done?*

I can't even remember what I thought Jeremy and I have in common. I look back through our old messages. He's a divorcee. Forty-six. Works at London University as some kind of sports administrator. Weekend custody of a boy and a girl aged thirteen and fifteen. We talk about our kids a lot. Two part-time parents trying to negotiate their way through their new normal. It's clear from scrolling back that we both just want to offload to an empathetic ear. Hardly the way great love stories are born.

And I'm meeting him for coffee in less than an hour. Definitely too late to cancel now.

I'm in and out of the shower in minutes. Cursing myself for ever saying yes to his suggestion we take it up a notch. Never again.

It's nearly four months since David announced our marriage was over. That's what it was, an announcement. Not a suggestion or a conversation. It was a fait accompli. An edict. When I think about that evening it plays out in my head like a bad soap opera, shot in high resolution, the colours too bright and jarring. I don't know how true my memory is, or if the endless reconstructions of it have shifted the reality.

It was a normal Monday. Betsy was galumphing around at her ballet class in the community centre up the road, and Zara's mum, Michaela, was taking them both home to have tea at hers. We used to take it in turns. It was bitterly cold, I remember. I had the radiators turned up high, and fir-tree-scented candles – my winter indulgence on dark evenings – alight on the mantelpiece. I was pottering around in the kitchen preparing a meal for just the two of us, David and me. Date night. I can even remember what it was. A comforting lasagne, made from scratch, and a tomato, onion and basil salad. Even a home-made dessert. Tiramisu.

All of these dishes were only half made when he arrived home from work earlier than usual. They never got completed. Never got eaten.

'I'm moving out,' he said when I asked him if he'd had a good day. I can remember what he was wearing. Black Levi's and a grey V-neck over a collared T-shirt. He doesn't have the kind of job where you have to dress up. He works in marketing. A good job, but nothing glamorous. A well-known range of domestic products.

I thought I'd misheard. I don't know what I thought he'd said, but it wasn't that. When I didn't respond he said it again. Slower. Louder. Of course, I assumed there was someone else. Someone I could fixate on. The enemy. He just kept reiterating that there wasn't. That wasn't what it was about. He'd thought it all through.

'Obviously, you and Betsy can stay here for now, but we'll have to put the house on the market . . .'

He had found a flat he wanted to buy, he told me. And a place to rent in the meantime while he waited for it to go through. He had it all worked out. No, he didn't want to talk about it. He'd agonized for weeks, but this was something he had to do. He was sorry. Truly sorry.

By the time Betsy got home, my marriage – her family – was well and truly dead.

Of course, I blamed myself. When I was eight, my mum and I came home from a day out buying new school clothes to find my dad gone. For me it was a bolt from the blue. One minute he was my loving, lovely dad, and the next he had disappeared from my life altogether. It was only years later that my mum told me he had been cheating for years. It was the lying that was the worst, she'd said. All the heartfelt denials and the tears that she knew were just bullshit. His absolute refusal to tell her the truth. When David and I got serious, I made him promise he would always be straight with me. That he wouldn't sugar-coat the truth if anything was wrong. And it seemed he had taken those words to heart.

I'm meeting Jeremy in Primrose Hill, halfway – give or take – between my home and his work. I drive because I want to be sure of making a quick getaway, and I have no intention of drinking anything other than coffee. I call Angie on the way to make sure everything is OK for this evening, and to tell her where I'm going and with whom, in case he turns out to be a serial killer. I spend an age trying to find a parking space so, consequently, I'm late, and Jeremy is already nursing a coffee himself when I walk in. He stands up to greet me. We both look like our photos.

He's smart, pleasant, nice-looking. Ordinary. My heart's not in it. I would rather be anywhere but here. I'm the opposite of sparkling company and I can tell that Jeremy thinks so too. After one coffee for me and two for him we agree to call it a night. Neither of us mentions meeting up again. I'm home by eight.

I'm not ready for this.

13

Betsy does not want to come to the flat with me. She tells me this tearfully when I go to pick her up from school on Wednesday.

'I hate it!' she cries, clinging on to her rucksack. Michaela gives me a sympathetic smile over Zara's head. 'I want to go home.'

Home. David's flat is now home. The word flashes in my head in garish neon. My daughter no longer thinks her home is with me.

'We can bake biscuits,' I say running a hand over her soft curls. Betsy loves baking. We used to watch *Bake Off* together religiously, David laughingly protesting from behind his iPad. I make a mental note to find out when the next series starts. 'We don't have to go out. We don't have to see anyone else.'

'I don't want to,' she says.

I crouch down so we're eye to eye. 'We can do whatever you want.'

'I want to go home,' she says, but less forcefully.

'You can't, sweetheart. Not yet. Dad won't be there. Felix can't babysit. He's not old enough.'

She gives me a wonky smile. 'He is in cat years.'

'Yes, but he doesn't know how to turn the oven on. You'd starve.'

Betsy laughs. I've won. This time.

On the way we stop off in Hampstead High Street at the chi-chi ice-cream shop. We choose our flavours – black cherry for me and peanut butter for Betsy – and take them to a table outside because all the ones inside are taken, pulling our coats tight around us. Betsy shovels in a mouthful, all traces of her earlier meltdown gone, then pauses with her spoon held high.

'Isn't that that horrible woman?' she says in a very loud whisper. I follow her gaze and spot Stella sitting across the alley, outside the bakery, deep in conversation with Jan – her of the shelf arse – over a couple of coffees. She's just far enough away that she, thankfully, doesn't seem to have heard Betsy's comment, but the moment is ruined.

'Don't stare at her,' I say. 'Hopefully she won't see us.'

'I don't like her,' Betsy says, jabbing her spoon into her container.

'Neither do I,' I whisper conspiratorially. 'Let's just pretend she's not there.'

Of course, as soon as you tell yourself not to look at something, it becomes literally impossible not to keep turning round every ten seconds. And, of course, as soon as I start doing that, it becomes inevitable that I'll accidentally catch their eye. In this case, Jan's. I force a half-hearted smile of acknowledgement on to my face. She blanks me and turns round to mutter something to Stella, who turns to look at me and then blanks me too. Jan turns back to add a glare into the equation, just for good measure. That hurts. I've never had any problem with Jan. I've barely even spoken to her. I've realized, though, that she and Eva are second in the hierarchy. Stella's loyal lieutenants. Katya and Anya are the young wannabes, waiting to earn their stripes. But it's now abundantly clear that if Stella blackballs someone, they're out. And I have definitely been blackballed.

'Finished?' I say with forced brightness to Betsy, thankful that she eats with all the decorum and restraint of a bulldog.

She grins back at me. 'Yep.'

'Let's go, then,' I say, leaving my own ice cream half finished. I steer her away from the bakery so we don't have to pass the Wicked Witches of the North.

I'm driving her back, a couple of hours later – she's clutching a Tupperware full of white-chocolate-chip cookies for her dad. The irony that he's left me but I am still somehow baking him treats is not lost on me – when I get a text from Angie. I know it's from Angie because Betsy grabs up my phone and tells me so. I dread to think what it might say, but I can hardly snatch the phone out of Betsy's hands.

'Something something is for something ring,' she reads, and for the first time ever, I'm pleased that spelling is not her strong point. I'm dying to see what it actually says. 'And then it says she had a look at something else,' she adds, losing interest.

'Oh well, nothing important,' I say, clueless. 'I might pop in there after I drop you.' I had already decided to do this. The card and the Polaroid are burning a hole in my pocket and I want to put them back in their rightful place.

For all I know, Al looks at them regularly. A little pick-up in a mundane day. I immediately regret mentioning it, though.

'Can I come?' she pleads, putting my phone back down. She has always loved going to visit the companies we clean for. It's a different – grown-up – world to explore. Not to mention that all my staff make a big fuss of her. They all find it hard leaving their own kids in the evenings, so any small human that makes an appearance is treated to the full force of frustrated parental affection. Plus, Tomas is teaching her how to swear in Polish, so there's that.

'Maybe next time,' I say. 'It's a bit late tonight.'

Once Betsy and I have said a tearful goodbye, David smiling blandly at me like we're two vague acquaintances and he can't quite place where he's met me before, I jab at my phone to bring up Angie's message.

Cartier receipt is for platinum ring. Had a quick look at the papers in there too. Might be interesting!! Ring me!

I send her a quick text back. *Be there in 5 x*

Angie is waiting for me at the top of the stairs, looking around furtively like an agitated owl. She beckons me into the offices.

'I just had a quick look. I've not got behind with work . . .'

'It's OK. So there's no clue who the ring is for?'

'No. Forget the receipt. It could be for his wife, or F, or anyone. It's the paperwork that might be worth a second look. It looks like it's personal, not business. Financial. I might have misunderstood – because God knows, finance isn't my thing – but I think they might have re-mortgaged their house . . .'

'Really? They're rolling in it. Why would they need to?'

Angie shrugs. 'Like I said, I only had a quick look. I might have got it completely wrong . . . But I thought it might cheer you up.'

'Shit . . .' I say. I can't deny I'm itching to see what's in there. Maybe Stella and Al are in financial trouble. Maybe their showy life is just that – a show. Maybe Stella is all fur coat and no knickers, as my gran used to say. I feel a satisfying rush of schadenfreude. Even if I could never let on to Stella that I know, I think it would make me feel less intimidated by her to know that she was a fraud. But there's no denying this feels a bit more invasive than just trying to establish if someone has a bit on the side. This feels like spying. I would be crossing a line. Sod it. I've crossed it already. Hopped back and forth over it several times.

'Same code?'

Angie smiles. 'Same. Luckily, Sharon's not on tonight, or she'd think the place was infested with spiders. She'd be handing in her notice. I'm going to do the kitchen. No one can get past me. And I'll block the stairs with the Hoover, just in case.' The tiny kitchen has a door right at the top of the stairs. If either Tomas or Amita head up to find Angie, they can't miss her in there.

'Is this really bad?' I say to her as she goes. She turns round and gives me her mega-watt smile. 'Only if they find out.'

Angie has left the key in the lock, so I crouch down behind Al's desk and open the drawer. Lift out the first ream of papers, which are enclosed in a plastic wallet. The front sheet shows just his name and address. 'Mr Alec J. Thornbury c/o AJT Music. Strictly Private and Confidential'. Alec J. Of course. He is AJT. So successful he has a multimillion-pound company named after him.

It's from a bank. A posh one, not your common or garden NatWest. The accompanying letter is addressed to Al. Further to your request blah blah blah. Raising finance. Three point five million pounds. Would Mr Thornbury please sign where indicated, in front of an independent witness. I flick further on. There's Al's signature, witnessed by Roman Fedorov, CEO of Alpha Recruitment, 4 The Close. Their neighbour. Jan's husband.

So far, so normal.

I shove the papers back in the wallet. Reach for the next batch. They're in a thick file. There are particulars for a stunning penthouse flat on the river in Battersea. Wraparound terrace. Floor-to-ceiling windows. State-of-the-art kitchen. Gym and swimming pool in the basement. Three and a half million. Various letters back and forth with a solicitor. OK, so they've raised some cash from their house and they're buying an investment property in up-and-coming Battersea. Maybe they're not quite on the breadline yet.

I'm so absorbed I wouldn't hear if Angie was shouting about man-eating tarantulas. I peer out from behind the desk. Everything is quiet. I can hear the faint noise of crockery clanking from the direction of the kitchen. I dig deeper into the drawer. Find another letter from the bank, this time about a new account in the name of Mr A. J. Thornbury. And another about a transfer of one million pounds from his joint account with Stella.

Something strikes me. I go back and look at the paper-work about the loan. Skim through the details. Angie's right, it's an additional loan on the house. The total now owed is just shy of ten million pounds. The monthly repayments are extortionate. Then I notice something else. The money for the flat – the three and a half million – has to be repaid by the end of this year. I take a few quick photos, start flicking through the rest of the pile.

'What have you found?'

I jump, throwing everything I'm holding up in the air.

'Jesus Christ.'

'Sorry, sorry,' Angie says. 'I just thought I'd better check on you.' She helps me scrabble everything back up, but the pages are all out of sequence now.

'I don't know.' I start putting them back in order. 'At least . . .' I reach for the stack I've already looked through. There's something hovering at the far edge of my brain. 'Hold on.'

I check back through them. Angie picks up the others and finishes straightening them up.

I recheck the contract for the Battersea flat. It's in Al's name only.

The remortgage is in Al's name only.

The new bank account is in Al's name only.

'Something's off with this,' I say. Angie looks at me, big-eyed. 'I just can't work out what.'

14

I'm sitting looking through the photos I took, waiting for the kettle to boil. Last night I fell asleep almost before my head hit the pillow, despite the twenty billion different thoughts that were buzzing round my brain. It was as if they blew a circuit. I had too much to think about, so better if I thought about nothing. I don't even remember dreaming.

I try to make sense of it but, if I'm being honest, I'm blinded by the amount of zeros after each number. If Al's taking out a loan against the house, then the house must be in his name. I'm pretty sure that if he and Stella owned it jointly, then she would have to sign too. I suppose he could have lived there before with his ex-wife, bought out her share when Stella came on the scene. I assume they didn't have kids, because I've never heard anyone mention them. Why would he burden himself with massively increased debts just to buy a new place? Why is he transferring money out of his and Stella's joint account? Something to do with tax, maybe? Perhaps he's a money launderer, although why he'd need to launder money the bank had legitimately given him I have no idea. I don't think that's how it works. I wish I'd stuck with *Ozark*.

There's a tap on my door. I didn't even hear anyone coming up the stairs. I stuff my phone in my pocket, stabbing at the buttons to hide the photos first. Gail is standing on my top step. It must be another working-at-home day.

'Hey. Come on in . . .'

'I don't want to disturb you,' she says, but she follows me inside anyway.

'It's fine. Tea? Coffee? The kettle's just boiled.'

'OK, then, coffee, please. It's looking nice in here.' I look round, trying to see the studio through her eyes. It does look homely. Lived in. 'Messy,' someone less charitable might say. Cramped. She sits on the sofa while I dig another mug out of the cupboard. 'It's only instant, is that OK?'

'I actually prefer it. Don't tell Ben. Our machine cost the same as a small car. He doesn't even drink coffee.'

She's probably not even joking, but I laugh anyway.

'So,' she says, 'I thought you'd like to know, I asked Stella about the book.'

I stop pouring out the water and look round. 'Oh. Tell me.'

'She brought it up, in a way. You're right – she's pissed off with you. I tried to mitigate it a bit, but she wasn't having it. I think it's a defence mechanism, if I'm being honest. If she can paint you as the villain, then it means Al hasn't done anything wrong . . .'

I don't even react. I know this is exactly what Stella is thinking, even if she doesn't realize it.

'. . . Anyway, she was talking about the book – it's a novel called *Murder in the Marais*, by the way, and she found it when she went snooping through his work bag one night. God knows why he took it home; he mustn't have realized – and how out of order it was, and I just asked her outright what you'd written. I mean, what whoever had written, obviously, but as far as she was concerned, I meant you.'

'It's OK. I understand.' I hand her the mug. There's nowhere to sit unless I perch next to her on the tiny sofa, which feels way too intimate, so I go back to leaning on the kitchen cabinets.

'So . . . wait, I wrote it down after I left, because I thought it might be important for you to have the exact wording.' She fishes around in her pocket, pulls out a folded piece of paper. '*Voici a Paris! Vers les etoiles et retour.*'

'I have no idea what that means. I mean, I recognize most of the words . . .'

'It's pretty basic and not even grammatically correct. It's definitely not written by a French person, anyway. More like Google Translate.'

Au revoir, Fifi, au revoir, Félice. Hello, Faith, hello, Fiona.

'Yes, I guessed as much. So . . .'

'It's basically meant to mean, "Here's to Paris. To the stars and back." I think.'

I'm starting to wonder if F is a would-be astronomer. She definitely has an obsession with the planets. 'Jesus. No wonder Stella's pissed off with me. I hope you know I would never write something that cheesy anywhere. Let alone in a book I was giving to a married man. To anyone.'

'You're preaching to the converted,' she says. She puts her coffee near her lips, puts it down again. Too hot. 'She told me off again for letting you move in in the first place. Anyway, for what it's worth, I told her I couldn't imagine

113

you genuinely making a pass at him. I said you were still hung up on your ex – I hope you don't mind?'

'I probably am,' I say. 'It's probably true. Um . . . are they happy, do you think? I mean, I know they're planning the wedding but . . .' This is as close as I dare come to telling her my suspicions. For all Gail's insights, I think she's the kind of person who likes to assume the best in people. Which is a great quality, don't get me wrong. But I think it means she'd rather not hear negatives.

Gail gives a wry laugh. 'I would never try to fathom the dynamics of anyone else's relationship. But yes, I think it works for them. And, who knows? Maybe after they're married he'll calm down.'

'I don't get it,' I say, but then I think maybe the drama is what gives them the passion. Maybe you need the lows, the fights and jealousies, to get the highs. Maybe a doomed marriage is one like mine that just plods along on an even keel. It's too depressing to think about. Because isn't that exactly what a relationship should be? Me and you against the world. Compromise and consideration. A united front. I'd always thought so.

'It wouldn't work for me either, but who are we to judge?'

'Well, I think I can a bit, since he dragged me into it . . .'

'True.' She pours a bit more milk into her coffee from the carton I've left on the coffee table. A jug was one of the things I considered surplus to requirements when I boxed up my worldly goods. I wasn't expecting to be entertaining. 'I don't think it'll happen again, though. And I know it's ghastly having her think you made a play for him, but it could have been worse.'

I'm not sure it could, from my point of view, but I don't say that.

'I'm just going to keep my head down. Try and forget about it,' I lie.

'Good idea. These things have a way of blowing over.' She wants everything to go back to normal, and I understand that. This is her home. Her life. She's done me a favour and now I need to return it by pretending everything is fine. All forgiven. I get it. I'd probably be doing exactly the same if I were her.

The thing is, I'm not her.

15

'What I can't get my head around is the wedding,' I say to Angie on the phone later. I've texted her over all the photos I took of the documents, and I've spent most of the morning since Gail left looking at them again, my face screwed up, as if that might help me make out the tiny, blurry print. There's only so far my fingers can stretch the pictures to read the fine type. I'm walking through the woods, towards the open spaces of the heath. I need to clear my head. 'Why is he going along with it if he's buying up sneaky flats and siphoning money out of their joint account?'

'Maybe that money is to pay for it? Maybe the flat is his wedding present to her? They sound like the sort of people who might think something like that was normal.'

'Then why is it in his name?' I pass a woman with a Jack Russell. We give each other that 'we don't know each other but it would seem rude not to, given as we're the only two people here' smile.

'Because it's a surprise. He'll transfer it into her name once the wedding's over.'

'Why is he buying her a flat as a present?' I'm not even concerned about the idea of Al spending three and a half million on a gift. They're nothing if not flash. It's more that it seems odd he would gift her something she could never show off, as opposed to, say, a Ferrari or a small yacht. 'It's not very romantic.'

'Because he's a flash git?' Angie says, and I guffaw.

'Well, there is that.'

'Even without the flat, why is he going ahead when he's got F on the side?'

'Because he's the kind of man who always has someone on the side. That's all F is to him. In his head, she's not a threat to his relationship with Stella. So long as Stella never finds out. But F . . . We can't keep calling her F, we need a name for her . . .'

'Fanny,' I say, without thinking. 'I will never unsee that Polaroid . . .'

Angie snorts. 'OK. My guess is that Fanny might not be satisfied with being a bit on the side and that's why she gave him a book with something written in it. She was marking her territory. Hoping that Stella might find it.'

I trudge on through the woods, going over it all again. What am I missing?

'Are you still there?' I realize that Angie has been talking and I haven't heard a word.

'Yes. Sorry, what did you say?'

'I said all this speculation is pointless anyway as you still have no idea who Fanny is.'

'I know. I'm wasting my time.'

'There'll be something,' she says, but it's not much comfort.

'Maybe.'

I distract myself for the rest of the afternoon by swiping aimlessly through Tinder, dismissing every potential mate without a second look. I'm lonely, but I can't raise either the courage or enthusiasm to start yet another conversation with yet another soon-to-be lost cause. Then I scroll through PrimeLocation, revisiting everything that comes up in the right area at the right price, even though I've already dismissed them all for what seemed to me good reasons.

I pick up the phone and call Rahina. It goes straight to voicemail, as it always does when she's with a client. I don't bother to leave a message. I should give myself a deadline, I decide. Even if I found the perfect house tomorrow and the sale breezed through without a complication, it would still take the best part of three months. I have no intention of renewing my lease on the annexe. No intention of not being my daughter's main caregiver for more than the six months I allowed myself. I make myself a promise – if I haven't found my dream home by the beginning of June, I'll settle for whatever I can get that's safe and in walking distance of her school.

As ever, whenever I call Rahina my finger hovers over the name that's next to hers in my contacts. Rebecca. Rebecca was the closest of my 'couple friends'. Married to David's best mate from his uni days. We hit it off immediately. She was funny and feisty and a bit clumsy. She and I soon became close. Not bosom buddies exactly, but we had a relationship that was outside of our coupledom. A coffee here and there. The cinema a few times. Playdates with our kids. I mistook it for real friendship. I let my old friends go. Gradually. Unconsciously. I got sloppy with returning calls, remembering birthdays, being free to chat on the phone, let alone meet up. I didn't mean for it to happen; it just did. And then, when they all eventually stopped trying, I told myself that that was how life went. You moved on. Mine and David's social lives were now inextricably linked. They'd merged. I never even realized until recently that I'd brought no one to the table. Rather than our old friends joining to make one big happy family, I had just adopted his. I didn't even notice it was happening. I think about sending Rebecca a text. Something short and sweet like 'Coffee soon?' but I know there's no point. Even if she could find the time for me, I don't want to torture myself by hearing about David's new life and, outside of our husbands' friendship, I can't now remember what we had in common.

For the first few weeks after David left, I told myself he'd be back. It was a midlife crisis. However much he protested that it wasn't, I was sure it was all about sex. Painful though it was to think about, I assumed he'd dip a toe into the scary world of dating – which had changed beyond recognition since we met – have a couple of soulless and empty encounters and then realize he'd made a huge mistake. He'd come crawling back. I told myself I'd forgive him. We'd get past it.

Of course, that hadn't happened, and now I knew it never would. I missed him – missed being a family, a team – so much I wore the feeling like a suit of armour. Weighing me down, stopping anyone else from getting close.

16

For want of anything better to do, I'm back at AJT Music the next Monday, rifling through the detritus on the desks in the hope of finding potential Fannys. Not a sentence I ever thought I would hear myself say. I forgot to warn Angie I was coming, but I find her on the first floor, in the open-plan office, singing to herself as she wipes down what bits of windowsill she can access.

'Very nice,' I say, when she gets to the end of what might be 'Chandelier' by Sia, although she might have just dropped a heavy weight on her foot. She jumps and turns round, clutching her chest.

'For fuck's sake, will you stop doing that.'

'Is that any way to talk to your boss?' I say, laughing

She raises a scrawny eyebrow. 'Is this a work visit?'

'This is as good as my social life gets these days. I couldn't stay away.'

'Any more news on you know what?'

I shake my head. 'That's why I'm here. I thought I could have a look for any females beginning with F. You never know.'

She throws her duster at me. 'Get on with it then. I'll start at this end.'

By the time I've dusted my half of the desks I've found Grant, Naomi, Jay, Kate, Andi, Sam, Tanya and Martha.

I'm guessing from Angie's silence that she's out of luck too. The work is strangely therapeutic. Back in the day, when I first started the business, it was just me and my first two employees, Angie and a woman called Martha, and I used to work alongside them every night at the one company we cleaned for. I'd chosen cleaning randomly, but in truth I'd always enjoyed it. Not in a 'does this small heap of cat hair give me joy or not?' kind of way, but because you saw results. You started with a messy space and ended up with a clean one. It was tangible, quantifiable even. I remember being exhausted but exhilarated that I was doing something for me, even though it really made no financial sense at that point. But I didn't want to go back to full-time work. I couldn't imagine spending all day chatting to people about medical-insurance claims, like I'd been doing before I got pregnant. I wanted to be there for my little girl. And David was earning enough so that I didn't have to. I was lucky. He used to tease me, call me Alan Sugar. I don't think he thought I'd still be doing it six years later.

'Nothing?' I say to Angie.

She shakes her head. 'I'll do the ground floor tomorrow. Maybe she's in Accounts.'

We both jump as the door swings open and a woman I've never seen before walks in. She stomps over to what, I assume, is her desk, picks something up and leaves again. She doesn't even acknowledge us. My heart starts racing. That's how easy it would be for Al to walk in and catch us snooping.

'One of us always needs to be on the lookout,' I say, once I'm sure she's gone. 'I might pop in again on Wednesday after I've dropped Betsy off.'

'Jesus, you really do need to get a social life.' She leans over and gives me a hug. I'm nearly crushed by her scrawny biceps. It's an unexpected and sweet gesture. She's not usually a hugger. Humiliatingly, I feel my eyes prick with tears.

On Tuesday I finally get around to sending out the reminders to all my office clients about their annual spring clean. Once a year they each get their employees to clear all their crap from their desks and the surrounding areas and we go in for a whole day or even two over a weekend and blitz everything. Wash the floors, clean the inside of windows. Take everything off shelves and put it carefully back again in exactly the same configuration. Empty all the cupboards. It's a big job, but it pays disproportionately well.

Then I do a mail-out to the few domestic clients I have. None of them are weekly – our services are expensive compared to a regular cleaner – but they've all used us in the past for a yearly spruce-up. I had hoped I might persuade a few of The Close's residents that they could do with a onceover, but I don't think any of them are going to be letting me into their house any time soon. What if I flung myself at their husbands? What if I wrote them cringey notes in French and accompanied them with photos of my hooha? Still, I order flyers detailing our services that I can distribute to the nearby streets. Might as well try and nab myself some one-per-cent clients while I'm here.

By the time it gets to six o'clock I'm itching for someone to talk to other than myself, so I take a quick shower and, even though it's against all my natural instincts to turn up somewhere unannounced, I force myself to head down to Gail's. Ben is away in Luxembourg for two nights and I know she likes company when he's gone. I take a bottle of wine, because I don't want her thinking I just show up so I can drink her top-notch stuff. I ring the bell and smile up at the camera, pulling the ends of my pony-tail to make it tighter.

'Hi!' she says, when she opens the door. She's dressed in her usual evening garb of high-end workout gear. I have no idea if she actually works out every night, but they do have a gym somewhere on the premises, apparently, and she's in very good shape, so something's working. I bran-dish the wine.

'Fancy a quick one?'

'Oh,' she says. 'Um . . .'

I've overstepped the mark. I should have waited for an invitation. I've probably broken some etiquette code and I'll be taken away and shot as a revolutionary. I take a step back. 'Don't worry. It was just a thought . . .'

'It's . . .' She pulls the front door closed a little. 'Stella's here, showing me ideas for her wedding dress . . .' Her voice is breezy, but she raises her eyebrows as if to signal why that might be a problem. Shit. I hadn't even thought of that as a possibility. She must have arrived while I was in the shower.

'Oh. Well, I don't want to disturb you,' I say awkwardly. 'Another time.'

She looks relieved. 'Yes. Lovely.'

And she shuts the door before I can even say goodbye. Back upstairs, I uncork the wine and climb up on to the kitchen counter to open the front window. It's a beautiful evening. Still and almost warm. The promise of good weather in the air. There are nearly two hours till I Face-Time with Betsy. She'll probably still be at Zara's. David usually collects her about half past six, by which time, hopefully, she's eaten and done her homework. I'm immensely grateful to Michaela for the way she's putting herself out to help my little girl carry on in her routine. I'm not sure I'd be so generous if it were the other way round. I need to make more of an effort to show my thanks, I remind myself. Buy her some flowers, at the very least.

The end of next week is the start of the Easter holiday, and – despite David and I always having agreed that we would reverse roles during the holidays, with Betsy stay-ing with me during the week and him at weekends (with the agreement that I could drop her round at his if I had a work crisis, unless he'd already told me he wasn't going to be there) – I know I have a battle on my hands. Betsy has made it very clear she doesn't want to spend more time in The Close than she has to. She wants to be able to see her friends and play with her cat. She wants to stay in the place she now calls home. And, of course, she wants me to be there too. It goes without saying that what she wants can't happen.

I wonder if I could get a last-minute deal and take us away somewhere, but it's my busiest time at work in terms of trying to drum up more business. It's so ingrained in people that spring is when you clean the bits of your house that you ignore the rest of the year (although, for some reason, this never occurs to them in February, when the weather is dreary; it's always a mad rush in April, and it'll be even more so this year because I'm so late with my mail-outs and flyers). Maybe, much though it pains me, I could suggest that David take the time off work. Although it'll probably be too late. Half his colleagues will already have booked their vacations to coincide with their kids' break.

I'm still mulling over all of this when I hear laughter. I peer out of the window, but there's no one in The Close. I take my glass through to the bedroom and look out of the window at the back, the one that overlooks Gail and Ben's back garden. Gail and Stella are ambling towards a little wrought-iron table with two chairs, where the last of the sun is hitting. They both have their coats on and Stella is carrying what looks like a couple of throws, while Gail has a wine bottle and two glasses. Stella's spiky heels sink into the grass as she walks. She reaches out and steadies herself on Gail's arm when she wobbles. They're obviously really comfortable with each other. I feel stupidly left out. The unpopular girl at school eating her lunch alone while everyone else gossips about her.

I make myself move away before they look up and see me.

17

OK. Something has happened. Maybe. I'm not sure.

I've found a potential Fanny. Except that she's not a Fanny, she's a Ferne. Of course, she might just be a random woman whose name begins with an F. Except that she looks exactly like Stella, just a ten-plus-years-younger, more natural version. And she lives here. In The Close.

Angie and I finished checking for possibles at AJT Music after I dropped Betsy off on Wednesday evening. She had already moved on from the top floor by the time I got there and had made some excuse to swap with Tomas so that she and I could forensically sweep the accounts and admin offices behind reception. We got briefly excited when we found a letter addressed to a Mr F. Freeman, in case the sender had unwittingly misgendered Fanny, but it soon turned out that F. Freeman was Frank and a man in his fifties, judging by a family photo on the wall. It was disheartening, to say the least.

'Fuck it,' I said to Angie. 'I give up. Why am I even doing this anyway?'

'Because if you weren't, you would literally be doing nothing with your life other than working and sleeping.'

'God,' I said with feigned indignation. 'Say what you think, won't you? Don't spare my feelings.'

She flashed me a smile. 'You did ask.'

*

I decided to give it up as a bad job. My business needed attention and, after I collected the 'Professional Spring Clean!' flyers from the printers I spent a whole day traipsing around the mansions of north-west London shoving them through letterboxes. At one pile the size of Southfork I was turned away by a burly, shaven-headed security guard before I could even enter the gate. At another, I was shouted at by a man in a vintage Aston Martin for using the main entrance and not the one marked 'Tradesmen'. One woman asked if I'd come to interview for the maid's job. It was an ego boost of a day, what can I say? As someone who never reads any leaflet that comes through her door, ever, I'm surprised at how much business can be drummed up in this way, though. I only needed a few takers to make a significant difference to my turnover. I shuffled back towards home, wishing the flat had a bath I could soak my aching limbs in and not just a shower. My messenger bag was, thankfully, considerably lighter since I had left home in the morning, now emptied of most of the flyers I had taken with me, and the sandwich and water I had consumed on the run. I would go out again tomorrow and I'd already decided Betsy and I could do some more this weekend. The weather was supposed to be fine and it would give us something to do away from the neighbours.

As I turned the corner into The Close, past the oh-so-welcoming 'Private Road: No Unauthorized Entry' sign (I secretly wanted to add 'Poor people will be ostracized' underneath, but I hadn't yet got up the courage), I decided to slip a flyer through the letterbox of number 1. The occupants (I had no idea who they even were, let alone what they looked like) didn't seem to mix with any of the others, so would – hopefully – not have heard the gossip about me. Yet. Feeling rebellious, I walked in through their 'Out' gate, on to the horseshoe-shaped drive. I dug in my bag for a leaflet and was just about to feed it through the letterbox when the front door opened and there was a woman, on her way out, by the looks of it, sleeping baby in a very expensive buggy behind her. I jumped guiltily.

'Oh. Hi.' She looked at me, confused. She was younger than most of the other residents – maybe twenty-five. But otherwise, the usual round these parts: slim, tall, big hair.

'Sorry,' I said, blushing. No one likes junk mail. Everyone hates the people who shove handfuls of it through their letterboxes. 'I was about to put this through your door.'

She reached her hand out and took it. Threw it on the doormat without looking at it. Not rudely, just on autopilot. 'Thanks.' I resisted the urge to ask for it back if she wasn't interested.

'If you do . . . need a spring clean or anything. I live here . . . on The Close . . . so I'd give you a neighbours' discount . . .' Shut up, Laura. 'Anyway, thanks.'

She pushed the buggy out and turned to lock the door. 'Ah, is that funny little car yours? Sunlight Cleaning?'

'Sunshine. Yes, that's me. Sorry it's such an eyesore.'

'It makes me laugh,' she said, smiling with dazzling white, straight teeth. 'It must be giving some of them palpitations.'

I'm not going to lie, I warmed to her then. 'I'm Laura,' I said. 'Number 6. Well, above the garage. Gorgeous baby, by the way.'

'Oh god, no. He's not mine. I'm the nanny.'

Ah. Now it made sense. 'Well, whoever's he is, he's lovely. That's a great age.'

She looked down at him fondly. 'It is. His name's Andrei. He's a sweetheart. When he's asleep. I'm Ferne, by the way. Listen, I'll mention the cleaning thing to them . . .'

I barely heard the last part. The first letter of her name jumped out at me in flashing neon a metre high. I looked at her properly for the first time as we both made to walk out on to the street. Long dark locks falling round her shoulders, high cheekbones, almond-shaped eyes, full lips. She was stunning, but what was more striking was that she looked exactly like a more natural version of Stella. That was what made me think she might be the one. If Al had a type, then here was a perfect candidate right under his nose.

And her name began with F.

I suddenly remembered that if she really was Fanny, I was more intimately acquainted with bits of her than I should be, and then I couldn't look at her any more. I had to try and dig some more, though, while I had the chance. I waited to see which direction she would turn in and then went the same way, away from Gail and Ben's and my comfortable sofa and a cup of tea. My legs were aching so much I could hardly shuffle one foot in front of the other.

'Don't you live that way? Ferne asked, looking slightly confused.

'I'm going to do a few more streets before I give up. Where are you taking him?'

'Just round the block to get some air. I don't like going on the heath on my own. It creeps me out.'

I decided to change the subject before she pinned me down on my exact route. 'How long have you lived here?'

'Since he was born, pretty much. You?'

I gave her a very brief version of what had brought me there. This wasn't about me. 'How do you like it?'

She leaned down to check on the baby. Adjusted his hat a little. 'It's OK. Good. Better than some other places I've been, I suppose. I wish more people had babies; it's nice when a few of you can all take them out together.' She started telling me about Sergei and Katherine, the couple she works for, and I had to stop myself from interrupting her to tell her we didn't have time for this. Luckily, she walked at a snail's pace, so we were getting nowhere fast. I waited until I thought I could politely step in.

'What about the other people on The Close? They're not very friendly, are they?'

Ferne shrugged. 'Of course they're not. We're the hired help. Well, I am. Not you. But you're not one of them. Some of the other staff are OK, though. Georgia, the nanny at number 3, is nice enough but she's only part-time because the kids are older . . .'

Number 3. That was Stella and Al. My ears pricked up.

'Oh yes, they have those two girls, don't they? Does she get on with them? Georgia?'

If she wondered why I was being so nosy, she didn't say. Ferne struck me as someone who loved a good gossip. 'They're brats, but that's hardly a surprise, given what their mum's like.'

'Is that Stella?' I said, as if I wasn't sure. I was

130

practically gagging with questions. 'Yeah, she seems like a bit of a cow.'

Ferne laughed. 'You've got that right. The housekeeper at number 2 is quite nice too, but they never give her a second off . . .'

Oh no you don't. 'He seems OK, though, Stella's other half. Al, is it?'

I'm not sure if I imagined it, but I felt as if she shot me a look then. I tried to act nonchalant. She stopped walking and bent down to fuss with the baby again. I noticed a sparkly, expensive-looking ring on the middle finger of her right hand. 'Yeah. Better than her anyway.'

'Aren't they planning some huge wedding soon? Is that them?'

I'd swear she blushed. 'I don't know. I don't really know them. Listen, it's been lovely meeting you, Laura, but I'm going to push my pace a bit. Get some exercise in while I can.'

I realized I'd have to let her go, otherwise I'd make myself look suspicious. 'Of course. Pop round any time for a cup of tea, if you're bored. Bring the baby.'

She waved a hand as she broke into a trot with the buggy, calling back over her shoulder. 'I will. Thank you. And I'll tell them about the cleaning. It could do with it. The regular cleaner's rubbish . . .'

'Oh yes,' I shouted after her. 'That'd be great.'

As soon as she turned a corner I doubled back to The Close, pulling out my phone to call Angie. It was hardly conclusive. Not enough to convict. But it was something.

18

April

I have three requests for quotations from my leafleting –
an all-time record – and one of them is from number 1,
The Close. Ferne must have put in a word for me. I
arrange to visit them all before the holidays start. It
doesn't look professional to turn up with a small girl in
tow. At the first, on Monday, I am shown around by the
housekeeper. Housekeepers are a bit like doctors' recep-
tionists. They know how much power they wield, and
they like to use it. I am left in no doubt that the decision
whether to use me or not is theirs and theirs alone. I
smile and make accommodating but non-committal
noises as she shows me the games room and the climate-
controlled cheese cellar. I promise to deliver a detailed
estimate the following day.

Next morning, at the second, I can't believe my luck
when the door is opened by Ferne herself, baby Andrei
clinging on to her like a limpet. No housekeeper here.
Katherine doesn't like the idea of someone being in
the house all day, getting under her feet, Ferne tells
me. Well, apart from Ferne herself, obviously, and she's
only temporary. Katherine and Sergei don't want the
baby to be brought up by nannies. Once Andrei is a

year old, in August, she'll be moving on and they won't replace her.

'That's unusual round here,' I say, in an attempt to bond about the privileged lives of our neighbours.

'Totally,' she says. She's making me a cup of tea while I bounce Andrei on my knee. He's a cute baby. Smiley. 'They're more down to earth than most, Katherine and Sergei. I've been lucky.'

'So . . . do you have another job lined up?' I try to look casual. Just making polite conversation. 'It must be hard leaving them behind when you've bonded.'

She looks at Andrei, who is making gurgly noises as I jiggle him up and down. 'It is. But I knew it was only ever going to be till he was one. And anyway, I'm giving up. Nannying. At least, the live-in kind.'

'Right. Yes, it must be unsettling. Never putting down roots.'

She hands me a mug of tea. 'Exactly. I'm getting too old.'

I laugh. 'What are you? Twenty-five?'

'Twenty-six. And I don't mean like that. I just mean I can't keep moving round from job to job and someone else's attic or basement or annexe for ever.'

'Yes, I suppose so.' She lifts Andrei out of my lap and sits down at the table opposite me. I'm sorry to let him go. 'What will you do, do you know?'

She gives me a big smile. 'Nothing for a while.'

'How lovely. Have you saved up loads, then? Sorry, that sounds really nosy. It's just . . . if you have the secret to being able to survive doing nothing, I'd love to hear it.'

Luckily, she doesn't seem to realize I'm interrogating her. 'God, no. You barely get paid anything on top of accommodation. It's like pocket money. I'm moving in with my boyfriend and I'm just going to take my time deciding what to do next, that's all.'

My ears prick up. I can almost feel them standing to attention, German shepherd-style. 'He must be doing well, if he can support you both.'

'He is,' she says, with a cat-that-got-the-cream smirk. I can tell she's dying to share more with me, but she stops herself.

I need to push it. 'What does he do?'

She looks awkward for the first time. As if she might give too much away. 'Oh . . . he works in the entertainment industry. I'm not exactly sure doing what . . .'

I think of AJT Music. Al's office with the gold discs. 'Lucky you. So where are you moving to?'

'Battersea,' she says, making the word sound as exotic as Barbados. 'Right on the river.'

The flat. It's her. It must be. She's moving into the flat that Al's buying. 'And . . . um . . . he's moving in too?'

If this sounds odd, she doesn't seem to notice, so caught up is she in her fairy tale. 'Of course. It's his flat.'

I nod, as if this is the most normal thing in the world, but inside, my mind is whirring. Where does this leave Stella?

And then it hits me. It's so obvious I can't believe I haven't worked it out before. Stella and Al's wedding is in August. Andrei will be one in August, and Ferne is moving into her new flat then. And – I assume – so is Al.

Stella can make all the million-dollar plans she likes, but there isn't going to be a wedding. After all these years, Al is finally going to leave. He's getting all his ducks in a row – the flat, the new bank account, the million-pound transfer – and then he's gone.

And Stella has no idea.

19

I get out of there as quickly as I can while still asking all the questions I need to ask (although not the ones I really want to) – number of bedrooms, number of receptions, number of bathrooms, level of clean required (inside cupboards? Take books off bookshelves? Empty drawers? Basement? Attic? Swimming pool? Red room? OK, so I made that last one up, although it wouldn't surprise me with some of these people). I'm tempted to ask for the full tour so I can check out her bedroom – although I don't know what I'm expecting to see; a framed photo of Al with a big heart drawn round his face, maybe – but I don't want to give myself away. Instead I give Ferne the hard sell with much talk of neighbourly discounts and preferential treatment. If it was up to her, I'm pretty sure we'd have a deal even before I've done a quote.

I call Angie as soon as I'm back home. I'm shaking as I scroll through to find her number. A part of me feels a kind of thrill that Stella is going to get her comeuppance, but another part – a bigger part – just feels horrified at the scope of Al's deception.

'Karma,' Angie says when I've finished telling her the whole story.

'I know, but . . . Jesus. Surely the punishment is meant to fit the crime where karma is concerned?' I'm up on the kitchen counter again, trying to push the window open.

It's stifling in here now the weather has warmed up into an early heatwave. 'I mean, what's going to happen to the house? He's taken that huge loan out against it, so I'm guessing he'll sell it once he moves out, to pay it back. Wouldn't he just have rented a flat for him and Ferne otherwise? It'd be way cheaper, surely.'

'I assume Stella owns half of it,' Angie's already told me she's in Tesco, and I can hear distant clanking and chattering. 'They've been together years, haven't they?'

'Hopefully. Her name wasn't on the papers for the loan, though, was it? Don't you think that's odd?'

'Well, she probably owns half by default . . .'

'They're not married, remember. Oh god, Ange. I don't know what to do. I wish I didn't have this information now.'

'She laughs. 'You don't. Not really. Not categorically, anyway.'

'I'm right, though, aren't I?' I say, hoping she'll say no, there could be a hundred different explanations.

'By the sound of it, yes.'

Fuck.

I try to concentrate on getting the two new quotes together, but my mind is wandering and I keep making mistakes. Stella might be ghastly. Jealous and vindictive. A Grade-A Mean Girl. But no one deserves this. Whatever this is. I assume Al loves his kids, even if he no longer loves Stella, so surely he wouldn't turf them out of their home? Maybe he's planning on letting them all stay there, living their luxurious lives – after all, the rumoured cost of the wedding would keep most normal people going for about twenty years. I tell myself that's it. He needed to free some cash to set up his bolthole, but he'll keep on making the huge repayments on the house, somehow find the three and a half million he has to repay by the end of the year, keep on funding all their lifestyles. But then I think about the new bank account, the massive sum transferred over from their joint account, the fact that he's still going along with the wedding plans as if nothing is wrong, and I know: Stella's life as she knows it is over. I know I'm being overdramatic. He's not going to make them live on the streets. And, let's face it, they'll probably still have a more pampered life than ninety-nine per cent of the population. But that's not the point.

Eventually, I give up trying to work. I have one quote finished and I drive round and drop it through the letterbox without ringing the bell. Quite often, this is the last I ever hear from a prospective client, so I try to forget about it as soon as it's done. I'm a bundle of nervous energy, so I leave the car near Golders Hill Park and stomp round the periphery, past the seemingly random selection of small animals in their enclosures and the donkeys in their field. Even in my agitated state, the sight of pre-school-aged children cooing at the kookaburras and lemurs makes me smile. I circle the whole place twice. By the time I arrive back at the car, sweating slightly, I know what I have to do.

Back home, I ring round all my office clients and remind them about their yearly deep-clean. Two of them book it in for upcoming weekends, so I email all my staff and let them know the dates. Deep-clean weekends are all hands on deck, or, at least, as many as we can muster.

Then I force myself to spend an hour trying to drum up new business and manage to get an appointment to go and meet the building services manager at a private doctors' offices in Marylebone on Friday. It's a bit outside my preferred area. All my ladies (I remind myself I must stop calling them ladies, now we have Tomas and Paul, but old habits die hard. It's probably breaking some kind of work practices code. I'll be carted off by the woke police) live locally – Queen's Park, Kilburn, Maida Vale – and I know part of what suits a lot of them about the job, apart from the flexibility, is the lack of hours – and cost – added on travelling back and forth. But needs must. I can't believe I'm going to come out of this with my contract with AJT Music unscathed, however I play it, and none of us can afford to be out of work.

That done, I scroll through the photos I took in Al's office. Email them to myself just in case I somehow lose them. I'm taking a huge risk. In fact, now I think about it, it's probably criminal, although I can't quite work out what the crime is. Snooping? Opening a locked drawer? I ask myself why I'm doing this, but I know what the answer is. Stella may be a cow, but no one deserves to have the rug pulled out from under them like this. No one deserves to have their life changed irrevocably by someone who hasn't given them the chance to grow a shell to protect themselves. I still don't fully understand what Al's up to, or why he doesn't just leave to be with Ferne, if that's what he wants, but I do know he's setting up a new life for himself. And for some reason, he's stringing Stella along about the wedding while he does it.

Don't get me wrong, I hardly think Stella's going to be

left destitute. Anyone who hasn't noticed a million pounds disappearing from their bank account is probably going to do OK without it. But I'm not sure anyone can get over the humiliation, the rejection. If I'm still struggling with David's out-of-the-blue announcement – and our split was fair and equitable in every way, despite everything – I can't imagine how I'd feel if he'd added a months-long calculated deception to that. And let's not forget they have kids. Ghastly, precocious, entitled kids but, underneath the make-up, designer labels and sneers, I assume they're actual children still. Stella deserves to know what he's doing. Not so much with Ferne because, let's face it, she definitely knows what he's capable of in that department. After all, she was a Ferne herself once. But the other stuff – the dismantling of her fabulous life – that's a battle she needs to know she's involved in.

And I'm the only person who can let her know.

I feel sick.

20

I watched Al leave for work twenty minutes ago. The Mini Mes have just been driven off to school by Georgia, the nanny, in the family 4x4. I already know that the drill is for her to return the car to the drive once she's dropped them off and then leave on foot for the day, until she needs to collect them in the afternoon. I assume Pilar is at home, doing the housework, or preparing meals, but otherwise Stella will be on her own. I need to act quickly because, most days, I see her leave the house at around eleven, dolled up to the nines, for the gym or shopping or whatever it is she does with her time. I also need to do this before I have time to change my mind. In the middle of the night I had the brainwave that I could do it anonymously. Print off all the photos and put them in a plain envelope addressed to Stella. Private and confidential. Light the touch paper and run as fast as I can. For about five minutes I felt relieved, and then I realized she'd just go straight to Al, and he'd know exactly who might have had access to his secret stash. Not only that, but he'd probably charm his way out of her thinking anything was wrong. And then he'd make sure that neither of us had a way to find out what else he was up to. Because I was sure there was more. If my gut was right – that he was getting out before the wedding – then he had to have everything set in motion by now.

I had no choice. If I was going to do anything with the information I had, I needed to be there to make sure she took it all in.

I hesitate with my finger on the bell. There's no turning back once I ring it. Of course, she might see it's me and tell Pilar not to let me in under any circumstances. In fact, standing here now, I feel as if that's the most likely outcome. I start to hope for it. I could tell myself I tried. Go back home and have a cup of tea, congratulating myself on my sound moral compass which led me to even attempt to talk to her.

I take in such a deep breath that I start to cough. Put a hand over my mouth to stifle the sound. Now my eyes are watering. I rub at them to dry them. Hook my hair behind my ears. Swallow noisily. Then I raise my hand again and ring the doorbell before I can change my mind. It echoes around their cavernous hall like a church organ.

Thankfully, it's Pilar and not Stella herself who opens the door, so at least it isn't slammed in my face again. She starts like a rabbit caught in the headlights when she sees it's me. No doubt she is recalling the dressing-down I assume she got when she let me in the last time. She places her round body in the gap between the door and the frame, as if she thinks I'm going to just barge right in.

'*Stella me está esperando*,' I say confidently, hoping that Google Translate gave me the correct meaning – 'Stella is expecting me' and not 'Stella is pregnant.' Pilar's face breaks into a big smile and she starts to babble away at me in Spanish, none of which I understand. I smile and nod and say '*Sí*' occasionally, because that sounds right, although for all I know I've just agreed to marry her son and have her grandkids. Somehow, she drifts backwards into the hall, and I follow, already feeling guilty for deceiving her.

'Pilar!' I hear, and it's as if an icy wind whips down the stairs.

Pilar seems oblivious and gives me a big smile. She says something that sounds like 'You friend here,' which might be slightly overstating the situation. I hear Stella inhale impatiently, and then a pair of black pointy high heels appears as she clomps down towards us. I brace myself. She stops dead when she sees me.

'You,' she says, managing to imbue the word with a considerable amount of loathing. She flicks a look at Pilar, who, from the expression on her face, seems to have realized that all is not as it seems. Before Stella has a chance to berate her, I jump in and start talking.

'It's not Pilar's fault. I lied to her and said you were expecting me. I just need a few minutes of your time, Stella. I have something I need to say to you and if, after five minutes, you want me to leave, I promise I will, and I won't ever show up unannounced again.'

'There's nothing you have to say that I want to hear,' she says, and I know she's not going to give me a chance. 'And I imagine Gail and Ben might want to reconsider your lease if they knew you were harassing me.'

Shit. I hadn't even thought of that. I ask myself what I'm doing here again. I need to turn this around quickly.

'I assume you know why Al's bought a flat in Battersea?' It's my best shot. If she knows about it, then all my theories must be wrong. I'm banking on her having no idea. I see it in her face. A flicker of confusion.

'Of course,' she says carefully. 'It's an investment. And it's none of your business.'

I don't believe her. 'How is it an investment if the money needs to be paid back in a few months? It's hardly a fixer-upper. I've seen photos.'

'Pilar, go and do something useful,' she barks at the housekeeper, flapping her hand at her dismissively. I hadn't even realized she was still standing there. We both watch her go, as if to make sure she really leaves. Not that she could be following most of what we're saying.

Stella turns back to me, a murderous look on her face. 'What exactly are you insinuating?'

I need to try and calm her down, get her to listen to what I'm actually saying. 'Stella, I'm not telling you this because I want to hurt you. I'm getting no joy from it, believe me . . .'

'Just spit it out. You have one minute before I kick you out.'

'I found a few things out. Accidentally. And I think you deserve to know about them. If you don't already. Which you might . . .'

'That we've bought a property . . . ?'

'That Al has. It's in his name only. He got the cash by taking a loan against this house. And he's set up a new bank account and transferred a load of money into it from your joint one . . .' Surely that's enough to get her full attention?

'What the hell are you doing, getting involved in our private business?' she says, but I can tell I've wobbled her.

She's dying to know more, and I need to make sure she decides to find it out from me rather than by running straight to him.

I put my hand out to touch her tanned arm and she flinches and snatches it away. 'Listen to what I'm telling you. I'll explain how I know later. But you need to take in what I'm saying. For your sake, and the girls' . . .'

This was clearly the wrong thing to say because her nostrils flare. I've reawoken the dragon. 'Get out. How dare you come in here trying to hurt my family because you have a pathetic little unrequited crush on my husband . . .'

She stomps over to the front door and opens it dramatically. Fuck. I should never have come. Let her wake up one morning and find her perfect life had crumbled around her. Now all I've done is created a whole world more trouble for myself. I'll almost certainly lose AJT Music as a client, possibly my little flat too, once she tells Gail her own warped version of what just happened. And it's all my own stupid fault. I think about refusing to leave until she's heard me out, but she's pulled her mobile from her pocket and she's probably about to phone the police.

'Out. Now.'

I edge towards the door. I know I've lost.

'If you want to know more, I have proof. It might be the only way you have to find out the absolute truth, not whatever version Al tells you when you put him on the spot.'

Stella lets out a sharp, over-theatrical laugh. 'I'm glad you think you know us both so well. Whatever would we do without you?'

'I have documents,' I say slightly desperately. 'Well, photos of documents. Proof, anyway.'

'I should report you to the police,' she says. 'You've obviously been snooping where you shouldn't be . . .'

'I didn't give him that book, Stella.' I might as well use all the ammunition I have if she's going to sell me out anyway. 'I didn't give it to him, which means someone else did. And I think I know who that someone else is.' I hadn't been intending to tell her Ferne's identity. I was hoping the news about the flat and the bank transfer would be enough. But it's all I've got now. I can see I've got her attention because she's silent for a moment. I know she's desperate to ask me who it is. Of course she is. I would be too.

'Leave. Now. I have a panic button here that would summon the police in three minutes . . .' She gently rests her fingers on a little white box beside the door. I'm pretty sure she's not bluffing. Although I'm not convinced about the three minutes – that seems a bit optimistic.

'It's OK, I'm going. If you'd rather not know what you're up against, that's up to you . . .'

I leave her with that and walk down the drive, my legs shaking. The door slams behind me.

I think I've just made everything worse.

21

Between leaving Stella's and going to pick Betsy up I sit in front of my computer, trying to concentrate on the quote for Ferne – already a day later than promised – but of course it's pointless. My mind is racing. I can't believe how stupid I was to think Stella would listen to me. That she wouldn't just kick me out and go straight to Al to demand to know what I was trying to tell her. I sit there like a criminal after a bungled raid, waiting for my punishment to catch me up. When I accidentally delete a column of figures I've spent an hour trying to work out I realize it's time to stop. They'll have to wait.

I don't want to bring Betsy anywhere near The Close so, after I pick her up from school, I take her to Regent's Park and we do her homework sitting on the grass in the sun, surrounded by people walking their dogs, then we walk back up to St John's Wood High Street and eat delicious bowls of food at The Good Life. I have no appetite, but I can't really afford to pay for food I then don't eat, so I just keep telling myself one more forkful, like I used to say to Betsy when she refused to eat her greens. Betsy, thrilled with this break in routine, shovels in the meal she doesn't even realize is super-healthy and prattles on about the upcoming Easter break. David has managed to take Monday, Tuesday and Wednesday off next week, and on Saturday they're going to stay with his brother and family down in Dorset for a few days. Betsy loves her older cousins with a passion and will be spoilt rotten – and I know it's absolutely the best place she could be at the moment, away from the toxic atmosphere surrounding my home – but my heart breaks at the thought of the time we could have spent together.

'Can you come too, Mum?' she says, spearing a chunk of sweet potato. I actually consider it for a moment. David's brother, Nick, and his wife, Jules, have always been more friends than in-laws. We used to spend whatever time everyone's busy lives allowed as a four, or as a seven with all the kids in tow. When David left they sent me a card saying he was a fuckwit and would come to his senses soon. Jules called me and said it was obviously some kind of sad midlife crisis and it would be over before I knew it, if I could bear to wait it out.

'Please don't meet anyone else yet,' she'd said. 'Not before he's got whatever he needs to get out of his system.'

Fat chance.

But, of course, family eventually won out. Not consciously, don't get me wrong. There's no way David would have made them feel awkward for still wanting to be friends with me. But, once it became clear that he was gone for good, that he was truly happy without me, our communications petered out. What was there to talk about now? And, like a lot of people, I think they started to find it uncomfortable mentioning David in front of me. In case I had a meltdown, I suppose. Or because what he got up to was now none of my business. Anyway, whenever we did speak, the elephant in the room kept doubling in size until it threatened to trample us all. We still talk occasionally. I'll call Jules before Saturday and just make sure she's up to date with Betsy World. And they send Christmas and birthday cards. Presents for Bets. But the thing about intimacy is that, once it's compromised, it's over, like a tyre with a slow puncture. You can patch it back together but there'll always be a point that will give under pressure. I understand. I just miss them.

I give Betsy a big smile. 'It's my busiest time at work.'

Luckily, she accepts that as the one and only reason. I tell myself I need to get a grip. Keep my head down and do nothing but work for the next few days so that I can give her my full attention when she comes back on Wednesday to spend the rest of the holiday with me. I need to plan days out, time spent away from The Close. Kentish Town City Farm, maybe? And the Tower? Betsy loves a bit of gore. Hopefully, the worst will have happened before then – I can't imagine Stella is going to hold back from asking Al what the fuck I was alluding to, or that he will take his time coming to hammer my door down to tell me to take my cleaning company elsewhere. I wonder if I should warn Gail. Get my side in first. She's definitely not vindictive, but she might feel she has to give me the requisite month's notice in the interests of neighbourly harmony. I wouldn't blame her.

'Mummy!' Betsy says loudly, and I start. By the tone of her voice, she's been trying to get my attention for a while. The couple at the next table look over at me. Bad mum.

'What, sweetie?'

She clunks her fork down into her empty bowl. Gives me a gummy smile. 'I've finished.'

*

Before I drop her back I take her to AJT Music to kill some time, where Tomas tries to teach her how to juggle with apples while I hole up with Angie on the top floor and tell her the latest.

'What were you thinking?' she says when I've finished.

'I have no idea,' I say. 'It just seems so wrong that he's going to surprise her with all of this. That she has no clue her life is about to fall apart.'

'Is this about you and David?' Angie says, and I scoff.

'Of course not. That was totally different.'

She raises her eyebrows at me. I ignore her. 'I have a couple of prospective new clients,' I say. 'Don't worry.'

'Stop changing the subject.'

Thankfully, Tomas and Betsy reappear then, my daughter eager to show off her prowess (if the employees of AJT Music wonder why their shiny, healthy Granny Smiths bruised so violently overnight, hopefully they'll keep it to themselves) and it's time to leave.

Having dropped Bets off, I head home, where I park my car out on the main road, cursing its stupid kitsch uniqueness, and practically tiptoe along The Close to home. If they don't see me, maybe they'll assume I've gone away for the night. Of course, for that to work I'll have to leave the lights off in my curtainless kitchen-cum-living room once it gets dark. It's worth it. I can make camp in my bedroom and only come out for snacks.

Once on the bottom stair, I allow myself to breathe out. I sneak a look over at number 3, half expecting to see Al glaring back at me, but the windows are blank. No clue as to whether they're in or out. The automated lighting system is set for the evening as usual, regardless. I fumble my key into the lock and bang through the door, slamming it behind me.

The first thing I see is a folded piece of paper on the floor. A note.

I pick it up, hands trembling. My name is written on the front in black biro. Capital letters. I edge over to the front window and cautiously look out. There's still no movement in Stella and Al's house. Heart pounding, I open up the piece of paper. No name, but I have no doubt who it's from.

I'll come over to talk more tomorrow 11 a.m. Please don't reply to this. If you're out, I'll try again at 2.

She's going to give me a chance.

22

Somehow, knowing that I have to face Stella again in the morning focuses my brain, and I stay up half the night finalizing the quote for Ferne, then, at six in the morning, after about three hours' fitful sleep, I sneak out and deliver it. I can hear baby Andrei crying when I walk up the drive to number 1, so I assume Ferne is up somewhere in the house. A tiny stab of guilt hits me in the ribs at the thought of what I'm about to do to her, but I squash it back down. She's hardly an innocent party here either.

I tidy the flat when I get back, throwing open the windows to let some air in. At some point in the middle of the night I was struck by panic that maybe the note was from Al. That he's made an appointment to come over and have it out with me, or worse. So I keep throwing glances over to their house in the hope of catching a glimpse of him leaving for work and, finally, at about twenty to nine, there he is, at the wheel of his sports Bentley. I'm so relieved I set the alarm for quarter past ten and go back to bed, fully clothed.

Up again, I shower and change into a flattering – but not too flattering – floral midi dress. My calves glow blue white but my feet – which have had a few days out in sandals – are pale brown, except for a T-shaped ghost shoe. It's a look. Stella is always an even hue of honey bronze. I can't imagine there's a tan line on her. I bet she doesn't even wear the paper thong they give you to protect your modesty while they hose you down in the salon. I had it done once – we were going on a seaside holiday, Devon, I think – and I felt like a hippo having a mud bath. Stella, I imagine, is the kind of woman who has no self-consciousness about hopping up on to a massage table, naked, on all fours, while some poor girl on minimum wage rips out the hairs from round her backside. So long as she looks immaculate when she leaves.

It's a beautiful, warm day, although the papers are predicting a return to freezing storms for Easter. I keep meaning to google 'things to do with kids on rainy days in London' because most of the plans I have for Betsy so far rely on sunshine. Or, at least, on the weather being dry. I leave the windows open, get out two of my prettiest mugs (I only have four here, so it's hardly a taxing decision) then start to panic about whether or not I should offer her a coffee, or if that makes it seem as if I think this is a social call. That she's a friend coming over to chat. I push them over to the side, by the kettle, out of the way. Line them up neatly. I'll play it by ear.

I hear footsteps on the stairs. My heart starts to pound. I thought I would see her coming across the road and that would give me a minute to compose myself, but my fannying about with the mugs means I took my eyes off the prize. I lift my hair off the back of my neck and flap it up and down. I'm sweating. Even though I know she's out there, I jump when she raps on the door.

Stella is dressed for the gym, long, skinny legs clad in Lycra, toned, tanned shoulders visible in a skin-tight coral vest, hair pulled up in a severe ponytail, which makes her eyes appear even more unnaturally slanted. She's not smiling.

'Hi,' I say nervously. 'Come on in.'

She refuses my offer of refreshments. 'Just show me what you wanted to show me, Laura.' The way she says my name lets me know she means business. This is not a social call. As if I ever might have thought it was.

'Of course. Right. Sit down,' I babble. She perches on the sofa. I grab my phone and squeeze in next to her. I've rehearsed over and over exactly what I need to say, what order to present the information in, but that's all gone out of my head now. All I can remember is that I should start at the beginning, so I scroll through my photos and bring up the letter from the bank about the loan.

'So, this . . . well, it's kind of self-explanatory, but it's a letter accompanying a contract for Al to take out a loan against your house. Three and a half million.'

There's the smallest intake of breath from Stella. An inadvertent gasp. I look at her, but her face is still impassive. Maybe, underneath all the Botox, it's struggling to express confusion. It's hard to tell. She takes the phone from my hand, zooms in on the letter, scrolling left and right to read the details.

'Where did you get this?'

This part I do remember. I need to engage her in the facts and not get sidetracked by the reason that I know them. 'I'll explain everything later, I promise. Can I just show you what else there is first?'

'No. Answer my question.'

I exhale noisily. 'From his office . . .'

'Ah. Do you make a habit of rifling through your

clients' personal belongings? I'm sure they'd love to hear about that.'

I don't want to show her how rattled I am. I reach my hand out as if to take back the phone. 'Of course not. I . . . if you don't approve and you'd rather not know, I completely understand . . .'

Neither of us says anything for a second. A stand-off. Then she gives the tiniest of nods.

'Show me.'

I take the mobile back, move on to the next picture. 'This is the contract for that loan. It goes on for pages. Basically, it says Al now owes around ten million on the house – does that sound right?' She doesn't react. Stares at the picture. '. . . But this extra bit is only short term. And he's signed it on the last page . . .'

I show her the signature page. Expand his signature for her to see. 'Um . . . is it . . . the house . . . is it in his name only?'

She makes eye contact then and I don't know how to react. It feels so intimate, given we both know how we feel about each other. We stay locked in a look for a few seconds while, I think, she decides how honest she wants to be with me. How much she wants to tell me. In the end, her need for the truth wins out. That's why she's here.

'Yes.' It's all she says, but it's a start. I want to ask her why. How can that be so, after all those years together? After two children? But I can wait.

'Right.' I move on to the next photo. It's the particulars for the Battersea flat. 'I'll show you these in a minute, but . . . here . . . this is the correspondence for the new flat. It's all going through . . . look . . .'

I take her through the half-dozen pages, expanding relevant bits – dates, signatures, any mention of his name. I've got her now; she can't take her eyes off the phone.

'Let me see the details,' she says, and I flick back to the estate agent's printout and hand her the mobile. She zooms in on every picture: the wide open-plan living room/kitchen with glittering views over the river through the floor-to-ceiling windows, the long, glass-walled terrace, the Morocco-inspired bedroom. It's nowhere near as spacious as their house, obviously. Not even half the size. Probably not even a quarter. But it screams of a different lifestyle. Sexier. Freer. Hipper. I don't rush her. I know the images so well, but I need to appreciate what it's like to see them for the first time. And to know that this is the place my husband has set up for himself and his mistress. His new life.

Eventually, she hands the phone back to me. There's the tiniest trace of a tear in the corner of her eye. Turns out she might be human after all. 'What else?'

'This,' I say, showing her the letter about the new bank account. The transfer from their joint savings. 'Did you know about this?' She says, 'No,' so quietly I can hardly hear her.

'And then this . . .' I scroll on to the card. The note inside . . . *I can't wait for our tomorrow. I love u 2 the moon and back!!!*

I point to the screen 'F. Her name begins with an F, see.'

She flicks forward. I say a quick thank-you that I didn't take a picture of the Polaroid. She lands on a photo of Betsy showing me one of her ballet moves, biting her bottom lip with concentration, one leg raised shakily out in front of her. She swipes back angrily. Her eyes flash at me. 'How do I know you haven't just set all this up? To make me think it wasn't you who gave him that book . . .'

I force myself to make eye contact again. 'Why? Why would I? Yes, it's been horrible having everyone turn against me, but . . . really? You think I would write whole contracts and fake letters from the bank? Just so you'd stop hating me? I didn't even know Al was short for Alec, let alone who you bank with. Look at the dates. I wasn't even living here when this started . . .'

She looks through the photos again, too quickly, taking nothing in.

'Who is she?'

I knew this would be her main focus. Find out who the enemy is. Channel all her hatred and anger towards them rather than her husband. I've already decided I can't risk telling her yet. She would go straight round there, making Ferne's life in The Close impossible. Threaten her with god knows what. And what if I'm wrong?

'I don't know. Does it even matter?'

'Of course it matters. You said you knew. Fucking bitch. I can make sure she never gets near him again . . .'

'Stella,' I say as gently as I can, 'Al's setting up a new life. He's leaving you.'

She whips her head round at that, as if it hadn't even occurred to her. 'Because some silly tart threw herself at him . . .'

'Yes, she's probably not very nice. But he's the one you're supposed to be getting married to. He's the one you have two kids with. He's the one who owes you

157

loyalty. And, by the looks of it, he's stripping your life out from underneath you . . .'

'She must have put him up to it . . .'

So this is how they're still together. Every time he strays, she pins all the blame on the other woman. It's classic. 'You need to protect yourself. And the girls. That's the only reason I'm telling you all this . . .'

'Don't tell me what I need to do.' she snaps.

'Do you want a glass of wine?' I need to calm her down.

She looks at me like I've offered her crack. I suppose it is only eleven o'clock in the morning. 'I just thought . . . well, you've had a shock . . .'

'Do you know how many calories there are in wine? I'll have a vodka. And slimline tonic. Ice and lemon.'

'There is no vodka. Or tonic, or ice, or lemon for that matter. I only have a cheap bottle of wine, but you're welcome to a glass. I'll join you.'

She shrugs, as if to say what choice does she have, so I get up and hunt out two glasses, get the bottle out of the fridge and pour us both a large one. Now I think about it, I'm not so sure this is a good idea. Maybe she's even meaner when she's drunk.

'How come you don't co-own the house?' I say as I hand her hers. I expect her to bite my head off, but instead she takes a long swig.

'Because he already owned it. He bought his ex-wife out of her share when they split. I've never even thought about it, to be honest, and then when we had children – well, that changes everything, doesn't it?'

'Not legally, I don't think. I don't know.'

She flushes pale, even with the tan. 'When we're married . . .'

'Stella,' I say softly, 'I don't think there's going to be a wedding –'

She cuts me off. 'But everything's booked. The deposits have all been paid. Why would he do that?'

I've been thinking about this. It *is* strange. Why would he be happy to throw all that money away? 'Who's been paying the deposits? You or him?'

'What do you mean? I've chosen everything. He said he wanted me to have the most fabulous day ever, to pick anything I wanted.'

'I know. But I mean, practically. Who has actually written a cheque or done a transfer or handed over cash for a deposit?'

She looks at me as if the answer is obvious, and I suppose in her world it is. 'He did.'

'And . . . um . . . have you got receipts? Have you looked at your bank statements and seen that the money has actually gone out?' I'm assuming the answer is no because, if she had, she might have noticed the tiny matter of one million going missing.

She attempts a frown. There's the tiniest puckering movement around the outside edges of her brow, like an overcooked lasagne. 'Al looks after all that stuff.'

Part of me wants to shake her. To say, *Are you so stupid that you don't even get involved with what's going on with your own finances?* Of course I don't.

'Right. Well, maybe that's where to start. Have a look through your joint statements.'

'I don't think we get statements. I've never seen one.'

Never? And she's never queried why? Jesus. The phrase 'taking candy from a baby' springs to mind. 'Maybe it's all online. Do you know?'

She looks at me, clueless. 'What about Ottolenghi? And Lewis Capaldi? Are you telling me Al's just going to cancel them at the last minute?'

'I'm guessing Al booked them, am I right? Have you met either of them? Have you spoken to them about it?'

She shakes her head. 'Al knows them through work. He's arranged everything.'

I risk putting a hand on hers briefly. She shakes it off like it's a muddy dog paw. 'I doubt he has. I doubt either of them know anything about it.'

She knocks back the last of her wine. I've barely taken a sip. Then she holds her glass out like a child. I lean over and pick up the bottle, fill her up again, with a bit less this time. I wanted to mellow her out a bit, but her getting slaughtered wouldn't benefit either of us.

'You don't know what you're talking about. Where did you get all this so-called information anyway?'

I've lost her again. I ignore the question. 'You need to find out what's going on. And I don't mean who she is. You need to find out if he's up to anything else. You owe it to your girls.'

'I'll kill him.'

'Information is power.' I don't know who said that first, but it sounds good at this point and I'll take any weapon I can get. 'Arm yourself with the facts before you say anything to him. Otherwise, he'll just make sure you never find out what he's doing. How much is the house worth?'

She looks at me blankly, but then again, she always looks fairly blank, so it's hard to tell if it means anything. 'I don't know. Ten million? Eleven?'

'You need to find out. My guess is that, once he's gone, he'll sell the house to pay off the flat. You need to know if there'll be anything left that you and the girls can use to buy somewhere. He has a responsibility for them, obviously, but if there's no money left . . .'

That's got her attention back on track. 'What do you mean, if there's no money left?'

'Theoretically. I have no idea, clearly. This might all be a drop in the ocean for him and he's planning to pay the mortgage on the house for ever so that you and the girls can live there. But if that's the case, it seems odd that he'd need to take out a short-term loan. Do you know how much is in your joint account?'

She shrugs. 'No idea.'

'Well, you're the only one who can find out.'

'How?'

'I don't know. Hunt through stuff at home or on the computer. Ask him questions . . .'

She nods. as if I've just said the most insightful thing ever. 'OK.'

'Don't let him realize you're suspicious. Not yet. He'll clam up. I mean, do if you want, but my advice would be not to. Not till you know exactly where you stand.'

'OK.'

I wait for her to get up and leave. I've shown her everything I have. I've done my good deed for the day. Now I just want her to go so I can get on with some work, or do some chores, or just veg out on the sofa. On my own. But she sits there, looking at me, as if she's waiting for me to tell her what to do.

'I think you need to go and process it all. It's a lot to take on.'

'You really don't know who she is?'

'No,' I say. 'You'll find out eventually. Just get yourself and the girls sorted first. That has to be the priority.'

'OK,' she says again. All the fight seems to have been knocked out of her. I'm sure not for long. I stand up, hoping she'll take the hint and, thankfully, she does.

'Send me those photos,' she says, handing me her empty glass.

'I can't. I mean, I don't think I should, just in case he sees them . . .' I doubt Al is taking sneaky looks through the contents of her phone, but I don't want to leave any kind of trail that could be traced back to me. 'I won't delete them, though. You can have another look any time.'

She gives the briefest of nods then sweeps through the door, slightly unsteady on her feet.

'A thank-you would be nice,' I say to her back, but I make sure I say it so quietly she doesn't hear.

23

Angie and I are having lunch. When I invited her, she told me it would be nice to mark her last day of freedom before the Easter holidays begin. Even though Bobby and Louis are now sixteen and fourteen, I get the impression they still run her ragged when they get the chance.

'Aren't they just out with their mates?' I asked her, and she laughed.

'No. All their mates are round mine. They know I'm a soft touch. I spend all day feeding and watering them, ferrying them around everywhere. Some of them even get me to do their washing.' I know from the way she says it that she loves it. Loves being needed. Loves knowing her kids are off the streets. She's all bluff.

'Lucky them,' I said. 'Do you want to do mine?'

We meet in the café by the boating lake in Regent's Park, not too far from where she lives, near Lisson Grove. It's where we always go – I say 'always'; this is maybe the fifth time we've ever had a purely social out-of-hours meet-up, just the two of us. I've been for a handful of raucous birthday nights out with a bunch of my employees over the years, a couple of weddings, and I take them all out for a meal every Christmas, but I've always shied away from mixing business with pleasure too much. I once knew I needed to sack someone – Jackie, her name was – because she kept letting me down, and all the others told me she was lazy and didn't pull her weight, and then I caught her out in an actual lie about being sick when she wasn't – but I found it almost impossible because we'd become really friendly outside of work. She had a daughter the same age as Bets and we'd shared countless playdates and confidences. I knew she was taking the piss. Relying on the fact that our friendship would protect her. It was messy and awkward but, in the end, I did it. I would have lost the respect of all the others if I hadn't. Of course, we haven't spoken since. Betsy still asks when she can play with Maya sometimes.

Anyway, I want to say thank you to Angie for being my partner in crime the past few weeks, but also she's the only person I can tell about my conversation with Stella, and I really need to get another perspective. Have someone tell me I'm not crazy to have told her (almost) everything.

'I'll be honest, I think you're crazy,' she says as soon as I mention going over there.

'Don't. I haven't told you the half of it yet.'

She listens in silence as I fill her in on the rest. 'You really think she's not going to go straight to Al?'

I put my head in my hands, elbows on the table. I've hardly eaten any of my cheese-and-onion panini. 'I don't know any more. Anyway, it's done now, so there's nothing I can do about it. Let's talk about something else.'

Angie fixes her dark eyes on me. 'Oh no you don't.'

She makes me take her through the whole thing again. 'She'll still be able to claim half the house, though, won't she? They have kids.'

'Half a huge mortgage, by the sound of it. I mean, I'm

sure he'll provide for them, but he's got to pay that three and a half million back somehow.'

'I imagine they'll still have a way flasher lifestyle than you and me,' she says, wafting a salt-and-vinegar crisp at me. She doesn't say it with malice. Angie is never mean. That's one of the reasons I like her so much.

'I know,' I say. 'Oh well, I've done my duty. It's up to her what she does with the information. Now can we talk about something else?'

Saturday and Sunday, it's the first of our office spring cleans. The finance company on St John's Wood High Street. I pitch in, happy to have the distraction. They're long days – we start at half seven and end about the same time in the evening – and only Tomas, Paul and I do the whole stint, the others doing a day or half a day in a carefully coordinated rota. We start off on Saturday morning, chatting and laughing as we methodically clear then refill small sections. I've taken countless 'pre' photos just in case we forget where something came from. By midmorning we're all silently getting on with our own patch. Some of these areas – the inside of cupboards, the floor underneath the photocopier – probably haven't been cleaned since this time last year. It's therapeutic. Almost a weird form of meditation. Repetitive movements. Wax on, wax off.

I'd forgotten how exhausting cleaning can be. By midafternoon, parts of my body I didn't even know I had are aching. By home time – a whole fifteen minutes earlier than I had anticipated, because we made such good progress – I can hardly move my back and my right arm is throbbing. It's a righteous feeling, though. A feeling of having actually achieved something. For the last hour, I fantasize about a deep, hot bath and a glass of wine, until I remember I've only got a shower and Stella polished off most of the only bottle I had. I don't have the energy to stop to buy some. I have a Pizza Express bake-at-home pizza waiting to go in the oven, so I fixate on that. I'll scoff it and then get into bed as early as I can – I have to do this all again tomorrow. Maybe I'll get in bed first. Eat under the duvet then go straight to sleep without even stopping to brush my teeth. By the time I pull into The Close, I'm practically drooling at the thought of both eating and sleeping. Maybe at the same time.

I turn the oven on to heat up as soon as I walk through the door, pour what's left of the wine into a glass and knock it back in one, then head for the shower, pulling off my grubby T-shirt as I go. I turn the water temperature up to high and wait for it to start steaming, dropping the rest of my clothes on the floor. I can pick them up tomorrow. Or never. I don't care at the moment. I'm just poking a tentative toe in to test the temperature when there's a rap on the door. I freeze. Maybe I misheard. Moments later, there's another. I decide to ignore it. I'm not expecting anyone, and everyone I care about has my mobile number if there's an emergency. I look down at it, next to my pile of discarded clothing. No messages. No missed calls. I'm about to step under the blissfully scalding water when there's another, louder knock. I peer round the bathroom door, trying to listen for clues, but the shower all but drowns everything out.

'Laura! I know you're in there. I saw your car outside.'

Shit. It's Stella. I could ignore her. Get into the shower and sing loudly so she might think I hadn't heard her. But then what? She lives opposite me; I can hardly avoid her forever. Fuck.

'Hang on!' I shout. I turn off the water and wrap myself in a towel, stomp over to the door and fling it open.

'Oh,' she says, looking me up and down.

'Hi,' I say, trying to manage my irritation. 'I was just getting ready for bed.'

Stella comes on in anyway. 'I've been watching for you to come home.'

'Right. Where's Al?' I peer down the stairs behind her, just in case he's going to rush me with an axe.

'At a gig. Work, apparently. I need to talk to you.'

My visions of sleep/eating crumble. 'I'm just going to . . .' I indicate the bathroom. 'I'll be five minutes. Do me a favour and stick that pizza in the oven, will you? It should be hot enough by now.'

She looks at me as if I've asked her to clean out my toilet, but then she gives the smallest of nods.

'Five minutes,' I say again.

There's a strange smell when I emerge from the bathroom, pink-skinned from the blistering water and dressed in my favourite pjs. Betsy chose them for me at Next and they have leaping cats on the soft, grey, baggy bottoms and one big glittery cat face on the short-sleeved top. I don't imagine they designed them with forty-something women in mind, but I love them. Stella is standing in the middle of the room with a pained look on her face.

'Is something burning?' I walk over to the oven and

throw it open. No way has my American Hot overcooked in the time it took me to have the world's fastest wash. Pungent black smoke rushes out. I shut it again quickly, turn it off before gingerly opening it again. Grab an oven glove and pull out the tragic remains of my beautiful pizza, plastic melted on to its delicious cheesy top and the cardboard underneath smouldering. I fling it into the sink, throw open the window. 'You didn't take it out of the packaging?'

She narrows her eyes at me. 'I'm not used to people asking me to cook their dinner.'

'You have two kids . . .' I say before I can help myself. I want to cry.

'I'm sorry. You can order one, can't you?'

'I can't afford to order one,' I say, holding back tears. I'm so tired, so hungry. 'And even if I could, they take ages. I've just worked a twelve-hour day, Stella. I want to eat something now and go to bed.' I know I sound like a child, but I can't help it.

She takes her mobile out of the pocket of her beautifully tailored jacket. For a moment I think she's going to call Dominos and order something for me but then she says, 'Pilar, put whatever's left from dinner on a plate and bring it over to number 6, please. Put . . . what . . . left . . . from . . . put . . . what . . . oh, for god's sake, put Taylor on. Taylor! God, that woman really needs to learn English,' she says to me while she waits. I bite my tongue to stop myself from saying she could try learning a few basic courtesies in Spanish. I busy myself with opening the door and flapping it back and forth to let some clean air in.

'Sweetheart. Can you explain to Pilar that I want her to

put the leftovers from dinner on a plate and bring them over to number 6? Not the main house, the servants' bit above the garage.' I swear she doesn't even flinch as she says that. 'Just because. And don't mention it to Dad when he gets back. I'll take you to Spielburgers . . .'

'Really, she doesn't have to bother,' I say, although I have no other food in the house that doesn't need assembling from scratch and I don't really feel like baking just now. Stella dismisses me with a hand. Negotiation over, she ends the call.

'We had a very nice filet de bœuf,' she says, pronouncing it *filay*.

'Right. Well, thanks.' I look longingly at the melted-plastic-crusted remains in the sink. 'Stella, why are you here? Only I really do want an early night. I'm working again first thing.'

She looks around. 'Could I please get a glass of something?'

'Water?' I say. 'Or I could make tea?'

'No alcohol?'

I shake my head. 'Sorry.'

She digs out her mobile again. Presses another number. 'Tayls. Give Pilar a bottle of white from the fridge to bring over too. That nice Gavi di Gavi. You're a sweetheart.' She ends the call. 'I know you like wine,' she says to me, as if she herself is about to make a great sacrifice by drinking something that contains calories just to please me.

I want to tell her to get to the point, but it's just occurred to me that she's being nice to me and I don't want to break that particular spell. I get another glass out of the cupboard in anticipation then flop down on the sofa, exhaustion making my eyelids heavy. 'So . . . um . . . what can I do for you?'

'I'd like to see those pictures again, please.' I've noticed that whenever Stella speaks, it's weirdly formal, as if she's an alien who's recently learned to mimic humans.

'Of course,' I say, looking round for my phone. It's still on the bathroom floor, so I drag myself in there to get it. Line them up. 'Here.'

We sit there in silence while she studies them. After a couple of minutes I hear footsteps on the stairs outside and Pilar appears at the door with a foil-covered plate and the bottle of wine. Stella ignores her, keeps her eyes fixed on the phone. Pilar looks back and forth between us nervously. Last time she saw me, Stella was throwing me out of their house like a bag of trash, and she probably got a telling-off. I get up and take the plate from her.

'*Gracias. Cómo estás?*' I say, dredging up some schoolgirl Spanish from my teenage holidays. She gives me a nervous smile and I realize she's probably ten years younger than I first thought, she's just worn out. She rattles off something I don't understand and I smile and nod and say *gracias* a few more times.

'Does Pilar cook for you every night?' I say after she's gone. I'm trying to locate a corkscrew. I'm strictly screw-top in this house.

'Mmm-hmm,' Stella says, engrossed. I find one, pour us each a glass, then peel the warm foil from the plate. There's the promised beef, in a rich, red, divine-smelling sauce, asparagus, some kind of creamy-cheesy potatoes. I find it hard to imagine either Stella or the Mini Mes actually eating any of this, except, maybe, the asparagus. I wonder if Pilar spends hours cooking Michelin-star-worthy meals every night only to throw most of it in the bin. I dig in, standing at the countertop. 'This is amazing,' I say, mouth full. It is. I may have to spend my evenings fighting with the foxes for scraps outside number 3 from now on.

Eventually, Stella drops my mobile on the seat beside her. 'I don't understand any of this.'

'I don't really either. But the fact that he's doing it all behind your back seems dodgy, don't you think?'

She nods. Holds her glass out for more wine. Now I have food and alcohol inside me, I'm in danger of falling asleep where I stand. I daren't sit down. 'Did you find anything at home? Did you look?'

She takes a sip. 'I've been through his study. Nothing. I told him I'd found a string quartet for the wedding and that I needed to pay them a five-thousand-pound deposit, and he just told me to give him all the details and he'd do it.'

I stop myself asking what kind of string quartet you get if the deposit is five grand. Gold-plated instruments? Caviar-encrusted bows? 'Can you check up with them to see if it's been paid?'

'That's a good idea,' she says, as if I've said something inspired as opposed to just common sense. 'But what if it hasn't, what do I do?'

'Nothing,' I say, stifling a yawn. 'But you'll know.'

'Yes,' she says. 'I'll do that tomorrow. You're working on a Sunday?'

'No rest for the wicked,' I say, then I try to suppress another yawn, but it escapes with a vengeance.

'I should leave you to get some sleep.' She stands up and I almost burst into tears with gratitude. I smooth the foil back over my now-empty plate, resisting the temptation to lick it clean, and hold it out to her. I don't feel bad about not having washed it up because there's no way in hell she'll end up doing it.

'Oh . . .' she says. 'No. I'll ask Pilar to come and collect it tomorrow.'

Really, though, you couldn't make it up. 'I'm at work tomorrow. Don't worry about it. I'll drop it over when I can.' I peel the foil off and put it in the bin, dropping the plate in the sink. 'Thanks for the food and wine.'

'You're welcome,' she says stiffly. 'Good night.'

''Night. Oh, and Stella . . .' I say as she goes. She turns round. 'You have to take all the packaging off first . . . the pizza. You take off the plastic and the cardboard and then put it in.'

'I see,' she says, looking at me in confusion, as if I've just explained quantum physics. 'Thank you.'

I pour the last of the wine into my glass, take it to bed and fall asleep before I drink it.

24

Sunday is more of the same, except that I take a break at lunchtime to FaceTime with Betsy, who tells me she is having 'the best time ever' with her dad and her cousins. I try to be pleased – like most parents, I just want my kid to be happy – but it's impossible to ignore the stab of anxiety that her comment brings. I need to get on and find a house for us both. I need her to start thinking of me as home again.

Even though I'm barely able to stand, I leave my car on the main road again and try to enter The Close unnoticed. The chances of Al being out and Stella wanting to have another look at the photos are slim, I'm sure, but I can't risk it. I nipped out earlier and bought another pizza and a bottle of wine, and I'm determined to enjoy them in peace. I don't put any lights on, even though it's dark. This time, I wait until I've put the pizza in the oven before I get in the shower.

I managed to fill Angie in on my visit from Stella while we did a tour of the three storeys with my cache of pre-photos, making sure everything was as it should be before we left. 'I wish I knew where she stands legally,' I said when I'd told her it all, and Angie had replied, 'In a loony bin, by the sounds of it,' which made me laugh but didn't help.

*

There's a knock on my door again. At first it penetrates my dream as the repetitive bang of a Hoover against a skirting board. Then I jolt awake as my subconscious suddenly cottons on that this is real. My heart is pounding. I feel as if I've only just fallen asleep. It's light, though. I groan and fumble for my phone. Nine forty-three. I've slept for nearly twelve hours. I close my eyes and lie back, not ready to get up. The pounding starts again.

I drag myself out of bed. 'What? Fuck!' I shout as I stagger to the door. This had better be an emergency. I fling it open and find Stella on my doorstep again. She looks immaculate. Full make-up. Sleek hair falling round her shoulders. Wide, floppy trousers. Vertiginous heels. I'm in the glittery-cat pyjamas again. I probably smell of last night's pizza and wine. I'm sure the flat does, because the dregs are still by my bed. Actually, I'm pretty sure some of them are *in* my bed.

'Stella. I was asleep,' I say, stating the obvious.

She visibly flinches at the waft of stale air that must accompany me. 'So I see.'

I wait for her to offer to come back later, but she just stands there, so in the end I invite her in. I open all the windows (by which I mean I open the two windows, front and back), and leave the door ajar.

'I spoke to the string-quartet person,' she says without waiting for me to ask why she's here. 'Not only has Al not paid the deposit, but he told them we'd changed our minds.'

'Oh,' I say. I'm desperate to go and clean my teeth.

'And then, last night, I asked him if he'd booked them yet and he said yes, it was all sorted.'

'Shit. I'm sorry.'

She crumples on to the sofa. I'm horrified to see a fat droplet plop out of her right eye and roll down her cheek. I stand there awkwardly. It's a bit like watching a bad actor cry. Her frozen face shows no emotion. It's as if someone has planted the tear there. A droplet of glycerine.

'What am I going to do?'

I fill the kettle. I need caffeine. I probably should be comforting Stella, but I'm scared she might snap and bite my fingers off, like a wounded pit bull. 'I think you need to find out what your rights are. Maybe talk to a solicitor? Gail might know someone who specializes in this stuff.'

Stella shudders. 'I don't want everyone knowing my business.'

I make two coffees without even asking her what she wants. 'They're all going to find out when you cancel the wedding.' It comes out a bit more direct than I'd intended. I'm nervous. She puts her head in her hands. Her thick, silky hair falls either side like the curtain coming down on a play. 'Sorry, Stella. I'm just being realistic.'

She looks up at me. 'It's OK. You must think this is funny, right? After everything that's happened between us. What do they call it? Karma.'

'I definitely don't think it's funny. I know how hard even a civilized divorce is on kids . . .'

She closes her eyes. 'My poor girls.'

'The thing is, he'll still have to provide for them, that much I do know. I mean, they probably won't be living in the luxury they're used to, but that won't be so bad. The rest of us cope,' I add, trying to make a joke out of it. 'You just need to get some proper advice.'

She sits there in stony silence for a long moment and I think I've offended her. I put her coffee down in front of her and go back to leaning on the counter. I'm scared to say anything else. Suddenly she takes a deep breath in.

'I will literally kill you if you breathe a word of this to anyone else.'

I look around as if there might be someone else in the room deserving of this comment. 'I'm not going to.'

'I mean it, Laura. I won't have my private business being tattled about like another piece of gossip.'

'I said I won't, OK. But you could find a solicitor in another part of London. There's no reason anyone would find out till . . . well, you know.' It occurs to me that she's hoping this will all go away somehow. That Al will change his mind. It should make me feel sad for her but, in fact, it just makes me irritated. She needs to grow up. Start seeing life as it really is.

She lets out a sob. 'What sort of man steals his children's future inheritance from them?'

'I don't know. Look . . . you can trust me. If you want someone to talk to about it . . . whatever . . .' A part of me wants to add, *If you tell your daughters to apologize to mine for the way they've been mean to her*, but of course I don't. Not now.

'Thank you,' she says, which, I suppose, is better than nothing.

'You at least need to start taking steps to protect yourself and the girls. Maybe play him at his own game.'

'What do you mean?' she says, looking up at me.

'I don't know. But if he's hiding money from you, then you can do the same, at the very least.'

176

That gets her attention. 'He'll notice.'

I think about it for a second. It probably is the sensible thing to do – the only thing she can do if she won't see a solicitor. 'Then we'll just have to find a way to make sure he doesn't.'

25

Of course it's very easy to make pronouncements like this, but it's another level altogether to actually have suggestions to back them up. It's obvious that Stella is clueless where their finances are concerned, happily playing the kept woman for their whole relationship.

'The first thing you need to do is set up an account in your own name, if you don't have one already – do you have one already?'

She shakes her head.

'– and ask for access to your joint statements. We'll figure it out from there.'

'How do I do that?'

Really? She's that helpless? 'Talk to the bank. You might need to show them ID.'

She looks at me and I think I see gratitude on her face. It's hard to tell.

'Thank you, for helping me.' I don't say anything for a moment. Is she actually going to acknowledge that she was wrong in the way she treated me? I hold my breath . . .

'I have an appointment at the salon,' she says eventually, combing her fingers through her thick hair. 'I should probably get ready.'

'Sure,' I say. 'Got to get your priorities straight.' I don't think she gets the sarcasm.

'Exactly,' she says, standing up and smoothing the creases from her palazzo pants.

'Stella,' I say as she moves towards the door. 'Maybe start watching what you spend a bit. Just . . . don't make any big purchases.'

She looks a bit confused. 'You're going to need all the money you can save. Setting yourself and the girls up with a new, secure life needs to be your priority now.'

'Right . . .' she says, but I'm not entirely sure she's taken in what I've said.

I try to busy myself with work once she's left but my mind keeps drifting off to Stella and the fact that there are two little girls – two mean little girls, I grant you – who have no idea that everything is about to come tumbling down around their ears. And their mother doesn't even know how to warm up a pizza. I can't just leave them to drown.

Concentration shot, I drag myself out to shove more leaflets through doors. I drive down to Avenue Road and hit the biggest houses in Primrose Hill. I turn the Stella problem over and over in my mind as I walk. Al is clearly intending to leave her with next to nothing. She has no independent source of income – she's never worked, so far as I can make out. I make a mental note to ask her if she has any secret skills but, beyond swanning about, bitching and spending money, I can't imagine what they might be – and no stash of savings outside the (probably vast) amount in their joint account, which may not be there for much longer. The immediate problem is for her to find somewhere for her and the girls to live. Somewhere safe and clean and warm – that's all that matters.

They don't need a pool and a sauna and a cinema room. Life as they know it is going to have to change.

So, she has two options, as far as I can see. Siphon off money from their joint account in the same way that Al has, but then he'll be on to her. Or she can find a way to build a nest egg gradually enough that he doesn't notice. Squirrel as much as she can away before he ensures it's all gone and there's nothing left to fight for. Maybe I'm doing Al a disservice, I think, as I trudge along Elsworthy Road, maybe now he's bought his flat and hidden away some cash, he'll leave the rest for her. But somehow, I doubt it. The way he's setting everything up in secret, the fact that he's still going along with the wedding planning, makes me think he's setting her up for a huge fall. This isn't just a man planning a new life with his mistress, this is making a statement. He wants to humiliate her. How has he ended up hating her this much? Actually, now I come to think about it, maybe it's not such a stretch to imagine.

What would I do in her situation? I ask myself, then I realize that's a ridiculous question. There are so many ways in which I could never be in her situation. Let's start with the millions. The complete lack of knowledge of finances. The inability to fend for myself in any kind of practical sense. She's like a throwback to a bygone age. The kept woman, trapped in her gilded cage. Sorry as I'm starting to feel for her, she makes me angry. How can a grown adult happily be so out of control of her own life, even if that life is a golden one?

I push a flyer through a brass letterbox and a snarly dog almost takes my fingers off from the other side. I jump back, massaging my hand. Stella obviously can't just transfer a huge sum out of their joint account in the same way Al has, because I assume he'd confront her straightaway and ask her what she was doing. He's clearly confident that she never bothers with bank statements but, like all guilty people, he is probably obsessive about checking all is as it should be. She needs a way to do it subtly. She still has several months, if my hunch is right, that he's going to string the wedding planning out right up to the date, the greater to hurt her. But, I assume, since she has no bank account of her own, she must make her many extravagant purchases out of this one, and he doesn't question that. A light bulb sparks on in my head. I stop dead in the street. It's not going to be enough, but it's a start.

I daren't go round to Stella's when I get back because, even though I can't see Al's car in the drive, he may be in there somewhere. And the Mini Mes almost certainly are, and I don't trust them enough not to say something to him if I suddenly show up. As I park my car, I see Eva up ahead, Cocoa trotting behind. I wonder if word has filtered through that I'm not the enemy yet. I assume Stella will have let the others know that I'm not the giver of the book. I take my time getting my stuff together so she has to pass me, plaster on my best smile. I imagine Eva is the kind of person who would want to apologize for a misjudged slight, but I want to show that all is for-given too.

There's a moment when she realizes she's going to come level with my car while I'm still there, fannying around. I see it in the sharp tug of Cocoa's lead as she crosses the road to the other side.

'Hi,' I say, putting on the most cheerful voice I can.

'Good afternoon.' She tugs at Cocoa's lead again, trying to get him to speed up, and she's off.

'Fuck's sake,' I say out loud, to no one.

I'm busying myself cleaning the flat ready for Betsy's stay. I have a giant Tesco order coming later, containing all her favourite things, and I need somewhere to put it all. Last night I willed Stella to make an unannounced appearance. I need a way to communicate with her. Something Luddite and cryptic that Al can't accidentally intercept. Maybe we should devise a code of things for me to hang in my kitchen window. A spatula means 'come over when you can'. A washing-up brush means 'the end of the world is nigh, get here now!!!' She'd probably get it all mixed up. Start battering my door down because I'd left a wine glass on the windowsill to wash up.

I'm changing the sheets on the bed when, finally, there's a knock on my door. I don't even stop to flatten my hair, I just fling it open, red-faced from the effort of wrangling the duvet cover. Finally.

Ferne is on my doorstep, with baby Alexei.

'Oh hi,' she says with a smile. 'Sorry, is this a bad time? Only you did say . . .'

I wipe my sweaty brow with an equally sweaty hand. 'No! Come on in. I'm just getting the place ready for my daughter to come and stay for Easter.'

She lays Alexei down on the sofa and he carries on sleeping. He's a very cute baby. I mean, they all are, I know. But I'm particularly partial to the chubby, smiley variety. 'It's nice in here,' she says, looking round.

'Tea?' She nods and I fill the kettle. 'Yeah, I lucked out, I think. I couldn't afford much. How have you been?'

We make anodyne conversation about our week, although obviously I leave out big chunks of mine, with the result that I make myself sound like an automaton who does nothing but work and, occasionally, sleep. A week or so ago, I'd have been thrilled to think I'd made a friend in The Close, but too much has happened. My brain keeps reminding me that this is the woman Al is setting up a new life with and telling me that I should be using that opportunity to get more information, but I can't think how without being rude.

'How's the flat purchase coming along?' I ask out of nowhere.

She lifts up her long hair, away from her neck, and lets it go again. It's a warm morning, and it's hot in here, even with both windows open. 'Good, I think.'

'Does he have a completion date?'

She shrugs. 'August the something.'

'Right. But they've exchanged?' If she wonders why I'm so obsessed by her boyfriend's affairs, she doesn't say. She just shakes her head.

'I don't think so. But the vendors don't want to move out till August, so . . .'

The timing makes sense. The wedding is supposed to be on the third. I'd put money on the fact that he's going to let Stella down right at the last minute for maximum humiliation. I wrack my brain for anything else I could usefully ask without giving myself away, but come up with nothing. Maybe I should just treat this as the social occasion it's meant to be. Relax, for once.

'Betsy's staying with her dad's family,' I say, changing the subject.

'That's nice. I mean, isn't it?'

We talk about this and that while we drink our tea, Alexei making snuffly snoring noises every now and then like a little cat. It's a relief, I realize, just to be chatting about not very much. Ferne tells me that her family are in Cornwall so she doesn't get to see them as much as she'd like.

'You're close to them?'

She nods. 'Very.'

'And do you want kids? Or is that a bit like someone asking me if I enjoy keeping my own house clean?'

She laughs. She really is very pretty, and it makes me a bit sad for a moment, thinking about how lovely Stella must have been before she started messing with her face. 'No, I do. I always have. But it's a bit of a sticking point. He – my boyfriend – isn't so keen. He already has two.'

I've noticed she always refers to him as 'my boyfriend' and not by name. Force of habit, I suppose. I remind myself I'm just having a friendly chat.

'Oh. I didn't realize. Do they live with their mum?'

'Yes,' she says. I can tell this is territory she doesn't want to stray into, because then she'd have to tell me that Al still lived with their mum too.

'Maybe . . . what's his name again?'

'Um . . . Alec,' she says, hesitantly. And, if I needed conclusive proof, there it is right there. I force myself not to react.

'Maybe Alec'll change his mind. You're young, you've got time . . .'

I stop short as I hear footsteps on the stairs. No. Not now.

There's a knock at the door. I give Ferne a forced smile and go to answer it. Of course it's Stella. Of course she would pick now to come round.

'I did what you . . .' she starts to say, and I practically roll my eyes right into the back of my head, trying to indicate that I have a guest. 'Stella! Hi! Come in!' I say over her with exaggerated enthusiasm. 'I'm just having tea with . . .' I stop dead at Ferne's name. I daren't even utter the F in case Stella puts two and two together. '. . . do you two know each other?'

Stella looks at Ferne as if she was shit on her shoe. Not because she has any idea who she really is, but because she's a nanny. The help. She's no doubt seen her coming and going from number 1 with the baby in tow. Ferne, on the other hand, looks as if she's seen a ghost. All the colour has drained from her face.

'I really need to talk to you. In private,' Stella says, completely ignoring her, which is downright rude, if you ask me. Ferne, of course, is just happy for the excuse.

'I have to go anyway,' she says, standing up and gathering her things. 'Thanks so much for the tea, Laura.'

She heaves baby Alexei up off the sofa. He's still sleeping and I'm sad I didn't get to have a proper cuddle. 'Any time,' I say. I need to try to act normal, not give anything away. Although, as usual, Stella is so self-absorbed she probably wouldn't even notice.

Ferne gives me a quick hug, waves a low hand at Stella, and she's out of there. I breathe a sigh of relief. Luckily,

Stella's not interested in my social life. The second Ferne's footsteps recede she tells me why she's here.

'So, I opened a bank account . . .'

'Great. Don't tell Al. Listen, Stella, I've had an idea. You need to set up a PayPal account . . .'

Nothing. Crickets. Tumbleweed.

'. . . that way, you can pay into it from your joint account and, if he asks, tell him you're buying things for the wedding, or clothes, or whatever you usually buy.'

She gives me a confused look. 'But I buy everything I want out of our joint account anyway. That's one thing Al has never been – so far. Stingy with me.'

OK, so she doesn't get what I'm saying. 'You won't be buying anything. It's your way of moving money out of your joint account. Building a nest egg. You definitely won't be buying anything,' I say again, just to make the point.

'But won't he notice?'

'It'll just say PayPal on the statements. Everyone uses it now, so tell him you set it up to make things easier. Just don't tell him you've bought something huge like a car or he'll be wondering where it is. Start small.'

I thought this plan was genius but, seeing her confused face, I wonder if she's got any hope of handling it without giving herself away. 'I'll help you. And you need to start selling stuff.'

'Selling what?' she says, in a voice that implies I might mean her children. Or fruit and veg on a stall at Chapel Market.

'Anything – jewellery, clothes. Stuff of Al's that he won't miss, even. You can sell it on eBay, they pay by Pay-Pal that's linked to your new bank account. Bingo.'

Stella sinks down on to the sofa and crosses her slim legs. 'Laura, I know you mean well, but selling the odd designer dress here and there is not going to set me and the girls up for a new life.'

'It's going to have to,' I say, a little too harshly. 'Because that might be all there is. Oh, and you're going to need to find a job.'

This may be too much too soon. Her mouth drops open like a hungry baby crow. I pretend not to notice.

'How do you pay the nanny?'

'In cash,' she says. 'She only does the school runs now, and a few odd hours here and there in the afternoons and the holidays.'

'Does she deal with Al at all?'

Stella shakes her head reluctantly. She can see where this is going. 'No. He's always at work . . .'

'Good. Then you need to get rid of her. Don't tell him, keep getting the cash out then pay it straight into your new account. Don't spend it. Can you find a way for the girls not to mention it?'

She scowls at me. 'Who's going to take them to school?'

'You are. Can they keep it to themselves?'

'I'd have to bribe them,' she says, and I think I'll tackle that one later. Taylor and Amber are going to have to learn that they can no longer demand whatever they want, whenever they want it.

'Well, just make sure the bribe is small enough to make it worth it.'

She blinks and a tear rolls down her cheek. 'My life is over, isn't it?'

'No,' I say gently. 'Your life as you knew it is over, that's all. Now you're going to have to live like the rest of us.'

I make her go and get her laptop and set her up on eBay and PayPal. I must tell her a hundred times that she needs to start small and to keep this to herself. We begin by transferring a random amount from their joint account to her PayPal. A trial run.

'So, he gets to take a million and I get twenty-seven pounds and ninety-three pence,' she says petulantly, peering at the screen.

'Just to see if it works,' I say. 'And that nothing flags up on the bank statement to say it's anything to do with you.'

'And what if it does?'

'You say you made a mistake. You were trying to pay for something. Fudge it. He's hardly going to be suspicious about twenty-seven pounds.' Then I tell her she needs to go and hunt out some stuff to sell. Their house must be a goldmine.

'Nothing he'll notice is missing,' I remind her. 'Bring it over here if you want and we can do it together.'

She sighs. 'Thank you.'

'Oh, and Stella,' I say as she leaves. 'Can you tell Eva and the others that you were wrong about me?'

'About what?'

Really?

'About me making a play for Al and being Public Enemy Number One.'

'Oh,' she says. 'That. Of course.'

I decide to push my luck. 'And Betsy is coming to stay

tomorrow. Maybe you could ask Taylor and Amber to apologize to her? And, you know, if at all possible, tell her her mother isn't a slut after all.'

Stella nods. I think I've knocked the fight out of her. 'I'll try,' she says, as if it might be beyond her capabilities.

It's a start.

26

David drops Betsy off on their way back from his family, with a bag full of dirty washing ('Sorry, I thought I'd kept on top of it'). He looks around at The Close appreciatively as we unpack the car.

'Nice place you've got here.' I'm hit with a memory of us moving in together for the first time. Into a tiny studio not much bigger than this one. We'd decided that we wanted to buy as centrally as we could afford, it didn't matter how small the flat. We'd been seeing each other for a year by that point, traipsing back and forth between his rented place in Hounslow and mine in Bounds Green. We hired a van and did the move ourselves, both crying with laughter and exhaustion when we realized that, once we both put all our accumulated worldly possessions into the space, there was no way of getting to the bathroom without some serious climbing skills. 'I'm glad we've got two sofas in here,' he said, collapsing on one of them. 'I'd hate not to have anything to sit on on the long trek from the bed to the fridge.' I remember us trying to cook our first dinner with a chest of drawers rammed in front of the sink. It was one of the happiest nights of my life.

He helps carry the luggage up the stairs, but I don't invite him in. Betsy is full of stories about things she got up to with her cousins, which thankfully removes the need for any polite conversation between David and myself.

'Anything I need to know?' I say as he leaves, hugging her goodbye. She runs off into the bedroom with one of her bags and I hear her arranging her toys on the bed.

'No, all fine. Oh, she's decided she's a vegetarian . . .'

I think of the big shop I did. Betsy's favourite sausages and chicken nuggets. 'Oh, for god's sake, David. You didn't think to tell me?'

'I just did,' he says.

'I bought loads of food . . .'

He shrugs. 'She'll probably change her mind again in a couple of days.' I'm reminded of how frustrating he always was to argue with. How passive and impossible to rile, calmly restating his point in ever more deliberate tones while I worked myself up into a frustrated frenzy. Some-times you just want a storm to clear the air.

'Meanwhile, what am I going to give her tonight?' I know there's no point, but I put time and effort – and money I can't afford to squander – into picking things that Betsy would most like to eat. Part-time parenthood does that to you. You want to ensure that the hours spent with you are perfect. Subconsciously or not, you want your home to be their favourite.

'I could pop to the nearest shop and get something?' he says, and for some reason that comment irritates me most of all. The calm logic of it. He might as well just say, *Why are you getting so worked up when there's such a simple solution?*

'I'll do it myself,' I say petulantly.

I fill the washing machine, then Betsy and I go for a trample in the woods. She holds my hand, which both fills me with joy and lets me know that she missed me, even as she's babbling on about how brilliant the last few days have been. Her cousins have a basset hound called Henry – a whiffy, cantankerous old thing with rheumy eyes and breath that could strip paint – and most of her stories involve him and the various outfits he allowed her to dress him up in. Of course, I'm fretting that I can't compete. No dog, no beach, no friendly playmates. I never used to be this anxious a parent. We're about ten minutes from home when my phone rings. Rahina. I answer immediately. Rahina is not one of those people who call for no reason.

'Hi,' I say. 'Anything?'

One of the things that makes her my favourite estate agent of all time (OK, so I have only ever dealt with two, but she wins hands down. She doesn't talk about a property having character when she actually means there's a hole in the roof, for a start) is that she never wastes time on inane pleasantries. So I know she won't be offended when I cut straight to the chase.

'Maybe. It's a flat . . .' she says, and my heart plummets back down with a thud. '. . . But hear me out.'

I want to say, *Don't bother*, but I don't want to be rude. And, besides, it's not as if she's been calling me every day trying to palm me off with unsuitable properties. 'OK.'

'It's ground floor and it has a garden. A nice one. And it's an absolute bargain. You know I wouldn't bother you with it unless I really thought you should see it. It's a ten-minute walk to the school. Tops. And it doesn't need any work. I mean, beyond whatever you might want to do cosmetically.'

'How much?' I try to keep the disappointed tone from

my voice. My heart is set on a house. A tiny house, but a house nonetheless.

She tells me, and it's right in the middle of my potential budget. Unlike the property I lost that was edging over the top and needed a complete renovation.

'Can you send me over the details?'

'We don't even have them yet. It's only come on this morning and I want you to see it before anyone. Before I even put it on the website. And, if it's not right, then fine, we'll keep looking . . .'

'OK,' I say. I don't want her to lose faith in me. I need to stay in the forefront of her mind so that when the perfect place comes up she'll do the same again. Call me before anyone else even gets a look-in. 'I could pop down this afternoon?'

'I've got the keys,' she says. 'Four o'clock OK?'

Betsy is beside herself. Going to see a potential new home for the two of us seems to be up there with dressing Henry in her ballet outfit in the excitement stakes. She took her whole ballet get-up to Dorset with her, I discovered when I helped her unpack – leotard, elasticated frilly skirt, little wrap-around cardi, tights, shoes. She also took a woolly hat and scarf – despite the temperature being in the high sixties – and only one pair of socks. I assume David left her to her own devices when she was packing. I try to manage her expectations by telling her you have to see lots of places before you find the right one, but her seven-year-old enthusiasm knows no bounds.

Rahina is waiting for us outside, looking summery in a fitted floral dress. Betsy hugs her fiercely. David and I used to call her the koala baby because of her love of hugging. I found her clinging on to the bemused postman once, after he'd been away on holiday for a fortnight. She'd opened the door and wrapped herself around his leg, and he was standing there with no idea what to do to get her off.

'So,' Rahina says, once the hellos are over. 'This is it.'

It's a nice-enough-looking building, I'll give it that. At least it probably was once. Yellow stone. Victorian, I'd guess. Mid terrace. Two storeys. Bay window. Tiny front garden behind a low wall, with just room for the bins. It looks a bit – a lot – unloved. The road is run-down – a betting shop on one corner and an intimidating-looking pub on another – but if it wasn't, then I probably couldn't afford to live here. There are two bells by the front door.

'Just be open-minded,' Rahina says. 'It's structurally very sound and the kitchen and bathroom are in really good nick, but the decor's a bit frightening. I think it'll put a lot of people off.'

She says it like a challenge. Like I'd be letting her down if I failed to see through a bit of naff wallpaper. She rattles the key into the lock. 'It's a share of the freehold, so the lease is still over nine hundred years . . .'

'Who's going to live here that long?' Betsy says, eyes owlish behind her glasses.

'You'd be surprised,' Rahina says with an indulgent smile.

Behind the front door is a neutral hall with a small table piled up with old mail. Rahina unlocks a door to the left. 'That one leads to the flat upstairs,' she says, indicating the other. 'There's an elderly couple living there. I say elderly – I think they're in their seventies, so they could be up there dropping acid and listening to the Grateful Dead, for all we know.'

We follow her through a tiny vestibule and into a decent-sized living room with the bay at the front. I'm temporarily struck dumb by the vivid purple walls and the sheer amount of stuff crammed into the space. China and ceramic knick-knacks and a row of glassy-eyed dolls. The ceiling is painted black. It's dark and dingy and reeks of tobacco. I want to cry.

'Does Ozzy Osbourne live here?'

Betsy, silent for once, reaches for my hand. We clasp our fingers together as if we both think something is coming to get us.

'OK,' Rahina says authoritatively. 'Try and imagine it empty and painted white. Look at the space. And the big window.'

'I'll take your word for it,' I say. I wander through to the small kitchen, which has a window and door on to a side return. Rahina follows me in. I try to concentrate on the units and ignore the dark green walls. She's right. They're neutral wood, and in pretty good nick. Back through the living room and along the hall there's the bathroom ('Put in three years ago. Ignore the walls!' Rahina barks before I go in.) and then the two bedrooms at the back. The bedrooms resemble a crime scene – I almost tell Betsy to stay back – but in the larger one Rahina takes my arm and steers me to a pair of French doors on to the back garden. It's tiny and overgrown, with mature climbers growing up the high walls. But the sun is streaming in and bathing the whole thing in light.

'Oh,' I say.

'Exactly,' Rahina says. 'It's west-facing. Safe. Private.'

She opens the doors and Betsy runs outside. 'Felix would love this,' she says.

'Do you want to have another look round now you've seen this?' Rahina says, and, leaving Betsy exploring outside, I agree.

'They hardly ever come up with gardens,' she tells me as we work our way back to the front room. 'And all it needs is a lick of paint. To get a house at this price it'd have to be falling down. Literally.'

It actually needs fumigating, but she's right. 'I know. I do. It's just . . .'

'You can afford it without crippling yourself,' she says. 'And it's part of someone's estate, so I don't think the family'll be haggling over money. They just want rid of it.'

'They didn't die in here, did they?' I say, even though I'm not in the slightest bit superstitious.

Rahina laughs. 'In hospital, I think. She was ninety-five.'

'Can I think about it overnight?' I say.

She nods. 'I'll hold it back till tomorrow afternoon. Just let me know yes or no.'

'I do appreciate this,' I tell her. And I do. I know she wouldn't do this for everyone.

'I'll email you over rough dimensions of the rooms in a bit,' she says. 'We haven't even had floor plans done yet.'

'Thanks. I'll call you tomorrow.'

'That place is scary,' Betsy says, too loudly, as we leave. Even so, I drive the route to her school on the way home just to double-check how close it is.

*

Later, when I'm making beans on toast for Betsy and promising her we'll pick up some veggie sausages tomorrow, my mobile rings and it's Angie, sounding breathless. 'There's a sealed envelope on his desk addressed to him and marked "Strictly Private and Confidential. To be opened by recipient only",' she tells me.

'Ooh!' I say. 'No clue what it is?'

'Nothing. Hopefully, I'll be able to find out tomorrow, after he's looked at it.'

'Everything OK your end?'

'Yes,' she says, probably wondering why I'm not engaging more. 'All fine. You?'

'I have Bets here. She's back from her holiday.' I give Betsy a big smile and she gives me one back. 'Auntie Angie,' I mouth at her.

'Ah!' Angie says, getting my message. 'Lovely. You two have a good time. I'll keep you posted.'

'Definitely. Good work. Thanks.'

I put off thinking about the flat till Betsy is asleep, tucked up on my side of the bed with Bruno in her arms. I try to approach it with my head and not my heart, comparing the measurements Rahina sent me with those of the house I lost. Apart from the kitchen and the second bedroom, there's actually not a huge amount of difference. The gardens are about the same size. It's walking distance to school. I know it makes sense; it's just hard to accept it. I wish Betsy hadn't seen it as it is. She'll have nightmares if I tell her we're going to be living there now.

By the morning, after going back and forth countless times, I've decided I have to be sensible and go for it. I'll offer lower than the asking price and if they accept – which

Rahina thinks they well might, because the family are keen to get hold of any cash from their crazy deceased aunt's flat and split it sooner rather than later – then it's fate and I'm meant to live there. I just won't mention it to Betsy yet. I send Rahina an email before I can change my mind.

Regret it immediately.

27

Stella is on my doorstep, and the two sullen-looking Mini Mes stand behind her, hands on hips like twin teapots.

'Taylor and Amber would like to ask Betsy to hang out with them,' she says through gritted teeth. I hadn't anticipated this. I'd hoped for an apology, but I'm not sure I'm happy about my daughter spending any more time than she has to in the company of these two precocious monsters.

'Oh,' I say. 'How nice.'

Betsy appears behind me like a dog who's heard the word 'walkies'. 'Hi!' she says eagerly, straightening her wonky glasses.

The Mini Mes both give her sickly forced smiles. 'They also have something they want to say, don't you, girls?'

'We made a mistake; your mum is not a slut,' they chorus in sulky unison. They've obviously been rehearsing. It's said robotically, completely without conviction, but Betsy takes it at face value and gives them a big grin.

'Can we play in the woods?' she says, and I immediately jump in with 'No! Stay where we can keep an eye on you. No further than the gate.' I don't trust them not to turn on her once they're out of sight. I swear, if they make her cry again, I'll kill them both.

Luckily, it's a beautiful day. 'Can I have your make-up bag?' Taylor says, and Stella digs in her Louis Vuitton. I look at Betsy and she's looking excited, so I leave it. So long as it keeps them occupied with something other than being mean, I can live with it. Just about. Stella hands it over. 'I do need to talk to Laura in private though,' she says.

Taylor snatches the bag. 'We'll sit on the steps outside.'

'I'm right here if you need me,' I say to Betsy as they lead her off, trying to keep the desperation out of my voice. Stella closes the door behind them and I open it again, just a crack.

'Coffee?' I say.

'Not that awful instant stuff. I'll have Pilar make a cafetière.' She fishes her phone out of her bag.

'No!' I say, more forcefully than I intended. She's going to have to get used to not being waited on hand and foot. 'You can have tea.'

She perches on the sofa. 'Do you have any matcha?'

'PG Tips,' I say, dropping a tea bag into a mug. 'I can't afford matcha, and neither can you any more.'

She's very pleased with herself when she tells me that she's signed up for online access to her bank accounts and that the trial PayPal payment just showed up as Pay-Pal and a series of numbers, nothing that overtly linked it to her.

'Of course, if he ever investigated it properly, he'd be able to trace it easily,' I tell her. 'The idea is never to make him so suspicious that he does.'

She nods. 'OK.'

'Just keep to fairly small amounts for now. We'll think of a way to do some big ones.'

More nodding. I put her tea down in front of her and

she delves into her bag again. Comes out with a Cartier box. Hands it over. I open it and I'm practically blinded by the bling. 'Wow!'

She takes it back from me, slips the ring on to her finger. 'He gave me this on our tenth anniversary, a couple of years ago. I thought . . . I could sell it.'

'Won't he notice?'

'I don't wear it much any more.' She waggles a hand full of glittering jewels.

'Great,' I say decisively, before she can change her mind. 'We need to find a jeweller's. That must be worth a fair bit.'

I can't help looking round at my things. How much easier life would be if I had a flat full of priceless artefacts to sell, but I'm not sure anyone else would pay good money for the misshapen brown ashtray Betsy made me when she did a pottery class last summer (excellent guidance for children there: encourage your parents to smoke, kids!) that David and I nicknamed – behind her back, of course – the flat turd. It's one of my most precious possessions. 'How does he seem . . . Al?'

'Like normal,' she says, taking a sip of her tea and grimacing.

'Did you want more milk in that?'

'No. It's just . . . it's fine.' She puts it back down. 'That's what makes this whole thing so hard to believe. It's not as if we're fighting . . . less than usual, even.'

Because he no longer cares enough, I think. I know that one. That's one of the sure signs it's terminal.

'Maybe you've got this all wrong . . .' she says hopefully. 'It might just be wedding nerves . . .'

I raise my eyebrows at her. 'I wonder how many men buy a secret bolthole and strip out their joint account because they're nervous about getting married.'

She looks at me, eyes watery.

'I don't mean to sound harsh, Stella, but you have to start believing it's true. You've only got a limited time to sort yourself out, and who knows what he might do next. Did you tell the nanny you don't need her any more, by the way?'

She shakes her head. 'I was waiting till after the holidays. She's doing extra hours in the afternoons while the girls are off . . .'

'Tell her today. Then take all the cash out that you would have paid her and put it in your new account, OK? They're very quiet out there, by the way.' I walk over to the door and peer out. Three little faces look up at me, one of them – my daughter – made up like a pantomime dame. Amber is painting Betsy's fingernails a vivid red and Taylor is scraping her hair back so tightly with a brush it looks like her eyes might pop out of her head.

'Everything OK?' I only look at Betsy. I know I'll be able to tell from her expression if she's under duress. But she gives me a big, lipsticky smile.

'Cool,' Taylor says, insouciant.

'Cool,' Betsy parrots.

I tell myself just to be happy she's still in one piece.

Betsy is on a playdate. I drove her down to Michaela's this morning so that she and Zara could spend the day gawping at the animals in the zoo. They've taken their sketch pads and packs of coloured pencils in their little backpacks and they've each made a list of their own 'big five' to immortalize. In Betsy's case: meerkat, warthog, lion, crocodile and tarantula. Michaela invited me to stay for a coffee, so we sat in her warm, messy, cosy kitchen.

'Where are the little ones?' I asked, when I suddenly realized it was suspiciously quiet in the flat. Michaela stretched her arms above her head, a sliver of soft, creamy skin appearing at her waist. She's one of those people who are totally comfortable in their own body. She sometimes reminds me of a cat in that respect.

'Staying with my mum and dad for a few days. It's bliss, but don't tell anyone I said that.'

'I honestly don't know how you cope with three on your own.' I'm always curious about where the kids' dad is, but I never feel I can ask. It's none of my business. She laughed. 'I'm not sure I do.'

Now, with a free day when I could be catching up with work before this weekend's marathon clean (of the four companies that share a building near Lord's Cricket Ground), I am standing outside a jeweller's near Hatton Garden waiting for Stella to show up, already late for our eleven o'clock appointment. I don't really have time for it, but she begged me to come along, as she's never had to do anything like this before ('Like I have either,' I said to her) and she's nervous she'll get bamboozled and accept way too low a price. And I have to admit I'm curious to see how it works, let alone find out how much she'll get.

I see her striding towards me. A model on her catwalk. She turns heads, not just because she's stunning – tall and slender in her skin-tight jeans and three-inch Louboutins, giant sunglasses covering half her face – but because she commands it. She walks like she's entitled to attention, and so she gets it. She's a self-appointed superstar. If there were a random paparazzo around, I guarantee they would jump out and take her picture. Just in case.

'We're a bit late,' I say as she gets close. We're actually nearly fifteen minutes late, but I don't want to put her in a bad mood by having a go. She waves a hand as if to say, *What does it matter?*

I ring the doorbell beside the heavily armoured glass door, peer through the decorative iron defences. A buzzer sounds and I push my way in. It's a tiny shop, rammed with display cases overflowing with boxes of twinkling diamonds mounted on rings, necklaces and bracelets, and with an equally tiny elderly man sitting behind one of them. Stella told me one of her friends sold something to him once and talked about him as being old school, always fair. I wait for her to speak. This is her rodeo, after all. She says nothing.

'We have an appointment,' I say. 'Stella Thornbury.'

He sticks out a hand for me to shake. 'Ah, the ring.' I nearly laugh because when he says it he's a dead ringer for Gollum, but I manage to hold it together. 'This is Stella,' I say. 'It's hers.' I feel as if I'm acting as her manager, trying to set up a deal on her behalf. Maybe she just doesn't like dealing with the little people. Gollum looks at her expectantly.

'Show him,' I hiss. She slides an elegant hand into her bag and slowly produces the Cartier box. Everything is a performance for her. Whereas for this old bloke, I imagine it's just another day in the office. He's about a hundred and ten, has probably worked here since he was fourteen. Even with one speculative valuation a day, five days a week, that would be, well, let's just say, a lot of valuations.

He spends an age looking over the box. Finally opens it and peers in. He takes out the ring and puts a little tubular magnifying glass to his eye, holding it this way and that. Then he weighs the whole thing on his old-fashioned scales and examines it all over again. Exhales loudly.

'Well?' Stella says rudely. She really does need to learn some common courtesies.

'Where did you get this?' he says, peeling the magnifying tube from his eye. I half expect his eyeball to follow.

'My husband bought it for me,' she says.

'Been married long, have you, love?'

She huffs. 'We're not actually . . . Why is this any of your business?'

I'm holding my breath, waiting for the big reveal. Maybe it's a rare find. Some kind of priceless treasure. Maybe this ring alone will help Stella set up her new life. The old man gives a hacking sort of laugh, showing his (mostly lack of) teeth. 'Don't like you much, does he?'

'What?' I say. I think I must have misheard, or he's making an ironic joke. Stella says nothing. She still has her giant sunglasses on, but I imagine she looks as confused as I am underneath.

'I'm sorry, Mrs, these are fake. The ring is eighteen carat, though, probably worth fifty quid, and I imagine the box set him back a tenner.'

Stella's top lip curls menacingly. 'You must be mistaken.'

'Expert, are you?' he says. 'If you think I'm saying this so I can rip you off, don't worry. I'm not interested in making you an offer. If I were you, I'd go and get a second opinion from one of the others. But I guarantee they'll say the same as me.'

Stella grabs the box from the counter, sticks her hand out for the ring. Gollum holds it out and she snatches it from his fingers and stomps out. He chuckles. I imagine he's seen this whole scenario many times before.

'Thanks for your time,' I say apologetically. 'She's just a bit upset . . .'

'Who can blame her? No problem, sweetheart.'

I follow Stella out on to the street and find her a few shops along, pacing up and down furiously. 'What does he know?' she spits as I get close.

'Quite a lot, I imagine. Let's go and ask someone else, though, just to be sure.'

'It's a scam,' she says.

'Stella, a scam would have been him telling you it was fake when it wasn't and offering you a fraction of what it's really worth. He didn't offer you anything. He didn't want it.'

'He's probably already phoned round all the others telling them to back him up so we go back there, tails between our legs, and accept a fiver for it.'

'Already? All of them?' I say, looking round at the countless other shops. She's being ridiculous, but I understand. It's embarrassment as much as anything else. Humiliation. 'Come on, let's just pick one at random.' I take hold of her arm and pull her along the street, stop about eight jewellers along.

'They might not see us without an appointment, but it's worth a try.' I ring the bell before she can tell me not to. Whoever is inside obviously decides we don't look like a pair of armed robbers because they buzz us in immediately. We go through the whole rigmarole again with another tiny, wizened man. This time, Stella is a bit less imperious, trying to charm him, as if that might affect his opinion.

'Well, it's definitely not Cartier,' he says before he even examines it closely. 'Is this the box it came in?'

'It is,' I say. 'Isn't it, Stella?' She nods reluctantly.

He goes through the whole production number with the magnifying glass. He's just as thorough as Gollum, turning it over and over, looking in different lights.

'Can't help you, I'm afraid,' he says eventually. 'The diamonds aren't real.'

'Would you give us anything for it?' I say. Stella shoots me a look. I ignore her. It's a test. If he offers us a pittance, then there's a possibility her scam idea could be true. I think I know what's coming, though.

'Not worth my reputation, love. Sorry.'

'I understand. Thanks, anyway.'

I avoid saying *I told you so* to Stella once we're back on the street. Instead I try to sound upbeat. 'OK, what else have you got?'

'I'm going to kill him. How could he humiliate me like that?'

I assume she means Al, and not the jeweller. 'I'm guessing it never occurred to him that you'd try to sell it.'

'Fucking cheapskate,' she snarls, hurling the Cartier box into a nearby bin.

'Hey! Get that back. That first bloke said the gold is worth fifty quid.'

She looks at me as if I've completely lost my mind. 'What use is fifty pounds to anyone?'

'Did you really just say that? What do you mean, what use?' I find myself raising my voice. She's so spoilt, so entitled. 'For some people – a lot of people – fifty quid would mean the difference between eating for the next couple of weeks or not.'

'Well, bully for them,' she says.

She's unbelievable. 'You need to drastically change your attitude to money, Stella. You can't swan round acting like a spoilt princess any more.'

She flares her nostrils, a sure sign trouble is brewing. 'Well, if a few pounds means so much to you, you have it.'

I stomp over to the bin. 'You know what, I will.' I root around. Somehow, the box has worked its way down into a mire of god knows what. I finally find it, hold it up like Excalibur. There's a homeless woman sitting on the corner with a sign asking for money. I open the box and hand her the ring. She looks at me as if I'm mad.

'The diamonds are fake, but the gold is real. If you take it to a scrap place, you should get a few quid.'

I turn and walk away before she says anything. I head back in the direction of the meter where my car is waiting. I don't even look back to see what Stella is doing.

28

I'm actually relieved to be working all weekend. I take Betsy with me first thing and assign her a job taking leather-bound books off the shelves at the solicitors', the first of the four companies we're tackling. I tell her how important it is that they all go back in the correct order, but they're all numbered volumes, so it's hardly rocket science for one of us to put right if she mixes them up. I'm happy it'll keep her occupied till her dad comes to pick her up for the afternoon at twelve. She's beyond excited. She's wearing her short dungarees with red leggings underneath and has tied her hair up in an old blue bandana of mine from when I tried (and failed) to pull off some kind of Stevie Nicks chic, so she looks ridiculously cute. She's been on cloud nine since Thursday, chatting away about Taylor this and Amber that. I can't bear to think they might be about to reject her all over again.

'Oh good, the child labour's arrived,' Angie says, giving her a hug. 'We can send you up the chimney later.'

I already know that the mysterious envelope on Al's desk has disappeared without a trace. Once Betsy is out of earshot and we're in the kitchen making everyone a coffee, I collar Ange about it again. Of course, it might be nothing. An over-officious business acquaintance trying to make their correspondence look important. But the overkill of 'Strictly Private and Confidential. To be opened by recipient only' has piqued my interest. I may be pissed off with Stella, but that doesn't mean I don't want to know what's going on.

'It's not in the drawer. Maybe he took it home. Maybe it wasn't anything he didn't want Stella to know about after all,' she says, getting the milk out of the fridge.

'Must be,' I say, trying to remember who has sugar and how much in this morning's team – Paul, Tomas, Catriona, Sharon and Amita.

Angie takes the spoon from my hand and deftly finishes the job. 'How's she behaving now?'

'I have so much to tell you. But not now. We need to get on with it.'

'Spoilsport,' she says, picking up four of the cups.

Luckily, we're not home enough all weekend for Betsy to wonder where her new friends are, but on Monday morning, once I've dragged myself out of bed, every limb aching, and I'm sitting with my laptop working out the wages for the past week, she announces her intention to call on Taylor and Amber. I haven't heard a word from Stella since Friday, and I haven't tried to contact her either. Her attitude shocked me. I know she's used to having whatever she wants whenever she wants it, but she needs to grasp that that's not going to be the case from now on. She needs to learn how the other half lives. Or not. It's nothing to do with me.

I think about saying no to Betsy, but then I decide to use this as a way to gauge Stella's mood without looking like I'm the one backing down. At half past ten, having checked that Al's car isn't on the driveway, we're standing on her doorstep, waiting for someone to answer, me clutching Stella's plate, which I still haven't returned. As usual, it's Pilar. I find myself wondering what will happen to her once this whole thing plays out. Al's hardly going to have space for her in his new flat, Stella won't be able to afford her. She'll lose both her home and her job in one fell swoop. Now that she's seen me and Stella together quite amicably, she gives me a smile and lets us in. I hand her the plate as if it's a VIP pass.

'*Gracias*,' I say as she lets us into the hall.

'Is that Stella with no clothes on?' Betsy says loudly, gawping at the painting.

'It's art,' I say, hoping that will satisfy her.

We wait in the stiff living room for Stella to appear. When she does she looks gaunt – not that she doesn't always look like she could do with a good meal, but this is different. She looks like she's spent the best part of the last two days crying. She looks, dare I say it, almost human. She gives me what looks like a nervous smile.

'Betsy wondered if Taylor and Amber wanted to play,' I say to explain my presence. I can't really imagine Taylor or Amber actually playing. They're more of the 'chill' variety.

'Oh,' she says, slurring, and I realize that what she actually looks is drunk. 'Pilar!'

Pilar, who is clearly hovering in the hall in case she's required to throw me out, appears immediately.

'Amber,' Stella says, pointing at Betsy. Pilar takes Betsy by the hand and leads her off. This isn't what I expected. I wanted to know what they intended to do and make sure Bets was happy with it. She seems thrilled, though, so I decide to let it go, just this once. What's the worst that can happen?

'I'll pick her up in a couple of hours, if that's OK?' I start to make my way to the door but then I turn back. 'Is the nanny here today or something?'

She steadies a hand on the wall. 'No. Why?'

'I . . . just . . . have you been drinking?'

'Don't give me a hard time, Laura,' she says huffily.

'I'm not. I . . . who's looking after the girls?'

She makes an attempt at pulling a face. 'The girls are fine. They're very mature for their age. Anyway, I only had a couple of sips . . .'

She staggers on her heels as she says this, which doesn't really back up her argument. I know the girls aren't in any danger. She's not steaming, just tipsy, and Pilar is here if there's an emergency. But I'm not keen to leave my own daughter here while she's in this state. If the house caught fire, she'd probably forget all about her while she tried to save a Mulberry handbag. Betsy, I know, would rather take that risk than have her playdate with her new friends cut short.

'Laura, please. Will you stay for a coffee?' Stella says out of nowhere. 'I . . .' She almost stumbles over the words, so alien are they to her. 'I owe you an apology for Friday.'

Wow. Stella apologizing. Wonders will never cease. I decide to accept it gracefully. Be the bigger person. Plus, getting some caffeine into her will help. 'That's OK.'

'Pilar!' Stella screeches again, and I jump.

'I'll stay if you make it. The coffee.' I say, smiling to show I'm (half) joking. 'No getting Pilar to do it. And then I'll take Taylor and Amber back to mine with Betsy for a bit, OK?' God help me.

She looks shocked, but then she says, 'Of course. Follow me.'

We walk back through the hall and behind the stairs into a vast kitchen. In here, everything is marble. The same brown floor. White-and-grey countertops. Grey-and-bronze splashbacks, every one with a different level of swirly patterning. It makes me go cross-eyed.

'Wow. You really like marble,' I say, putting out a hand to steady myself on a table.

'This one's Statuario,' she says, stroking the countertop. 'Italian. It's the best quality. It cost a small fortune.'

I assume in her world that means she likes it. Expensive is the new tasteful. 'Right.'

There's an oven that looks like the control deck for the *Starship Enterprise*. A massive stove with seven burners. Something that looks like it's exclusively for baking pizzas. Built in the wall is a gadget I assume to be a state-of-the-art coffee machine, from the way Stella is jabbing at the buttons on a remote. I watch for a moment, amused. Clearly, she has never used this particular piece of equipment before.

'Is that new?'

She presses another button. Nothing. 'No.'

'Shall we just have instant?'

'I don't know if we . . .' She starts opening and shutting random cupboards. It's apparent she doesn't even know her way round this kitchen. She's saved by Pilar wandering in, a pile of washing in her hands.

'How does this thing work?' Stella says, flapping her

hands at the wall. Pilar thankfully gets her drift, presses one button on the machine and it starts gurgling.

'You do mine, at least,' I say, when the endless rumbling stops and hot coffee starts streaming out of the spout. 'Did you watch what she did?'

Stella shakes her head. Pilar puts the now full mug on the counter and stands another in its place. She raises a hand to press the button.

'No!' I bark, and they both jump. 'Stella.'

Stella points a long finger, and I'm reminded of ET. It hovers vaguely over the control panel. She moves it in one direction and Pilar gives her a surreptitious shake of the head. The finger moves slowly sideways. Pilar's eyebrows suddenly shoot upwards and Stella stabs at the nearest button triumphantly. The low growling noise starts again. I can't help but laugh.

'Well done. *Gracias*, Pilar.'

Pilar gives me a smile and goes off towards, I assume, some kind of utility room with her pile of washing. Stella manages to find the milk but, when she asks if I want sugar, the look on her face is so despairing that I say no, even though I do.

'So,' she says, once we're seated either side of the long kitchen table. 'I'm sorry I overreacted on Friday.' I wait to see if there's more, but that's it. Still, it's an apology, which is a big deal for Stella.

'Thanks,' I say. 'I appreciate that.'

'Please don't give up on me, Laura. I need your help.' It's the most vulnerable I've ever heard her sound. Of course, it's the alcohol talking, but it still resonates. 'I have no idea how to fend for myself.'

'You can learn,' I say, more gently. 'If you want to.'

She dabs at the corners of her eyes with her fingers. Takes a gulpy breath. 'I just . . . I don't know what I'm going to do without him.'

'You'll manage,' I say. 'It'll be OK.'

'I don't just mean practically. I love him, Laura. We're supposed to be getting married. I mean, I know he's a shit . . .'

'. . . but he's your shit,' I say, and she rewards me with a watery smile. 'Exactly. I still can't quite believe this is happening.'

'I know. I understand, I do. But right now, you need to focus on you and the girls.'

She nods. 'Will you still help me?'

I exhale slowly. I've been thinking about this. Even though I feel awful for her, I need to stand up for myself. 'I will. But we have to establish some ground rules.' I jab at the table with my finger to emphasize each point. 'No more attitude. No more "what use is fifty quid to anyone?" You're not better than everyone else; you're one of them. The girls too. No special privileges.'

'OK,' she says.

I'm not finished. 'No more drinking in the day. And you really are going to have to speak to Eva, Jan, Anya and Katya and whoever else you've bad-mouthed me to. I'm not doing anything till they stop treating me like I've done something wrong. You don't need to tell them everything, just that you were wrong about it being me who gave Al the book.'

She combs her fingers through her abundant hair. Sweeps it to one side. 'I'll talk to them today.'

'Then we have a deal,' I say. I have no idea what I'm letting myself in for.

I just hope I don't come to regret it.

'And then we played being Kylie and Kendall Jenner. I was the nanny. I was taking Stormi to play with Psalm and Saint, and Taylor and Amber were closing the Victoria's Secret show in Milan. It was rad.'

Have I collected the wrong child? I run through a checklist: wayward curly hair. Wonky glasses. Lopsided grin. No, this is her. But some kind of dystopian future version where her personality has been replaced with inane facts about D-list celebrities. If this is what happens in a couple of hours, I dread to think what she'd be like after a whole day. Giving Morgan a run for her money, I imagine.

'You've had a nice time, then?' I tell myself just to be grateful that they haven't been being mean to her.

'Rad,' she says again.

We wait while Taylor and Amber remonstrate with their mother in the kitchen. I've explained to them that she's not feeling too well and she needs a lie-down, but I imagine they can see straight through the white lie. They're not happy about being dragged across the road to mine for a couple of hours, especially as it's now raining so they won't even be able to play on the steps. It'll be the four of us holed up in one room. Trust me, I feel like protesting too. But I don't see what else I can do. Pilar shouldn't have to handle them as well as keeping an eye on Stella.

'Right,' I say as soon as we get in. 'Who wants to bake cupcakes?'

Silence. Betsy, who would ordinarily be in her element,

takes her cue from her new, sophisticated friends and scowls at me. Tough crowd.

'Well, good, because that's what we're going to do.'

'That's stupid,' Taylor says. 'We could just go and buy some.'

'Where's the fun in that?' I say, slightly desperately. I gather up the ingredients. Spread them out on the kitchen counter. Measure out the sugar and margarine.

'Mix those together,' I say, handing the bowl to Taylor. If I can get her to engage, the other two will follow. She looks at Betsy as if to say, *You'll pay for this*. I don't want to undermine the strides my daughter has made trying to get these two to accept her, but I refuse to indulge them in any more games where they are the superstars and she is the hired help. Or any more make-up sessions, for that matter. 'It's easy, look,' I say, as if her reluctance is caused by fear, not loathing. She jabs the wooden spoon into the bowl. A single grain of sugar flicks out on to her black (Armani) T-shirt and she squeaks as if she's been hit square in the face with a cricket ball. She slams the spoon down.

'We're going to get dirty.'

'Oh no!' I say. 'Shall I call the police, or will you?'

Betsy lets out an involuntary snigger and then looks mortified. Taylor glares at her then me in turn, nostrils flared, just like her mother. I'm worried I've gone a step too far, but then Amber sticks a finger into the sugar-and-marg mixture and flicks it at her sister.

'Whoops,' she says, looking at Betsy and laughing. Betsy practically wets herself with relief that she's allowed to find it funny. She snorts.

'Girls . . .' I say.

'I'm telling Mum,' Taylor says, picking up a handful and slinging it at her sister. Amber scrapes it off her top and slings it back. It plaps on to Taylor's cheek. There's a collective intake of breath. Everything stops for a split second. And then Taylor starts laughing. She dips her hand into the bowl again, and then it's chaos. Every woman for themselves. I know I should step in and tell them off about food wastage and making a mess, but it's such a relief to see them behaving like actual children, even naughty ones, and not worrying about whether they look cool or their make-up stays in place, that I haven't got the heart to interrupt the moment. I can make them clear it all up once they run out of steam. For now, I'll let them play.

29

Stella is looking pleased with herself. I can tell because her overly smooth face is cracking round the edges and her mouth is stretched sideways like the Joker's. This, I have come to realize, is her attempt at a smile.

We haven't seen each other since our chat last week, except for casually in the street, because Al had a few days off work leading up to the Easter weekend, so I've been keeping well out of the way. But we devised a very sophisticated communication code before we parted and this morning there was a red bra hanging in her dressing-room window, which means 'the coast is clear and I need to talk to you urgently'. (A blue one would just mean 'the coast is clear if you need to talk to me'.) Not owning any bras that aren't either black or flesh-coloured, I have agreed to signal with tea towels. Today is the first time either of us has attempted contact and I'm over there like a rat up a drainpipe as soon as I see the flash of red.

Betsy has gone back to her father's because school started again today. On Saturday Eva appeared at my door with a huge Easter egg for her and an apology for me. Of course, I accepted both (I had no choice about the first, because Betsy had practically snatched it from her hand and started unwrapping it before Eva even had her foot through the door). She had even brought some dog-friendly chocolate for Betsy to feed to Cocoa while she reiterated to me how sorry she was. I decided not to give her a hard time about being so ready to believe unsubstantiated gossip, but to let her off the hook. She hardly knows me, and Stella was her friend; we've probably all been guilty of that one. We weren't going to be best mates. I was wary of her now, loathe to trust anyone who would drop me so readily. But we could be civil. As she left, she told Betsy she was welcome to visit the dog any time. The smile on my daughter's face made forgiveness much easier.

Now I'm standing in Stella's kitchen, waiting to hear what's so urgent. Whatever I thought she was going to say, it wasn't this.

'I have fifteen thousand pounds in my new bank account. Well, fifteen thousand plus, because I've been paying in the money I used to give the nanny.'

'What? No, Stella, remember we said little, regular amounts. Nothing that Al would really notice. Not yet.'

She puts a mug under the spout of the coffee machine. Stares at the buttons for a moment. I have to stop myself from intervening. Eventually, she presses the correct one and the beans start to grind noisily. If it wasn't for what she'd just told me, I'd give her a round of applause for this breakthrough.

'It's fine,' she says. 'He knows all about it.'

'What?' I'm confused. I wait for her to explain herself.

'He must have been checking the statements, because he suddenly asked me if I'd got PayPal. Really casually. Because of our trial payment, you know. And guess what I said?'

'No idea,' I say. 'Tell me before I have a heart attack.'

'I came up with it on the spot, and I was so proud of myself. I said, yes, because I'd finally found the perfect designer to make my wedding dress, and that's how she wanted to be paid. I told him he wasn't allowed to deal with this one because everything about my dress had to be a secret from him till the big day. And then I said I was going to use it all the time now, because it was so easy to get your money back if anything went wrong. He liked that.'

'He's OK that your wedding dress is going to cost fifteen thousand pounds?' I say, aghast. I pretty much missed everything she said after that.

'That's just the deposit. I told him it's forty-five thousand and the designer wants a third upfront.'

I stand there with my mouth open, like Jacob Marley when he undoes the bandages holding his face together. I can't seem to close it. 'I could live on that for a year. Two. Easily.'

Stella shrugs. 'I'd originally told him it was going to be about forty, but she's charging extra because it's so late in the day. Which, to be fair, would probably have been the truth. And he knows I've been meeting designers for months and I couldn't make up my mind, so . . .'

'So, what? As far as he's concerned, he might lose fifteen grand?'

'Exactly. I suppose he's assuming he'll never pay the balance. But he knows if I'm going to keep thinking the wedding is on, I'm going to have to organize a dress, and that's one thing he can't cancel behind my back because I'd have to go for fittings and stuff, so I'd find out.'

I sit down on one of the kitchen chairs. Maybe she can pull this off after all. 'That might be genius.'

'It is, isn't it?' she says. 'And, do you know what? It gave me a thrill. I felt powerful.'

'I'm proud of you,' I say.

'I know, right? I am too. I thought I could do the same with the bridesmaids' dresses next.'

'Don't get carried away.' I can't help myself. I can't believe she's smart enough not to blow this somehow.

'I won't.'

'Stella . . .' I'm starting to feel as if we're getting on. I want to try to understand what's happening. 'Have you got any idea why he's being so vindictive? I mean, why he's still pretending the wedding's going to go ahead. Why he's hiding all the money . . . ?'

'Of course not. He's just a bastard, I suppose. You know,' she says, peering at me and changing the subject, 'You could look fabulous if you had fillers. And maybe a bit of Botox for these . . .' She indicates the side of her eyes, meaning, I assume, the fan of fine lines I have radiating outwards from mine.

'I'm fine. Really.'

'You need to make the best of yourself. Show your ex-husband what he's missing.'

'If David decided he wanted me back purely on the basis of the fact that I had a few less wrinkles on my face, then, in all honesty, he can fuck right off. And besides, it was my personality he decided he didn't like . . .'

'Still –'

I interrupt. 'Still nothing. Who says I want him back anyway? Who says I want to spend my life with a man who thinks being with me is worse than being alone . . .'

'I didn't say you should take him back, just make him regret what he's done. It'll make you feel better.'

'I don't want him to regret it. I want it not to have happened in the first –'

Before I can continue with my rant, my phone beeps with a message. I glance down at it. Rahina. 'Did you get my email?'

'Hold on . . .' I say to Stella. What can be so urgent that she's sent me a text as well as an email? I jab at my phone. Skim-read Rahina's missive. The words 'good news' jump out at me and then 'accepted'.

'Fuck,' I say out loud.

'What is it?'

I read through the email properly. Just to be sure. 'I've had my offer on a flat accepted.'

'You're buying a flat?'

'Apparently,' I say. 'I don't even like it. I just need a proper home for me and Bets. I should go and deal with this.'

'Congratulations,' she says. 'I wouldn't know where to start.'

'Well, I'm sure Al won't leave you stranded. You'll have time to work out what you can afford.' It occurs to me that Stella doesn't have a hope in hell of getting a mortgage. She has no income of her own. Hopefully, Al's settlement will be reasonable, because I'm not sure anyone reputable would even rent her somewhere. There's no evidence she could pay the rent. 'Did you manage to find out how much is in your joint account? I mean, I don't want specifics, I'm not being nosy – but if he splits whatever's left with you, will you be able to buy yourself a place? A normal place, I mean, not . . .' I wave my hands around the space '. . . like this.'

'Not much.' I have no idea what 'not much' means in Stella's world. A million? Ten? I certainly can't imagine it means the same as in mine. 'His salary is still being paid in. I suppose he thinks if payments suddenly start getting rejected, then I'd want to know why.'

That doesn't sound good. 'You need to go through and cancel any regular outgoings — not essential things like gas and electric, obviously. But anything else. And then pay those exact amounts into your PayPal every month. Exact, OK? Anything you can that he won't notice. And Stella, no more weekly massages or facials or nails or whatever it is that you do. Take what you usually spend on stuff like that out and pay it into your own account. Everything PayPal or cash, OK?'

She looks at me as if I've suggested she give up eating, although, come to think of it, she'd probably prefer that to giving up her pampering. 'I'm serious.'

She blinks at me slowly. I think I've lost her. 'Tell you what, I'll go through it all with you, OK? And if you want, I'll come over and we'll go through all your stuff to see what you can sell . . .'

'I'm not sure I can go through that humiliation again.'

'It doesn't have to be jewellery. You must have loads of designer clothes, right? Shoes? We'll put it all on eBay. Like I said, I'll help.'

'Thank you,' she manages to say. 'I'd appreciate that.'

'I really do have to go and deal with this now, though. Will you be all right?'

She nods unconvincingly. I wonder if I should find Pilar before I leave, but then I think Stella's going to have to get used to standing on her own two feet. 'I'll come back tomorrow, if you want. Don't forget to signal.'

I rush out, leaving her there. Halfway across the hall, I realize I don't have my phone in my hand. I step back into the kitchen. Stella is still sitting slumped at the table, head in her hands.

I take a step back out again. 'Stella,' I call, loudly. When I walk back into the kitchen, she's sitting bolt upright, pretending to be looking at something on her own phone. 'Sorry . . . I forgot my mobile . . .'

I grab it up. 'Thanks. See you soon.'

I go into efficient mode and call Rahina, the mortgage adviser at the bank and the conveyancer who dealt with the sale of my marital home. Rahina tells me that the family didn't even flinch at my low offer. I try to be grateful for my stroke of luck.

I'm loath to tell Betsy about the flat yet. I think she'll panic about living there, with the black ceilings and the reek of decades-old tobacco. It will probably all fall through anyway, if the grieving nieces and nephews get wind of the fact that they have grossly underestimated London prices, I tell myself. And, if it doesn't, I decide, I won't mention it till it all goes through and I've been in with an industrial-sized tin of white paint and a fumigating spray and blitzed the lot.

I remind myself I need think with my head. I suddenly feel overwhelmed with how much I have to do, especially when I check my work emails and find one from AJT

Music asking if we can fit their spring clean in this weekend, and another from one of the local houses I quoted for saying they'd like to book in for the cheaper of the two options I presented them with, and a very specific list of dates and times. I decide I need to start delegating a bit more, something I have always found almost impossible. But I know how time-consuming even the most straightforward home purchase can be.

'I have so much to tell you,' I say to Angie when she answers my call. 'But not now. I'm in a bit of a rush.' I do tell her quickly about the flat, and she's so pleased for me I can't help but start to feel more upbeat myself.

'So, it's not the dream home you imagined in your head, but if it's got enough space, it's in the right area and the neighbours aren't crack dealers, then it could be,' she says.

'I don't know about the last one yet,' I say with a laugh. She's right, though. 'You should start an advice column. Ask Auntie Ange.'

'No one could afford me. My opinions don't come cheap.'

She's happy to coordinate with all the others to get everyone's availabilities for the upcoming weekends. 'Leave it all with me,' she says, and I wish I'd done this earlier. 'But you owe me big time. I want detailed updates of life in The Close next time I see you.'

I wouldn't even know where to start because so much has happened since I last filled her in, but I tell her it's a deal anyway. I do tell her about number 7's application for permission to build an iceberg basement – two underground storeys and an additional six thousand square feet of leisure centre, car parking, servants' quarters and a dedicated hairdressing space, according to the plans which are being bandied about The Close by the furious neighbours.

Angie laughs. 'Maybe you could move in there. They wouldn't even notice you.'

I decide to take twenty minutes out and go for a walk round the block to clear my head. Things keep randomly popping into my brain, like the fact I'm going to have to shell out for new carpets that I can't afford, because god knows what's living in the existing ones. I remember they were grimy. A shade of red that's straight out of a brothel in an episode of *The Sweeney*. I wonder if there's a stunning wooden floor underneath that no one thought to mention. Unlikely. I need to ask Rahina if I can get in and have another look round, because I can't actually remember anything except the colours, the smell and the garden. But I'm almost scared to, in case I realize I'm making a horrendous mistake. Better now than later, I suppose.

I'm deep in thought as I reach the end of the road and I almost bump into Ferne, pushing the baby buggy as I round the corner. We both jump like startled cats.

'I was about to call round,' Ferne says, once we've recovered our composure. 'They want to book in a cleaning date.'

Blimey. It never rains but it pours. I don't think I've ever had a sixty-six per cent success rate from domestic quotes before. Maybe I'm pricing myself too low.

'Oh, that's great, thanks.' I'm pretty sure she must have put in a good word for me, and it turns out I'm right. She offers up a few dates and I make a note of them in my phone, promising to email her later on. They don't want to do a weekend, which complicates everything massively in terms of staff availability, but needs must, so I'll make it work somehow. We're chatting away about nothing, and I'm making random faces at baby Andrei to make him laugh, when a flash car pulls up beside us (I want to say it's a Ferrari, but I have no idea. It's one of those uncomfortable-looking, totally impractical but beautifully sleek things, anyway) and the window rolls down. Katya leans across from the driver's seat.

'Laura! I was hoping to bump into you,' she says, all smiles, as if she's forgotten that she blanked me last time our paths crossed. Like everyone else on the street, she has some kind of Spidey sense for underlings and she doesn't acknowledge Ferne at all.

'Hi,' I say, and then I've got nothing.

'I just wanted to say I'm really sorry. I can't believe we all got it so wrong. Typical Stella.' She rolls her eyes exaggeratedly to let me know she's joking.

I force myself to smile. 'That's OK. No harm done.'

'Good. Well, pop round any time. It would be nice to catch up.'

'What was that all about?' Ferne says, once Katya's mean machine purrs off again.

Annoyingly – because I would love to see her reaction – I can't tell her, in case she lets Al know that I'm no longer going along with his phoney explanation for the book. 'Oh, it's nothing. You know what they're like . . .'

Ferne nods. 'Rich girls' club.'

'Exactly.' It occurs to me that soon she'll be joining. Hopefully, she'll remember what it's like to be one of us little people. Throw us a few crumbs from on high.

*

It's the weekend, and the AJT Music deep-clean. A couple of weeks ago, I would have been thrilled to have the chance to sift through Al's office with a fine-tooth comb, but I feel as if I've already found the mother lode in there, so now it's just another cleaning job. I'm only pitching in on the Saturday morning this time, because I'm damned if I'm missing a weekend with Betsy when David's had her all week. She came along with me first thing this morning and spent an hour or so wiping down windowsills, her tongue poking up out of the corner of her mouth as she concentrated on getting right into the corners, and then Michaela popped by with Zara and the two younger ones to whisk her away to theirs for a couple of hours. She managed to use her new favourite word at least four times before she left, whenever anyone asked how she was getting on.

Angie and I have opted to do the executive offices together, to give us a chance to catch up in private.

'I just feel as if I can't leave them all to drown. I mean, she's ridiculous and spoilt and a bit of a bitch, but she has no idea. I think, left to her own devices, she'd sit in that house, still ordering all her food from Fortnum's, still being waited on hand and foot by Pilar, having her Botox and eyelash extensions and manicures, until the bailiffs showed up and threw them all out on the street.'

'My heart bleeds.'

'If it was just her, then I think I'd leave her to get on with it. But there are kids . . .'

Angie interrupts. 'The kids who were so mean to Betsy?'

'I know. Still kids, though.' I want to get off the subject. I don't even really understand why I'm doing what I'm doing. Except that I remember what it was like to be eight and suddenly find your father had exited your life with no warning. What it was like to be forty-two and suddenly find your husband was doing the same.

'You're too soft.'

'You can talk,' I say, and I know it's true. Angie might be tough as nails on the outside, but she has a soft centre, especially where children are concerned.

She shrugs. 'Maybe. Just don't let her turn you into another person who does everything for her. Like you said, she needs to learn to stand on her own two feet.'

'I won't,' I say, brushing a strand of hair away from my eyes with the back of my hand. 'Promise.'

'Rad,' she says, with a smirk.

As I'm cleaning Al's desk – all the bits and pieces have been moved to a box on one side, as with all the desks, so we can polish them properly for once – I decide it would be foolish not to check his locked drawer one more time, just in case there's anything new.

'Keep a look out for a minute,' I hiss to Angie. Maggie is meticulously wiping down the louvre blinds at the other end of the main office, while Jean and Catriona tackle the kitchen and Tomas and Paul take on the toilets, everyone's least favourite job. She screws her face up as if to say, *Really? This again?* The key is, thankfully, in the same place, so I don't think he can suspect anyone has been going through his things. Or that I am on to him, hopefully. I huddle down in the kneehole of the desk, out of sight of the main office, and go through the documents systematically. There's nothing new.

I put everything back where it should be. Angie is idly flicking through the box on the desk into which Al (or his assistant, I assume) has haphazardly thrown everything in sight to clear the way for us. She opens an envelope, pulls out the contents, dismisses them. Does the same to another. Then another. She takes her time reading this last one, hands it to me, looking at me expectantly. It's obvious straightaway what it is.

'Shit,' I say.

30

Inside is a copy of a contract. And a letter from an estate agent laying out the terms for the sale of number 3, The Close. The letter reiterates that the sale is to be completely confidential, not advertised on their website but offered privately to prospective clients only. That viewings are only to be held on certain dates and with the prior agreement of Mr Thornbury only. The first is booked for 2 May. This coming Thursday. That all business will be discussed with Mr Thornbury and Mr Thornbury alone. There's a suggested sale price that makes my eyes water, but it's not much more than I now know Al owes to the bank. The letter is dated a couple of days ago.

'He's put the house up for sale,' I tell her – although she's read the letter herself, so she must already know – taking photos of every page. 'He's selling it out from under them.'

I'm too knackered to hang up the red tea towel when I get home and, besides, I couldn't discuss anything in front of Betsy, who has all the discretionary skills of a parrot. Michaela dropped her back after lunch and she spent the afternoon playing in the reception area with Jean's ten-year-old daughter, who had refused to go to Sharon's with the rest of the 'little kids', as she called them. She's a sweet, serious girl and a good antidote to Amber, so I left them to it.

On Sunday, there are enough staff available so that I don't have to pitch in, at least until after I drop Betsy back at her dad's when I pop in to do a last walk-through, making sure everything is as it should be. Thankfully, this morning we saw Stella's whole family pile into their Bentley and I remembered she told me it was Al's mother's eightieth birthday and they were taking her to lunch. Anyway, it means there's no question of Betsy demanding to go over there – something I'm keen to avoid when Al is about. He might start to wonder how Stella and I have suddenly become matey, or at least civil, with each other, and I certainly don't want to open that particular can of worms.

First thing Monday, though, the red tea towel is up, flapping in the breeze of the open window. Stella is going to have to find somewhere to live for her and the girls, and fast. It's unimaginably cruel, what Al is doing to his family. I find it hard to believe that he'll go through with it, but the evidence is there in black and white (and garish colour, because he's somehow managed to have a photographer in to capture the full glory of their house. I spent quite a while last night poring over the pictures I'd taken with my phone, enlarging them with my fingers, fascinated by the rooms I've never seen before – the swimming pool, the state-of-the-art gym, Stella and Al's stadium-sized bedroom, which looks like something Hugh Hefner might have thought was overstated, with opulent drapes, deep pile, dark grey carpet, black silky bedding and 'erotic' monochrome photographs on the wall behind the bed).

By the time Stella appears, I'm pacing anxiously. I have so much I need to be getting on with, but I'm finding it impossible to concentrate. Angie has emailed over a rota of people for the two house cleans – including a plan for midweek at number 1, which leaves enough people free to leave early and cover the usual evening's work – but other than that I've spent most of the morning rehearsing in my head how I am going to break the news to Stella.

'Sorry, been dropping the girls off at school,' she says when I open the door. She says it like it's an achievement, like she's expecting praise for her selfless service. I decide to indulge her.

'Good for you.'

She perches on the sofa as I fill the kettle. Now she's here, I don't know where to start.

'So, what's so urgent?' she says.

I pluck the red tea towel from the window. 'Can I ask you a random question? What are you doing this Thursday?'

She looks at me, confused. 'Why?'

'Just indulge me,' I say, spooning coffee into mugs.

'As a matter of fact, I'm going to the spa at The Sanderson for the day.'

'When did you book that?'

'Al booked it for me, actually. Very unlike him.'

Ah. I exhale noisily.

'What?' she says. 'What's going on?'

I slosh milk into the coffee, sugar in mine, and then I plonk a mug down in front of her. 'I found something . . .' I say. I sit on the sofa next to her, pull out my phone. I need to just say it; there's no way to sugar the pill. 'Al has put the house up for sale. They're doing viewings on Thursday. I wondered how he was going to make sure you were out of the way.'

'No . . .' Her eyes flood with tears.

'It's all here, look . . .' I hand her my mobile, watch while she scrolls through the photos.

'He's had a fucking photographer in the house?' she spits. 'When the hell was that?'

I shake my head. 'God knows.'

The edges of her face screw up. I almost make myself laugh, thinking that she resembles a Cornish pasty. I should make a list: foodstuffs that Stella's frozen face resembles. It's not funny, though. None of this is funny.

'What am I going to do?' she says.

A thought hits me. It's hardly a long-term solution, but it's certainly a delaying tactic. 'What if you don't go to the spa? Tell him you're ill. He'll have to cancel everything.'

'That's funny,' she says, although I can't tell if she really means it.

'Of course he'll just rearrange, but you'll know as soon as he organizes for you to be out of the house for a day.'

'He'll be furious.'

'Probably. But, if you're ill, what can he do?'

Meanwhile, she tells me, she has earmarked a large pile of designer clothes – both hers and Al's – as well as bags and shoes, for us to put on eBay. It feels too much like hard work, but I know she needs all the money she can lay her hands on, and soon, so I trail after her to her house, to show her what to do. For which, read 'do it for her'. Luckily, The Close is empty, so I don't have to worry about anyone wondering why me and Stella are suddenly hanging out together.

It's the first time I've been upstairs chez Stella – although, of course, I have now seen photos. She leads me through the Fifty Shades of Black bedroom (I try to avert my eyes from naked – I assume – Stella on the walls. I'm pretty sure it's her, at least; I don't like to ask), through an adjoining bathroom the size of my studio – more marble, and gold-coloured taps. Maybe they're actual gold; I wouldn't be surprised. I can see that the other side is a mirror image, so I assume this is 'hers' and that is 'his' – and into a vast wardrobe-lined dressing room. There are mirrors everywhere, reflecting off each other to give you a front, back and side view of yourself in any outfit. I can't imagine anything worse. There's a dressing table with a looking glass surrounded by lights and expensive-looking jars featuring names I've never even heard of on top. Piled on a chaise longue is a mountain of clothing. I assume this is the reason I'm here.

'Won't Al notice if all this just disappears?'

She shrugs. 'He never wears any of it any more. The same with me and my stuff.' She flaps a hand, and I see another, much smaller heap of what looks like dresses and bags. 'Right,' I say. 'OK.'

It takes us over an hour and a half to photograph everything. Stella insists on modelling half of it, and I take pictures that cut her head off, just in case. Then I show her how to set up an eBay account (i.e. I set it up while she reads *Vogue*), link it to her PayPal account, then start the painstaking process of listing all the items.

'You do one,' I say, after I've sweated over five or six.

'Oh gosh, no, you're so much better at this than me.'

Two can play at that game. 'Only because you haven't tried.'

'Please, Laura,' She flaps her eyelashes at me, pouts the fishy lips. 'I'm hopeless at anything with computers.'

I imagine this is how she always gets her way. Plays the helpless little lady. Well, that one's not going to cut it any more. 'No. You need to learn how to do this stuff.' I hand her the laptop. Sit back.

See, this is why I could never be a teacher. After fifteen minutes, I have to sit on my hands to stop myself grabbing the computer back and doing it myself. I must tell her the same thing twenty times. I don't know if she's deliberately not getting it to make a point, or she really is this useless. At this rate, we're going to still be here when Al gets home from work.

'I think I've done it!' she announces suddenly. I've almost drifted off. I peer over her shoulder. Thank god.

'Fab. Now the next one . . .'

'You're so much quicker than me,' she whines, but I stand my ground.

'I won't be now you've got the hang of it. Keep going.'

She sighs. I sit there, impassive. 'Go on, it won't do itself. The sooner you start, the sooner you'll finish.' Maybe I could have been a teacher, after all. I certainly know all the clichés.

'You need to buy a load of packing stuff. Just get brown paper, and tissue paper – cheap tissue paper, not fancy stuff – and Sellotape,' I say, once she's reluctantly back to it. 'And put everything somewhere he won't see it. Not in here.'

'I've thought of that. Everything's going in one of the

spare bedrooms upstairs. It has a lock. He'd never have any reason to go in there.'

'OK. Good.'

'Oh, and I'm taking the girls for bridesmaid dress fittings tomorrow.'

I wonder if I've misheard. 'You're . . . ?'

She laughs, and I realize I don't think I've ever heard her laugh before. It's a sort of dry honk. No joy in it whatsoever. 'I haven't gone crazy. It's the only way I can transfer the money without them giving away the fact that they don't know anything about it. I can't afford to bribe them any more, can I?'

'What did you have to get them for them not to tell him about the nanny, by the way?' I realize I'm talking about her girls like they're a pair of experienced blackmailers, but I think perhaps they are.

'You'd be proud of me,' she says, more animated. 'They're desperate for a miniature pony, so I told them I was going to arrange for them to keep one of the ones we've booked for the wedding. By the time they find out there's not going to be a wedding, and so no pony either, it won't matter what they say to Al . . .'

She looks at me, waiting for praise. I don't even know where to start with the morality of this one. The idea that you would promise your small daughters a pony to keep a secret from their father. Let alone the fact that you were actually conning them in the first place. 'Gosh,' is all I can manage. 'Whatever it takes, I guess.'

'I knew you'd be impressed.'

I change the subject. 'How much does a bespoke bridesmaid's dress cost in these here parts anyway?'

Stella shrugs. 'I've told him fifteen thousand each.'

'Oh my god, Stella! It would take me months to earn that.'

The look on her face is priceless. I may as well have said something in Mandarin. 'But you have your own business . . .'

'Cleaning,' I interrupt. 'I have a tiny cleaning business, and most of what comes in goes on wages. It keeps my head above water, that's all.'

'And what about your ex-husband?'

'He's good,' I say, because he is. I can't fault him on that. 'He pays maintenance for Bets, and he'll contribute to our living costs once she's back with me full time. But it's not as if he has loads of spare cash knocking around. He just has a normal job. Nothing flash.'

'Well, then, I'm lucky, I guess,' she says. But we both know that's not true.

31

May

Of all the things that hurt about David leaving, it was somehow the fact that he'd been viewing flats to buy, that he must have had our place valued, sat down and worked out exactly what he could afford to offer, that hit me the most (he'd left aside precisely half of the potential profit for me, and half of our savings). We'd been lucky – well, 'lucky' is definitely the wrong word; I don't know what the right word is, but bear with me – in that, being an only child, he'd inherited his parents' house when they died in quick succession. Not a pile, by any means. A modest three-bedroom home in Kent, but nearly all paid off by his mum and dad's careful planning. And we'd bought the maisonette using most of the money from its sale. With a big mortgage on top, obviously. But it gave us a chance, and it meant we had a hope in hell of getting two places once we split. He told me his intentions the day his offer was accepted. He didn't want to be going behind my back, he'd said. He wanted to be upfront, like he'd promised. No deceptions. Our idea of what constituted a deception clearly differed. I'd lain awake at night obsessively picturing him and our besuited, ruddy-cheeked, wine-bellied bank manager poring over our finances in secret, both agreeing to keep it from me for now. Mistresses come in all shapes and sizes.

I obsessively check Stella's eBay items. Of course, not much is happening, as it never does until the last few hours of any sale, but, when I click on her, the seller, I see there are new listings. A Mont Blanc pen. A silver paperweight. A pair of men's Tom Ford sunglasses. I feel proud, like I did the first time Betsy tied her own shoelaces. She did it all by herself. That's my girl. I leave the blue tea towel hanging, just in case Stella needs me, and I get on with work.

I feel as if I've neglected Gail a bit. Since the time I showed up unannounced and Stella was there, I haven't been round and, lately, I've been too scared of what I might say, what I might give away. I've avoided her on the drive a couple of times, waiting until she got into her car and drove away before leaving myself. I feel bad. Not that I think she will have given it a second thought, but she was the only person who gave me the benefit of the doubt when I was blackballed. So, the next time I see her pottering in the front garden, watering the hedge round the fountain in the early evening, I go out, as if I'm going for a walk.

'Hey,' I say, feigning surprise at seeing her.

She pushes her fringe out of her eyes with the inside of her elbow. 'Laura! How are you?'

'Good,' I say. 'I've found a flat. They've accepted my offer.'

'That's fantastic news. Do you want to come in and

have a glass of wine to celebrate. Or . . . oh . . . were you on your way somewhere?'

'No. Just a walk. I'd love to. If you're free, I mean . . .'

'Look at us pussyfooting around like two teenagers who fancy each other,' she laughs. 'Isn't it funny how, when you're a child, you just assume everyone is happy to play with you, and then you somehow lose that.'

I think about Betsy and the Mini Mes. 'It gets knocked out of you, I suppose.'

She turns off the hose. 'I'm going to make a resolution to live like an eight-year-old. We'd all be far less anxious if we did that.'

I follow her into the house and through to the kitchen. 'Um . . . you don't have any white, do you?' I ask as she reaches for a bottle of red.

'Of course.' She roots around in the fridge. 'Don't tell me you'd have preferred white all this time?'

'Well . . .' I say, and we both burst out laughing.

'Here's to living like eight-year-olds,' she says as she pours me a glass. I clink it against hers. 'If you don't like what you're being offered, just say so. Life would be far easier if we were all a bit more honest.'

'Here's to that,' I say. She opens the glass doors and steps out into the garden, and I follow. It's incredible out here. There's a stone patio with a table and chairs and two rattan loungers, an epic area of pristine grass (I've seen a gardener hard at work a couple of times a week) surrounded by blossoming rhododendrons of all colours, and behind them a row of tall fir trees. Over to the left, out of sight of my bedroom window, is an azure swimming pool.

242

'Wow.'

'Lovely, isn't it? One of these days, Ben and I are going to have to have the downsizing conversation, but I don't think I can bear to leave this.'

'Not yet, surely?'

'Once we're both too decrepit to manage the stairs.' She laughs, showing her perfect veneers. 'Come and sit over here, it gets the last of the sun.'

She leads me across the lawn to the table where I watched her and Stella share a bottle. It's idyllic. Almost silent, except for the birds.

'Oh no!' she says as we sit down. 'I've just realized that means you'll be leaving us.'

I screw up my face. 'Sorry. Not for a few months, and that's assuming it all goes through smoothly. Anything could go wrong.'

She takes a sip. 'What's it like? Tell me everything.'

'It's . . .' I start to say, and then suddenly I'm biting back tears. 'It's awful.'

Gail laughs, thinking I'm making a joke, but then a loud sob escapes me and she puts her glass down, alarmed. 'Laura . . . what?'

I dab at my eyes with my sleeve. 'Sorry. God . . .'

'Has something happened?'

'No. I mean, apart from the flat . . . I'm being stupid. I should be happy that I've found somewhere . . .'

She reaches out a hand and touches my arm. 'You're allowed a wobble.'

'That's all it is,' I say, getting my breathing back under control. 'I just need to keep reminding myself why I'm doing it.'

'Because you're a good mum . . .' Gail says.

I manage a watery smile. 'Don't. You'll set me off again . . .'

Gail produces a tissue from somewhere and hands it to me. I rub at my eyes. 'It'll be fine,' I say decisively. 'I just need to get my head around it.'

'Well, you'll be missed. By me and Ben, at least. I can't speak for the rest of them.'

'It's got better. I think Stella called the dogs off.'

'I'm glad. You might be gone before the wedding.'

'Lucky me,' I say. I mustn't give anything away.

We sit in companionable silence for a moment. I watch a jay hop cautiously towards a bird feeder. 'Do you think my separation would have been much more difficult if we hadn't been married?'

Gail wafts a fly away from her glass. 'In what way?'

'I don't know. Dividing the spoils? If David had been difficult, I mean. Which he wouldn't have been.'

She shrugs. 'I know nothing about family law, but I imagine if you have a child together, the father has a duty of care. I mean, maintenance for the child obviously, but also a responsibility to make sure they have somewhere decent to live and such.'

'Keep them in the style to which they've become accustomed, that kind of thing?'

'Well, I'm sure it depends, but yes.'

I thought so too. I'm still confused as to why Stella won't see a lawyer. Get her ducks in a row. No one would have to know, but she could at least find out where she stands. Make plans before it's too late and it's all academic because everything is gone anyway. I resolve

244

to mention it to her again. Press her a bit, now we're getting on.

I'm in her kitchen. Before I ended up here, I drove to Tesco and bought big bags of macaroni and cheap cheese. No more Fortnum and Mason delivery. No more filet de bœuf. She's going to squirrel away the money and buy budget from now on. And she's going to learn to cook, because Pilar is not going to be there for ever. Stella has complained every step of the way, like a sulky toddler, and I'm beginning to wish I had never started this.

I've fetched a Pyrex dish from home and I'm knocking up my own smaller portion for Betsy and me to share tonight. I talk Stella through every step of the way (I assume nothing, once I realize she doesn't even know how to boil pasta. Me instructing her to tip it into the water: 'How long would you think it has to cook for?' Stella, shrugging her shoulders: 'Half an hour?' – then, noticing my expression: 'A minute?') and I try to ignore the massive pile of washing-up we're creating by using two of everything. Just this once, I'll let Pilar clean up. Otherwise, I'm pretty sure I'd end up having to do it.

'What about before you met Al? Didn't you have to fend for yourself then?' I ask, stirring the sauce. I know nothing about her background. Maybe she was just left by aliens at the age of twenty-seven. Fully formed, but with no life skills whatsoever.

'I was married before,' she says, casually.

'You were . . . ?'

She nods. I indicate to her that she needs to keep stirring. 'I got married at twenty-one. Andrew.'

'I had no idea,' I say, although, why would I?

'We split up when I met Al. One of those things.'

'Right. Did you never ... I mean, you and Andrew weren't big on cooking?'

She gives me her weird fishy smile. 'He liked to do it. Or we'd eat out. Whatever.'

Ah, so she's always been a princess. 'And you've never worked? Anything?'

She wafts a hand. 'Oh, a bit of modelling, you know.' She says it in a way that makes me think, if I asked her what campaigns she'd done, she wouldn't be able to provide an answer. I can't imagine she ever had the drive, or work ethic, to make a go of it, even if she had the vital statistics. So she really does have zero experience of earning her own living.

'What did Andrew do?' I stir my pasta into the sauce. She does the same, watching my every move, as if there's a trick to it.

'He worked in the financial sector. He had a good job, but he never quite made it.'

Probably because he had to leave early to go home and cook dinner every night. She sounds quite wistful when she speaks about him, though. There's obviously a fondness there.

'He was older, you know. Very handsome. Very kind. But he just lacked that drive.'

'Are you still in touch?'

She shakes her head. The horse tail swishes. 'Oh god, no. There's nothing deader than an ex-love. Isn't that what they say?'

'Something like that. And before Andrew, what?'

'I lived at home.'

'Put the bread in the food processor,' I say, and she looks at me as if I've asked her to split an atom. I point at it. 'Are your parents . . . ?'

'Still alive. They live in Dorset.' She's wrestling with the lid of the Kenwood. Pilar walks through, watching us nervously. I smile at her.

'Look,' I say to Stella, twisting the top off. Before she can take it from me, I twist it back on again so she's forced to do it for herself. 'So could you maybe go and live with them for a bit? You and the girls? While you sort yourself out?'

I have to play 'Guess the expression' again, because something moves bits of her face around, but it's unclear what. I think it's a grimace. 'I don't think so. They live in an apartment complex for the over-sixty-fives. I mean, it's nice, they like it. But, you know . . .'

'I know I've said this before, Stella, but you really do need to get some professional advice. You need to know where you stand –'

'I don't want to talk about it,' she says, cutting me off. That told me.

'Make a salad to go with it,' I say, once we've scattered breadcrumbs and Parmesan on top. 'And put it in the oven for about twenty minutes. Not too high.'

Silence.

'Do you know how to turn the oven on?'

She gives me a 'whatever' look. I approach the 'command module of a space ship' cooker and poke a few buttons. 'OK, this'll do. Come and have a look.'

She comes over obediently and watches what I'm doing. 'Will you remember that?'

'Of course,' she says, as if I'm the idiot.

'OK. I need to go and collect Bets.'

'What do I put on the salad?' she says as I go to pick up my own mac and cheese. 'We didn't buy any dressing.'

'We didn't need to buy dressing. You can make dressing. Do you know how to make dressing?' I realize I'm talking to her like she's four years old, but I'm in a rush now and I really can't be doing this. She shakes her head and I see her eyes tear up. 'Oh, for god's sake.'

Of course, she doesn't know where anything is, so it takes me five minutes to locate the oil and vinegar before I can show her how to put it together, adding a bit of soy sauce, honey and lime juice that I find along the way.

'Put everything in the fridge for now,' I say as a parting shot. 'You know where that is, right? You put it in the oven when the time comes, and then you can let Pilar serve it like usual so Al doesn't know you made it. OK? Let me know how it goes.'

'He's expecting steak au poivre,' she says sulkily.

'Well, lucky him, he's getting something much nicer.' I leave her standing in the bombsite of a kitchen. I don't hold out much hope.

Betsy declares my mac and cheese 'the best thing ever'.

'Is it rad?' I say. I've decided gently teasing her might be the way to help dissipate her obsession with the Mini Mes. I've already had to talk her down from thinking she was going to call on Amber after tea.

Betsy just grins, oblivious to my sarcasm. 'Totally.'

I wonder if all her little friends are saying it now. If all the other mums are having to cope with rad this and rad that, no idea where it's come from. I hate missing out on the daily sea change of what's in and what's not in her social circle. The ebb and flow of what they're all playing and who they're all in love with. You don't get that through FaceTime; you don't get the subtleties.

I reach out a hand to ruffle her curls. 'Good.'

'So?'

I'm back in Stella's kitchen. The blue bra was flying this morning and I won't lie: I'm desperate to hear how her first ever adventure in haute cuisine fared. Not to mention how she pulled off her sabotage of Al's prospective buyer's viewing day. From my perch by my front window I watched as he stormed out of the house at about quarter past nine, phone glued to his ear and a thunderous look on his face.

'Well . . .' She's dressed in skinny jeans so tight they're making my eyes water, with three-inch-high wedges. Perfect for relaxing at home. She's making me a cup of tea at my request, and every fibre in my body is straining to take the teaspoon out of her hand before the whole thing turns to syrup. 'First of all, he said, "What on earth is this?" when Pilar brought it out. So I said, "I asked Pilar to do it for a change. It's a treat," because, you see, he likes to stay in shape, so he's very conscious about what he eats . . .'

I can't help wishing she'd told me this yesterday, but anyway.

'. . . But then he tasted it and he said it was delicious!

249

And the girls loved it too, after I told them the calories weren't too bad . . .'

I don't know where to start. That her eight- and ten-year-old are concerned about calories? That she's lying to them, because, trust me, that thing had a shitload? I don't say any of this. I just resolve that the next thing I show her how to cook will have a nod to healthy, at least on the surface. There's no point teaching her if the family are then going to refuse her offerings.

'Excellent. And this morning?'

She finally takes out the tea bag. Pours in some milk, which turns it a deep mahogany colour with a thick tannin slick on top. The edges of her face crinkle. 'That doesn't look right.'

'You left it in too long. Start again.'

'Why didn't you tell me?'

I raise an eyebrow. 'I'm telling you now. Start again.'

She does as she's told. 'Rinse the cup, or all that scum'll still be there,' I say, once she's poured the liquid away. My new strategy is just to assume she literally knows nothing about anything, which doesn't seem to be far from the truth.

'He had Pilar go in and make the bed as soon as we were up, and he was walking round fluffing up cushions and straightening things. It was so obvious, really. He thought I was leaving for the spa about twenty past nine, so he made some excuse about going into work late – which he never does, he's there by nine every morning. He likes to say one of the reasons he's so successful is that he puts in the hours. Anyway, I'd arranged for one of the girls' friends' mums to collect them because, obviously, he would have noticed that Georgia wasn't here if I suddenly said I had to do it, so they went off at the usual time and then I started saying I felt unwell, and doubling over with stomach cramps. I told him it was period pains – he won't know the difference – and then I said there was no way I wanted to go to a spa on the first day of my period, especially when the pains were so bad. I knew he wouldn't want details – he's squeamish about stuff like that. He got really huffy about how it was all booked, and he'd done it as a treat, and I said I'd phone them and explain and I was sure they'd let me rearrange under the circumstances, but meanwhile, I was going back to bed. You should have seen his face . . .'

It's the most animated I've ever seen her. She's almost enjoying it, and it makes me happy to see. She deserves a bit of luck. 'I saw him leave. He was on his phone, looking furious.'

'Ha!' she says. 'He hasn't seen anything yet.'

32

I've been invited to another drinks party. This time, it's Katya and Guy at number 2. I am truly back in the fold. Praise the lord. Katya actually came to my door and invited me herself and, while I was tempted to tell her to go fuck her party and all who sail in it, I found myself saying yes. Curiosity won out. To see inside their house. To watch them all interact. To see Stella and Al together for once, playing the happy couple.

Katya was sweet in the same blank way she always is. She's a Stepford Wife, I realize. Programmed to be pleasant, bland, harmless. An unchallenging adornment on Guy's arm. I found myself mirroring her tone, saying thank you, I'd love to come, as if I, too, had been brainwashed. This time, I know the uniform. Jeans, strappy sandals and a T-shirt. Unfortunately, my efforts do not make me look like an off-duty supermodel, more like I couldn't be bothered to find anything nice to wear.

Last night I sat glued to my laptop as the first of Stella's eBay auctions raced to a close. A couple of things didn't sell, a few went for disappointingly low amounts, but there was a last-minute flurry of activity on two bags – a vintage Chanel and a Hermès – and a pair of Cartier cufflinks that shot the prices through the roof. As the seconds ticked down to nine o'clock I looked over the road and saw Stella at her dressing-room window, waving frantically at me, giving me a manic thumbs-up. It was the most excitement I've had in months.

I wait until I see Gail and Ben leaving the house before I head down myself. I want to make sure I have someone to talk to. I've discussed with Stella how we need to be. Civil and polite, but not so friendly that Al wonders what's been going on. He still thinks that she thinks I gave him the book. He wouldn't understand a thawing on her part.

Katya and Guy's housekeeper – a woman in her fifties who I have somehow never seen before with short curly hair, tiny eyes that blink rapidly in the light like a mole who's never seen the sun – lets me in and indicates I should go through to the garden. I walk slowly to take in the details of the house. It's weirdly similar to Stella and Al's. Too much marble, too much gilt, bad artwork. I already knew money didn't buy taste, but it doesn't seem to buy individuality either. There's the usual unmistakable hint of chlorine in the air from the underground swimming pool. I head through the living room (white grand piano. No point asking which of them plays, because the answer will almost certainly be neither) and out into the vast conservatory. The doors to the garden are open, but the evening is cool, so the early arrivals – Gail and Ben, Jan and Roman, Bill and Anya – are gathered here with Katya and Guy, flutes of fizz on the go. They're mid-conversation, so I hover on the periphery, waiting for a hiatus to announce myself. I'm grateful when the housekeeper reappears with a glass of champagne on a silver tray and presents it to me like a trophy.

The chat seems to be about Jan and Roman's impending departure. They're moving their soon-to-be-empty nest to the south of France. For a year at first and then, maybe, permanently. 'Obviously, you're all welcome. Any time,' Jan says, with a crack in her voice. I wonder if these are the kind of people who keep in touch. Maybe if there's a villa in the Midi involved. I almost make myself laugh, imagining their faces if I piped up and said, *Ooh, thanks, I'll be over for Christmas*, but I manage to keep it together. There's a lot of talk about friends they all have in the area, one-upmanship for whoever knows the most impressive people. 'Have you met the Parker-Rothmans?' Bill offers up. 'He's something big in F1 and she's the heiress of Rothman Hotels.'

'Henry and Sophia?' Jan jumps in. 'Of course. They came to dinner with Philip and Alexandra when we were in Nice. Do you know them? The Marquess and Marchioness? Charming people.'

It's a bit like Top Trumps. The 'Minor Royalty and Rich People' edition.

'Just make sure whoever you rent the house to are our kind of people,' Guy says, as if he's making a joke, but I'm pretty sure he means it. They all laughingly toast to that, and then Katya finally sees me standing there.

'Oh, Laura! I didn't realize you were there. You must think we're all ignoring you!'

Well, it wouldn't be the first time. Katya gives me a kiss that lands somewhere in the air near my right ear. She pulls me towards the group, and Gail and Ben greet me warmly.

'Laura is leaving us too, sadly,' Gail says, although I'm not sure any of the others will care. 'She's found a flat to buy.' I can almost see them glazing over. Probably thinking they don't really need to bother with me any more if I'm moving soon anyway. They're spared the necessity of feigning interest by the appearance of Stella and Al, all smiles, like the world's happiest couple. Behind them are Eva and Rafa, making it a full house. Weirdly, apart from Gail, Stella is the person I'm happiest to see here. But I notice a couple of flicked looks – Katya and Eva – between me and Stella. Is the ceasefire holding? I go over in my head what we rehearsed. Civil but distant. I smile politely. Hold back from the cheek kissing. Al, oblivious, gives me a salacious once-over and says, 'Hello, Laura,' in a way that makes even my name sound like an attempt at seduction. I can hardly look at him, I'm so sickened by the things he's doing. Stella is doing a great job of acting as if everything is as it should be, holding on to his hand and laughing at his lame jokes. Looking at him like he's her everything.

Inevitably, the talk turns to the wedding.

'What's the latest?' Eva asks. Al rolls his eyes indulgently. Starts a side conversation with Roman about Boris Johnson. The other men drift towards them and they form a revolving mass that edges slowly towards the garden, where they can light their cigars. It's like a teenage school dance. With added Cubans.

'I found my dress designer,' Stella says, hitting the exact showy-offy tone she always uses. The other women gasp.

'Finally!' Jan says. 'And they can do it in time?'

'For the right price,' Stella smirks, and they all guffaw.

'Who is it?' Anya says, breathless. 'Is it Sarah Burton?'

'Top secret,' Stella says. 'I want it to be a surprise for Al on the day. I had my first fitting too . . .'

She actually looks as if she's enjoying this.

'Tell us how much,' Katya says.

'No, forget that, tell us what it's like,' Gail interrupts, and I'm reminded how she's the best of them, the most down to earth in a land of people who are all living in the stars. Not for the first time, I wish Stella would confide in her.

Stella describes in detail a dress that doesn't exist while all the women ooh and aah in all the right places. She keeps looking over to check that Al isn't listening in, as if she actually believes what she's saying is true and secrecy is imperative. He, on the other hand, couldn't be less interested. He knows the dress will never be worn. He just doesn't realize that Stella knows that too. For a moment, I detach myself and watch the two of them, each the ruler of their separate group. Confident, charismatic, commanding. Imperious.

Even though the atmosphere is friendly enough, no one really speaks to me, beyond the initial pleasantries. I hover on the edge of conversations, smiling politely and interjecting here and there. No one asks about my new flat or expresses a sadness at me leaving. I know I've only been here a couple of months, but it's as if, in their minds, I've gone already. I wonder if Katya and Guy would even have invited me if they'd known they were going to be able to forget all about me so soon. I'm not saying that in a self-pitying way. I couldn't care less, so long as they're polite to both me and my daughter. It's just interesting. The lack of curiosity about anyone who's not truly one of them. But you can bet your life that if I suddenly married a stonkingly wealthy man and we moved into Jan and

Roman's house, they'd be all over me like wasps at a barbecue.

At one point I'm coming back from the loo (marble, natch, and one wall of framed 'artistic' photos of Katya. The narcissism of these people knows no bounds) when I bump into Stella coming the other way. We smile like two people who are actually happy to see one another. She briefly touches my arm. I almost jump with surprise.

She speaks in a loud whisper. 'How am I doing?'

'Well. Great, actually.'

'It's exhausting,' she says.

'Just keep showing off and they'll never realize anything is wrong.' It's a risk; she might take offence. But, actually, she just laughs her dry, rasping laugh. It sounds as if it's rusty from under-use.

'You're so funny.'

I've never really thought about Stella having a sense of humour. I can't imagine her kicking back watching a comedy, or her and Al chuckling over stupid in-jokes, laughing till they cry about some shared memory that no one else would understand. David used to make me laugh, and I him. Even the way he proposed became a funny story. I was reading in the living room of our shared flat one afternoon and I could hear him doing something behind me, but in that way where you know someone is trying to be quiet. I looked in the blank reflection of the TV and I could see he was taking a photo of the back of my head. I waited for him to show me, to see what the joke was, but he didn't even mention it, so that piqued my interest. When he went to the loo later I looked at his phone. In the picture he'd propped up a piece of paper behind me with the word 'Will' written on it in marker pen. And I just knew. I'd discovered his big surprise. There would be three more photos taken in random places. Three more words held up behind my unsuspecting back. A triumphant glee when he finally showed them to me in sequence. Anyway, to cut a long story short, a week or so later when we were lying in bed and he told me – all pleased with himself, and buzzing with anticipation – that he wanted me to look at some pictures on his phone, I whipped mine out and said, 'Hold on, I just want to show you this first,' and flashed him a photo of him sleeping with a sheet of paper bearing the word 'Yes!!' on the pillow next to him.

'Yes, what?' he'd said, roaring with laughter, not at all bothered that I'd ruined his big moment. 'I was just going to show you some holiday snaps.'

With everything that's gone on, I'd forgotten that. That was one of the things that was good about us, the way we used to crack each other up. And then we didn't. It just stopped. And I didn't even notice.

'Thank you,' I say. 'I try.'

I'm the first to leave. I can feel the evening is winding up, and I don't want to be the one who outstays her welcome. There's always one at any party. When I announce I'm going Gail and Ben say they'll call it a night too, so we walk back together. The air is sweet with the smell of honeysuckle.

'It's so nice that everyone's getting on now,' Gail says as we say goodnight on the drive, and I just say, 'Yes, isn't it?' And leave it at that.

*

Having my little team rock up to The Close is bizarre, to say the least. The collision of two planets. The usual plan with any house clean is that we all meet on the corner of the street ten minutes before we're due so that we don't arrive in dribs and drabs. This time, it makes sense that they all come to mine rather than irritate the inhabitants by lurking messily. Angie is the first to arrive, at a quarter to eight. I'm still dressed in my pyjamas, shovelling in the last of my granola.

'I was terrified I wouldn't be able to find it,' she says as I let her in. 'And then I didn't want to wait outside in case one of them called the police or set the guard dogs on me.'

'It's fine,' I say. 'I just need to throw some clothes on.'

I nip into the bedroom to get dressed, leaving the door open a little so we can chat.

'This is cute,' she says, by which I assume she means my flat. 'I could live here.'

I sniff the armpits of yesterday's T-shirt. Pull it over my head. 'It might get a bit crowded with the boys.'

She laughs. 'I meant on my own. They can stay in Lisson Grove. Think how peaceful it would be. Ooh, who's that?'

I peer round the door, and she's looking out of the front window. 'Woman, tall, skinny, big hair, anywhere between twenty-five and sixty, definitely had work . . .'

'That could be any of them.' I look over her shoulder. 'That's Eva. If you'd said she had a big brown dog with her, I would have known . . .'

Angie shrugs. 'Which one's Stella's?'

I point over at the house, show her the window we use

to communicate. There's just time to fill her in on the latest before I hear heavy footsteps clump up the stairs outside and Tomas and Paul appear at the door. My studio suddenly feels tiny. Lilliputian. They shuffle in, filling all the available space, arms held stiffly in front of them to avoid knocking anything over. There's no time to offer them a coffee, so we all just stand there, waiting for the final two arrivals, Catriona and Amita.

'Nice place, Mrs Anderson,' Tomas says.

I don't even bother to correct him. 'You know it's just this bit, right?'

He nods. 'Nice.'

Paul, who almost never says anything, smiles approvingly. I know the two of them share a house with six others in Kilburn, all students. I imagine my studio looks luxurious in comparison. I'm already dreading them graduating and getting proper jobs. I'll need to replace them each with about eight people.

Catriona and Amita traipse up the drive together and I herd the others downstairs so we can head straight over to number 1. As we unload all our supplies from my car, Stella's front door opens and Al emerges. I poke Ange in the side and give a surreptitious head flick in his direction. He waves a hand as he gets into his car, looking a little confused at the sight of my merry band of cleaners.

'Exactly as I imagined him,' she says. 'Exactly.'

Ferne opens the door to us, Andrei in her arms. She steers us away from the kitchen, where Katherine and Sergei are still finishing their breakfast, and up the stairs. I've already explained to her that we always start at the top and work down. The others look round in awe at the opulence. Personally, I feel as if I've seen enough marble to last me a lifetime. Even if I won the lottery, I would have a ban on it in my home. Ditto faux Greek columns, gold leaf and arty semi-naked black-and-white photos of myself. And no cinema room. What sane person gets up from their perfectly comfortable armchair in front of the telly to go and sit on a different armchair in front of a different telly two minutes down the hall? Why? Just get better speakers.

The third and highest storey has three bedrooms, each with attic space off it, a small bathroom and a room that has been converted into a living space for Ferne, with a microwave, fridge, TV and seating area. She's slightly apologetic that we're going to be cleaning up after her, but I tell her it doesn't make the slightest bit of difference to us. And, besides, I can't say I'm not curious to find out more about her. Two of the bedrooms are unoccupied, with just a spare bed and little else. We've agreed to vacuum all the attic space we can easily access, but they still won't take long. Tomas and Paul have offered to handle any potentially spidery areas and, even though Angie has no fear of arachnids, she's claustrophobic, so that suits her. I set them on the unused rooms, with instructions to move on to the other storage areas when they're done. I give Catriona the bathroom, Angie and Amita Ferne's living room, and I take her bedroom. It's her room that's going to take the longest, but I'll get to have a poke around before any of the others finishes what they're doing and comes to help me.

It's nice up here. Light and simply decorated, with walls painted in pale chalky greys and greens. The floors are a rich reddish wood. Obviously, the obligatory interior designer didn't stray this far up; it's all way too tasteful and understated. Ferne's bedroom is definitely the room of a young romantic. There's a string of pink, feathery fairy lights woven into the iron bedstead, a battered teddy bear on the bed, and the mirror is ringed with cards covered in hearts or flowers. I have a quick scan of them. All signed 'A'. Soppy messages that range from 'To my beautiful baby girl' to 'You and me, always and 4 ever.' It's all very teenage.

There's nothing much else to see in here, short of rifling through the drawers and wardrobes. Everything is cleared away neatly for our convenience. I tell myself I don't need to dig deeper. I already know what's going on. I need to stay professional. I'm relieved when we're ready to move down to the floor below.

Betsy is dangling Felix in front of the phone, making him wave his paw at me. He's clearly not impressed. We're FaceTiming at bedtime. Thanks to Sergei and Katherine's aversion to having us around while they're at home, we were instructed to finish at six, so it's been a relatively short day. Even so, I'm knackered. Already in my PJs, M&S lasagne down, glass of Sauvignon Blanc on the go, steadfastly not looking out of the front window in case the red bra makes an appearance. I'm planning to be asleep by nine.

'And then Michaela plaited my hair . . .' She turns round to show me.

'Michaela's there? I look at my watch. Five past eight. 'Is Zara staying over?'

Betsy shakes her head. 'She's at her gran and grandad's. She missed ballet . . .'

'Oh. Is Michaela babysitting you?' I suppose David must go out sometimes, although I always assumed he saved it for the nights Bets was with me. Maybe it's a work thing and he had no choice about the day.

'No,' Betsy says casually. 'She's just here.'

It hits me like a freight train. I actually gasp from the force of the blow to my chest. 'Does that often happen? Michaela comes over when Zara and her brothers are at their grans?'

Betsy shrugs. 'I suppose.'

And I know. I try telling myself it's probably a recent thing. Not that that still doesn't hurt. But then I'm flooded with a rush of memories all at once: Michaela offering to take Betsy after school unasked, Michaela and David sharing a look when we were all watching a school play together, Michaela letting slip that she knew where his new flat was when I was sure I had never mentioned it. Things I never gave a second thought to, but my subconscious has clearly stored them up for just this moment all the same.

And I know that I was lying to myself when I said him leaving for no reason was the worst.

This is the worst.

33

I manage to get off the phone without letting Betsy see there's anything wrong. I'm devastated, but I'm raging too. No wonder she was so fucking happy to help out. No wonder she didn't want payment. I need to speak to someone. To offload. I try calling Angie, but her phone is turned off. She's probably flaked out already. Gail is away for a couple of days. I flick through my contacts. There's no one else. No one who would understand why this is such a big deal. Before I really know what I'm doing I hang the red tea towel in the window. I tell myself I'll take it down when I go to bed. There's almost no chance Stella will see it between now and then anyway. Or be able to act on it immediately, even if she does. I pour myself another glass of wine and wait. I feel numb.

Not even five minutes later I hear soft footsteps on the stairs and a tap at the door. Stella is standing there, a look of expectation on her face. Of course, she thinks I have some more breaking news about Al. She would never imagine this was about me. She takes one look at me and the edges of her face crinkle, a sure sign that she's concerned. Or laughing, though that seems unlikely. 'What's wrong?'

I burst into tears.

Stella grabs me by the arm. 'Laura, what is it? What's happened?'

'David'sseeingsomeoneandIthinkhehasbeenallalongand she'smyfriend.' It all comes out as one long wail.

'Say that again. David's what?'

I take a gulpy breath. 'He's seeing my friend. And, I don't know, but I think she might be the real reason he left.'

She leads me towards the sofa. Wrangles me into a sitting position. 'Of course she was,' she says. 'No man ever leaves unless he's got someone else on the go. It's a law of the universe.' She opens a cupboard and helps herself to a wine glass, pouring herself a large measure and topping mine up.

'No,' I say. 'Not David. He swore he'd be honest with me. He knows how I feel about stuff like that. Lying.'

'Mmm,' she says, unconvinced. She sits down next to me.

'He made this big deal about how he knew he had to be truthful with me, and how he would never just up and leave, because of what happened with my dad . . .' I've never talked to Stella about my dad, or anything personal, come to think of it. Her focus has always been firmly on herself. 'He left overnight with some other woman. Out of the blue. I never really saw him again after that.'

Stella puts her arm round me stiffly. 'I'm sorry. Maybe David thought he was being kind. Trying to spare you . . .'

'But he promised!' I howl. I know I sound ridiculous. Naïve.

'Why do you think it's not a recent thing? Maybe he was telling the truth and this happened later?'

'No. I know. I just do.' I wipe my eyes with the hem of my top. Stella gets up, goes into my bathroom and comes back with a wodge of toilet paper. I take it gratefully. Blow my nose. 'Thanks for coming over, by the way. Where does Al think you've gone?'

'I told him I was going up to the meditation room for an hour before bed.'

I let out a strangled half-laugh. 'You have a meditation room? A whole room just for meditating in?'

Stella shrugs. 'Doesn't everyone?'

And then I really start to laugh, and so does she, rasping like a rusty old saw.

'We also have a yoga room,' she says.

'A different room? You couldn't do yoga in the meditation room?'

'God, no,' Stella says. 'What would the neighbours think?'

I don't know if it's because I'm feeling so on edge anyway, but I can't stop laughing. And neither, it seems, can she. It's hysteria, I know it is, but it feels good. Cathartic.

'Does it matter?' she says, once we've finally calmed down. 'If he left you for someone else or just left? The end result is the same.'

'I feel stupid.'

'You're not the stupid one.' She divides the last of the wine between our two glasses, swigs hers back in one. 'I should go.'

We hug goodbye. It just happens, and I don't even hesitate. Stella's natural stiffness feels softer. Her shield has dropped.

'Get some sleep,' she says as she leaves.

Next day, cleaning the house where Ferne lives, while she looks after baby Andrei as we tackle the vast ground floor (cinema room: tick, gym: tick, walk-in humidor: tick), all I can think about is that I'm lying to Stella. I know who Al is leaving her for. I try to imagine finding out that David left me for someone else but not knowing her name. What she looks like. Stella knowing won't change anything, but it might make her feel more in control, less of a patsy. I know I'd be throwing Ferne to the lioness, but, nice as she seems, she's stolen someone else's husband out from under their nose. I owe it to Stella to be honest with her. I just have to get up the courage first.

34

'Don't do it,' Angie says. She's come back to mine with me for a glass of wine and pizza, and then Sunshine Cleaning is going to treat her to a cab home because she's just worked two ten-hour days on the trot, and she's worth it. 'What's the best that can happen? She'll make Ferne's life hell and you'll feel guilty.'

'I'm going to persuade her not to say anything. I'll reason with her that, if she does, Ferne'll tell Al and everything will blow up. He'd know she knew the wedding was off. She wouldn't get the revenge she wants. Or the money.'

Angie slides another slice of pizza on to her plate. 'You think she'd be that rational? It'll come back and bite you. Because if she goes off at Al, he's going to want to know how she found out.'

I know she's right, but I can't shake the feeling that Stella deserves to know the truth.

'Don't play God,' she says.

'I'm not. I'm just making sure she has all the pieces of the puzzle. I'm just thinking how I wish someone had told me.'

'What difference would it have made?'

I push the hair out of my eyes. 'Funnily enough, that's what Stella said.'

'See!' Angie says triumphantly.

I stack our plates up, carry them over to the sink. She starts to rinse them and I slap her hand away. 'Don't you dare.'

'Force of habit. If I didn't do it all at home, we'd be on one of those documentaries about hoarders in a week. Trapped in our flat by dirty dishes.'

'Those boys are never going to leave home,' I say indulgently. 'The point is, I shouldn't be keeping a secret from her.' I look over towards Stella's house. 'Oh, your cab's here.'

'I'm leaving,' she says, standing up and stretching her arms in the air. 'I'm going to fall asleep before I get home, I know it.'

'You're welcome to stay on the sofa.'

She looks at it. It's nowhere near big enough for an adult to stretch out on. 'I'll take my chances in the taxi. Thanks, though.'

We hug it out. 'Think about it,' she says, her face in my hair.

'I will,' I say. But I've already made up my mind.

I try not to grill Betsy when I pick her up on Wednesday afternoon, but I can't help myself. We're taking Cocoa for a walk, at her insistence. I was reluctant to call round at Eva and Rafa's, but Betsy happily flung herself at their front door, while I hung back, smiling apologetically. Eva was all smiles, her earlier attitude erased now that I'd been declared innocent. I wasn't buying it, though. If she could switch it off that easily, she could switch it back on again if an edict was issued. We can be friendly, but we're not friends. Not when her friendship is conditional on someone else's opinion.

'We'll keep him on the lead,' I called as Cocoa shuffled out of the front door, tail wagging.

She handed Betsy a well-loved tennis ball. 'No need, he won't go anywhere.'

Betsy puffs up to about three times her normal size with pride as she walks him along the street towards the woods. I snap a picture on my phone. Think about sending it to David, but then remember how angry I am with him. He doesn't deserve to see it.

'How's Zara?' I say to her, as casually as I can.

'OK,' she says. She unclips Cocoa's lead and watches him shamble off.

'Does Michaela ever bring them all with her when she comes in the evenings?' Who knows, maybe she's doing David a favour by babysitting them all at his place?

Betsy screws up her face. 'No. Just her.'

'Right. And Dad's always there?'

'Of course,' she says, throwing the ball in Cocoa's direction. It lands right by his feet. 'Good boy.'

'I think you're meant to throw it so he can run for it. And . . . um . . . is that a recent thing?'

'What?' she says, not making it easy for me.

'Michaela coming over.'

She throws the ball again, this time in the opposite direction from where Cocoa is sitting. He wanders off towards it. 'No.'

There's nothing else I can ask. Betsy would have no idea if Michaela used to visit the flat David briefly rented when he first left and was waiting for his purchase to go through – she was living with me during the week – or indeed whether he was already seeing her before we separated. She'll just get anxious if I keep asking questions.

I don't want to have to see him when I drop her off later, but I can hardly just leave her in the foyer. As I pull up outside, my anger starts to bubble up to the surface; my mouth fixes into a thin, tense line. I manage to smile at the concierge, who Betsy greets like he's her husband back from the long war. She fills the silence after he's phoned David to come down, chattering on about walking Cocoa while I focus on my breathing. In. Out. I don't want to cause a scene in front of my daughter and this portly stranger. The lift door opens. I can't look at him. I hug Betsy, remind her I'll see her on Friday.

'Everything OK?' he mouths over her head.

'Yep,' I manage, and then I turn and walk out before I can say any more.

By Thursday morning I've made up my mind. I tried to calm myself down last night by flicking through Tinder (fuck him, there are men who want me; even if we end up just meeting up for meaningless sex, that'd show David. Not that there's been any meaningless sex since he left. Or any sex at all, for that matter). Thankfully, I didn't strike up any conversations. Start any more relationships that I would regret immediately. Then I browsed Stella's latest eBay auctions: three men's watches, vintage cufflinks and a gold cigarette case – all Al's, I assume. Stella must have quite a healthy bank balance by now – certainly a lot more robust than mine has ever been – but still not enough if he isn't going to provide them with a home. I started wondering if Ferne had any idea that her knight in shining armour was planning to leave his family with nothing, maybe not even a roof over their head. Would she be as starry-eyed if she did? Or maybe she was encouraging him. All the more for her.

I see Stella heading off with Taylor and Amber on the school run, stacking the boot with brown-paper-wrapped parcels bound, I assume, for the post office, only just stopping myself from calling down to ask her if she knows where it is, and what to do when she gets there, although I've talked her through it at length ('Take a ticket from the machine and then wait till your number's up.' 'What number?' 'The number on the ticket.' Sometimes I swear she's doing it to wind me up. I said to her, 'What do you do when you need to send someone a birthday present or something?' and she gave me that blank, confused look and said, 'Pilar,' as if that would explain everything, which, I suppose, it did). I hang the red tea towel. She'll see it whenever she gets home. I need to do this before I talk myself out of it. She trusts me enough to listen to my advice now, I'm sure of it. If I tell her not to go straight round to Ferne and accuse her, she'll understand why that makes sense.

I try to do the rotas while I wait, but my mind keeps racing. It's impossible to concentrate, so I snatch the tea towel down again and take myself for a stomp through the woods to use up some of my nervous energy. Up ahead, I see Katya stretching out before or after a run, so I change direction and head down a different path.

Thirty-five minutes later Stella's car is back in her driveway and my distress signal is back in place. I run into the bathroom for a quick shower. My bravado is dwindling by the second, trickling down the plughole with the soapy water. I decide that I'll give Stella fifteen minutes after I get out and, if she hasn't shown up by then, I'll rethink.

Fourteen and a half minutes later I hear footsteps on the stairs. My heart starts pounding and I rehearse in my head what I'm going to say.

'What?' she says as soon as I open the door. 'Are you OK?' I'm touched by the fact that she came so quickly, thinking it might be about me again.

'Yes. I mean fucked off, angry and disappointed. But, yes. I'm fine. I have to tell you something.'

Here's where I'm going to massage the truth. For all my insistence on honesty, I can't bring myself to confess to Stella that I've known who F is all this time and I haven't told her.

'Sit down,' I say.

'You're frightening me now,' she says, doing as I tell her. I sit next to her.

'Before I tell you, I want you to promise me that you won't do anything rash . . .'

She looks at me. 'What? Jesus. Yes, OK. Just tell me.'

'Promise.'

'I promise. Whatever it is, tell me, Laura.'

I take a deep breath. Way too deep. I start to cough. Stella sits there, looking torn between concern and irritation. Eventually, I get myself under control. 'I think I know who Al is seeing.' I wait for her to ask how I found out, so I can give my practised speech about finding a photo of the two of them together when I cleaned her room in Sergei and Katherine's house, but she goes straight in for the jugular.

'Who?'

'She's called Ferne. She's the nanny at number 1 . . .'

Stella cuts me off. 'Number 1 here? The Close? He's seeing some tart who lives right on our doorstep?'

I nod, even while I'm flinching at the harshness of the word. Stella is incandescent. 'A fucking nanny? The hired help is going to steal money away from my children?'

'Stella,' I say sternly. 'Al's the one who's responsible for that.'

'But she knows about them, right? If she lives here, she must see us every day. It's not like he can have told her he's separated or glossed over the fact that he has two daughters.'

I sigh. She's right. Pleasant as Ferne seems, she can hardly claim innocence in this. 'That's true. I hadn't thought of it like that.'

'How old is she?'

I knew she would fixate on this. 'I don't know. You've probably seen her around with the baby. Late twenties?'

Lucky for me, she doesn't seem to remember her being here. In my flat. She lets out a sob. 'Why this one? What's she got over all the others?'

I put an arm around her bony shoulders. 'I don't know. It might just be timing. How many have there been?'

'Three that I know about. It's anyone's guess. But not like this. Not planning to set up home with them.'

'I'm sorry, Stella. I really am.' She leans into me, cries on my shoulder. I find myself stroking the thick, glossy hair. My heart goes out to her. No one deserves this.

'I won't say anything,' she says finally. 'I wouldn't want to drop you in it.'

'Thanks,' I say.

'You're a good friend, Laura,' she mutters into my arm-pit. I almost laugh. If you'd asked me a couple of months ago who would be the least likely person in the world ever to say these words to me . . . But, actually, I'm touched. 'And I don't have many good friends.'

'Well, that's not true, for a start,' I say. 'They all love you round here.'

'They love what they think I am.'

It's the most perceptive thing I've ever heard her say.

'I'm sure they'll still be here for you.' I'm not convinced that's true, even as I say it.

I feel rather than see her shake her head. 'I doubt it. What will we talk about? What's on three for two at Lidl?'

'Don't be a snob,' I say gently.

'I'm not. I'm saying they will be.'

'Not Gail.'

'No, maybe not Gail. But when are our paths ever going to cross?'

We sit there quietly for a second, and then I have an idea. I ease her head off my shoulder and jump up. 'Come on.' I put out a hand to pull her to her feet.

'What? Where are we going?'

'Three-for-two shopping,' I say triumphantly. 'We can go to the big Sainsbury's on Finchley Road; they have a car park. I'll tell you what your budget is and you have to buy enough food for the family for the whole week. I'll show you how exciting three-for-twos can be.'

'No, Laura,' she says petulantly. 'I appreciate the offer, but . . .'

'But what? It's better than sitting round here moping. You may as well learn how us plebs survive.'

She rasps a laugh. 'All right. I give in. Let me get changed first.'

'No. Rule number one: no one gets dressed up to go food shopping. You look fine. We'll take my car.'

She gives me a look. Opens her mouth to say something. I interrupt. 'What? The Sunshine Cleaning mobile not good enough for you?'

'I was going to say mine's bigger. We can fit more in.'

'Nice try,' I say, laughing. I grab up my keys. 'Let's go.'

Taking Stella to the supermarket is a bit like I imagine it would be to take the queen to bingo. They know why they're there, they understand the principle, but they have no idea what to do. I'm sure Stella must have wafted round the food halls at Harrods or Fortnum's before, picking up an artichoke here or a jar of truffle butter there, but a real-life, no-nonsense, basic food shop, never. Thank goodness I eased her in gently and didn't go straight for Aldi. It would have blown her mind. She's overwhelmed by the choice, gravitating to the most expensive version of whatever is on the list I forced her to make while we were in the car. I add up all her choices on my phone as we go along so I can show her how much more they would have cost than the things we actually buy once we get to the checkout. I probably should have consulted Pilar first, and I hope she's not upset with me for the slightly random ingredients she's about to be presented with. As with all my trips to the supermarket, the list goes out of the window as soon as I see what's on special offer. Stella starts off bemused and defensive, but after a few minutes I'm having to talk her down from buying eight aubergines because they're flogging them off at two bags of four for the price of one.

'You'd have to use them all by tomorrow. They're on the verge of going off.'

'I can freeze them,' she says confidently.

I resist the urge to say, *Do you even know where the freezer is?* 'You'd have to make something out of them first. You can't just stick them in whole.'

She looks at me, clueless. 'Like what?'

'I don't know. What were you going to make with them tonight?'

'How do I know? Pilar would come up with something.'

'But we might not have bought whatever else she needs to go with them. And then, by the time you do, they will have gone off. Planning is everything.'

She rolls her eyes at me. 'I thought you wanted me to buy bargains.'

'Only if you know what you're going to do with them. Otherwise, you'll end up throwing them a—'

I stop talking as Stella gasps and clutches my arm. I glance over to where she's looking as she ducks behind a fresh-bread display. 'What? What are you doing?'

'It's Bill and Anya's housekeeper.'

I look back and there's a vaguely familiar-looking woman pushing a trolley. 'Oh yes.' I smile and wave. She waves back. 'Why are you hiding?'

'She can't see me here. What will she think?'

'That you're buying food for your family? Come out. What are you doing?'

She shakes her head violently.

'You're being ludicrous,' I say. I look over, and the woman – I don't know her name – is moving closer.

'Stella, look!' I raise my voice. 'They have sea-salt-and-rosemary focaccia!' I pick it up and wave it at her. Bill and Anya's housekeeper looks over. Smiles vaguely at Stella and moves on. Stella grabs the bread out of my hand and flings it in the trolley. 'For god's sake. Now she's going to tell all the other housekeepers that I do my own food shopping.'

I pull a mock-horrified face. 'No! Oh my god, Stella! How will you ever show your face again? Next thing you know, they'll think you have to wipe your own arse too. Stop being so ridiculous.' I snatch the focaccia out of her trolley. 'Oh, and you can't afford that. Way too expensive.'

I wait for her to throw a tantrum but instead she cracks a painful-looking smile. 'You're right, I am ridiculous.'

'Fucking ridiculous,' I say, laughing with relief.

She honks a laugh. 'Ludicrous. I'm a fool.'

'Yes,' I say. 'Yes, you are.'

Her laughter subsides. 'I really am, though, aren't I?'

'No,' I say, trying to sound convincing. 'At least, you were, but you're becoming less so by the day.'

'Well, that's something.'

I put a hand out and rub her upper arm. 'I think of you like someone who's been brought up by wolves. You just need to learn how the real world works.'

'I appreciate what you're doing for me, Laura. I really do.'

'No problem,' I say. 'That's what friends are for.'

Because that's what we are now, I think. Friends. We trust each other.

35

My flat purchase seems to be sailing through alarmingly smoothly, leaving me little reason to panic and pull out. I push it to the back of my mind, only thinking about it when my solicitor needs me to. Keeping my head firmly stuck in the sand. But when we agree a date to exchange in a couple of weeks' time I realize I need to be grown up about this and at least go and visit it a second time before it's too late. I arm myself with a tape measure, a pad and pencil and a list of questions. Rahina meets me at the front gate, a big smile on her face.

'Ready?' she says, waving the keys at me.

'As I'll ever be.' I look round at the street. It's even rougher than I remember. Bins overflow with rubbish bags. A young man is hunched over in a shop doorway, out cold. Maybe I've become rarefied, living in my miniature ivory tower. I've lost touch with my reality. Inside, the stench has got worse, if anything. Weeks of no one opening any doors or windows. I hold my breath for as long as I can and take photos. I don't bother taking any measurements because that would mean getting up close and personal with the furniture, and god knows what's living in there.

'They are going to take everything away when they leave, aren't they?' I knew I should have been paying more attention.

Rahina smiles behind the hand she's using to cover her mouth. 'They are. They're going to get a house-clearance firm in to take everything. Carpets, curtains, the lot.'

'Thank god.' I'm struggling to believe that, in eight weeks or so, this will be mine. I push all thoughts of The Close, with its silence and the smell of the woods and the heath in the air, out of my mind, remind myself why I'm doing this. This area is Betsy's home; it used to be mine. We were happy here. I force myself to think about her playing happy families with David and Michaela. 'I don't think I need to see anything else at the moment,' I say. We've only been here for ten minutes. I need to get out.

I've timed my visit to coincide with my workers starting for the night, and I feel as if I've been neglecting them lately, so when I leave I pop into the four-storey, four-company offices and check up on Paul, Amita and Maggie there before heading round to AJT Music and finding Angie on the top floor, wiping down the kitchen surfaces. She gives me a hug, holding her rubber-gloved hands away from me as she does so.

'Everything OK?' I say, trying to feign an interest in work for a minute.

'All good.' She flicks the kettle on. I fill her in on everything: the flat, Michaela, the fact that I think me and Stella are friends now. She's a mime of exaggerated expressions. Sympathy, incredulity, scepticism. She offers up her opinions (remember why you're buying it, you and Betsy need a home; you've got absolutely no proof it was going on while you and David were still together, so don't torture yourself; fuck me, really?) and lets me get it all off my chest, which is what I need, really.

'Did you look in his drawer lately?' She knows what I mean immediately. Al's locked drawer, where he keeps all his personal documents. She shakes her head.

'Shall we do it?'

I nod. 'Not that I'm expecting to find anything, but I wouldn't want to miss it if he's up to anything else.'

'Wouldn't want to let your new best friend down,' Angie says with an exaggerated smirk. She's teasing me. I know she's not being snarky. I've started walking towards the offices when I hear the lift ping. I stop in my tracks, just in case, and Angie bumps into me from behind. I turn round to look at her just in time to see Al stride out into the corridor. My heart stops, starts, thumps so hard I feel as if you could see it through my chest. I prepare myself to say hello, but he doesn't even look at us, just walks through to the main office. Jesus. That was close. I grab Angie's arm, flick my head towards the kitchen. We – or at least I – can hide in there till he goes. He knows I own the company that cleans here, obviously, but I don't want to remind him of the fact that I have unfettered access to his office after hours. I can't even bear to think what might have happened if he'd arrived two minutes later. I feel almost light-headed with relief when I hear 'Laura? I thought that was you I saw out of the corner of my eye.'

It's him. He's turned back and he's heading towards me. I force a smile. 'Hi! How are you?'

'Good,' he says. Without Stella to witness it, he's lost the flirty tone. He just sounds friendly. 'Operating on the coal face tonight?'

'Something like that,' I say, trying to keep the nervous stammer out of my voice. 'Just checking everything's OK.'

'I like that you have that personal touch,' he says.

'You're working late.' I try not to sound as if I care.

'Forgot my phone,' he says. 'Actually, I need to run. I'm late for a dinner. Nice to see you.'

'You too,' I say, but he's already on his way to his office. I look round for Angie, but she's retreated to the kitchen. I go and stand in the doorway, waiting to see him leave again, eyebrows raised at her to let her know the danger's not over. Thirty seconds later, he's back, stuffing his phone into his jacket pocket.

'Nice to see you,' he says, galloping down the stairs.

'And you,' I say insincerely. 'Jesus,' I say to Ange once he's out of sight. 'Fuck.'

Angie keeps watch while I locate the key to Al's desk drawer. Neither of us is joking about now; we both know only too well that we're taking a big risk. It's obvious pretty quickly that there's nothing new there. I find the other key and check the metal box.

'Nothing,' I say. 'Which, I guess, is a good thing.'

Feeling slightly deflated, I lock the box and then the drawer. The smaller key escapes my hand and disappears under the desk before I can catch it. 'Damn.'

I look, but I can't see it. 'Keep watch.'

'No shit, Sherlock,' Angie says.

I crawl under. It must have found its way into the tiny gap beneath the drawers. 'Fuck's sake,' I say huffily. I roll on to my side and try to force my fingers underneath. I feel something hard. 'Got it.' I scrabble it out, then, turning on to my back, I start to scootle out from my hiding place, leaning back so I don't hit my head. A glint of metal catches my eye as I do. There's a key Sellotaped to the underside of the middle drawer. 'Ange!' I say urgently.

'What?'

'There's something . . .' I go to grab it then realize I need to do this carefully. I gently pick at one side of the tape until it releases, leaving the other end attached. Then I peel the key off it. I need to make sure it goes back in exactly the same place. It's an old key. Small. I clamber out and look around the room.

'Look!' I say in a stage whisper. I wave the key at her.

'What the fuck?' she mouths.

We both look round the room as if something we've missed will suddenly jump out at us. Apart from the desk and the bookcase, there's a small two-seater sofa with an ornate, solid wooden table at one end topped with a lamp and a few bits and pieces – a cactus in a pot, a little action figure and a bowl with several carved silver balls inside – another in a corner by the window with some kind of sculpture on top, and that's it. I check through the drawers again, just in case I've missed another lockable box, but there's nothing.

Angie takes the key off me. Turns it over and studies it. 'Maybe it's for something at his house?'

I take it back. 'No. Why would he have gone to all the trouble to hide it under the desk? It's not as if anyone here is likely to have access to his home. It must be here somewhere.'

'It's not like there's many options,' she says.

We both stare vacantly at the space, willing a secret panel to reveal itself. Angie suddenly strides across to the little table by the window and pulls it away from the wall, peering behind it. Taking my cue from her, I move to the one beside the sofa.

'Nothing,' she says, just as I pull mine out and spot a cubby hole with a drawer underneath at the back.

'Look! He's put it facing the wrong way so you can't see the drawer.' I spin the whole thing round and scrabble the key into the lock. It fits. 'Jesus Christ. Keep an eye out.' Angie moves to stand in the doorway, flicking quick little looks between me and the main office. I open the drawer. There's an envelope. A large white one with 'Strictly Private and Confidential. To be opened by recipient only' written on it. And underneath it, a thin cardboard file.

'Look,' I say, holding it up for Angie to see.

'That's the one I saw on his desk.' I put the file aside for now, open the envelope, pull out a sheaf of paper, look at the top sheet, look up at Angie.

'What the fuck?'

36

It's a letter from a private medical facility. I have to read it three times to take in what it says. It's dry. Factual. Confirming that Miss Taylor Thornbury and Miss Amber Thornbury cannot be the children of Mr Alec Thornbury, although they do share the same mother and father. It doesn't say what was provided for them to reach this conclusion but on the sheets below are incomprehensible figures and medical speak.

'I don't . . .' I say, handing the letter over to Angie.

She scans the letter. 'Jesus Christ. I take it you didn't know about this?'

'Of course not. What does it even mean?'

'Well, that Al isn't the girls' father –'

'I know that,' I interrupt. 'But . . . I mean . . . who is?'

'Fuck knows. The same person, according to this.'

I flop down on the sofa. I can't take it in. 'Why didn't she tell me? What's in the file?'

She reaches in and pulls it out. Looks inside. 'Same. Different lab. He must have had it done twice, just to be sure.'

'What's the date on that one?'

'January twenty-first, 2019.'

Only a few weeks before I moved to The Close. 'So that must be when he decided to move out. Why he's being so cruel.'

'You kind of can't blame him,' Angie hands me back the letter and I snap a photo of it before putting it back in the file. 'I mean, it looks as if this was all news to him. Although he must have suspected something to have got the tests done in the first place.'

'She's been lying to me . . .'

Angie puts the letter back in the envelope and replaces it in the drawer with the file.

'So . . . what?' I say. 'She had an affair? For more than two years, apparently, since they have the same father.'

'I guess so. How did she think he would never find out? I mean, why take that risk? You'd better put this back.' She hands me the key and I get up and crawl back under the desk, replacing it exactly where I found it.

I'm starting to get angry. 'All that stuff about him stealing his daughters' inheritance. All her fucking self-righteous "how could he do this to me?" bullshit.'

'They kind of are his daughters, though,' Angie says, playing devil's advocate. 'He's been their dad their whole lives . . .'

'But under false pretences. I know it's not fair on them, because none of this is their fault, but it does kind of explain everything.'

Angie thinks for a second. 'So Ferne isn't so much the love of his life as the bit on the side he happened to have when he found all this out. Timing is everything.'

'I wonder if she knows,' I say, straightening the small table. 'She mentioned he had kids and she didn't imply there was any complication, but then she hardly knows me.'

Angie leans over and tweaks it by a millimetre. 'I imagine he wants her to believe she's the love of his life, not that she was just in the right place at the right time. Or the wrong time. You know what I mean.'

'He's still a bastard, let's not forget . . .'

'They're all as bad as each other, if you ask me,' she says. 'I told you you should never have got mixed up in this.'

I have to stop myself storming straight over to Stella's when I get back, despite the fact there's no blue bra giving me the all-clear. Angie's advice was to just back off, leave her to sort out her own mess, but I've worked myself up into a state of righteous indignation on the way home. She had me feeling so sorry for her. Thinking she was misunderstood and that we were friends. Helping her basically steal stuff from Al because she had me convinced that he was one hundred per cent in the wrong. Around Swiss Cottage, I had a heart-stopping panic that I may have done something criminal, aiding and abetting by helping her sell his belongings on eBay. Does setting up a PayPal account to knowingly siphon money from someone's bank count as a crime? Definitely, I would say.

Gail saves me from myself by popping her head out of the front door as I walk past and asking if I have five minutes. I'm tired and grumpy, but I don't want to appear rude so I follow her into the kitchen and she's opening a bottle of wine before I can protest. Not that I would. I'd drink the whole thing at the moment if she'd let me.

'I wanted to ask you a favour,' she says, handing me a large glass of white. 'I'm trying to pick my dress for the wedding of the century and I'm having trouble choosing.

I ordered four from Net-a-Porter and now my head's spinning and I don't know which one I should keep, if any. Can I give you a fashion show?'

Oh god. I keep forgetting that no one else knows any of what's going on with Stella and Al. It suddenly strikes me how incredibly selfish it is that they're letting everyone spend fortunes on outfits they don't even want and they'll end up never wearing. It doesn't matter that they can afford it. Well, it does a bit, but it's the principle.

'Of course.'

She goes off and I hear rustling coming from another room. There's no sign of Ben, so I assume he's away for work again. I sip my wine and wait, my eyelids drooping. Finally, I hear heels clip-clopping across the floor.

'Blimey.'

Gail is in a kind of frilly, floaty get-up with a ruffle at the neck. I can't even describe it properly. 'You have great legs,' I say, because she does and I can't think of anything positive to say about the outfit.

'This is my least favourite,' she says eventually. 'I don't know why I'm even showing it to you, really.'

'OK. Good. Yes, it's awful. Is it expensive?'

She names a price that's more than my company would charge for six people spending two twelve-hour days cleaning your house. My eyes start to water. 'And the shoes are practically the same again.' I hadn't even noticed the shoes, but they're lovely. Nude. Open-toed. Achingly high with a small platform. Red soles, of course.

'The shoes are gorgeous,' I say, figuring she could wear them anywhere and with anything. That needs to be my tack, I decide. Helping her pick something that's flattering but that she can wear to something other than the wedding that never will be.

'I'm getting them whatever,' she says, already unzipping the dress.

We go through the process three more times. Number two looks fabulous on her, but I struggle to imagine it anywhere other than at a multimillion-pound outdoor wedding, and it will almost certainly be out of style by next summer. Three is my favourite. The most understated. It shows off her stunning figure and it wouldn't look over the top at a garden party. Four is nice, but it doesn't really suit her, and it's a bit OTT on the design front. I'm sure it's the height of fashion, but it looks as if the designer threw in every idea they'd ever had and then added a few more. I don't even ask the prices after number one. I don't want to know.

'Definitely number three,' I say, once she's back in her normal clothes. 'Do you have to get it now, though? There's still more than two months to go.'

'One less thing to think about,' she says, and I decide not to push the point.

'Well, it looks amazing, so you'll get a lot of wear out of it.' I'm pretty sure that, unlike Stella, Gail won't have a 'wear it once and bin it' policy. And she'd at least have the good grace to donate it to a charity shop if she did.

'Exactly,' she says, proving me right. 'Good, that's settled, then.'

'Is there anything you want to tell me?' I'm giving away how angry I am, even though I told myself I wouldn't. First thing this morning, after a restless, sleepless night, I hung the red tea towel in the window and paced around as I waited. Stella arrived, all smiles, brandishing a Pyrex dish containing a large portion of moussaka.

'I made it with Pilar yesterday,' she said, holding it out proudly. 'I thought you and Betsy could have it tonight.' It was such a sweet gesture that I almost forgot why I'd summoned her over with such urgency. 'You have to heat it on one hundred and eighty degrees centigrade for twenty minutes,' she parroted. I was surprised it didn't come out in Pilar's thick accent. 'Al and the girls loved it,' she added, probably confused about why she wasn't getting the reaction she'd expected. Any other day, I'd be dying to ask her what Pilar made of her sudden desire to cook, but now is not the time.

Now she stands there, open-mouthed. 'What? What are you talking about?'

'Anything?' I say. 'Maybe something that slipped your mind, that might have made me think twice about helping you?'

She puts the dish down warily. 'You're worrying me, Laura. What have I done?'

'Just be fucking honest with me,' I snap.

'I'm going to leave now. I was just trying to play along with your silly attempts to force me to cook, but obviously you've got out of bed the wrong side . . .'

'I know, Stella. I know about Taylor and Amber . . .'

'What about them?' she says haughtily, but there's the trace of a nervous twitch around her mouth.

'And so does Al.'

She gasps in a breath. A hand flutters to her neck. Now I've got her. 'What are you talking about?'

'You tell me.' I don't know why I don't just come out and say it, but I want to hear it from her.

'Laura, please. Whatever you think you know, just tell me. I can't . . .'

I pick up my mobile, scroll through my photos. Find the one with the most recent letter on. I hand it to her. Watch as she expands the text. She sinks down on to the sofa, all the colour drained from her face.

'Well?'

'Well, what? You know everything now.'

'Hardly,' I snap. 'Ordinarily, I'd think this was none of my business, but you've made it my business, so I figure I deserve an explanation.'

She looks at the picture again. 'I don't understand. If he's only just found out . . .'

I grab the phone out of her hand, scroll forward, wave the screen at her. 'Here. That letter was the second test. He had one done in January too.'

She stops my hand and looks closely. 'No . . .'

'Yes. So is this why you wouldn't see a solicitor? Because you thought if you fought him he might bring out the big guns and find out about this?'

She nods. 'If he's found out already, it explains everything. Why he's leaving. Why he's being so mean . . .'

'I'll be honest, I don't blame him.' I'm being too harsh, I know I am. But I can't help myself. I feel stupid. Taken in. Played.

'He's their father,' she says. 'He always has been.'

'And what does the man you had an affair with think of that? Can't he provide for them? Or is he not rich enough for you?'

'You know nothing about it,' she says, the steely look returning.

'I know I don't, because you haven't told me! Instead you laid it on thick about how Al was trying to ruin his daughters' lives and how devastated you were!'

We sit there in angry silence for a moment. A stand-off. I can hear the birds singing outside, and the sound of Eva's voice calling Cocoa to heel. Finally, Stella speaks. 'No one knows,' she hisses. 'No one.'

'Except for Al now.'

She shakes her head. 'He's never even taken the girls to the doctors'. Why would he even suspect?'

I think of Taylor and her sister, how like Stella they look. The Mini Mes. Stella's genes must be strong. Now I come to think of it, neither of them do look much like Al, apart from the fact they're both tall for their age, and dark. But so is Stella. Well, not tall for her age, but you know what I mean. I can't help thinking of the Oscar Wilde quote: 'To have one kid by someone other than your husband may be regarded as a misfortune, to have two looks like carelessness.' Or something along those lines. 'So, who's . . .' I break off as Stella gives me a look that could freeze vodka. 'Sorry, none of my business.'

No wonder Stella is so suspicious of any woman who comes within a mile of him: she's projecting her own past behaviour. Don't they say that the people who are most insecure about their partner's fidelity are the ones who have strayed themselves? Because they understand the impulse. I have a million questions I want to ask. Mainly about the paternity of the Mini Mes. Does their real father know about them? Was she still seeing him right through her first pregnancy and Taylor's birth, and then he hung around and got her pregnant again? It's mind-boggling.

It's as if Stella can read my mind. She glares at me. 'I didn't have an affair, if that's what you're thinking.'

Now I'm really confused. 'Of course not. Virgin birth. You're right, it's none of my business . . .' I say self-righteously, even though I'm dying to know.

'It was an anonymous arrangement. Al and I were desperate to have children, but we were having difficulties. I was fine, but his count was . . . low. I went to an agency. Found a donor who looked like him . . . we didn't have sex.'

I stand there, mouth open. 'And they did it without ever talking to your partner?'

She gives me a tight smile. 'Money comes in handy sometimes.'

'He didn't wonder what you'd spent it on?' I have no idea how much she might be talking, but I imagine it was significant, and Al definitely seems to be in charge of the finances in their house.

'I told him I was going to a clinic where they did things that maximized a woman's chances of getting pregnant. Luckily, he's so squeamish about that kind of thing he didn't ask for details. And, in a way, it was true.'

Shit. 'Wow . . . and you've never worried he might find out. Like, if one of them was ill or something . . . ?'

'Of course I have,' she snaps. 'But it was worth it to get my girls, and I figured he'd get over it eventually. I did it for both of us. It's not as if I cheated on him. It's not as if every time he looked at them he'd be seeing the face of my lover. I don't even know who the man is.'

There's a twisted kind of logic in what she's saying. Not that I think I could ever take the risk of living with that unexploded bomb in my house myself. 'So they do have the same father?'

'Same donor, yes.'

I stretch my back. It's aching from standing up for so long. 'Jesus Christ.

'He'll use it against me. Especially if he's looking for ways to screw me over so he can run off into the sunset with that bitch.'

I'd almost forgotten about Ferne, I was so engrossed in Stella's bombshell. She's right. Where once Al might have reasoned that Stella did what she did for both of them, that they have their girls, who were desperately wanted, now he probably just sees it as an excuse to cut off support. And he'll get away with it too. I'm sure a court would argue that he mustn't leave the girls to the wolves, but I doubt they'd listen to Stella insisting that he needs to keep them in the extravagant style to which they've become accustomed either.

'You're screwed,' I say helpfully.

'Please don't give up on me.' A tear plops out of the corner of her eye and lands on her smooth, plumped-up cheek. I feel awful, but I know I have to stand my ground. There is no black and white any more. No clear-cut right and wrong.

'I'm not judging you. I know you thought you were doing the right thing. But I can't help you any more, I'm sorry.'

Stella stands up. She flares her nostrils. Pouts her lips.

Tosses her mane. In a flash, the frosty expression that she always used to use with me is back.

'Fine. If that's how you want to be . . .'

'Stella . . .' I say, although I'm not sure what I want to say next. She's not listening anyway. She swoops up the Pyrex dish and storms out without looking back.

37

I try to bury myself in work. Spring-clean season is more or less over, but I go into overdrive pursuing new contracts, chasing any I have already pitched for. Nothing. It's a competitive market. Any old idiot can buy a can of Pledge and call themselves a cleaning firm these days, it seems. I chip away at my potential profits, going lower and lower until I would practically be paying for the privilege if anyone took me up on my offer, but still no results.

Half-term is here and, with it, the promise of a week with Betsy. I've managed to come up with strategies to avoid her calling on Amber thus far since my falling-out with Stella, but a whole week seems insurmountable until I remember that Stella once told me they always go to France in the May break. The prospect of a whole seven days without worrying about bumping into either her or Al feels like a holiday in itself. Who needs the beach? In the end, they leave on the Friday morning, clearly deciding taking the girls out of school is worth it to beat the rush. I breathe out as they drive off, the car weighed down by their Louis Vuitton luggage, and it feels as if it's the first time I've truly let go in days.

Michaela is waiting for Zara when I get to the school. I've avoided her since Betsy let slip about her and David. It's such a surprise when I see her that I don't know how to arrange my face. She greets me warmly, exactly like she always has. I bristle. There's so much I want to ask her, but this is not the place. And I don't want to be like Stella, assuming guilt before I've actually seen proof. She must pick up on a change in the atmosphere. My pheromones aren't as obliging as my face. 'Everything OK?'

'Sure,' I say unconvincingly. 'I'm just in a bit of a rush. I need to dash off as soon as she comes out.'

We stand there in silence for a second and then I can't help myself. 'Going anywhere for half-term?'

Michaela smiles like the cat that got the cream. My cream. 'The kids are going on holiday with their cousins so, no. I'm having a blissful week of doing nothing.'

Except my ex-husband, I think but, thankfully, don't say.

Betsy comes flying out of the door with Zara in tow. She throws herself into my arms then hugs Michaela with the same intensity. Koala Baby strikes again. I look away.

On Monday morning I'm getting a picnic lunch ready for us to take to the park because it's a beautiful day and Betsy wants to spend it watching the outdoor trapeze school. She lives in hope that someone will fall off and break something so she'll get to see paramedics in action. Something catches my eye and I glance over at Stella's house as a car pulls into the drive. I watch as a man in a suit gets out. He lets himself in, silences the alarm and then I see the electronic shutters go up on all the ground-floor windows. Of course, an estate agent. He must be doing the viewings today. Pilar followed the family to France on Saturday, after giving the house a thorough clean, no doubt. Stella is safely out of the way. Even though this is nothing to do with me any more, I snap a photo on my phone, wishing I could spend the day watching. Ten minutes later, while Betsy is fussing around, trying to decide what to take in her little backpack, I see the first potential buyers pull up in a Rolls-Royce. Three people get out – a couple (him: forties, dark suit, large watch, her: twenties, big hair, fishy pout) and a normal-looking woman in her thirties, probably some kind of property finder – and look around, sizing up the street. I'm hit with the urge to run outside and start making a show of myself somehow to put them off. I wonder what Al is intending to tell the neighbours if any of them spots the stream of strangers and asks what was going on. Maybe he's hoping they'll have forgotten by the time they get back.

The estate agent comes out to greet them and ushers them into the house. I'm sure he's under strict instructions to be discreet. I watch as they go inside, shutting the front door. They're still there by the time we finally get our act together and set off.

Later, once we're back home, sleepy from the sun and fresh air – two students fell from their trapezes and into the netting, which, to Betsy's disgust, held up, so no injuries – I peer out of the front window while Betsy crashes out on the bed. The estate agent's car is still there, and there's another next to it. A gold-coloured Bentley or Mercedes. I take more photos. I think about Stella and Al on their holiday, presenting a glamorous united front to everyone they meet, the resentments and deceptions simmering just under the surface. I'd be terrified I'd have one glass of wine too many and blurt it all out. Or maybe they've had a civilized conversation after the girls have gone to bed one night, discussed their issues like adults. Fat chance.

After another ten minutes or so the prospective buyers exit the front door. They're the spitting image of the earlier couple: he's a good fifteen years older than her; plastic surgeons have run amok with both their faces. I take pictures. The Close is deserted. There's no one but me to see them leave.

The agent hangs around, so he's obviously expecting another viewer. I'm struck with a ridiculous thought. I run into the bedroom – Betsy is still passed out on the bed, Bruno snuggled under one arm. I pull out my one good dress and heels, untie my hair and shake it down. I prod Betsy awake. She peers at me, sleepy-eyed. 'Why are you all dressed up?'

'I just have to pop over the road for a sec.'

'Will Amber be there?' she says, sitting up.

'They're in France, remember. They have someone looking after their house and I have to talk to him quickly.' She looks confused, as well she might. 'I'll be two minutes, tops. You can watch me out of the front window.' I don't really like leaving her alone, but she'll be able to see me the whole time. I have no intention of going inside.

'Do you like him? The man who's looking after their house. Is that why you're wearing that . . . ?'

'No. I don't even know him. It's a long story. Do you want to come with me?'

She shakes her head. Yawns.

'Two minutes, OK? Shout if you need me. I'll hear you.' Parent of the year, right there.

She nods and follows me out to the steps. Sits on the top one, Bruno still under her arm.

I don't want the agent to see which house I came from, so I wait until he wanders inside, leaving the door open, and I'm over there, ringing the bell, looking back over my shoulder to see Betsy watching on. He looks a bit confused when he sees me standing there, checks his watch.

'Ms . . . ?'

I tell myself to project confidence. You are rich enough to afford a house like this.

'Hello.' I extend my hand, which he shakes limply. His palm is sweaty. A blob of white shaving cream clings to the underside of his pimply pink chin. On close look, he's only about twenty-five. He looks like a rabbit caught in the headlights. 'I don't have an appointment. I already live on The Close . . .' I wave my hand in the direction of the woods. 'And Alec – Mr Thornbury – mentioned they were selling up just before they left for France. I've always loved their house. I . . . we . . . my husband and I . . . have often said we'd snap it up if it ever came on the market . . . it's on at . . . what?' I wrack my brain for what the letter said. 'Ten?'

I leave it hanging. He probably thinks I'm a nosy neighbour, but he won't want to lose any opportunity.

'Tim Sergeant. I have appointments all day, but I could slot you on to the end . . .' he says hopefully.

'Oh, it's OK. I know the house inside out. I particularly love the yoga and meditation rooms. And the art! They have such wonderful art, although, of course, that won't be staying. I just wondered if you could confirm the price.'

'Ten point five,' he says casually, as if he doesn't

actually think he could work his whole lifetime and never be able to afford it himself. Him and me both. Three lifetimes.

'Million?' I say, then curse myself. As opposed to what? Billion? Ten pounds fifty? It's a higher price than they'd originally agreed. 'That's actually very reasonable. It's what? Seven thousand square feet?'

'Six two.' Tim Sergeant says. 'Could I take your details?'

'Oh. Sorry, I didn't introduce myself. 'Jan . . .' I realize I've forgotten her and Roman's surname. 'Abramovich. I live at number 4 . . .'

He asks for my number, so I make something up, and then I ask him for his card.

'Let me speak to my husband,' I say. 'But we're very interested . . .'

'I've been asked by Mr Thornbury to keep the sale discreet . . .' he says nervously as I make to leave.

'Of course. Don't worry. Not a word, not even to Mrs Thornbury.'

I'm saved by another car pulling into the drive. Another couple who would look right at home here climb out languidly. She's about seven feet tall and one inch wide, he's older (*quelle surprise*), short, squat and hirsute. They both drip gold like Mr T. on a night out. I smile a hello then turn right out of the gate, as if I'm heading to number 4, raising an eyebrow at Betsy as I go. She watches, confused, but thankfully silent. I wait for them all to go inside before I sneak home. I write '10.5' on the back of Tim Sergeant's card and pat myself on the back for a good bit of detective work. Then I put the card in a drawer; no idea what to do with the information.

38

Gail and Ben are having a last-minute garden party. 'Now that everyone's friends again, and the weather's so beautiful,' Gail says when she pops up to invite me and Betsy. She's slightly behind the curve, as ever, but I don't disabuse her. Stella and Al are expected back on Friday, she tells me, so she's hoping they'll come along, and everyone from The Close is invited, as well as a few families from neighbouring – equally posh – streets.

'Lovely,' I say, because what else is there to say?

I offer mine and Betsy's services on the day, and she accepts gracefully. We've had a quiet half-term, just the two of us and the occasional walk with Cocoa. Without Stella and Al around, everyone seems more relaxed, less aware of how their everyday actions will be judged. No one else seems to have noticed Monday's stream of house hunters or, if they did, they don't mention it. On Wednesday I watched as the gold-Bentley couple returned for a second viewing. I had to duck down behind the sink so Tim the estate agent didn't see me while I tried to take more snaps. They all looked very matey now. Yesterday I called him, blocking my number. Jan Abramovich here. I asked if there had been any offers, because my husband and I were still thinking it over, and he very smugly said yes, there had. I asked if they'd offered the asking price and he got a bit shifty so I could only assume the answer was no.

'The offer hasn't yet been accepted,' he said. 'But the buyers are in an excellent position, so it may move very quickly once Mr Thornbury returns. It would definitely be worth your putting in a bid asap.' He said 'asap' like it was a word, not a series of letters. I thanked him. Told him we'd have a firm decision after the weekend and that, by the way, we'd be cash buyers. I could practically hear him salivating, drool hitting his starched collar. 'Well, of course, that's very interesting, Mrs Abramovich. I'm sure I can delay any decision till Monday, but I can't guarantee after that.'

'Of course,' I said. I didn't know how much time I could string him along for. Or for what purpose, really, either. It could only delay things so long. I just didn't want Stella to come home to a fait accompli, even if I was pissed off with her. 'It would be useful to know what the other party has bid,' I said, trying again.

'I shouldn't really tell you,' Tim said, but he loved me now he'd seen the colour of my cash. 'But let's just say, if you went to nine seven five, you would be in a favourable position.'

So the Gold Bentleys had knocked a cool million or so off the asking price and no one seems to have batted an eyelid. I remembered Rahina once saying to me that, with the really high-end stuff, agents just pluck a figure out of the sky; it's not really based on anything concrete like square footage. After all, what price can you put on a passenger lift to all floors or a temperature-controlled under-the-floor wine cellar?

Betsy is almost hysterical at the prospect of a party in one of the big houses, until she remembers that all her party outfits are at her dad's (by 'all', I mean two, and by 'party outfits', I mean her favourite skirt, which is a pink-and-blue striped skater that she usually teams with stripey tights in a different colour combination, or her one good dress that she has worn to every christening, wedding and birthday for the past two years. Luckily, she's not a fast grower, but it's still getting so short she looks as if she's auditioning for *Geordie Shore* when she wears it and so has lately taken to wearing trousers underneath). I convince her that casual is best. I'm pretty sure I've got the hang of the dress code and almost everyone will be in the skinny jeans/T-shirt combo, with the odd summer dress. Satisfied, she picks her cut-offs and a pink top with a cartoon dancing crocodile on the front and 'Croc 'n' Roll' emblazoned across it. Earlier in the day, I'd helped Gail string up more lights in the garden and arrange a cluster of chairs and tables on the lawn. Ben fussed around with a large wood burner and made Betsy's day by letting her help him build a test fire, meticulously stacking it up with kindling he'd brought home from the woods. He declared her the best fire starter ever, and then, when she wasn't looking, he rebuilt the whole thing. When we went back upstairs for a nap I noticed Al's car in their driveway. I wondered if Stella could sense a change in the air. The faint trace of a stranger's perfume. I didn't go anywhere near gold-Bentley man but I'd put money on him reeking of Eau Sauvage.

Betsy and I have a fight over make-up while we get ready. My little tomboy has spent a couple of afternoons with the Mini Mes and now she thinks contouring is de rigueur for seven-year-olds.

'They'll think I look like a baby,' she wails.

'You are not wearing blusher, and that's it. Even I'm not wearing blusher, and I'm forty-two.'

'Amber said her mum said you'd look better if you wore more make-up,' she says, and I have to stop myself from saying, *Well, Amber and her mum can both fuck off.* Instead I compromise with lip gloss.

For all I know, Taylor and Amber will be back to ignoring Betsy anyway, sneering at her from afar. Who knows what Stella's been filling their heads with since our fight? I realize that this applies to me too. Maybe she's this minute letting Eva, Katya, Anya and Jan know that I'm officially back on the blacklist.

I've promised Gail and Ben that we'll arrive early, so at five past six we're standing on their doorstep, frazzled and tetchy. We're the first, but then everyone turns up in quick succession and no one seems to be ignoring me so I finally start to relax. Being Gail and Ben, they have invited all the housekeepers and nannies and live-in gardeners, but the other householders have clearly interpreted this as meaning staff can come along if they're providing childcare, and there's a kind of apartheid with nannies and children on one side of the garden and employers/parents on the other. None of the housekeepers or gardeners seems to have been given the night off. There's a group of three nannies, one of them Ferne, bouncing baby Andrei on her hip. My heart starts pounding. I hadn't for a second thought that Sergei and Katherine would come along. They've always kept themselves to themselves. They're not part of the inner circle but, of course, Gail would never leave them out. I should have known. I smile over at her and she waves back. I have no idea if Stella and Al are going to show up at any minute – hopefully, they're too tired after their journey and have decided to give it a miss – but, if they do, this is not going to be good.

A couple of glasses of champagne later and I'm starting to feel better. There's still no sign of them. Betsy is happily playing with some children of around her age who I've never seen before and I'm guessing are the offspring of one or both of the only two couples I don't recognize. Everyone is being friendly, although I'm mainly hovering on the periphery of conversations, as usual, an observer rather than a participant, but that suits me fine. It's a beautiful evening and I'm content to just take it all in. I get talking to one of the two waiters, Louis, and he tells me he's the son of one of Gail's work colleagues and he's grateful for the chance to earn some extra cash before he goes to uni in the autumn. He's off to study finance and business.

'You'll be living somewhere like this in a few years in that case,' I say, and he screws his face up. I laugh.

'Sorry, no disrespect . . .' he says.

'None taken. I'm an outsider here too. I'm the lodger.'

'Do they all have the same plastic surgeon,' he says, and I realize he's flirting with me, even though I'm a good twenty years older than him. It's ridiculous, but I decide to just go with it. What's the harm?

'They've definitely all had the same hair extensions.' I say, and he snorts. 'That's what I'm going to do in my next life. Get trained in how to put fake hair on rich people.'

'Damn,' he says. 'I should change my course.'

'That, or teeth. Learn how to do those big white veneers

that look like your granny's falsies. Well, great-granny, in your case.'

It's a fun way to pass the time. Flattering, even. But then I feel it. An almost imperceptible ripple as all heads turn towards the patio doors. Al is first, suntanned from his holiday, wearing a beautifully tailored pale blue jacket over a faded T-shirt and jeans. Loafers and no socks. Behind him, Stella, in a tiny denim skirt and a coral vest top, all long, tanned limbs, and then the Mini Mes in almost identical outfits. Three high, dark, gleaming ponytails. If you could ignore the fish lips and padded cheeks for a moment, they'd look like they were in contention for World's Most Beautiful Family. I look over to Betsy and she's standing with her mouth open, gazing in wonderment.

'Who are they?' my companion says. Even he has picked up on the change in atmosphere.

'They live across the street,' I say, without looking round. I watch as all the men gravitate towards Al and all the women towards Stella. Each of them is a head taller than all the others in their respective groups. It's almost like watching two maypoles with the dancers flocking round. Taylor and Amber glide over to the small band of kids who were happily running around a minute ago but are now standing warily, waiting to be told what to do.

Louis picks up on the fact that he's lost me for the moment. He probably thinks I'm as in awe of the Thornburys as everyone else obviously is. 'Well, I'd better do my duty . . .'

I give him a smile. 'Yes. Lovely chatting to you.'

I'm left standing there with no one to talk to. I think

about going over to where the kids are, but I don't want Stella to see me talking to Ferne. I could join the group of satellites orbiting her, but I have no idea what kind of reception I'd get. So I just stand there, looking like a spare part. I wonder if I should go and find Gail – she's disappeared into the house, probably checking on the caterers. I'm watching the women lapping up the details of Stella's Insta-worthy vacation when I see her give a slight double take on spotting Ferne. Her nostrils flare like an angry pony's.

'Are there staff here?' I hear her ask incredulously. 'I thought Gail was joking.' Clearly, the invitation was not handed on to Pilar.

'Only a couple of the nannies,' one of the others – Anya, I think – says. 'Which is a good thing, really, because they can look after all the kids.'

'So long as that's all they're here for,' Stella says. Apparently, new, more humble Stella didn't survive our falling-out. I see her flick a glance towards Al, but he's deep in an anecdote. If he knows Ferne is only a few feet away, he's not letting on. He's practised at this. 'Really, it's too much. How are we supposed to let our hair down with them watching us?'

'Mine's only here so the children could come for a while,' one of the non-Close women says apologetically. 'She's taking them home soon.'

'Mine too,' the other one says, a bit more defiantly. 'Gail was very keen on all the children coming.'

Stella fixes her beady eyes on Katherine. 'How about yours? Will she take the baby home soon?' She's in danger of giving herself away or, at least, looking unhinged in front of the whole neighbourhood. Katherine doesn't bat an eyelid. She's not the slightest bit in awe of Stella.

'Oh, he'll sleep through anything. And I'm going to take him off her hands soon anyway, because I don't want to take advantage. She's not on duty, she's a guest. In fact, I might go and grab him off her now . . .'

She strides off, leaving the others clucking like a clutch of chickens in her wake. I watch as Katherine makes her way over to Ferne – the older children now seem to be doing some sort of catwalk show, which involves Taylor and Amber being the models and everyone else pretending to take photos – and chats to her before lifting Andrei out of her arms. I look back at Stella. She still hasn't taken her eyes off Ferne.

I know I have to do something – for Ferne's sake as much as Stella's. And for Gail's. I don't want her party to be ruined because two of the guests end up fighting to the death on her flawless lawn. Stella and I haven't even said hello yet. We haven't communicated since she stomped out the other week. But I decide I have to take my life in my hands and I force myself to march confidently over to the group and hook my arm under one of hers.

'Stella, can I borrow you for a second?' I say, smiling manically at them all. I start leading her away before she can protest. 'Calm down,' I mutter, still with a forced smile plastered to my face. Then: 'Let's go over here!' loudly, for everyone else's benefit.

'What the hell?' she says, trying to wrestle her arm away.

'You're giving yourself away,' I hiss. 'Just come over here and take a few deep breaths.'

'I thought you didn't want to help me any more,' she says petulantly.

'I don't,' I say. 'But it would give me no pleasure to see you make a fool of yourself either. Look happy. Pretend to be laughing.'

She cackles noisily, then glares at me. 'Satisfied?'

'It'll do. Let's sit here.' I wrestle her over to a small wrought-iron table with two chairs. 'Right, just stay here till you feel calmer.' She flicks a glance straight back over at Ferne, who, now relieved of baby Andrei, is throwing herself into playing fashion shows with the kids. She pretends to fuss over Taylor's hair. Practises a pose with Amber. 'She's playing with my fucking children,' Stella spits.

'I know,' I say. 'Don't watch. Talk to me about something. Anything. How was your holiday?'

'Fine,' she says tetchily.

'Whereabouts in the south of France –'

'Laura,' she interrupts and I jump. 'You don't need to do this. You don't have to sit here making phoney conversation with me. Everything's fine.'

'Hardly,' I say. 'You're about to rip Katherine's nanny's head off her shoulders in front of all our neighbours. So, unless the definition of "fine" has changed . . .'

I'm relieved that she laughs for real then. 'Fair point.'

I make a split-second decision. I need to get her attention away from the immediate problem of Ferne. Dig my phone out of my back pocket. 'Listen. I didn't know whether to tell you this or not, but while you were away, they had viewings . . .'

'I assumed they would,' she says, engaged now. I show her the photos. 'These people . . .' I pull up the picture of the Gold Bentleys '. . . have put in an offer. At least, I think it's them.'

'Bastards,' she says, peering at the image as if she might be able to magic them to life so she can question them. 'How do you know?'

I tell her about my interaction with Tim the estate agent, about Jan Abramovich. She honks a big, genuine laugh at that bit, and everyone looks round at us. 'Stella,' I say quietly. 'What if you told Al the whole story about the girls? As if you assume he doesn't know any of it. Like a big confession. As if you can't live with it on your conscience any more. Explain to him it was a donor and not an affair. It might make a difference.'

'Why would he believe me?'

'Why wouldn't he? If he thinks you have no idea what he's planning. About Ferne.'

We're interrupted by the arrival of Taylor, come to complain that some of the other kids want a turn at being the models, and isn't that unfair? Stella reaches out a hand and gently smooths her perfect ponytail. 'Why don't you let them have a turn?' she says. Taylor pouts.

'You should have a go at being one of the photographers,' I say. 'That way you can have a career that lasts beyond twenty-five and you get to eat what you want.' Taylor raises her immaculate (microbladed? Surely not. She's ten years old) eyebrows at me. Rolls her eyes. She turns back to her mother. 'Me and Amber are the only ones who are going to be models in real life, so we're the ones who need to practise.'

'Maybe you should play something else now,' I say. She really is a little madam. 'Betsy wants to be a vet, so why not play that and you can be one of her patients. A sick warthog, maybe.'

I hear a loud noise and realize it's Stella laughing again. Taylor flashes her a betrayed look. 'That's just stupid.'

'Tayls . . .' Stella says.

'Sorry,' Taylor says sulkily.

'Laura's right. Time to play something else. Let everyone have a turn at doing what they want.' Taylor flares her nostrils in the exact way her mother always does. 'Fine,' she says imperiously. She's used to getting her own way. But, however spoilt or self-obsessed she is, she certainly doesn't deserve the mess that her life is about to become. Not the lack of riches – that will probably do her good – but the truth about her father, the fact that the man she's always thought of as her dad is about to cut her off, I assume emotionally as well as financially. You'd have to be a monster not to feel for her. I try to imagine what it would do to Betsy if David suddenly stopped wanting to have anything to do with her. It's unthinkable. It would break her heart.

'Taylor,' I say as she turns away. She looks back, tossing her hair. I give her a big smile. 'Thanks.' Her face relaxes slightly. Not quite a smile, but the grimace is gone. She turns and walks off. Walks, not stomps. It's a victory of sorts.

Stella looks down at her hands, which are resting on the table. She twirls her mega-watt engagement ring round her finger. I assume that one is genuine. Bought when Al was still inclined to make grand romantic gestures. 'Please let's stop fighting, Laura. I don't have anyone else to talk to.'

I close my eyes briefly. 'I don't know, Stella.' I don't want to get sucked back into her orbit. I feel for her, I really do, but I don't know if I trust her. Scrub that: I don't.

'Whatever I've done wrong in the past, I have to be able to move on and work out what's going to happen in the future.'

'You will –' I start to say.

Stella interrupts. 'You're the only real friend I've got. I mean, I have friends, lots of them, but you're the only one who really knows me. Knows everything . . .'

I open my mouth to protest again, but she's looking at me so intently, tears pooling at the corner of her eyes. You know that Christmas advert with the puppy in a cardboard box, abandoned on the street, silently pleading for love? That. Despite all my better instincts. I can't just walk away.

'It's fine,' I say gently. 'Come round on Monday and we'll talk about it then, once Betsy's gone back to David's.'

'Thank you.'

'Now you need to get back to your adoring audience and start showing off about your holiday again. We need to act as if everything is normal.'

'Very funny,' she says lightly.

'And, Stella . . .' I say as she gets up. 'Stop giving Ferne filthy looks. You'll give yourself away.'

She nods. I get up and follow her back, but I veer off and go over to where the kids are playing. I've had enough of the adults for this evening. They do indeed seem to be playing vets. Betsy is wearing one of the nannies' jackets as a lab coat and appears to be in charge. She's in her element. Taylor is the nurse. The others – Amber and the two boys and one girl from round the corner – are the injured animals. It resembles a First World War battlefield with Old MacDonald as the soundtrack. I lie down on the ground next to them and start to moo mournfully, ignoring the confused looks from my grown-up neighbours. It's the most fun I've had in ages.

39

Sunday night comes round way too quickly. Once again, I couldn't look at David when I dropped Betsy off. Gave him monosyllabic answers to his questions. I'm sure he must realize something has changed. The world's most smooth-running divorce has hit a speed bump. I wonder if he knows Betsy must have let something slip. Whether he's ever asked her not to tell me. Whether Michaela has.

I check the rotas for the week, swapping a couple of people around to accommodate two late requests and then, unable to get 18-rated videos of David and Michaela together out of my head, I go on to Tinder and end up striking up a conversation with Danny (forty-eight, divorced, one son, neat beard and kind eyes in his picture). After a few exchanges we're both just ranting about our exes, but at least it's cathartic. Eventually, I ask him if he thinks David was seeing Michaela before we separated, because why wouldn't a man who doesn't even know me, let alone either of them, have an opinion? 'Probably,' he replies. And then he adds a smiley face and a 'Sorry', as if that might help.

On Monday morning I watch as Al leaves and then Stella takes the girls to school. I hang the blue tea towel, just in case she's not sure what time to come round, and when she gets back she comes straight over without even going home first, armed with two oversized Starbucks coffees and a bag containing pastries.

'Are you drunk?' I say as she plonks the bag on the kitchen counter. 'You've brought something that contains calories.'

She ignores me. Gets out one of the pastries and takes a substantial bite. 'I wish I knew when he was going to do it. How long I have.'

I've noticed the eBay sales have dried up. Either she's lost heart or she's running out of things of Al's to sell. 'How much have you got saved up?' She tells me and I actually gasp. I couldn't cobble that much cash together if I spent the rest of my life trying to do it. 'How did you get it up to that much?'

She shrugs. 'I told him I needed to pay the balance on the bachelorette party.' By 'bachelorette party', it turns out she means the week in a villa near Rome she had booked for herself and her closest girlfriends – Eva, Jan, Anya and Katya. Gail had claimed busyness at work – in a few weeks' time. 'He saw all the details when I first reserved it, so he had no reason to question the amount, although he did ask if I really had to pay so soon. I told him they'd had an enquiry from the Beckhams and I couldn't risk losing it now all the girls had booked their flights.'

'Dare I ask how much?'

'A hundred and fifty,' she says casually. 'I lost the deposit, but . . . you know . . .'

I should be immune to it by now, but it still renders me speechless for a moment. That she could find it so easy to get her hands on such vast sums of money. That she was going to blow it all on a holiday in the first place. 'You were paying for the whole thing?' I say, once I've taken it in.

'Of course. Except the flights.'

'Will the rest of them get their money back for those?'

She looks at me as if she has never even considered this. 'I don't know. They can't have been very expensive.'

'I'll take your word for it.'

'This is why I wish I knew what he was planning. How can I tell them the bachelorette is cancelled without giving away that something's wrong?'

'It's all going to have to come out soon. You know that, don't you?'

She nods wearily. 'I know.'

I put down my half-eaten pastry. 'If they're your friends, they'll support you.'

'Maybe.' She doesn't sound convinced.

'You need to start looking for somewhere to live. You have enough money now.'

She drains the last of her coffee. 'Not for round here.'

'Well, no. You definitely can't afford to live round here. You need to start looking at areas you can afford.'

Stella looks out of the window. Lets out a big sigh. 'Where I grew up,' she says quietly, 'it was so . . . dull. My parents were – are – kind, but they're ordinary. Very ordinary. Does that sound harsh?'

She looks at me. It does a bit, if I'm being honest, but I shake my head. I want her to keep talking. It's not often she opens up.

'Mow the lawn on Saturday, wash the car on Sunday, TV with a nice cup of tea every night. Just the three of us, sitting there in silence. Even our house was boring. A little square box in a cul de sac of other identical little square boxes, with tiny identical back gardens and tiny identical weeping willows on the front lawn. It was stifling . . .'

I don't know where to start. How many people wish they'd had a safe, stable upbringing like that? Boring is the best a lot of people could hope for.

'I couldn't wait to get away, but I couldn't afford to get away either. And I wasn't clever enough to go to college. That's why I got married so young. If I hadn't met Andrew, I'd probably still be there. Living in one of those houses with some tedious man, going to the WI . . .'

'I doubt it,' I say.

'I won't go back to being that person.'

'You're not going to. Just because you won't be super-rich. Just because you won't be living here . . .'

She puts her head in her hands. 'It's all too much.'

'I know,' I say. 'But the more you start to plan, the easier it'll be.' I need to stop her wallowing. Get her back to laying the foundations for her future. Every time I mention looking for somewhere to live, she goes into a decline, so I need to give her a break from that for a while. Steer her into more positive waters. 'What do you want to do today?'

She looks at me, confused. 'What do you mean?'

'I don't know . . . what have you never done?'

'Um . . . should we have the Oud Renewal massage at the Mandarin Oriental?' she says. 'I've always wanted to try it . . .'

'I meant more like filled up your car with petrol or baked a cake. Life skills. Things you've always paid other people to do for you.'

'I can put petrol in my own car, thank you,' she says huffily. 'I'm not completely useless.'

'Change a plug? Sew on a button? I don't know.'

'Are you thinking I could get a job as a lady's maid?' She doffs an imaginary cap and curtseys. 'Will that be all, m'lady?'

'Well, it would be better than nothing,' I say, relieved that she's at least finding it funny. 'You could live in. The girls could be scullery maids. Tell you what, we'll make ourselves lunch. You can help me make a quiche. How does that sound?'

'Riveting,' she says. 'I can hardly contain my excitement.'

In the late afternoon I head down to St John's Wood. I drive past my new flat, trying to ignore the shabby surroundings. It's two minutes' walk to the shops, I tell myself, ten to the school, fifteen to her dad's. I repeat it like a mantra. Half an hour ago I got an email from the conveyancer saying we were almost ready to exchange contacts, assuming there were no last-minute complications. The point of no return. Or no return without a financial penalty at least. She's asked me to decide on a completion date. The date when it will finally be mine. It makes me feel sick to think about it.

The drive from there to Al's office takes me past David's block and then the flats where Michaela lives. Betsy will be there having her tea, post ballet. I could drop in and surprise her. I won't, of course, because that would mean seeing Michaela and I don't think I'm ready to pull that off without giving away how hurt I am yet. I picture Michaela's place. The warm, earthy colours, the muddle of kids' toys, the slight smell of the Body Shop grapefruit shower gel the whole family uses. Does it feel like a second home to David now? Does he have a favourite spot on her soft, baggy sofa? A shelf in her bathroom cabinet? His preferred side of the bed?

'Here, look . . .'

For a change, I am keeping watch and Angie is rifling through Al's drawers. Like many a woman before her, apparently. I look over. She's waving a white A4 envelope at me. I take it from her, slide the papers out.

'He's accepted that offer on the house. Well, I assume it's the same one. Nine point five million.' I read on. 'We note your request to complete the sale by 16 August. That's two weeks after the wedding is supposed to be.'

'Well,' Angie says, 'you've got to admire his organizational skills.'

'So Stella's got until then to move out. Maybe. That's, what? Ten, eleven weeks?'

Angie nods. 'About that. To find somewhere to live and a job. I know I said she was a cow, but I don't envy her.'

'She needs to get on with it,' I say.

'She needs more than that,' Angie says, pushing a tanned hand through her short hair. 'She needs a miracle.'

40

June

I'm forcing Stella to look at flats. At least to look at details of flats on PrimeLocation. We've dismissed Hampstead, Highgate, St John's Wood and Primrose Hill as being too expensive. At least, I have. She's resisting. She keeps bringing up things like proximity to the girls' school, and I have to remind her that it's unlikely the girls are going to be staying at their five-thousand-plus-a-term-each establishment. (No way can we assume Al will pay now he knows they're not his.) I'm trying to talk up other, less glamorous areas and make her consider them. We're in her garden, under a giant parasol, drinking mojitos in the early afternoon.

She clears her throat, something I've realized she does when she's about to make an announcement. 'I've been thinking. You were right. I have to stop burying my head in the sand. It's all going to come out one of these days anyway, like you keep telling me . . .'

'I'm glad you've been listening,' I say jokily.

She pulls a face. A tiny line appears on her forehead. Tiny, but there. 'You look good today,' I say. 'Did you stop the Botox?'

'You told me I couldn't afford it any more. I look like an old crone already.'

I laugh. 'It suits you. You almost look human. Give it a few weeks.'

'You are hilarious,' she says drily.

'Pleasure. Anyway, you were saying . . .'

She sucks in a breath. 'I need help. Not . . . you've been amazing, I'm not saying that . . .'

I put her out of her misery. 'You totally do.'

'So, I've made a decision. I'm going to start by telling the others. I can't keep stringing them along about the wedding. Just the women. I don't trust the other men not to tell Al. Well, maybe Ben wouldn't. A few heads have got to be better than two, right?'

'Right,' I say. 'What's brought this on?'

'Last night. I felt bad . . .'

Last night was a 'girls' dinner' at Anya's. I was there. Invited as 'part of the gang', as she put it. I'm not going to lie, I was happy not to be left out, flattered that I was included. We ate in their fairy-light-festooned conservatory, waited on hand and foot by their exhausted-looking housekeeper, who had probably already done a full day's work before we even arrived. I say we ate – I mean, I did. Even though the meal was basically salad followed by salad with a tiny bit of grilled fish on the side, followed by salad of the fruit variety, I was still the only one to actually move the food from the fork to my mouth and not just round and round on the plate. Anya and Bill's house conforms to all the norms of The Close: marble, gold, dodgy art. So now I've seen Anya in all her naked black-and-white glory too. I'm getting to know these women far more intimately than I'd like. There was much talk of the wedding, of course. Stella played her part beautifully, but

322

I could see she was uncomfortable when Katya started asking about the bachelorette, wanting more details about the house Stella had found for them all, and the rest of them started twittering away about how much they were looking forward to a week away without their husbands and what they were going to get up to.

'I'm scared I'm going to get caught out,' she says now. 'And, you know what? I don't want to give Al the satisfaction of being the one to drop the big bombshell. I want to get my side of the story in first, take the wind out of his sails. Plus, I can't keep expecting you to drop everything and worry about me. You have enough on your plate. These women are my oldest friends, and friends are meant to support each other, right?'

I'm struck with a tiny jolt of anxiety. I'm sure it's one hundred per cent the right thing to do, but I realize that, ridiculously, I'll miss being the only keeper of Stella's secret. Well, apart from Angie, who Stella doesn't even know about. I'll miss being needed. 'Do you think they'll be able to keep it to themselves, though?'

'We'll soon find out,' she says.

'And, if they don't?'

She looks at me evenly. She's made up her mind. 'Then I'll know where I stand. It's time to try to work out who my friends really are.'

41

If an alien came down and landed in the middle of the small gathering in Stella's garden, they would go back and teach their offspring that human females were tall, with abundant glossy hair, huge plumped-up cheeks and protruding oversized lips that didn't quite fit their mouths. I would be paraded as some kind of a runt: a short, curly-haired, laughter-lined, thin-lipped freak. These are the Lulu Lemons, it would say. They wear a uniform: yoga pants and strappy vest tops, which all have their tribal name stamped on the outside. Except for the runt who seems to be from an inferior caste known as the Gaps.

We're sitting round a large glass-topped faux-wicker table, under the massive umbrella, because the sun is fierce. Me, Stella, Eva, Katya, Anya, Jan and Gail. We debated long and hard about inviting Jan, because Roman is Al's best friend in The Close and she might feel conflicted about not telling him, but Stella was adamant she should be included. They're all looking at the two of us expectantly, mouths open like a pond full of hungry koi.

We wait for Pilar to put down a tray with a cafetière and seven tiny cups and saucers. 'Help yourselves,' I say, doing just that. In any other circumstances, I would automatically pour one for everyone, but here that would just confirm my lowly status, so I sit on my hands and wait it out.

'Stella has something she wants to tell you,' I announce, once everyone has a drink. I squeeze her arm encouragingly.

'I . . . I don't know if I can . . .' she says. 'Will you tell them, Laura?'

Shit. 'OK, well, first she needs you all to promise not to breathe a word of this to anyone. Not your husbands. Especially not your husbands. Not yet. They'll all find out in a few weeks anyway. And don't talk about it in front of anyone, including your staff. Stella's relying on you all. Anyone uncomfortable with that?'

Of course, no one would own up if they were now, not without finding out what the enticing bombshell is first, but it needed to be said. I don't want anyone to be able to claim later that they didn't realize the importance of secrecy. They all make agreeing noises.

'Stella, dear, are you OK?' Gail says softly. Stella nods.

I breathe out slowly. 'You're sure you want me to be the one to tell them?' I ask Stella, and she gives me a weak smile. 'Please.'

'Right. I'm just going to say it. Stella has found out that Al is planning to leave her and set up home with someone else. So the wedding won't be happening . . .'

There's a collective gasp and then a cacophony of voices about taking him to the cleaners and names of divorce lawyers. Gail reaches out and puts a hand on Stella's arm. Stella just sits there, looking at the floor.

'There's more . . .' I say. This is the really tricky bit. I'm not sure how much detail to go into and it's such a juicy bit of gossip that I really don't know how any of them are going to keep it to themselves. But Stella is adamant she wants them to know everything. I lay it on a bit thick about how much Stella and Al wanted children and how she didn't go off and have an affair, she found an anonymous donor through an agency who agreed to father two babies. By the end I've made her sound like Mother Teresa, selflessly doing battle with a turkey baster to save her marriage. Katya is in tears. I tell them that Al has found out, that it's kicked off his scheme to destroy her. How he has no idea how it really went down, that she did it for them, just that he has been bringing up two girls who aren't his. Now there's not a dry eye in the house. It looks like the world's greatest miracle. Five frozen faces with tears rolling from their eyes. Statues come to life. The Virgin Marys of N2.

While I've got them on side I tell them about what we've been trying to do. How we're afraid Al is planning to leave Stella and the girls with nothing. About the loan and the flat in Battersea and the sale of the house. How Stella has been squirrelling money away for the future, but she's still going to have to lead a very different life from now on.

To give them credit, none of them says anything critical. In fact, none of them says anything at all. It's as if they're rudderless, now their leader is down. They don't know how they're meant to feel without her giving them the nod of approval. The queen is mortally wounded and the whole hive is in danger of imploding.

Gail, of course, has a mind of her own. 'Oh, Stella,' she says gently, 'why didn't you tell us sooner?'

'I wanted to,' Stella says at last. 'I just . . . I didn't know how.'

'Does this mean . . .' Katya flaps her long eyelashes, a robot rebooting. '. . . you're going to be poor?'

I suppose someone had to say it. 'Yes!' Stella says dramatically.

'No,' I say at the same time. 'She already has more money in her bank account than I've ever seen. She's just going to need to get a job . . .'

I might as well have said, *She's going to need to find food in your bins from now on.* Every one of them except Gail drops their mouth open again, like a frog catching flies. 'But, of course, that's not as easy as it sounds.'

'Who is she?' Eva says. 'Do we know her?'

Stella is about to speak, but I jump in. 'It doesn't matter. It's happening and we need to work out what Stella is going to do.'

'You poor girl,' Gail says. 'Of course we'll all help you.'

The rest of them all sit there staring at us. I wonder if it's even really gone in. Finally, Jan speaks. 'Did you say Roman witnessed the loan document?'

'Um . . . yes,' I say. I'm relieved no one has yet asked how we found all this out. I'm not sure their loyalty to Stella would extend to keeping quiet about me poking around in people's private things.

'I see,' she says with a sneer. There's no telling what she's thinking. Anya and Katya – both of them second wives of much older men themselves – just look dumbstruck. Could this happen to them? Aren't they supposed to be the winners? The one he ends up sticking with because he can't face the hassle (or the demands for alimony) another messy separation would bring. They're meant to be the default long-game victors.

'So . . .' I say eventually. This is pointless. 'Stella just wanted you all to know. As her closest friends. And, you know, if you have any ideas about what she might be able to do, because we're all out . . .'

'What I don't understand,' Eva says, 'is how Laura got involved in this . . .'

Ah. I'm about to open my mouth to explain myself when Stella gets there first. 'It's a long story. I'll explain it all one day . . . I'm indebted to her.'

'Well, personally, I'm just glad Stella had someone she could confide in,' Gail says. 'I completely understand why she felt she couldn't tell any of us.' I give her a grateful smile.

Jan speaks up again. 'I have to go, I'm afraid, my Pilates instructor will be here any minute.'

'Don't forget, don't cancel your flight for the bachelorette yet. Not if Roman'll notice,' I say. I can't help myself. It just needs one of them to accidentally let something slip and Stella will be rumbled.

The others take their cue and can't jump in with their own excuses quickly enough. Now they've heard the goss, they just want to get out of there, in case Stella's problems are a virus they might be in danger of catching. I should have known they were all too self-obsessed to be of any use. Only Gail stays put, waiting until the others round the corner to the side gate before she says, 'Shall we have a drink?'

Stella volunteers to go and get something, which must be a first. She looks shell-shocked, as if the fight has gone out of her.

'Do you think they'll keep their mouths shut?' I say, turning to Gail.

She gives a sad little laugh. 'Probably for now. They won't want to give their own husbands ideas.'

'I wonder who'll be Queen Bee once Stella's gone . . .'

'If Jan wasn't leaving, it'd be a fight to the death between her and Eva.'

'You should stage a coup,' I say jokingly. 'Bring about an age of enlightenment.'

She stretches her toned arms above her head. 'Too much like hard work.'

Stella appears at the back door with a tray carrying what looks like three giant mojitos. 'Poor Stella,' Gail says quietly.

'I know. What's she going to do?'

Gail shakes her head. 'I have no idea.'

'I made them all by myself,' Stella says as she arrives, handing us each a drink. I take a sip. It's pretty much just pure rum.

'OK, don't apply for any mixologist jobs,' I say, and I'm gratified to hear her rasping laugh.

An hour later and two more of Stella's mojitos down, we're basically all slaughtered. I hug them both like true friends and stagger back home to sleep it off. I wake up at six, disorientated, not knowing if it's morning or afternoon for a few minutes, until I realize I'm on the sofa, legs hanging off the edge, and with all my clothes on. I stagger up wearily and into the shower. I think about the afternoon and what we've achieved. Was it worth it? Now we have five more people who might give the game away to Al, and not one of them came up with a helpful suggestion. Or even an unhelpful one. And I am most definitely out of ideas.

42

Days pass. A week. Two. The day after what is now officially known by Gail and me as 'the fiasco in Stella's garden', I waited in. I thought at least one of them might call round to ask if there was anything they could do. If Stella was coping. Or even just for more gossip. The name of Al's bit on the side, for example. But, apart from Gail, who has been talking to Stella every day, offering a shoulder to cry on, it's as if they've all gone into denial. As the days went by, I started to think I might have imagined the big revelation completely.

I've exchanged on my new flat so the countdown has begun to when it will be all mine. Gail and Ben have offered to let me stay in the annexe for the last two weeks for free while I make it habitable, which is kind beyond any of my expectations. I thought about protesting, but I talked myself out of it. They were happy to do it; I should just accept gracefully. I haven't told Betsy yet. Not until I can show her her new home without the black ceilings and the smell. Until it looks less like a place where someone might sacrifice chickens and more like somewhere her cat might want to live.

Stella is no further forward with a home of her own. Or a job. Or a plan. I think the reaction – or lack of it – from her friends threw her. I won't lie, it threw me too. I was expecting hysteria, shock, an outpouring of sympathy, or even disbelief or thinly disguised disapproval. Not blank incomprehension. Not shell-shocked self-interest. She's heard from them all, of course. None of them is treating her any differently. In fact, that's what's so odd about it. They're all still inviting her for drinks or meals, suggesting facials or trips to Bond Street, but not one of them has asked if she's OK. I don't think they're being nasty; they just can't compute what they've been told. I doubt they're even discussing it among themselves, because that would make it real.

I'm still trying to make her look at houses to rent – she could offer to pay a year in advance, I realized, which would hopefully have most landlords overlooking the fact that she has no income. Gail and I could be references. But I made the mistake of asking her how much it would cost to rent a house like hers, just as a starting point. I knew she could never afford it, but I thought we could ease down from there. When she told me, I thought I'd misheard her and I made her repeat it. It was the same amount the second time. Thirty thousand pounds. Maybe thirty-five. Per month.

'Who . . . ?' I said, mouth open. 'I mean . . .'

She shrugged. 'People like us.'

I didn't have the heart to point out that she was no longer a person like her. 'OK,' I said brusquely. 'Well, then, we need to look for something that's what? A fifth of the size of this. That should be doable.' I clicked away manically at PrimeLocation.

'Look, there's a house – a whole house – in the Vale of Health.'

Stella looked over my shoulder. 'It's in a terrace . . .'

'So? It's got three bedrooms . . .'

I could see she wasn't interested, even though, to my eyes, the house was gorgeous. I scrolled down, clicked on another. 'How about this one? Semi-detached, not a terrace. Little garden, look . . .'

She peers at the listing. 'Finchley? Where would the girls go to school?'

'I don't know. They must have schools, right?'

'Not good ones,' she said, as if she were an expert.

'O-K.' I kept looking. 'Swiss Cottage? No? Childs Hill?' She shook her head. 'Belsize Park?'

'Too dull,' she said petulantly.

'Fuck's sake, Stella. You have to be realistic. Belsize Park is lovely.'

'I don't want to live in Belsize Park. I want to live here.'

'Well, you can't!' I practically shouted. 'You have to get your head out of the sand!' An idea occurred to me. 'Come with me.' I rattled off a swift text as I chivvied her out of the house and into my car.

'Where are we going?' she huffed.

'You'll see.'

We drove without speaking. My patience was wearing thin. She seemed unable to acknowledge real life. I had no idea what was actually going through her brain about where she and her girls might be calling home in a few short weeks. I didn't want to get into another argument with her so I turned the radio up poundingly high. Sang along to Beyoncé. Jack, the junior from Rahina's office, was already waiting for us outside when we arrived. Stella looked around at the street anxiously, as if worried she might be jumped by a gang of feral youths as soon as she put a Louboutined foot outside.

'What are we doing here?' she asked nervously. I could tell she was feeling sheepish. Wanting to be back in my good books.

I smiled at Jack. 'Hi. Thanks for this.'

'Can I leave you to it?' He handed me the keys. I was slightly nervous to let myself in, but I didn't want Stella to see that. Anyway, I was going to have to get used to it. 'Of course. I'll drop them back in a bit.'

We watched him saunter along the road, hands in his pockets. 'This is where I'm moving to.'

She actually gulped. 'This house?'

'Just the ground floor,' I said, unlocking the front door.

'Gosh,' is all she could manage. I opened the door to the flat and beckoned her to go ahead of me. The smell was incrementally worse every time and I almost laughed when I saw the moment it smacked her in the face. But then I remembered that this was going to be my home and that made it suddenly seem not so funny. Stella put her hand over her mouth and nose. Looked round, eyes wide.

'You can't live here.'

'Of course we can,' I said, with more confidence than I felt. 'We have to, because we can't afford anything else.' I nearly added, *That's how the world works*, but I thought that would be overkill and tip over into being patronizing. 'And, you know what, we're lucky because I'm able to buy it. With a huge mortgage, it goes without saying.'

'Can I even afford this?' she said.

'Not to buy, no. Because no one will give you a mortgage. But you could afford to rent somewhere much nicer, until you get on your feet. Come and see the garden.'

She shook her head. 'No. You've made your point. I get it. Let's go.'

'I take it you won't be coming round for tea, then?' I said, trying to lighten the atmosphere. She didn't laugh. It must have struck a nerve, though, because we now have appointments to view two houses tomorrow. It's a step in the right direction.

Jan is sitting on my sofa.

I'm so preoccupied with wondering how she can sit on her protuberance without rolling around like a Weeble that I haven't even started to wonder what she's doing here. We are not the kind of acquaintances who call on one another.

Of all the women in The Close, she's the one I feel I know least well. The one I find most intimidating. Obviously, compared to a hostile Stella, she's a pussy cat, but then so is a rabid Doberman. I don't think we've ever been alone together, ever exchanged more than a few words since the ceasefire.

I offer her coffee and she refuses. The rumour has probably got round that I only have instant. Not even a Nespresso. I make myself one anyway, as a distraction. I wish she'd just get on with it and say whatever she's got to say.

Finally, she speaks. 'I'm grateful for the help you've been giving Stella. I'm glad she had someone to talk to.'

I stir the sugar into my coffee. I want to say, *She could*

have talked to you if you'd had the good grace to ask her how she was, but what comes out is: 'Thank you. I appreciate that.' Why do I feel as if she's softening me up for something?

'I misjudged you. We all did, really.'

'Yes,' I say. I'm not letting her off completely.

'I wish to tell you something,' she says, with that weird formal tone they all use. 'I think it might be helpful.'

'OK.' I lean against the counter. I feel as if I need to steady myself for something.

'I've thought long and hard about this, Laura. It wasn't an easy decision. Roman is Al's closest friend . . .'

All of a sudden, I'm hanging on her every word. 'Go on.'

Jan gives a little cough. 'Could I have a glass of water?'

'Of course.' I just want her to get on with it and tell me whatever it is she has to tell me. I don't even wait until the tap runs cold before I fill a glass and hand it to her. She takes a sip. 'That afternoon at Stella's . . . you mentioned that Roman had witnessed the loan Al took out to buy the flat. I'll be honest, I was furious that he'd never mentioned it. I mean, they do things like that for each other all the time, but I couldn't shake the idea that Roman knew Al was planning to go off with that woman. Or at least that he was doing something that he didn't want Stella to know about. He must have asked Al why he needed the money. So I confronted him about it . . .'

For god's sake. I thought I'd drummed it into all of their heads not to mention any of this to their husbands. Jan takes another sip of her water. I have to stop myself from shouting, *Get on with it!*

'He was very cagey. Denied knowing anything. So I

took a chance. Told him what I knew about Al having a mistress and the new flat. I thought he'd just confirm that that was what he knew too, but . . . well . . . he hadn't the slightest, it seems. He told me that a couple of years ago Al came to him to ask to borrow money. Two and a half million. The business was going through a rough patch, he said. I suppose we've all been there. He begged Roman not to tell me so that Stella wouldn't find out. And he didn't. Because he trusted Al when he said he would pay it back . . .'

I say nothing. I don't want to interrupt her flow. I can't work out where this is going yet.

'I'm going to deal with that one later. And then he told me that a few months ago Al came to him and said the business wasn't recovering but he'd worked out a way to repay his debt. He asked Roman to witness his signature on a contract with the bank so he could take out a loan against the house. The plan was, he said, that he was going to buy a smaller place for Stella, him and the girls to live in, and then sell the house and pay Roman back. From the profits. Again, he asked Roman to promise to keep it to himself, to let Stella have the fairy-tale wedding she so desperately wanted before Al had to break the news to her. Again, Roman said yes. Why wouldn't he? Al was his best friend and he felt bad for him. But he said he told him he was proud of him, that he'd found a way to work out his difficulties, to still provide a fantastic life for his family . . .'

She pauses, as if she's trying to get things straight in her head.

'But, you see, what I told him made him realize that

that wasn't the case. Al wasn't buying the flat for them all to live in; he was buying it for him and . . . her. Roman had no idea. So I said, "Where's Stella going to live?" And he said, "I suppose Al will sell the house and whatever's left after he's paid me back will go on a home for her and the girls." He said it was sad, he felt awful for Stella, but these things happen and so long as they were all looked after it was just one of those things . . .'

She looks at me expectantly. I still can't quite put the pieces together.

'So I told him that there wasn't going to be anything left. That Stella had found out the whole thing was mortgaged. He was never going to be able to pay Roman back. Anyway . . . at that point Roman snapped. I think he could get past the way Al was treating Stella, but once he knew he'd been trying to screw him over too, that was it . . .'

'So Al's been propping up AJT for years, by the sound of it.'

Jan nods. 'I had to stop Roman going straight round there to confront Al, but I don't know how long I can hold him off, to be honest.'

I go and sit on the sofa next to her. She shuffles along on her space-hopper behind. 'I knew he must be living beyond his means, because why else would he have borrowed more from the bank, but I didn't know it was this bad. You really do have to get Roman to keep it to himself until we can work out what this means . . .'

She gives me a pained look. Up close, her face is even weirder. A Frankenstein's monster of a thing. 'I know. That's why I've come to you now.'

337

'Do you have any suggestions?' I ask hopefully.

'None whatsoever. I thought you were the person with all the ideas.'

I ignore the slightly barbed comment. I get the feeling she still blames me somehow for upsetting the equilibrium. As if, if I hadn't been here, they all would have carried on as normal and it would have somehow worked itself out.

'I appreciate you telling me, Jan. And for what's it's worth, I think you did the right thing.'

She stands up. 'I should go. Please keep me informed.'

'Of course,' I say. 'Thanks again.'

I never would have thought Jan would be the one to come through. That she might turn out to be the saviour. Now I just have to work out how this information changes things. What to do next.

43

July

As it turns out, I don't have to wait too long for a plan to come together.

Al has announced he wants to have a pre-wedding celebration. A party for their nearest and dearest. No kids, just the grown-ups. Obviously, I am not invited.

It also happens to be on the night before the men are supposed to be leaving for the bachelor weekend in Monte Carlo and a couple of days before building work is due to start on the 'Wedding Village'. It's the point of no return. Stella would wake up and wonder why her husband to be wasn't packing his swimming trunks, and there was no sign of the builders.

Oh, and thanks to Angie's snooping, I also know it's the night before he's due to both exchange and complete on his new flat. His new home. Contracts are signed and ready to go. From the photos Ange has been sending me of his secret correspondence, it's clear that he was hoping this would have happened a few days earlier. That there was a last-minute hold-up on the part of the sellers. Nothing alarming. Just a routine delay that has thrown his perfectly planned schedule somewhat. He won't be able to make his announcement and then swan straight off to his new love nest, Ferne in tow. But he can't delay telling Stella the wedding is off any longer, either. This has to be it.

It's the week before Betsy's summer holidays start. A few days before my own flat is also mine. I've arranged with David that she'll go to Dorset with him for two weeks while I get the place sorted, and then she and I will move in together for good. Our roles will be reversed. He'll have her every other weekend and the occasional weekday evening. We're going to try to be as flexible as we can, for her sake. Which will be interesting, because I'm still struggling to speak to him. Still struggling to not start hurling accusations and telling him he's a duplicitous bastard every time I need to ask him if Betsy has enough clean socks. I decided I had to bring things to a head.

'Is Michaela going too?' I asked when he called to tell me it was booked. I wished we were having the conversation face to face. I wanted him to have to look me in the eye.

'Is . . . ? Um . . . no. Why would you say that?' he stumbled. He always was a shit liar when he was put on the spot.

'You don't have to lie to me any more, David.' In truth, I didn't think she would be, because Betsy would never have been able to keep it to herself if she was there, but I wanted to force him to be upfront with me. 'I don't care, I just want to know.'

'No. She's not. I would have discussed it with you before taking Betsy on holiday with someone else.'

'I'm just going to ask you this once,' I said. 'And I would really appreciate the truth. Had you started seeing her before you left?'

Silence.

I waited.

Eventually, he sighed. Which was all I really needed to hear. And then he spoke. 'Yes. Not for long . . . that's not why . . .'

I know I'd told him I didn't care, but of course I'd been lying. I hung up while he was mid-sentence.

Al's pre-wedding bash is to be a meal. In the garden, if the weather holds up. Catered, of course. All the usual suspects will be there: Jan and Roman, Eva and Rafa, Katya and Guy, Anya and Bill, Gail and Ben.

Obviously, we have no idea what Al is actually planning, but we have our own ducks in a row, regardless. I have spent an inordinate amount of time with the ladies of The Close since Jan's revelation, discussing exactly how we should play our hand. I could teach a masterclass on why Louboutins are better than Choos and how to keep one's staff in line. With the men too, because we need them to be onboard. Roman has been good to his word – at least so far as I know – and has not given the game away to Al. It's turned out that he's not the only one of them to have been burned. When Eva filled Rafa in on the whole story he confessed that he too, had lent Al money to bail out the business – one million pounds – and that Al had fed him the same line about paying it back by downsizing, as he had Roman. They want their money back and they want it back now. They do not want him to spend what should rightfully be theirs on a love nest for him and Ferne.

The plan I have come up with is this: I want Al to show

his hand. I want him to show himself at his worst. His cruelty. His selfishness. The other husbands are all a bit disapproving of Stella. Maybe they're just projecting how they think they would feel if the same thing happened to them, but they're struggling to accept that her fate is anything other than her own fault. (Of course, I'm not including Ben in this. In fact, that should be a given. If I say that all the men or all the women have behaved unreasonably, I'm excluding Ben or Gail. They're two of the sweetest, least judgemental people I've ever met.) It's so unfair. Stella did what she did for both her and Al's sake. Yes, she should have told him. Yes, she handled it badly. But her crime is a lamb to his sheep. I want them to see him in all his true, vindictive colours. So, I have persuaded them to hold fire until the night of Al's dinner. Until he does whatever he's going to do, says whatever he's going to say. Until he puts into action the plan he's been hatching.

And then, and only then, will they hit him with the big one. That they're delivering letters to his solicitors from theirs first thing the following morning. Letters that say that the purchase of the flat cannot go ahead because the money Al has borrowed is owed to them. Al will have to pull out on the day he is due to exchange and complete. He'll have to use the money he's borrowing to pay off his debts. And he'll still have to sell the house in The Close because he'll have to pay the bank back somehow. They'll want their three and a half million by the end of the year regardless, especially once they realize he hasn't bought a property with it that they could seize if he defaulted.

It's not going to help Stella secure her future – she still

hasn't found a place to live, by the way. We've looked at three houses so far. At the first, in Gospel Oak, she sniffed her way round like a truffle-hunting pig with a pained look on her face. 'It smells. Doesn't it smell?' she said about five times. 'Everything smells of something,' I'd said, giving the estate agent a Pollyanna smile. 'No, but this smells like . . . I don't want to sound rude, but . . . let's just say it's not what I'm used to.' I think what she meant was it smelled of normal family life. Laundry and comfort food. People living on top of one another instead of spread out, each with fifteen hundred-odd square feet to themselves if they wanted it. I'd found it comforting, but she refused to even consider it. The other two were worse. She was downright rude about the space, the decor, the area – but Al won't be able to swan off into the sunset and a new fabulous life either. He might still have Ferne, but he'll have precious little else. And do I believe she's the love of his life who he would happily live in poverty with? Hardly.

I'll be honest, I've come to like all my neighbours a bit more these past few weeks. Their loyalty to Stella, even now they know she is no longer going to be one of the chosen few, is quite touching. We'll see if it lasts once the trappings have actually gone. Once she's a working mum, living an ordinary life.

44

The stage is set. It's a steaming-hot day, the third of a brief heatwave. I spent the afternoon in Stella's back garden with her and Pilar, arranging things to Al's specifications. He wants it to be perfect, he'd said to her. He wants it to be the most special night ever. I asked her what she said in return and she told me she'd answered: 'Oh, it will be, I'll make sure of that.'

Taylor and Amber, being at private school (at least, for now), have already broken up and been dispatched to stay with friends in Suffolk for a few days. They have no idea, of course, that life as they know it will be gone for ever when they get back.

We strung fairy lights above the table and put out brightly coloured jars for candles. Pilar swept the patio as we lined up white wooden chairs with deep magenta cushions and decorated the table with stupidly expensive flowers delivered by a stupidly expensive florist. I pointed out to Stella that she had beautiful blooms growing in her garden she could have used and so pocketed some more cash, but she told me Al had placed the order himself and she wasn't about to get his suspicions up at this late stage of the game.

Now I'm back in the flat, waiting for the signal that all is clear. I have Stella's spare key and clear instructions of which room I should head to to get the best view and be able to hear the conversation. It turns out I shall go to the ball. I'm not missing it for the world. I can't stop pacing and I'm trying to resist the urge to pour myself a large glass of wine to calm my nerves. I need to have my wits about me. I force myself to have a shower and make myself presentable. I'm not going to stay hidden all evening.

Afterwards, I hover by the front window, watching for the arrivals. The instructions are seven thirty for eight and, at exactly seven thirty-two Gail and Ben exit the house and cross the road. Gail gives me a surreptitious wave as they pass. Next come Bill and Anya, smart in simple summer clothes that scream of expensive fabrics. Katya and Guy and Eva and Rafa follow, bumping into a tense-looking Jan and Roman, who are also on their way. I wait, taut as a horse in the starting stall. Eight minutes later (not that I was counting, but every one lasted about an hour, it seemed) I get a text from Stella. The first one we have ever exchanged because, after tonight, it won't matter if Al knows we're in contact. All it says is 'Now'.

I'm over the road as fast as my heels will carry me. I know that everyone will be in the garden, but there's an outside chance that Al has wandered back inside to use the loo or one of the caterers has strayed from the kitchen for a snoop around. I know I have to be quick. As I tiptoe through the hall, I can hear the rumble of conversation from outside. I creep up the stairs, turn to the left and along to the second room at the back. It's a spare bedroom dominated by a large brass-headed bed with about four million throw cushions in various shades of lavender piled on top. There are patio doors on to a small balcony

345

and they've been left open. Beside them is an ice bucket containing an open half-bottle of champagne and a bottle of sparkling water and, nearby, two glasses. On a covered plate there are sumptuous-looking sandwiches from Paul. It's such a sweet gesture, and can only have been Stella. She knows I might end up being hidden here for hours. It makes me smile. I pour myself a small glass, take a bite of a sandwich, then lay down on my stomach and shimmy out through the open balcony door like Ant Middleton on a mission. The table is right below me. I can see the guests milling about with flutes of fizz. There's a wash of chatter and I can only make out odd words: Brexit, Henley, Meghan. The atmosphere seems forced. Everyone is too bright, too happy. Only Al, unaware, is his usual relaxed self, topping up glasses, making a big show of being attentive to his wife. I'm just starting to get stiff, my elbows sore, when he taps the side of his glass with something and announces he wants to make a toast. Is this it? I practically feel a collective intake of breath. I peer over as far as I dare. All eyes are on him.

'Welcome, all,' he says pompously. 'Thanks for coming to celebrate with us. To the best friends a man can have. And a woman,' he adds. 'Hahaha. Mustn't forget my beautiful bride-to-be. Actually, let's toast Stella.'

He raises his glass. They all mirror his action with a few mutters of 'To Stella'. They seem to have momentarily forgotten they're meant to be acting as if nothing is wrong. I shift position, careful not to knock into my glass. Everything has gone quiet, everyone waiting to see what Al is going to say next, but he's just smiling away, waving to the caterers to start bringing out the starters.

Stella saves the moment by making an announcement of her own.

'To Al,' she says. 'My wonderful husband-to-be.'

This time the response is more robust. They're back on script.

'OK, everybody, let's eat,' Al says, ever the magnanimous host. Earlier, Stella will have put out name cards. She at one head of the table, Al at the other. Five people each side. 'Boy, girl, boy, girl' in that tiresome way posh dinner parties do things. Or so I've heard.

The caterers – two young women in muddy-brown artisanal aprons – bring out plates of jewel-coloured salad, works of art in miniature, with slices of slightly melting grilled goat's cheese on top. I'm salivating. I snake backwards into the bedroom, chomp a few more bites of sandwich. I'm pretty sure that nothing will happen now until they've eaten, so I shuffle over to lean on the side of the bed. It's tempting to get on and lie down, but I'd be asleep within minutes. That's if I could even fit on there with all the soft furnishings. I pour myself a large glass of sparkling water and flick idly through my phone.

I haven't looked at Tinder for weeks, so I amuse myself swiping through. Left, left, left. Only left. I see that I have a message from Danny – *How are you doing?* – but, when I look at it, it's over three weeks old and it feels weird to reply now. As if I'd have to think of a blisteringly witty reply that it might have taken me a fortnight to come up with. I play solitaire and try to read a book, but it's hard to concentrate. The main course has arrived – turbot, apparently – and I can hear Bill relating an anecdote about a meal he and Anya had at Scott's a few nights ago above the clank of cutlery. I check my phone. Almost nine o'clock. The turbot is cleared. Everyone oohs and aahs over the dessert as it appears – tarte tatin and salted vanilla ice cream. I hear Al's voice above all the others and my heart stops.

'Everyone . . .'

I crawl back on to the balcony. It's a still, quiet evening. Now it's dark, the candles and fairy lights are magical against the trees. There's a smell of cut grass and earth mixed with night-scented flowers. I'm going to miss this place, I realize with a sharp pang.

'The caterers are about to leave us to it, so I'm sure we'd all like to show our appreciation.' There's a round of applause. False alarm.

Even though it was in the high twenties earlier, I'm a little bit chilly now. There are two gas burners either side of the dining table to keep the guests cosy, but I'm regretting not bringing a cardigan. There's a knitted throw on the bed under the cushion mountain, so I tug at it gently, trying to free it. There's a crash as a lamp falls from one of the bedside tables on to the floor, followed by a pillow avalanche. I freeze. Everyone outside has gone silent.

'One of the caterers must have dropped something on the way out,' Stella says eventually. 'I'm sure it's fine.'

'I'll have a look on my way to the little girls' room,' Jan says, and I hear the scrape of her chair on the tiles. I breathe a sigh of relief. A few seconds later I hear her footsteps on the stairs and she appears at the door.

'Is everything all right?' she hisses.

'Yes. I knocked something over. Sorry.'

'Not long now, hopefully,' she says, and I give her a thumbs-up.

'How's Roman doing?' I say as she turns to leave.

'You can imagine,' she says.

Once I've heard her go back outside, announcing to the group that it was indeed the caterers, dropping a tray, but thankfully nothing was broken, I creep back to my vantage point. Unless this whole evening is a MacGuffin, then Al must be going to make his move soon. Time is running out.

The clatter of cutlery has come to a slow standstill. I smell the cedar-tinged smoke from a cigar. 'Everyone for brandy?' Stella says. There's a murmur of assent and then the sound of spoon on glass.

Al clears his throat. Stands up. 'I have an announcement to make.'

My heart starts to thump in my chest. Here goes.

45

I lean further over my parapet. All eyes are on Al.

'Thanks so much for coming, all of you. My dearest friends. I can't think of who I would rather share this evening with. Or the next few days in Monte Carlo, eh, boys?' He laughs heartily and everyone else gives it a good go of laughing along with him. He's loving this. He looks as if he can hardly contain himself long enough to spin the story slowly enough for maximum impact.

'Seriously, though, I want to share something with you all that I've never shared with anyone else . . .' He pauses for dramatic effect. He's commanding the stage. Transfixing the audience. Stella flicks a surreptitious look up at me. 'Stella and I have been together for what? Twelve years.' He smiles at her indulgently. 'We've been through everything together, side by side. Well, except for a wedding ceremony, of course. Not yet, anyway. Only two more weeks until the big day. Can you believe it? Finally. We had our two beautiful children. Some of you – Roman, Jan, Eva, Rafa – probably remember how desperate we were to be parents. How hard we tried. Practice makes perfect, ha ha. And it was all worthwhile. Stella always used to say she wanted a fairy-tale wedding one day, but I could never see the point. Then, a year ago, I looked at my perfect little family and I knew I wanted it too. I wanted to make us official. So I got down on one knee and proposed. And luckily, she said yes . . .'

He raises his brandy glass at Stella and everyone else follows suit. Then he takes what – from my bird's eye view anyway – looks like a massive swig.

'But then something happened. I wanted to surprise her. Do something for her that I thought she might like. You all know how she only has her mother and father. No one else. No brothers or sisters. She always thought there might be cousins somewhere, but she'd never met any of them. I thought I could trace her family and – if I found anyone – invite some of them to the wedding. I thought that would be the best wedding present I could ever give her. More family . . .'

He takes a breath and looks around each of his audience in turn. I have to say, I'm fascinated to hear how Al's suspicions came about. We've never been able to work it out.

'So I did a bit of research, but I was getting nowhere. Then a colleague at work suggested one of those genealogy websites. Ancestry DNA, that kind of thing. If you have any family who've also been on there, they tell you. First cousins, second, sixteenth. Whatever. Obviously, I couldn't get Stella to spit into the tube. It would spoil the surprise. So then I had a brainwave. I could ask Taylor to do it. All the same connections would be there, just one step removed . . .'

Ah.

'So that's what I did. Of course, you know what Tayls is like. I had to bribe her to keep her quiet.' More hearty laughing, but now it's starting to sound hollow, like he can no longer keep up the pretence of it being real. 'And then we waited. And, to be honest, I forgot about it for a while. We started planning the wedding . . .' He keeps giving Stella little looks now, as if he's trying to read her reaction. She's playing her role to perfection, mouth slightly open in shock.

'The perfect wedding. And then, one day, the results came and there *were* people there on Stella's side. Cousins. I couldn't quite work out from their relation to Taylor exactly who they were to Stella – all that first cousin once removed and second cousin's mother's aunt stuff. But I knew I could find out. I was elated. But then, after a while of staring at the results, I suddenly noticed something. There were no Thornburys on there. No names I recognized from my own family – and you know there are lots of us. Maybe no one from my side had ever done one of those tests. Or they'd all set their privacy settings high – what did I know? But Tayls had relatives on there that I'd never heard of. Scores of them. Close ones too. Can you see where this is going yet?'

They all stare at him. To him it must look as if no one quite knows how to react. Stella wrings her napkin in her hand, dabs at her eyes. Al smirks. His big moment has come.

'I realized that the only reason that could be is because Taylor is not related to me . . .'

He fixes his gaze on Stella. Take that. If he's confused by the fact there aren't any gasps of shock, he doesn't show it. He's revelling in his revelation.

'And so, my friends, I ordered a paternity test. Not just

on Taylor, but on Amber too. And do you know what the results were? Not only is Taylor not my daughter, but neither is Amber. And what's more, they have the same father. It's just not me. Which means I've been bringing up some other fucker's children for the past ten years. And not just any other fucker. A fucker who was shagging my wife.'

He's dropped his bomb. He looks around to survey the damage. Where I'm sure he expected gasps of outrage and shock, there's nothing but silence. I can see Roman sitting poker straight, tense, waiting for his own big moment.

'So . . .' he says, a little more hesitantly. He must suspect all is not quite as it should be by now. 'What I've gathered you all here to tell you is that there isn't going to be a wedding. There isn't going to be a happy ending. Stella, tonight is our last supper. I'm leaving you. Or, to be more precise, you're leaving. Because this house is mine, let's not forget that. And I've just sold it. You're on your own. I'm not giving you a penny.'

He looks at her triumphantly. He's played his best hand.

'Well,' Stella says, brushing imaginary crumbs off her lap. 'I'm glad you got that off your chest. Now, would anyone like another brandy?'

Al opens his mouth to say something. Shuts it again. Looks around at the others, confused. I wish I was down there, so I could see his expression properly. Roman gets to his feet. Here goes. 'That's what you would call old news, my friend. We all know that Stella used a donor . . .'

'Ah!' Al interrupts. 'Now I get it. Now I understand. That's what she's told you. Why you're all acting like this,

353

how she's got you on side. But I'm pretty sure she didn't tell you this . . . Just give me a moment, Roman, and then you can say your piece . . .'

Roman sits back down. There's the tiniest ripple of confusion. Stella looks up at me, frowns. I shrug. I've got no idea what he's going to say, but we might as well hear him out before we play our trump card.

Al stares straight at Stella. 'I forgot a chunk of the story. The best bit. You're going to like this. Once I found out that the girls weren't mine, I went back to that damn genealogy site. I studied Taylor's relations, the ones on her father's side. And finally, something clicked.

'I know who their father is, Stella. Shall I carry on, or have you told them that part?'

46

Gail is the first to speak. 'She had an anonymous donor, Al . . .'

Eva is next. 'Yes, I'm sure you could have worked out a family name, but that doesn't mean anything.'

Rafa reaches out and puts a hand on her arm. 'Let him say what he has to say.'

I agree. I have no idea where Al is going with this. What justification for his behaviour he's managed to cobble together now he knows he's been rumbled, but I'd like to hear it. Like to hear how low he can go. I edge forward to the front of the balcony. I no longer really care if he sees me, I just want to make sure I hear every word. Stella is sitting perfectly still, her eyes never leaving Al's face. The others look a bit lost now that the script has been thrown out. They flick glances between Stella and Al. Gail looks up at me and I shake my head: I don't know what's going on either.

Al puffs up his chest. Pours himself another brandy. 'There was a name that reoccurred. It became obvious pretty quickly that it was significant. Cartwright. Does that mean anything to any of you?'

I can't take my eyes off Stella. She gulps. She's rattled. I have no clue why.

'No? Stella?'

Stella mutters something. I can't hear what.

'Sorry, Stella, what was that? Do say it again . . .'

'Al . . .' Ben says, a warning note in his voice.

Al ignores him. Keeps his eyes on Stella. 'Shall I tell them?'

Stella looks at him. 'Andrew,' she says more clearly. 'My first husband, Andrew. Is that what you want me to say? That was his surname. But it's hardly uncommon . . .'

The others are exchanging looks. 'Don't treat me like a fool, Stella. That's gone on long enough. You think I didn't look further than that? That I didn't find out that Andrew has a sister, Deborah, and she's listed on that site as Taylor's aunt? How do you explain that?'

All eyes flick back to Stella. 'Stella?' Jan says. 'Is there any truth in this?'

You could hear a pin drop. Stella briefly closes her eyes and then opens them again. 'I did it for us. I didn't have an affair with him, you're wrong about that. I used Andrew as a donor because I wanted the girls to look alike. But I wasn't sleeping with him. They're your daughters, Al. They're just not your DNA.'

'Well, that's the fundamental problem, isn't it? They're actually not my daughters.'

I don't know what to think. Stella used Andrew as the donor? Why would she bring that complication into their lives? And why didn't she tell me?

'Does it really make a difference, Al?' Gail says. 'Once you knew the girls weren't yours, does it matter who the donor was? They're just a donor . . .'

'Maybe it shouldn't,' Al says. 'Maybe I could have got past bringing up some fucking loser ex-husband's children as my own . . .'

356

Stella interrupts. A tear escapes and rolls down her cheek. 'I just asked him because he looks a bit like you, that's all. And I didn't want to risk using someone who might have god knows what in their family history . . .'

'How noble,' Al says, unmoved. 'And to ensure that, did you have to sleep with him? I mean, surely there are more sophisticated methods these days? Even ten years ago.'

'I didn't . . .' Stella says. She looks around at the others for support, but most of them are looking at the table.

'You didn't . . . ? What? Know how? Think it mattered?'

'Sleep with him,' Stella says.

'Really?' Al says, polishing off the brandy in one long swig. 'Because that's not what he told me.'

I stand up out of my hiding place. Al glances up and sees me. Looks away. For the first time, he looks as if he has emotions other than just anger. He looks devastated. 'What he actually told me,' he says, 'is that Taylor was an accident. That you'd been sleeping together ever since you left him for me. That you told him you never would have left at all if his career had taken off. If he could have kept you in the style you thought you deserved. And, when you realized you were pregnant, you were so desperate for a child that you decided to keep her and pretend she was mine. And then, two years later – when you and he were still in the middle of your affair, just for the record – you decided that she needed a brother or sister. And he agreed to go along with it if you made it worth his while. That's what actually happened, isn't it?'

'Stella?' Jan says.

'I imagine the romance died pretty quickly once you paid him off. Or did you just discover contraception?'

Anya looks back and forth between them. 'Is this true? Stella?'

'Oh, for god's sake,' Stella says loudly, the meek, hard-done-by front completely gone. 'What difference does it make any more?'

47

When Angie told me she would come and help me clean and fumigate my flat once I took possession, I hadn't expected her to turn up with my whole workforce in tow, but here they are on my doorstep, minus Sharon, who is at home looking after all the kids. So far, I've managed to go inside and open all the windows and then stand in the tiny garden trying to appreciate that it is now mine. I would have killed for this a few months ago, I told myself, but I didn't feel it. Yes, Betsy and I could finally be reunited, but did I really want her living in this dingy, smelly, cramped space on a slightly rough-around-the-edges street? As if she can sense my lack of enthusiasm, Ange takes charge, allocating jobs to each of my rubber-gloved colleagues. She provides them all with paper face masks – a genius idea I wish I'd thought of for myself – and we all go to work scrubbing and sweeping. At lunchtime I go and get pizzas from Dominos and a few bottles of wine for us to share at the end of the day because it's the least I can do. Then I remember I don't have any glasses, so I nip into Poundland and get twelve and a bumper pack of cheese-and-onion crisps. I find them all crammed into the garden when I get back, sitting on the flagstones chatting and laughing in the sun. The place already smells better.

I haven't seen Stella or Al since Thursday evening. Gail

tells me she's been there, skulking at home while the men went to Monte Carlo, regardless. Al included. Their original plan had been to go without him, but – and even though, understandably, their generosity doesn't extend to letting him off his debts, and quite rightly so – the revelation about Stella and Andrew has changed everything. Al is no longer the villain. At least, no more so than Stella herself. As Angie said to me all those weeks ago, they're as bad as each other. She tells me Al has instructed the bank to repay Roman and Rafa what he owes them with the money he borrowed, without them having to resort to lawyers. So they're all friends again, although I'm pretty sure neither of them will be offering to lend him money in the future. He's pulled out of the flat purchase – no more love nest – and he's pushing ahead with the sale of the house – under threat of death from the bank, I imagine – so he can pay off his debt to them. He'll be OK – he must have a decent chunk of the million he transferred from his and Stella's joint account left, but what's going to happen with him and Ferne I have no idea.

By the end of the day my flat is clean, every corner swept, every cupboard scrubbed. Tomas offers to come back and paint the ceilings because he could practically do it sitting down. I can do the rest, but the ceilings mean going up a ladder, something I'm pretty much incapable of without coming over all light-headed. I insist on paying him this time and he agrees graciously. I hug each and every one of them when they leave.

I haven't told Betsy that she'll be moving in with me when she gets back from her holiday yet. She'd want to know all the details and then have nightmares about having to live in the creepy house of horrors. I'm collecting Felix from the cattery on the day before they get back, though, and he and I will be moving in. Then David is going to bring her over so she can see her new bedroom with the smart white bed, desk and chest of drawers that hopefully will have arrived by then, and we'll take it from there. I know from countless conversations with her that she wants yellow walls, so that's what I'm going for. Buttery, sunny, happy.

I go down there every day, throwing open the windows, burning citrus-scented candles, trying to infuse a new aroma into the fabric of the place. Either I'm becoming immune to it, or the stench has almost gone. I turn the radio up and sing along as I sand down window frames and skirting boards. Sadly, there was no beautifully neglected wooden floor under the rotting carpets, just hardboard on top of old lino. Now the lino has been scrubbed, it's almost bearable in a 1940s-kitchen kind of way, so I order a huge rug that will just leave a small border round the edge. Tomas paints all the ceilings in a day and offers to do the walls, but I know I can't really afford to pay someone else to do them. It's a daunting task. I'm not sure how I'm going to achieve everything before Betsy gets back, but the thought of her motivates me and I get up at five every morning, crawling home late at night with an aching back. I'm neglecting my business, neglecting everything, but I'm on a mission.

I park my car on the street and half drag myself up the stairs to the annexe. It's hard to believe I'll only be living here for another week. It seemed like an eternity, but suddenly it's over in the blink of an eye. It makes me feel panicky when I allow myself to think about it but, thankfully, at the moment, I'm too tired to dwell on anything beyond sleep. I'll miss The Close, it turns out, but I'm also relieved to be leaving it behind. It's bittersweet. I'm halfway up the steps when I hear Stella calling my name. As ever, she has the knack of pouncing when I'm too tired to defend myself. She's the last person I want to see. I think about ignoring her. Going inside and slamming the door in her face. But it would only be prolonging the inevitable.

'What do you want?' I can't even pretend to be civil. On Thursday evening, after it all happened, I left without going out into the garden. I had nothing I wanted to say to her. Nothing more I wanted to hear. She'd made an idiot out of me, as she had everyone else.

'Do you hate me?' she says. If I didn't know better, I'd say she genuinely sounded as if she cared.

'I don't hate you, Stella. I can't be bothered to hate you. It's too much effort and I'm too tired. I'm moving away, so we won't have to bump into each other any more. Let's just leave it at that.'

'I'll miss you. I mean it. I enjoyed all those things we did together. The cooking and that silly trip to the supermarket.'

'Good. Well, hopefully, it'll come in useful. I really do need to go and get some sleep . . .'

'I still don't know where we're going to live. Me and the girls . . .'

'I can't help you any more. I'm not judging you. I just . . . I really need to concentrate on me and Betsy now.'

'Can we at least be friends?'

I can't let it happen. Can't let myself get dragged back into her world yet again. 'I don't know. I don't think so.'

I turn and walk on up the stairs before she can say any more.

I'm slathering undercoat liberally on the living-room walls by quarter past six next morning. Trying to keep the noise down in case I upset the upstairs neighbours, although I've barely seen them so far. They seem like a nice couple. Retired but hardly retiring. They go walking, they told me. They do their ten thousand steps every day, regardless. And she volunteers at the local Oxfam Books a few days a week while he helps out walking the up-for-adoption dogs at The Mayhew. They have a son and a daughter and three grandchildren and a cat who doesn't go outside. I haven't yet asked them if the old lady who owned my flat was a devil worshipper or just a heavy-metal fan. We'll get to that.

The sun is out and blazing through the east-facing bay window. It's already starting to look like a different place. I keep the radio on quietly, listening for movement upstairs. By eight o'clock I need a break so I walk down the road to get a coffee, stretching my aching back as I go. When I round the corner on the way back I see four people standing on my doorstep. They're all dressed in pink. My first thought is that the couple upstairs are doing Airbnb and a hen party has turned up. As I get closer, though, I recognize Katya, then Jan, Eva and Anya. They're all wearing matching boiler suits with the legs rolled up to show their ankles and Converse on their feet.

Their hair is tied up in elaborate scarves. They all look like Rizzo from *Grease*.

I can't help the big smile breaking out on my face. 'What on earth . . . ?'

'We've come to help you,' Eva says. 'Just tell us what to do.'

'The outfits . . .'

'Anya found them. Aren't they great?'

Katya holds up a big wicker Fortnum's basket with what looks like three bottles of champagne poking out of the top. 'We brought a picnic. We figured you wouldn't have supplies.'

'Oh god. I actually love you all. This is so kind.' I'm almost brought to tears by the gesture. 'Come in . . . How did you . . . ?'

'Stella told us the address,' Jan says. 'But she didn't think she should come too.'

'No,' I say. I'm a bit lost for words.

'Gosh, isn't it great, girls?' Eva says as I let them in and they all ooh and aah unconvincingly. But they're trying. We decide to paint for an hour before taking a break for fizz and some of the snacks they've brought (taramasalata, aged Parmesan, caviar and quail's eggs. You couldn't make it up. If my flat has started smelling too pleasant, this should soon sort it out). It's a bit like teaching kindergarten. Not one of them has a clue. Anya squeals like a baby when a blob of paint lands in her hair. Jan, whose (fake) nails are about a foot long, has to hold the brush as if she's holding her phone and flap it sideways at the wall. There's paint all over the – thankfully – soon-to-be-rug-covered floor. But somehow, sections of wall get covered. It's patchy, but I can make it work with the top coat.

The living room is done by the time we stop for refreshments. We're all a bit giggly by the time we recommence, but I can see they're flagging already. It's a bit too much like hard work, and none of them has ever done any work, let alone the hard stuff. I don't trust any of them with the kitchen or the bathroom. There are too many fittings that I don't want to get covered in paint. So I do those myself while Jan and Anya give my bedroom a once-over, Katya does Betsy's tiny room and Eva tackles the hall.

By early afternoon we've finished an undercoat on the whole place, we're all half-cut and they're flat out. They saved me a couple of days, there's no doubt about it. I tell them all to leave me to it. I can't thank them enough, but I don't want them to overdo it. I can see that none of them has the strength to argue, but then Katya comes back in from the garden and tells us she's just arranged for us all to go and get massages at the Mandarin Oriental. 'My treat,' she shouts when I try to protest. I want to say no, but the idea of someone's warm oily hands digging into my protesting muscles is too much for me. I will probably only ever get one chance to experience somewhere like this, and it couldn't have come at a better time. I decide just to accept graciously. So what if I can never reciprocate? I don't think the thought would even cross Katya's mind.

48

August

Gail is throwing me a leaving party. I have a self-drive van and Tomas and Paul booked for tomorrow to collect my few belongings from The Close and then the stuff that's in storage. I'll spend my first night at my – now fully decorated – flat tomorrow. Today I had a locksmith come in and put locks on the windows while I cleared the garden. Dragging the bags loaded with dirt and leaves, destined for the dump, through my bedroom and hallway, I realized I probably should have started with this. And that, as a cleaner, I should probably know that.

Because I'm the guest of honour I resist the urge to go down early and help Gail get everything ready. I watch her from the back window, pottering round the garden making everything look just so. Having missed the Pink Ladies visit because she was at work, she came down at the weekend with Ben and they helped me finish the job. I'm not going to lie, the flat-of-horrors looks lovely. Brand new.

I wait until I see Katya and Guy strut over from number 2 and then I run down and join them. Jan and Roman are next. I finally met their daughter, Sophia, this week. I've seen her gliding past in her smart VW Beetle many times. I assume she has feet, but she never seems to go anywhere on them. But Jan invited me round for a coffee and she was there when I arrived. On her way to get into her car, naturally. She was polite and poised. Perfectly nice. The coffee was a little strained. I hadn't expected it to be the two of them. Jan and Roman. Roman makes me nervous. I felt a little as if I was in a job interview or being checked out by an overprotective father as a potential suitor for one of his offspring. They leave for Marseilles in a couple of weeks.

Bill and Anya arrive next, Sergei and Katherine a couple of minutes later. Sergei has baby Andrei in his arms. It must be Ferne's night off. I haven't seen her since everything blew up. I imagine she's keeping a low profile. I have no idea where she and Al are intending to live. I thought about dropping in on her, but it felt too complicated. I don't know what she knows about what, and I don't want to make things any worse by saying something I shouldn't. It feels strange without Stella or Al here. Unbalanced, as though no one knows what the pecking order is any more. More of a democracy and less of a sovereign nation.

'AJT Music is going under,' Gail tells me when we're alone for a second. 'It's in so much debt and there's no one left to prop it up.'

I know I should feel the tiniest smidgen of pity for Al. He built that business up from nothing. I know how that works, how much of your time and attention and love you have to put in, even in a tiny enterprise like mine. But actually, all I feel is panic that I'm about to lose one of my biggest clients. I try not to give my self-interest away.

'What will he do?'

She shrugs. 'I'm sure he'll land on his feet.'

Later, when I'm fussing over Andrei and no one else is in earshot, I ask Katherine how Ferne is.

'She's left,' she says.

'Already? I thought she had another couple of weeks. He's not had his first birthday yet, has he?'

'She had a family emergency,' she says, handing Andrei over for me to hold. I realize I've been holding my hands out for him like a toddler in a sweet shop. He gives me a huge, gummy smile and my heart melts. 'So I told her it was fine. We must have owed her holiday anyway, because she never really took any time off.'

'I'm sad I didn't get to say goodbye. Is she still moving in with her boyfriend?' I put on my best ingenuous face.

Katherine looks around and then leans in closer. 'Do you not know? She was the one Al was seeing . . .'

I try to look surprised. 'Gosh. No . . .'

'She couldn't stay here after . . . you know . . . I had no idea about any of it.' She drops her voice to a whisper. 'I only found out when she told me she was leaving. She didn't really have a family emergency. She just wanted to get away.'

'I don't blame her,' I say.

'You know today was supposed to be the big wedding day?' she says, and I realize I'd totally forgotten. I wonder what Stella is doing. Whether she's at home across the road, listening to us all party. I feel an almost overwhelming urge to go over and check up on her. I know how lonely it is to feel as if you're the only person who's excluded.

Roman collars me while I'm en route to the loo, picking my way across the grass, slightly tipsy.

'Laura. Do you have a moment?' he says, and I jump half out of my skin.

'Um . . . sure . . .' My bladder is bursting, but I don't like to say so.

'My company needs new cleaners. I've suggested Sunshine Cleaning.' He hands me a card. 'This is who you need to contact, but I've told them I'd very much like them to use your services.'

'In Marseilles?' I say gormlessly.

He smiles indulgently. 'The London office.'

I'm completely taken aback. 'Oh. Of course. Thank you. You didn't have to . . .'

So it's no wonder the coffee felt like a job interview. In a way, it was. Roman must already have known about AJT. That I would lose a contract. I don't even know where his headquarters are. How large. If I have the staff to cover it. But I know I can make it work somehow.

'It's fine,' he says brusquely. 'Just do a good job.'

'I will. Definitely. Thank you.'

Later, once Katherine and Sergei have taken Andrei home, the rest of them toast me. I blush and stammer and tell them I'm going to miss them. Suddenly, I'm swaddled in some kind of group hug. Pointy fake boobs dig into my sides from all angles, I'm spiked with bony elbows, fishy lips plant kisses on my head. A false nail accidentally pokes me in the eye. It's not exactly comfortable, but it's strangely comforting. I'm accepted. Then Jan and Roman, Eva and Rafa, Bill and Anya, Guy and Katya, one by one say their goodbyes and Ben goes off to start clearing up the kitchen, leaving me and Gail to drink into the small hours.

I'm going to miss them.

49

There's a hammer pounding at my brain and an insistent ringing in my ears. I force my eyes open and squint at the clock. My mouth feels furry. Eight oh five. Weren't . . . shit . . . Tomas and Paul were meant to be arriving at eight.

'OK, OK,' I shout, staggering out of bed. I catch sight of myself in the mirror as I pass. Either I didn't take last night's mascara off or I've gone ten rounds with someone in my sleep. 'Can you give me ten minutes?' I yell through the door. 'I overslept. Maybe go and get some coffees somewhere? I'll pay you back.'

'No problem!' one of them yells, Tomas, I think. I hear them stomping back down the stairs, the whole place shaking. I throw myself in the shower. A memory comes back to me. Me saying I should go because it was already one in the morning and I needed to get up at seven, Gail insisting we have another glass because it was the end of an era. Despite how awful I feel, I smile. I have no recollection of what time I went to bed.

Thankfully, I packed yesterday, except for a few essentials. By the time Tomas and Paul get back with three scalding coffees everything is ready to go.

'No offence, Mrs Anderson, but you look terrible. Are you ill?' Tomas says. Paul is sniffing the place like

Hannibal Lecter. I can't imagine what it smells like. I should have opened the windows.

'Hangover,' I say. There's no point trying to cover it up. It must be so obvious. 'They had a leaving party for me.' Tomas and Paul laugh like this is the funniest thing ever. Their boss is human after all.

'We'll take care of you,' Tomas says, handing me one of the coffees. 'First, paracetamol.'

'I've packed them. I have no idea where.'

Paul digs around in the pockets of his combat trousers. Produces a couple of fluff-covered pills. I check the writing on the side before I swallow them, just in case he's got them mixed up with some kind of recreational horse tranquillizer. 'Thanks.'

They run up and down the stairs with my boxes and cases. Usually, I would be fretting about not helping. I'm not very good at watching people work. It makes me feel antsy. Lazy. Disrespectful. I could never have a cleaner myself, even if I could afford one. I'd have to go out for the day every time they came, otherwise I'd end up washing the floor alongside them. But today I let myself off. Remind myself that Tomas and Paul are grateful for the work and more than capable of shifting my paltry belongings without me helping.

It takes them less than ten minutes. I give them directions to Big Yellow Storage. Tell them to call me when they've finished emptying out my space and I'll meet them at the flat. Meanwhile, I need to scrub my studio clean. Finished, I post the key through Gail's letterbox. There's no sign of her so I assume she's still asleep. I'll see her next week, anyway. We're having lunch. I take one last look around The Close, breathe in the clean, earthy air. And then I get in my little yellow car and drive away.

I arrive at the flat with more coffees and a big bag of goodies from Greggs that Tomas and Paul devour between them with all the decorum of a pair of feral cats who have stumbled across the bins out the back of KFC. We unload my worldly goods. Half of the marital spoils. I got the bed, the bedside tables, a two-seater sofa and a small coffee table, along with a few pictures and fifty per cent of the contents of the kitchen. To be honest, I don't have room for any more. Most of Betsy's stuff is at her dad's. I've chosen a white duvet cover with sunflowers and cushions with bees, two things she loves, to match the yellow on the walls.

Later, once the boys have gone (I bought them some more food to take home. I couldn't help it, they always look so hungry), and I've been on a trip to the cattery, I FaceTime her.

'Guess where I am,' I say, once she's told me about her day's adventures. She's been having a great time, for which I'm thankful.

'Timbuktu,' she says, giggling.

'How did you know?' I say with a straight face. 'You've spoiled the surprise.' I pan the camera round her new bedroom. 'What do you think of this?'

'I love it,' she says, wide-eyed. 'Where are you?'

I ignore her question. 'How about this?' I whip round and there's Felix asleep on a little wicker chair.

'Felix!' she squeals.

'I've moved into our new flat. Felix is living here too now.'

'Where is it?' she says, jumping up and down. This is the tricky part. I walk through to the living room, camera held aloft.

'Remember that place you came to see with me?'

Her face falls. 'The creepy place?'

'Turns out it wasn't creepy at all. It just needed painting.'

'It smelled,' she says, channelling Stella, only in this case she's right.

'It did. But now it doesn't. At least, it doesn't smell bad. And look how nice it looks.' I turn round three hundred and sixty degrees to show her.

'Does Felix like it?'

'He loves it. He's already found his favourite snoozing spot.'

'In my room?'

'In your room.' This is good. She's not throwing a tantrum. I'd been afraid she might. 'Dad's going to bring you to see it when you get back.' I don't want to push the idea of her moving in before she's seen it for herself. I don't want her to feel railroaded.

'What if I don't like it?' she says.

'Then we'll sort something out,' I say. Of course, she's going to be moving in whatever, there's no question of that. But I'm confident enough that she'll forget all about the creepy flat when she sees its new identity that I've decided I can risk letting her think she has a choice.

'I miss you, Mummy,' she says, and I feel a tear well up. I blink it away. 'I miss you too, baby.'

*

I spend the evening getting the kitchen straight. I'm falling asleep by nine, my hangover still not quite shifted. Usually, I find it hard to sleep in a new place, all the unfamiliar sounds creeping into my subconscious and making me feel unsettled and anxious. Tonight, I get into bed next to my purring cat – who seems to be completely unfazed by his new surroundings – and next thing I know, it's the morning.

David brings Betsy over as soon as they get back. I pick her up and twirl her round. She looks tanned and happy, although one arm of her glasses appears to be held on by Sellotape. I've swept the small patch of ground out the front in an attempt to make it look more welcoming, but I know I need to show her the inside as soon as possible.

'Everything OK?' I say to David as I lead them through the communal hall.

'Great,' he says. I think he's nervous around me since I confronted him about Michaela. Good. Let him sweat. I open the door and let Betsy edge in ahead nervously, my hand on her shoulder. She stops dead in front of me.

'Wow. Is this the same place?'

'Nice, isn't it?' I say, knowing she's sold.

'It's brilliant.' She beams at me and my heart soars.

'Not rad?'

Betsy gives me a look that I'm sure I'll become only too used to in a few years. 'No one says "rad" any more.'

David snorts. I catch his eye over her head and we give each other a 'isn't our daughter cute?' look. One we used to give each other all the time. I remind myself that this is important to me. Civilized co-parenting with the only other person in the world who can possibly love our girl as unconditionally as I do. I suddenly realize I don't feel angry with him any more. I don't feel upset. I don't feel anything. I've let go, moved on. I give him a smile and he smiles back, relieved.

'Shut the door so Felix doesn't get out,' I say. 'He needs to stay in for at least three weeks till he gets it into his head that this is where he lives now.'

'Where is he?' Betsy says excitedly. 'Where's my room?'

I lead her down the hall. David veers off into the kitchen as we pass it and I hear him turn the kettle on. I'm glad he feels relaxed enough to do so. Betsy gasps as we go through the door. It's the time of day when the sun streams through the back windows. It's like being inside a sunbeam. The hefty ginger cat sprawled out on her duvet only complements the colour scheme. She picks him up, squeezing the life half out of him.

'This is the best room ever,' she declares, and I swallow down the lump in my throat.

At her insistence, she and David go back to his to collect Bruno and all her favourite bits and pieces so she can move in with me tonight. They return an hour later with all her books, most of her toys and half her clothes. She's home.

50

One year later

The house is magnificent.

It's in a private close. Not *The* Close, but nearby. This one has only six mansions set among a riot of green, each one different, sold and rebuilt many times by people who don't want to live in a house that's been lived in before. They want one built to their own exact specifications. Either that, or they're money launderers and construction is a great way to legitimize money.

The one I'm going to sits on the curve at the end. Prime position. It's a modern glass box. Vast. The light reflects off it at all angles so it blends into its woody surroundings. The drive sweeps round behind an architectural cluster of silver birch trees and out the other side. I've been here before, but it never fails to take my breath away.

Today, as a mark of respect, I have left the Sunshine Cleaning mobile at home and taken a taxi. Betsy – who's first time it is – stands at my side, mouth open. She's half a head taller, full set of teeth, but she's still my unique little tomboy. She's more sure of herself, less in awe of more sophisticated girls. For the moment, she's decided she thinks make-up is stupid, worn only by lame-os. 'Lame-os' is her new favourite word. On the other side of her is my date. An actual human date, not a virtual Tinder hook-up, although that is how we met. It's Danny of the facial hair, kind eyes and messy divorce. We started talking again when I contacted him and apologized for ignoring his earlier messages, told him I'd been straightening my priorities out. We've been seeing each other in the flesh for a couple of months. We're taking it slowly, but the fact that he has accompanied me today has earned him many gold stars, especially as I've warned him that all the males here will be alpha, waving their Rolexes and their huge bank balances in his face like a bunch of erect Bonobos. The fact that he's a paramedic will earn him zero kudos unless he tells them he stems people's bleeding wounds with old fifty-pound notes he finds down the back of his sofa. He doesn't seem fazed. Betsy likes him, loves to ask gory details about his work, although she'd still always rather it were just her and me or her and her dad. He and Michaela have moved in together, and I think she's finding it hard adjusting to there always being three other kids vying for his attention. Betsy and Zara have fallen out, but when she's there they're required to share a bedroom. My ex-sister-in-law, Jules, told me David was finding it exhausting having three more kids more or less full time. He looks like he's run ragged, apparently, in their new, practical flat, without so much as a porter, let alone a concierge. Although I will confess to having enjoyed a moment of schadenfreude, what I actually felt was sad for Betsy that her relationship with her father has become so complicated. I avoid Michaela if I can. She's kind to Bets and for that I'm grateful, but I don't want to be her friend.

The street is already clogged with Rolls-Royces, Bentleys, Mercedes, Porsches. Smartly dressed drivers, in for the long haul, stand around in groups, chatting. Despite the amount of vehicles, the air smells clean, fresh. I can hear voices coming from the back garden – I say back garden, it's more like a football pitch with very expensive landscaping – and music from a string quartet. I give our names to an official-looking woman at the gate and she points us to the side entrance. Luckily, it's a perfect day. Sunny. Warm, but not too hot. Still. So all the festivities can take place outside, as planned. I lead Betsy and Danny round to the back. I already know what to expect when I get there. I've been involved with every step of the planning, every decision that was slightly larger and fancier than the last. It's about as over the top as you can get without falling down the other side.

Because this – finally – is Stella's wedding.

We only started talking again about six months ago. Brokered by Gail, of course. Stella was still on The Close, living in Jan and Roman's house rent free, because they felt they couldn't leave her and the girls with nowhere to go. We met up for tea, the three of us, in Gail's back garden. It was strange to be back. Although I've seen Gail regularly, I've avoided The Close. We started to meet up on neutral ground. Mainly just me and her, but sometimes one or all of the others too.

I've met Bill and Anya's little boy, now a chubby eighteen-month-old. After they all found out the truth about Ferne, Anya decided on a nanny who was both stocky and maternal when he came home with them six months ago. I know that Jan and Roman are about to return from their year in Marseilles. (Roman came good on his word, by the way, and I managed to get the contract for cleaning his firm's offices in Paddington. It's some kind of recruitment, don't ask me what. But whatever it is, it's clearly very lucrative. They own the four-storey building they occupy. And clearly, Roman is dripping in cash. I even put my prices up, knowing they were already predisposed to hire me and assuming they would knock me down, but they didn't. Not only that, but I approached the company who moved into AJT's old space and they agreed to use us for continuity's sake. I've expanded, taken on six more people. Business is booming. I've employed Angie as a full-time coordinator/supervisor. She's desperate for the gossip from today. Gobsmacked that it's happening at all.) I know that Eva and Rafa are about to become grandparents, which has prompted her to have another face lift, so her eyes are now practically vertical on her face. That Katya and Katherine are both pregnant. Andrei is running around and making the occasional monosyllabic pronouncement. He is still, gratifyingly, always thrilled to see me. Hormones aplenty have been flying round The Close. Maybe what happened to Stella and Al prompted people to try to solidify their own marriages. The gold-Bentley couple – Dima and Monika – are fitting in nicely, apparently. I'll meet them for the first time today.

Stella cried when she saw me, but a bit of distance had made me immune to her emotional manipulations. She apologized profusely and I agreed to accept it without any more discussion. There was no point going over the same ground. Otherwise, she was exactly the same – self-obsessed, entitled, occasionally funny and disarming. It was actually quite refreshing. So much has changed in my life, but there was Stella, still being her old ridiculous, charismatic self. I knew I was never going to allow myself to be sucked back into her orbit again. I knew too much about her. About the way she uses people to get what she wants. But that didn't mean we couldn't be friends again. And we are. Real friends. Equals, finally.

There are two giant circus tents in the garden. Pristine, as if it's their first ever outing. One is set for a meal with gleaming silverware and glistening glasses on the flower-strewn tablecloths. The other has a parquet dance floor and bar. An ice sculpture – life-size and horribly photo real – of the bride and groom sits on a plinth in the middle. A fake stream has been created linking the two, complete with trees and actual real live ducks quacking away on the water. I'm looking forward to the ice sculpture melting later and the ducks running riot, all the guests cowering in the corners so they don't get their Jimmy Choos wet. There are jugglers on stilts and fire eaters mingling with the crowd. In front of the tents, on the lawn, there are rows of white chairs facing an arch that appears to be built entirely from candyfloss. I can't remember what it really is, but I know it cost a fortune. This is where the ceremony will take place. Stella got the hump when I asked her what ducks had to do with her circus theme, by the way. 'You have animals in circuses,' she said haughtily. I decided to leave it in case she thought she should go for more authenticity and booked a pair of tigers.

I see Gail and Ben in a huddle with Eva and Rafa and lead Danny and Betsy over to them, eager to find the security of friendly faces. It's the first time any of them will have met Danny, and I am both nervous on his behalf and terrified he'll somehow show me up. You see a new partner in a completely different light when you see them through the prism of your friends' gaze. Gail will have warned them all, I have no doubt – 'Laura has a new boyfriend' – so they'll all be looking to see who's standing next to me as soon as they spot me in the crowd. He already looks slightly strange to me today, in his suit, with his hair neatly slicked back. I'm sure he thinks the same about me. Posh dress-up dates have not been on our agenda thus far.

For all of her new maturity, Betsy has not lost her marsupial instincts. She clamps on to Gail, who makes a big fuss of her and then turns to Eva and insists on knowing where Cocoa is.

'He might come to the party later,' Eva says with a smile.

'What happened to your eyes . . .' Betsy demands, so I take that as my cue to introduce Danny. I've talked about them all so much that he already knows who's who. When I introduce Gail, he envelops her in a hug. He knows how fond I am of her. She gives me a wink over his shoulder, which – I assume – means she likes him.

Gradually, the others drift over. A reunion of sorts, although I saw most of them at Gail's a couple of weeks ago. They've all been on the bachelorette together since. A week in a fully staffed trullo in Puglia. All except Gail, who claimed work ('I can never retire,' she told me. 'What excuse would I have to get me out of things?'). I see Pilar and wave, and she beams at me. She's happily settled in the rooms above the double garage now that Stella has moved in full time. She's been living at Jan and Roman's with Stella for the past year – paid for by Stella's secret savings, now that she didn't have to spend money on rent. A lot of the guests, I don't recognize – friends and family of the groom, I assume. The other inhabitants of this particular close are here. I can guess who they are. They have that same look, that same confidence as my former neighbours. Stella is once again living in the grandest, most impressive house in a clutch of grand, impressive houses. It'll take her a while to become the crowned queen, but I have no doubt she'll get there.

Danny is telling someone that he's a paramedic and, no, he doesn't work in the private sector, he works for the NHS, for the fifth time, when the jazz band falls silent and we're all instructed to take our seats. This takes an age. People finish their conversations and their drinks, stubbornly ignoring the hovering waiters with trays for the empties. I can picture Stella sitting inside getting furious because everything isn't running to her very precise timetable. Shouting at someone to get it sorted.

There's an ear-splitting note from a giant organ on a plinth outside the patio doors. Everyone falls silent as 'Here Comes the Bride' strikes up. The groom steps out from where he's been hovering nearby and takes his place. We all crane our necks to look for Stella.

She comes out on the arm of her father, a tall, distinguished-looking man in his seventies. Round here, you would easily be forgiven for thinking they're the happy couple. She had another boob job about a month ago, so her humungous cleavage actually enters the garden a considerable while before the rest of her does. She's rail thin. Almost six foot in her heels. The train of her closely fitted dress could clothe a whole family. In layers. The dress itself cost thirty thousand pounds. She told me this proudly, as if I'd be impressed by how cheap it was, compared to the one she was planning on wearing for her wedding to Al. The Mini Mes follow in matching silver frocks. Poised. Rehearsed. Finally on the catwalk.

Stella reaches her groom, takes his hand. The ceremony begins.

51

She's not marrying for love. It's a decision she's made with her head and not her heart. But she likes him. He's a nice man. Kind. And that counts for a lot.

He's twenty-five years older than her – sixty-four. He's been married twice before. Grown-up kids. He's average-looking. Groomed to perfection, of course, but you wouldn't pick him out in a crowd. He likes golf and art and current affairs. Stella would never even have noticed him, had she not been set up on a date with him by Bill and Anya.

And known in advance that he was very rich. Very, very, very rich.

It sounds awful. It is. It definitely wouldn't work for me. But I don't think she's deceiving him. I don't think he's under any illusions. She gets the status she so craves with someone who is only ever going to treat her with kindness. He gets his third trophy wife. She doesn't have to look for a house to rent now that Jan and Roman are back, or a job. Her girls are secure in their private school. Timing is everything. She spends her time pampering herself, shopping, going to the gym. It's just like the old days.

He – Ted – knows all about Taylor and Amber's parentage and couldn't care less. In fact, I think he's probably relieved that there isn't another man around making demands to see them, negotiating a complicated relationship with his new wife. They both like to travel and eat fine foods and acquire beautiful things. They enjoy each other's company. There are just no fireworks – on her part, at least; I can't speak for him. Who knows? Maybe that's a good thing? They're building a future on a rational assessment of their compatibility, not on how much they want to rip each other's clothes off. Maybe that's the sensible thing to do if you're in for the long game.

And now she's living in this glass dream house. Taylor and Amber are happy. They're fond of Ted, he buys them stuff. I'm sure I should have put a 'because' in that sentence somewhere. He leaves all the parenting decisions to Stella, which means the girls are pampered and spoilt. A year of living rent free has meant they barely noticed a change in their circumstances. But they must miss Al – Stella finally told them that he wasn't their real dad, that he wouldn't be coming back. They took it remarkably calmly. Too cool for school. Personally, I think they're bottling it all up until they hit their teens and then they'll probably both go crazy with drugs and resentment. They're a pair of unexploded bombs, but at least they're still wearing Gucci.

Al, well, who knows where Al is? He's moved away is all we know. Living in a hovel with Miss Wife-Stealing Nanny 2019 like two star-crossed lovers, hopefully, Stella said. Eating soup out of a can and shagging each other in front of the gas fire. I hope, for his sake, he bounces back. His punishment feels disproportionate when you look at how Stella has got off scot free for her own mistakes. Although the way he has turned his back so completely on the two girls he brought up as his daughters for all those years means my sympathy has limits.

The ceremony is short. No need for drawn-out declarations of love here. Ted's daughters – one a woman around Stella's age, the other younger, courtesy of wife number two – look slightly po-faced throughout the whole thing. There was much talk of a pre-nup once the engagement was announced, but Stella put her expensively clad foot down. She had had one man try and leave her with nothing, she'd said. She'd be damned if she was going to let it happen again.

You'd be forgiven for thinking she'd learned nothing. That she still valued wealth and status over everything else. But I don't believe that's true. She's been kind to me over the past few months. She's put herself out. She came over when I first found out David and Michaela were moving in together. I was side-swiped by my reaction. I had no idea I still cared, that he still had the capability of hurting me. I thought I'd moved on completely, but it turned out I was mistaken. Admittedly, she was the third person I called, after Angie and Gail, both of whom were at work, but she got straight in the car and drove over with two bottles of Prosecco. Sat uncomplaining while I cried into her hair. Actually, that was the night I finally got back in touch with Danny, drunk on fizz and indignation.

'Sorry I've been ignoring your messages,' was the first thing I wrote. He'd contacted me a couple of times by then just to see if I was OK. 'But I'm drunk and I've just found out my ex is moving in with my former friend.'

'Not the friend who you thought he was seeing before

you split????' he'd sent back. No recriminations for the months I'd left him hanging. 'Bastard.'

'Utter bastard,' I replied. 'Both of them.'

'Well, if it makes you feel any better, my ex-wife has just started seeing her personal trainer. He's five years younger than her and his name's Adonis.'

I'd laughed for the first time all day. 'You're joking,' I sent.

'Not even. He's Greek.'

We talked like this for weeks before we finally decided to meet up. Jokey. Indulging the other in their resentments about their former partners. It probably wasn't the most healthy way to start a relationship, but by the time we had a coffee in Marylebone one afternoon I felt as if I knew him. And as if I'd got all my sadness about David out of my system. From that moment on, neither of us really mentioned our exes at all. It was as if we'd purged ourselves of them.

Stella sees me and comes over as fast as her train will allow. She hugs me, hugs Betsy. Betsy runs off to play with Taylor and Amber, now their duties are over. No more letting them torture her with make-up and hair accessories. These days, she's confident enough to put her foot down.

'Happy?' I say to Stella.

'Happy,' she says.

'Are you smiling, because I can't tell. Nothing is moving.' The Botox is back with a vengeance.

She rolls her eyes. She's used to me taking the piss. I think she actually likes it. 'I'm smiling on the inside.'

'Have you told Ted? Because he might not realize . . .'

'Where's Danny?' she says, ignoring me.

I look round, and he's deep in conversation with Gail and Ben. They're all laughing, so it seems to be going well. Or there's something in the wine. 'Over there. Come and meet him.' I grab her hand and pull her behind me. 'Danny, this is Stella . . .'

He smiles and shakes her hand. He has a lovely open smile. It's one of my favourite things about him. Stella leans in towards him. 'If you ever treat my friend badly, I will kill you.'

Thankfully, he realizes she's joking and laughs. It could have gone either way, because she didn't really give away any clues. 'Nice to meet you too. Congratulations, by the way.'

'He's cute,' she whispers to me later.

'It's early days,' I say. 'But yeah, I like him.'

Back home later, just me and Betsy (Danny is yet to stay over. It feels wrong with Betsy in the next room, at least until I'm sure if he's more than my transitional relationship), we flop on the sofa, fresh from our showers, pyjamas on. The party will still be going on, but they announced no kids after 7 p.m., which actually seems like a good idea to me, and gave me the perfect excuse to get away before it got messy. Right on cue, at about ten to, the nannies started to arrive to collect their charges, and that was my prompt to leave. Felix curls up between us, purring, content, snoring like an old steam train. We look through the day's photos on my phone.

'I should send this to Angie,' I say of a picture of Eva

looking particularly pained. Not that I want to encourage my daughter to make fun of the way people look, but I do get nervous that she'll start to think the things her surrogate aunts do to their faces are just what it's normal for women to do. So I indulge in a bit of gentle mickey taking here and there. With Angie, obviously, it's different. She's met Stella a few times, and even Jan, Eva, Katya and Anya once, at my place on my birthday. She's obsessed by their ever-changing features, their expanding and contracting (mostly expanding) chests. She finds them all hilarious and ridiculous at the same time.

'Send her the one of Auntie Stella's new boobs,' Betsy says, yawning, and I laugh, even though I shouldn't.

It's a hot late-August night. I can't open the front window because of the traffic noise, not to mention the possibility that someone might climb right through it and steal all my meagre possessions. I'm sweltering, though. Betsy is falling asleep where she sits. It's been a long day.

'Bed,' I say, and for once she doesn't argue. Because she's so tired, she even lets me tuck her in. I turn the fan on in the corner of her room. 'Love you,' I say as she closes her eyes, already out for the count.

'Love you too,' she mutters.

I make myself a cup of tea and take it out to the little back garden. It's still not quite dark and I can hear various of my neighbours pottering around, drinking, laughing. Even though I can't see any of them because of the high brick walls, and I've never spoken to any of them beyond a hello in the street if I see a familiar face, I like the sense of community you feel just from knowing there are all these different lives going on in proximity to your own.

It's never quiet. Aside from the traffic and the neighbours, there's the sirens and the beat of music from the pub on the corner. But my garden is an oasis. Betsy and I spent hours out here in the spring, planting up pots and the thin beds around the edges of the flagstones. It's a riot of colour. Although, if I'm being honest, it still smells a bit of take-outs and traffic and cat wee.

I stretch my feet on to the other wrought-metal chair. Lean my head back and look at the sky. Felix wanders out and sits washing himself and watching me. He can't go anywhere beyond the garden, because the walls are too high, but he doesn't seem to mind.

My phone beeps with a message. Angie. *Blimey. Wouldn't like to bump into her on a dark night!* It makes me laugh.

I drag myself inside. I need to get some sleep. I'm supposed to be dropping Betsy off with David and Michaela first thing, because the wedding has eaten into his weekend time with her. She doesn't want to go. Since Michaela became a fixture, she never wants to go. It's something we're going to have to address one of these days.

'I want to stay here with you,' she said to me yesterday as we got ourselves ready for the wedding. 'I want to stay home.'

It still gives me a thrill every time she says that word. She loves it here. She loves the noise and the chaos and the fact that she's near all her friends and her school and her ballet class. And because she loves it, I've come to love it too. That's one of the reasons I'm in no rush with Danny. Or anyone. Because what matters at the moment is that she and I are together. That I'm back where I'm supposed to be, living with my daughter. That I'm back in my own life. Shabby and imperfect as it may look from the outside – and from the inside too most of the time, let's face it – it's enough. In fact, it's more than enough. I don't need anything else.

Acknowledgements

As this is book number ten I thought it was about time I did some more comprehensive thank yous to the amazing team of people who contribute so much behind the scenes. So here's to Maxine Hitchcock, my fabulous editor, super-woman Louise Moore, Claire Bush, Gaby Young, Clare Parker, Liz Smith, Lee Motley, Christina Ellicott, Beatrix McIntyre, Alice Mottram, and everyone else at Michael Joseph and Penguin Random House.

And to my agents and their teams: the wonderful Jonny Geller at Curtis Brown, along with Ciara Finan, Kate Cooper and Nadia Farah. Peter Macfarlane of Macfarlane Chard for relentlessly drumming up interest in the film and TV rights, and Melissa Myers at WME for never minding that every time she asks me if I want to go to LA and write something I say no.